FIELD OF FANTASIES

Baseball Stories of the Strange and Supernatural

Edited by Rick Wilber

NIGHT SHADE BOOKS
NEW YORK

For my wife, Robin, my daughter, Samantha, and my very special son Richard Wilber Jr., who's my regular companion at Tropicana Field where we cheer on the Tampa Bay Rays.

Night Shade books may be purchased in bulk at special discounts for sales promotion, corporate gifts, fund-raising, or educational purposes. Special editions can also be created to specifications. For details, contact the Special Sales Department, Night Shade Books, 307 West 36th Street, 11th Floor, New York, NY 10018 or info@skyhorsepublishing.com.

Night Shade Books™ is a trademark of Skyhorse Publishing, Inc.®, a Delaware corporation.

Visit our website at www.nightshadebooks.com.

10 9 8 7 6 5 4 3 2 1

Library of Congress Cataloging-in-Publication Data is available on file.

Cover design by Rain Saukas
Cover photos from Thinkstock and iStock

ISBN: 978-1-59780-548-3

Printed in the United States of America

Contents

∞

Introduction

∽

THIS COLLECTION CELEBRATES the merger of baseball and fantasy in short fiction, reprinting stories that range from classic works of the 1940s and 1950s to stories so new that they have only appeared in digital form before their print appearance in this book.

The stories range from very-short to novelette length, from the ambitiously literary to the ambitiously genre, from humorous to poignantly serious, from deeply ironic to touchingly earnest and honest; and yet they all fit perfectly here, for what brings them together is baseball and fantasy, the national pastime at its strange and supernatural best.

Baseball fiction has been popular since the game was spelled with two words—"base ball"—in the mid nineteenth century. By the post–Civil War years, the emergence of the dime novels of Zane Grey and others told stories of players and games and leagues that didn't exist anywhere except in the writer's imagination. But those works of fiction were intended to seem real, aimed at giving the reader the feeling of being immersed in the lives of real ballplayers playing the real game. Most of these stories were aimed at younger readers, too, and were meant to lead those readers toward a proper life, so the heroes were often uncompromisingly moral young men and women.

That began to change with the arrival in the 1940s through 1970s of adult baseball fiction, some of it very ambitious in the literary sense and all of it meant to engage and entertain adult readers—sometimes for dramatic effect, sometimes for political and social commentary, and often for comedic effect. Baseball really was "the national pastime" for much of that era, and so any number of short stories and novels emerged, a good number of them with fantasy elements. Some of these included Valentine Davies's comedy radio play and film, *It Happens Every Spring*, Douglass Wallop's *The Year the Yankees Lost the*

Pennant (which became 1955's famous musical, *Damn Yankees*), and Philip Roth's ambitious *The Great American Novel*. The highlight of the era, of course, is 1952's remarkable novel, *The Natural*, by Bernard Malamud, which can be seen as the first major mainstream success at novel length, blending baseball and fantasy.

During this period a number of excellent blends of science fiction and baseball were published, too, with several of the top authors in the field incorporating their interest in the pastime with their work in science fiction. That's a trend that continues today, but in this collection I have, for the most part, avoided the overtly science-fictional and focused, instead, on the fantastic, the supernatural, and the strange.

Some of the best of the post-war baseball fantasies were short stories that appeared in the top magazines of the day, including "My Kingdom for Jones," by Wilbur Schramm, which appeared in the *Saturday Evening Post* at the height of that magazine's popularity in 1944, and Jack Kerouac's 1955 "Ronnie on the Mound," which appeared in *Esquire*. Both of these stories are reprinted in this collection.

More baseball fantasies appeared in the 1960s and 1970s. Robert Coover's much-lauded 1968 novel, *The Universal Baseball Association, Inc.*, was an important precursor to what would become a major trend, as was his terrific 1971 short story, "McDuff on the Mound," from the *Iowa Review*, and the very famous "The Mighty Casey," by Rod Serling. These two stories offered alternate takes on the famous "Casey at the Bat" poem by Ernest Lawrence Thayer, as did Ray Bradbury's poem, "Ahab at the Helm." Both stories and the poem are in this anthology.

In that same period, Max Apple's 1975 story, "Understanding Alvarado," took on an alternate history of Fidel Castro's baseball skills, something that would be done very successfully nearly twenty years later by John Kessel in "The Franchise" and Bruce McAllister in "The Southpaw." All three of these stories are reprinted in this collection.

And then came W. P. Kinsella, surely the most influential of these baseball fantasists, beginning with his 1980 "Shoeless Joe Jackson Comes to Iowa," and continuing today. From a wealth of Kinsella short stories, I have chosen the very funny and effective "How I Got My Nickname," from *Spitball Magazine*, originally published in 1983.

For other stories from the 1980s, I have also included the highly praised 1984 story, "The Hector Quesadilla Story," by T. Coraghessan Boyle, which appeared in the *Paris Review*, as well as the excellent "Baseball Memories," by Edo van Belkom, which appeared in *Aethlon: The Journal of Sport Literature*, in 1989.

With the embrace of baseball fiction—often fantastic in nature—in literary reviews, and the appearance of magazines like *Elysian Fields Quarterly*, the short-lived *108* magazine, and *Aethlon*, the number of stories for those interested in baseball rose from 1990 forward. The wealth of excellent stories makes choices difficult and at one point I had a list of eighty-four "must" include stories, which I finally narrowed down to the twenty-two you see here.

During the 1990s and into the new millennium, an increased interest in counterfactual (or "alternate history") stories brought a new element into baseball fantasy. One of the top magazines in the science-fiction and fantasy field, *Asimov's Science Fiction*, printed a number of these stories, and several of them appear in this collection; but other publications, too, published baseball alternate-history stories. Among the very best of these are those by Harry Turtledove, the writer generally said to be the master of the alternate-history form. Known primarily as a prolific novelist, Turtledove's short stories often appeared on tor.com, the online magazine run by Tor Books. Turtledove's "The House that George Built," from that site, is included in this collection.

A number of women writers have published excellent baseball fantasy of one kind or another in the last twenty years. Among the best of these many fine stories are "The Further Adventures of the Invisible Man" by Karen Joy Fowler (whose 1998 novel, *The Sweetheart Season*, made a significant contribution to the literature), "How to Read a Man" by Valerie Sayers, "Diamond Girls" by Louise Marley, and "Pitchers and Catchers" by Cecilia Tan. All four stories are in this collection.

Other outstanding baseball stories with elements of the strange or supernatural in more recent years include the minimalist "Baseball," by Ray Gonzalez; "Lost October," by David Sandner and Jacob Weisman; the very famous "Arthur Sternbach Brings the Curveball to Mars," by Kim Stanley Robinson; the disarmingly satiric "My Last Season with the Owls," by Ron Carlson; a wonderful tale of a curveball that really, seriously hangs, "The Hanging Curve," by award-winning editor and writer Gardner Dozois; and my own "Stephen to Cora to Joe," which appeared in *Asimov's Science Fiction* in 2000. All of these stories are to be found in this anthology.

Finally, the most recently published story to appear in this collection is "A Face in the Crowd" by Stephen King and Stewart O'Nan. Originally published as an e-book in 2012, this is the story's first appearance in a print edition and it's in the lead-off spot in the anthology.

In total, these great stories range from the openly strange and fantastic to the more subtly ambiguous. The writers range from the little known to the hugely popular, and from those with famous literary reputations to those best known by the cognoscenti of genre writing. They are a diverse group, with diverse interests and ambitions; but what brings them together in this collection is their appreciation for elements of the fantastic and how they mix with the game of baseball to create a useful tool for storytelling. It is a tool offering a deep cultural history that allows for irony, humor, ghostly apparitions, slickfielding horses, vampires, the challenges of childhood, the retelling of famous players and poems and tall tales from the pastime, a new way to look at what might have been, and—most of all—a great way to entertain, inform, and prod readers of all kinds.

Rick Wilber
April 2014

Stephen King is one of the best-selling and most-honored authors of his generation. His first novel, *Carrie*, was published in 1974 and some fifty novels later he remains at the top of the best-seller lists. Stewart O'Nan is an award-winning novelist and is, like King, a notable fan of the Boston Red Sox. King and O'Nan followed the Red Sox closely in the remarkable 2004 season and their book, *Faithful*, was an extraordinary success. In 2012, King and O'Nan collaborated again on "A Face in the Crowd," published first in e-book form. The story is a vintage example of the supernatural in baseball, as a man learns some hard lessons about life and death and the Red Sox. This is the story's first appearance in print.

A Face in the Crowd
ᛜ

Stephen King and Stewart O'Nan

THE SUMMER AFTER HIS wife died, Dean Evers started watching a lot of baseball. Like so many snowbirds from New England, he was a Red Sox fan who'd fled the nor'easters for the Gulf Coast of Florida and magnanimously adopted the Devil Rays, then perennial punching bags, as his second team. While he'd coached Little League, he'd never been a big fan—never obsessed, the way his son Pat was—but, night after night, as the gaudy sunset colored the West, he found himself turning on the Rays game to fill his empty condo.

He knew it was just a way of passing time. He and Ellie had been married forty-six years, through the good and the bad, and now he had no one who remembered any of it. She was the one who'd lobbied him to move to St. Pete, and then, not five years after they packed up the house, she had her stroke. The terrible thing was that she was in great shape. They'd just played a bracing set of tennis at the club. She'd beat him again, meaning he bought the drinks. They were sitting under an umbrella, sipping chilled gin-and-tonics, when she winced and pressed a hand over one eye.

"Brain freeze?" he asked.

She didn't move, sat there stuck, her other eye fixed, staring far beyond him.

"El," he said, reaching to touch her bare shoulder. Later, though the doctor said it was impossible, he would remember her skin being cold.

She folded face first onto the table, scattering their glasses, bringing the waiters and the manager and the lifeguard from the pool, who gently laid her head on a folded towel and knelt beside her, monitoring her pulse until the EMTs arrived. She lost everything on her right side, but she was alive, that was what mattered, except, quickly, not a month after she finished her PT and came home from the rehab, she had a second, fatal stroke while he was giving her a shower, a scene which replayed in his mind so often that he decided he had to move to a new place, which brought him here, to a bayside high-rise where he knew no one, and anything that helped pass the time was welcome.

He ate while he watched the game. He made his own dinner now, having tired of eating alone in restaurants and ordering expensive takeout. He was still learning the basics. He could make pasta and grill a steak, cut up a red pepper to crown a bag salad. He had no finesse, and too often was discouraged at the results, taking little pleasure in them. Tonight was a pre seasoned pork chop he'd picked up at the Publix. Just stick it in a hot pan and go, except he could never tell when meat was done. He got the chop crackling, threw a salad together, and set a place at the coffee table, facing the TV. The fat at the bottom of the pan was beginning to char. He poked the meat with a finger, testing for squishiness, but couldn't be sure. He took a knife and cut into it, revealing a pocket of blood. The pan was going to be hell to clean.

And then, when he finally sat down and took his first bite, the chop was tough. "Terrible," he heckled himself. "Chef Ramsay you ain't."

The Rays were playing the Mariners, meaning the stands were empty. When the Sox or Yanks were in town, the Trop was packed, otherwise the place was deserted. In the bad old days it made sense, but now the club was a serious contender. As David Price breezed through the lineup, Evers noted with dismay several fans in the padded captain's chairs behind the plate talking on their cell phones. Inevitably, one teenager began waving like a castaway, presumably to the person on the other end, watching at home.

"Look at me," Evers said. "I'm on TV, therefore I exist."

The kid waved for several pitches. He was right over the umpire's shoulder, and when Price dropped in a backdoor curve, the replay zoomed on the Met Life strike zone, magnifying the kid's idiotic grin as he waved in slow motion. Two rows behind him, sitting alone in his white sanitary smock with his thin, pomaded hair slicked back, solid and stoic as a tiki god, was Evers's old dentist from Shrewsbury, Dr. Young.

Young Dr. Young, his mother had called him, because even when Evers was a child, he'd been old. He'd been a Marine in the Pacific, had come back from Tarawa missing part of a leg and all of his hope. He'd spent the rest of his life exacting his revenge not on the Japanese but on the children of Shrewsbury, finding soft spots in their enamel with the pitiless point of his stainless steel hook and plunging needles into their gums.

Evers stopped chewing and leaned forward to be sure. The greased-back hair and Mount Rushmore forehead, the Coke-bottle bifocals and thin lips that went white when he bore down with the drill—yes, it was him, and not a day older than when Evers had last seen him, over fifty years ago.

It couldn't be. He'd be at least ninety. But the humidor that was Florida was full of men his age, many of them well preserved, near mummified beneath their guayaberas and tans.

No, Evers thought, he'd smoked. It was another thing Evers hated about him, the stale reek of his breath and his clothes as he loomed in close over him, trying to get leverage. The red pack fit the pocket of his smock—Lucky Strikes, filter-less, the true coffin nails. *L.S.M.F.T.*, that was the old slogan: *Lucky Strike Means Fine Tobacco*. Perhaps it was a younger brother, or a son, Even Younger Dr. Young.

Price blew a fastball by the batter to end the inning and a commercial intervened, hauling Evers back to the present. His pork chop was tough as a catcher's mitt. He tossed it in the trash and grabbed a beer. The first cold gulp sobered him. There was no way that was his Dr. Young, with his shaky morning-after hands and more than a hint of gin under his cigarette breath. Nowadays they'd call his condition PTSD, but to a kid at the mercy of his instruments, it didn't matter. Evers had despised him, had surely at some point wished him, if not dead, then gone.

When the Rays came to bat, the teenager was waving again, but the rows behind him were vacant. Evers kept an eye out, expecting Dr. Young to come back with a beer and a hot dog, yet as the innings passed and Price's strikeouts mounted, the seat remained empty. Nearby, a woman in a sparkly top was now waving to the folks at home.

He wished Ellie were there to tell, or that he could call his mother and ask whatever happened to Young Dr. Young, but, as with so much of his daily existence, there was no one to share it with. More likely than not, the man was just another old guy with nothing better to do than waste his leftover evenings watching baseball, only at the park instead of at home.

Late that night, around three, Evers could easily see why of all the possible punishments prisoners feared solitary confinement the most. At some point a beating had to stop, but a thought could go on and on, feeding and then feeding on insomnia. Why Dr. Young, who he hadn't thought of in years? Was it a sign? An omen? Or was he—as he feared he might when they told him Ellie had died—gradually losing his grip on this world?

To prove those doubts wrong, he spent the next day running errands around town, chatting with the clerk at the post office, and the woman at the circulation desk of the library—just small talk, but still, a connection, something to build on. Like every summer, Pat and his family had taken off for the Cape and Sue's folks' place. Evers called their machine anyway and left a message. When they came back they should really get together. He'd love to take them all out to dinner somewhere, their choice, or maybe a ballgame.

That evening he prepared his dinner as if nothing had happened, though now he was very aware of the time, and ended up rushing his grilled chicken so he could catch the first pitch. The Rays were playing the Mariners again, and again attendance was sparse, the upper deck a sea of blue. Evers settled in to watch, ignoring where the pitch was, focusing instead on the third row just to the left of the umpire. As if to answer his question with a cosmic Bronx cheer, Raymond, the team's mascot, a creature with blue fur not found anywhere in the natural world, flopped across the seats, shaking his fist behind Ichiro's back.

"You're going shack whacky," Evers said. "That's all."

The Mariners' ace, Felix Hernandez, was going for them, and King Felix was on. The game was fast. By the time Evers cracked his nightly beer, it was the sixth and the M's were up by a couple. It was then, just as King Felix caught Ben Zobrist looking, that Evers saw, three rows deep, in the same pinstripe suit he was buried in, his old business partner Leonard Wheeler.

Leonard Wheeler—always Leonard, never Lennie—was eating a hot dog and washing it down with what ESPN's *Sports Center* smartasses were pleased to call "an adult beverage." For a moment, too startled for denial, Evers defaulted to the outrage the merest thought of Wheeler could call up from his gut even now. "You controlling son of a bitch!" he shouted, and dropped his own adult beverage, which he'd just been bringing to his lips. The can fell into the tray balanced on his lap and knocked it to the floor between his feet, where the chicken, instant mashed potatoes, and Birds Eye string beans (also of a color not found in the natural world) lay on the carpet in a foaming puddle of beer.

Evers didn't notice, only stared at his new television, which was so state-of-the-art that he sometimes felt he could simply pick up a leg, duck his head to keep from bumping the frame, and step right into the picture. It was Wheeler, all right: same gold-rimmed glasses, same jutting jaw and weirdly plump lips, same head of flamboyant snow-white hair that made him look like a soap opera star—the mature lead who plays either a saintly doctor or a tycoon cuckolded by his sleazy trophy wife. There was no mistaking the oversize flag pin in his lapel either. He'd always worn that damned thing like a jackleg congressman. Ellie once joked that Lennie (when it was just them, they always called him that) probably tucked it under his pillow before he went to sleep.

Then the denial rushed in, swarming over his initial shock the way white blood cells swarm into a fresh cut. Evers closed his eyes, counted to five, then popped them wide, sure he'd see someone who just looked like Wheeler, or—perhaps worse—no one at all.

The shot had changed. Instead of a new batter stepping in, the camera focused on the Mariners' left fielder, who was doing a peculiar little dance.

"Never seen *that* one before," one of the Rays' announcers said. "What the heck is Wells up to, Dewayne?"

"Li'l crunk move, I 'spec," Dewayne Staats vamped, and they both chuckled.

Enough with the sparkling repartee, Evers thought. He shuffled his feet and managed to step on his beer-soaked chicken breast. *Go back to the damn home plate shot.*

As if the producer in his gadget-loaded broadcast truck had heard him, the shot switched back, but only for a second. Luke Scott hit a bullet to the Mariners' second baseman, and in the wink of an eye, the Trop was gone and Evers was left with the Aflac duck, who was plugging holes in a rowboat even as it plugged insurance.

Evers got halfway up before his knees gave way and he collapsed back into his chair. The cushion made a tired wooshing sound. He took a deep breath, let it out, and felt a little stronger. This time he made it to his feet and trundled into the kitchen. He got the carpet cleaner from under the sink and read the instructions. Ellie wouldn't have needed to read them. Ellie would have simply made some half-irritated, half-amused comment ("You can dress him up, but you can't take him out" was a favorite) and gone to work making the mess disappear.

"That was not Lennie Wheeler," he told the empty living room as he came back. "No way it was."

The duck was gone, replaced by a man and his wife smooching on a patio. Soon they would go upstairs and make Viagra-aided love, because this was the age of knowing how to get things done. Evers, who also knew how to get things done (he'd read the instructions on the can, after all), fell on his knees, returned his sopping dinner to the tray in a series of plops, then sprayed a small cloud of Resolve on the remaining crud, knowing there'd probably be a stain anyway.

"Lennie Wheeler is as dead as Jacob Marley. I went to his funeral."

Indeed he had, and although his face had remained appropriately grave and regretful throughout, he'd enjoyed it. Laughter might be the best medicine, but Dean Evers believed outliving your enemies was the best revenge.

Evers and Wheeler had met in business school, and had started Speedy Truck Rental on a shoestring after Wheeler had found what he called "a gaping hole the size of the Sumner Tunnel" in the New England market. In those early days Evers hadn't minded Wheeler's overbearing manner, perfectly summed up by a plaque on the man's office wall: WHEN I WANT MY OPINION, I'LL ASK YOU FOR IT. In those days, before Evers had begun to find his own way, he'd needed that kind of attitude. Wheeler, he sometimes thought, had been the steel in his spine. But young men grow up and develop their own ideas.

After twenty years Speedy had become the biggest independent truck rental outfit in New England, one of the few untainted by either organized crime or IRS problems. That was when Leonard Wheeler—never Lennie except when Evers and his wife were safely tucked into bed and giggling like a couple of kids—decided it was time to go national. Evers finally stood up on his hind legs and demurred. Not gently, as in previous disagreements, but firmly. Loudly, even. Everyone in the office had heard them, he had no doubt, even with the door closed.

The game came back on while he was waiting for the Resolve to set. Hellickson was still dealing for the Rays, and he was sharp. Not as sharp as Hernandez, though, and on any other night Evers would have been sending him brain-wave encouragement. Not tonight. Tonight he sat back on his heels at the base of his chair with his bony knees on either side of the stain he was trying to clean up, peering at the stands behind home plate.

There was Wheeler, still right there, now drinking a beer with one hand and holding a cell phone in the other. Just the sight of the phone filled Evers with outrage. Not because cell phones should be outlawed in ballparks like smoking, but because Wheeler had died of a heart attack long before such things were in general use. He had no *right* to it!

"Oh-oh, that's a *loo-oong* drive!" Dewayne Staats was bellowing. "Justin Smoak smoked *aaa-alll* of that one!"

The camera followed the ball into the nearly deserted stands, and lingered to watch two boys fighting over it. One emerged victorious and waved it at the camera, pumping his hips in a singularly obscene manner as he did so.

"Fuck you!" Evers shouted. "You're on TV, so what?"

He hardly ever used such language, but had he not said that very same thing to his partner during the argument over the expansion? Yes. Nor had it just been *Fuck you*. It had been *Fuck you, Lennie*.

"And what I did, you deserved it." He was dismayed to discover he was on the verge of tears. "You wouldn't take your foot off my neck, Leonard. I did what I had to do."

Now the camera returned to where it belonged, which was showing Smoak doing his home run trot, and pointing at the sky—well, *dome*—as he crossed home plate to the apathetic applause of the two dozen or so Mariner fans in attendance.

Kyle Seager stood in. Behind him, in the third row, the seat where Wheeler had been was empty.

It wasn't him, Evers thought, scrubbing the stain (that barbecue sauce was simply not going to come up). *It* was just someone who looked like him.

That hadn't worked very well with Young Doctor Young, and it didn't work at all now.

Evers turned off the TV and decided he'd go to bed early.

Useless. Sleep didn't come at ten or at midnight. At two o'clock he took one of Ellie's Ambiens, hoping it wouldn't kill him—it was eighteen months past the expiration date. It didn't, but it didn't put him to sleep either. He took another half a tablet and lay in bed thinking of a plaque he'd kept in his own office. It said GIVE ME A LEVER LONG ENOUGH, A FULCRUM STRONG ENOUGH, AND I'LL MOVE THE WORLD. Far less arrogant than Wheeler's plaque, but perhaps more useful.

When Wheeler refused to let him out of the partnership agreement Evers had foolishly signed when he'd been young and humble, he'd needed that kind of lever to shift his partner. As it so happened, he had one. Leonard Wheeler had a taste for the occasional young boy. Oh, not *young* young, not jailbait, but college age. Wheeler's personal assistant, Martha, had confided to Evers one rum-soaked night at a convention in Denver that Wheeler was partial to the lifeguard type. Later, sober and remorseful, she'd begged him never to say a word to anyone. Wheeler was a good boss, she said, hard but good, and his wife was a dream. The same was true of his son and daughter.

Evers kept mum, even keeping this nugget from Ellie. If she'd known he intended to use any such scurrilous information to break the partnership agreement, she would have been horrified. *It's surely not necessary to stoop to that*, she would have said, and she would have believed it. El thought she understood the bind he was in, but she didn't. The most important thing she didn't understand was that it was *their* bind—hers and little Patrick's as well as his own. If Speedy went nationwide now, they'd be crushed by the giants within a year. Two at the outside. Evers was dead certain of it, and had the numbers to back it up. All they'd worked for would be washed away, and he had no intention of drowning in the sea of Lennie Wheeler's ambitions. It could not be allowed.

He hadn't opened with *Fuck you, Lennie.* First he tried the reasonable approach, using the latest spreadsheets to lay out his case. Their market share in New England was due to their ability to rent one-way and at hourly rates the big boys couldn't match. Because the area they covered was so compact, they could rebalance their entire inventory within three hours, where the big boys couldn't and had to charge a premium. On September 1, move-in day for the students, Speedy owned Boston. Spread the fleet thin trying to cover the Lower 48 and they'd have the same headaches as U-Haul and Penske—the same lumbering business model they purposely avoided and undersold. Why would they want to be like the other guys when they were killing the other guys? If Wheeler hadn't noticed, Penske was in Chapter 11, Thrifty too.

"Precisely," Wheeler said. "With the big boys on the sidelines, this is the perfect time. We *don't* try to be like them, Dean. We chop the country into regions and do what we already do."

"How does that work in the Northwest?" Evers asked. "Or the Southwest? Or even the Midwest? The country's too big."

"It may not be as profitable at first, but it won't take long. You've seen our competition. Eighteen months—two years tops—and we'll be absolutely killing them."

"We're already overextended, and now you want us to take on more debt."

As they went back and forth, Evers honestly believed in his argument. Even for a publicly owned company, the problems of capitalization and cash flow were insurmountable—a judgment that would prove devastatingly true two decades later, when the downturn hit. But Lennie Wheeler was used to having his way, and nothing Evers said would dissuade him. Wheeler had already talked with several venture capital concerns and printed up a sleek-looking brochure. He planned to take his proposal directly to the shareholders, over Evers's protests, if necessary.

"I don't think you want to do that," Evers said.

"And why's that, Dean?"

He'd tried, really tried, to do this ethically, honorably. And he knew he was right; time would prove it. In business everything was a means to one end—survival. Evers felt it urgently then and still thought it true today: He had to save the company. Hence, the nuclear option.

"I don't think you want to do that because I don't think you'd like what I'd take to the shareholders' meeting. Or should I say, whom."

Wheeler laughed, a sick little chuckle. He stared at Evers as if he'd pulled a gun. "Whom?"

"We both know whom," Evers said.

Wheeler slowly rubbed a hand up the side of his face. "I was wondering why you walked in here like you'd already won something."

"We're not winning anything. We're avoiding a mistake that would lose us everything. I'm sorry it came to this. If you'd have just listened to me—"

"Fuck you, Dean," Wheeler said. "Don't try to apologize for blackmail. It's bad manners. And since it's just the two of us, why don't you roll those spread-sheets tight—that's the only way you'll get them up that narrow ass of yours—and admit the truth: you're a coward. Always were."

Within a year, Evers bought him out. The split was expensive, and, in retro-spect, a better deal than Wheeler deserved. Lennie left New England, then his wife, and finally, in an ER in Palm Springs, this earthly vale of tears. Out of respect Evers flew west for the funeral, at which, not surprisingly, there were no lifeguard types, and, of the family, only the daughter, who dryly thanked Evers for coming. He didn't say the first thought that had come into his mind: *Sarcasm doesn't become fat girls, dear.* A few years later, after a thorough vetting of the numbers and fueled by Bain Capital, Speedy actually did go national, using a streamlined version of their old regional plan. That Evers had been right—that it ended with Speedy's lawyers filing the same Chapter 11 briefs as their vanquished rivals—was little vindication. He came out of it with a goodly sum, however, and that was.

The funny thing was that with a minimum of digging—an offhand question or three to Martha, a keen read of her blinking—Wheeler could have bought him-self an ironclad insurance policy. When Evers realized this, he gently dropped her, which, because they both had a conscience, was actually a relief. Their fling had run its more than pleasant course, and rather than fire her, he kept her closer, making her his executive assistant at double the salary, working beside her day in, day out until, eventually, she accepted a lavish early retirement package. At her farewell party, he made a speech and gave her a Honda Gold Wing and a peck on the cheek, to raised glasses and warm applause. The affair ended with a slide show featuring Martha on her old Harley Tri-Glide, while George Thorogood sang "Ride On Josephine."

It was a rare moment for Evers, a happy parting. Beyond the silly intrigue, he'd always liked Martha, her brash laugh and the way she hummed to herself as she typed, a pencil tucked behind one ear. What he said in his speech—that she wasn't merely an assistant but a dear and trusted friend—was true. Though he hadn't spoken to her in ages, of all the people he'd worked with, she was the only one he missed. Drowsing now as the Ambien kicked in, he wondered hazily if she was still alive, or if, tomorrow, he'd turn on the game and find her behind home, wearing the sleeveless yellow sundress with the daisies he liked.

He rose at eight—a full hour past his usual time—and stooped to pick the paper from the mat. He checked the sports page and discovered the Rays had the night off. That was all right; there was always *CSI*. Evers showered, ate a healthy breakfast in which wheat germ played a major role, then sat down to track Young Doctor Young on the computer. When that marvel of the twenty-first century failed (or maybe he just wasn't doing it right; Ellie had always been the computer whiz), he picked up the telephone. According to the morgue desk at the Shrewsbury *Herald-Crier*, the dental bogeyman of Evers's childhood had died in 1978. Amazingly, he'd been only fifty-nine, nearly a decade younger than Evers was now. Evers pondered the unknowable: was his life cut short by the war, Luckies, dentistry, or all three?

There was nothing remarkable in his obituary, just the usual survived by and funeral home info. Evers had had absolutely nothing to do with the drunk old butcher's demise, just the bad luck to be his victim. Exonerated, that night he raised an extra glass or four to Dr. Young. He ordered in, but it took forever, arriving after he was well in the bag. *CSI* turned out to be one he'd seen before, and all the sitcoms were stupid. Where was Bob Newhart when you needed him? Evers brushed his teeth, took two of Ellie's Ambiens, then stood swaying in front of the bathroom mirror, his eyes bleeding. "Give me a liver long enough," he said, "and I'll move the fucking world."

He slept late again, recovering with instant coffee and oatmeal, and was pleased to see in the paper that the Sox were coming in for a big weekend series. He celebrated the opener with steak, setting the DVR to capture whatever malevolent spirit his past might vomit up. If it happened, this time he'd be ready.

It did, in the seventh inning of a tie game, on a key play at the plate. He would have missed it if he'd gone off to do the dishes, but by then he was poised on the edge of the sofa, totally into the contest and concentrating on every pitch. Longoria doubled to the gap in left center, and Upton tried to score from first. The throw beat him but was wide, up the first baseline. As Sox catcher Kelly Shoppach lunged toward home with a sweep tag, directly behind the screen a scrawny, freckle-faced boy not more than nine rose from his seat.

His haircut was what used to be called a Dutch boy, or, if you were taunting this particular fellow at school, a soup bowl. "Hey, Soup!" they used to hound him in gym, pummeling him, turning every game into Smear the Queer. "Hey, Soupy. Soup, Soupy!"

His name was Lester Embree, and here in the shadowy Trop he wore the same threadbare red-and-blue striped shirt and bleached, patched-at-the-knees Tuffskins he always seemed to have on that spring of 1954. He was white but he lived in the black part of town behind the fairgrounds. He had no father, and the kindest rumor about his mother said she worked in the laundry at St. Joe's hospital. In the middle of the school year he'd come to Shrewsbury from some hick town in Tennessee, a move that seemed foolish, a dunderheaded affront to Evers and his cadre of buddies. They delighted in imitating his soft drawl, drawing out the halting answers he gave in class into Foghorn Leghorn monologues. "I say, I say, Miss Pritchett, ma'am, I do declayuh I have done done dooty in these heah britches."

On-screen, Upton leapt to his feet, looking back at the sprawled catcher and signaling safe just as the umpire punched the air with a clenched fist. A different camera zoomed out to show Joe Maddon charging from the dugout in high dudgeon. The sellout crowd was going wild.

In the replay—even before Evers paused and ran it back with the clicker—Lester Embree and his doofy bowl cut were visible above the FOX 13 ad recessed into the wall's blue padding, and then, as Upton clearly evaded the tag with a nifty hook slide, the quiet boy Evers and his friends had witnessed being pulled wrinkled and fingerless from Marsden's Pond rose and pointed one fish-nibbled stub not at the play developing right in front of him, but, as if he could see into the air-conditioned, dimly lit condo, directly at Evers. His lips were moving, and it didn't look like he was saying *Kill the ump*.

"Come on," Evers scoffed, as if at the bad call. "Jesus, I was a *kid*."

The TV returned to live action—very lively, in fact. Joe Maddon and the home plate ump stood toe to toe and nose to nose. Both were jawing away, and you didn't have to be a fortune-teller to know that Maddon would soon be following the game from the clubhouse. Evers had no interest in watching the Rays' manager get the hook. He used his remote to run the picture back to where Lester Embree had come into view.

Maybe he won't be there, Evers thought. *Maybe you can't DVR ghosts any more than you can see vampires in a mirror.*

Only Lester Embree was right there in the stands—in the expensive seats, no less—and Evers suddenly remembered the day at Fairlawn Grammar when old Soupy had been waiting at Evers's locker. Just seeing him there had made Evers want to haul off and paste him one. The little fucker was trespassing, after all. *They'll stop if you tell 'em to*, Soupy had said in that crackerbarrel drawl of his. *Even Kaz will stop.*

He'd been talking about Chuckie Kazmierski, only no one called him Chuckie, not even now. Evers could attest to that, because Kaz was the only friend from his childhood who was still a friend. He lived in Punta Gorda, and sometimes they got together for a round of golf. Just two happy retirees, one divorced, one a widower. They reminisced a lot—really, what else were old men good for?—but it had been years since they talked about Soupy Embree. Evers had to wonder now just why that was. Shame? Guilt? Maybe on his part, but probably not on Kaz's. As the youngest of six brothers and the runt of their scruffy pack, Kaz had had to fight for every inch of respect. He'd earned his spot as top dog the hard way, with knuckles and blood, and he took Lester Embree's helplessness as a personal insult. No one had ever given him a break, and now this whingeing hillbilly was asking for a free pass? "Nothing's free," Kaz used to say, shaking his head as if it was a sad truth. "Somehow, some way, somebody got to pay."

Probably Kaz doesn't even remember, Evers thought. *Neither did I, till tonight.* Tonight he was having total recall. Mostly what he remembered was the kid's pleading eyes that day by his locker. Big and blue and soft. And that wheedling, cornpone voice, begging him, like it was really in his power to do it.

You're the one Kaz and the rest of them listen to. Gimme a break, won't you? Ah'll give you money. Two bucks a week, that's mah whole allowance. All Ah want's to get along.

Little as he liked to, Evers could remember his answer, delivered in a jeering mockery of the boy's accent: *Ifn all you want's to git along, you git along raht out of heah, Soupy. Ah don't want yoah money, hit's prob'ly crawlin wit' fag germs.*

A loyal lieutenant (not the general, as Lester Embree had assumed), Evers immediately brought the matter to Kaz, embellishing the scene further, laughing at his own drawl. Later, in the shadow of the flagpole, he egged Kaz on from the nervous circle surrounding the fight. Technically, it wasn't a fight at all, because Soupy never defended himself. He folded at Kaz's first blow, curling into a ball on the ground while Kaz slugged and kicked him at will. And then, as if he'd tired, Kaz straddled him, grabbed his wrists, and pinned his arms back above his head. Soupy was weeping, his split lip blowing bloody bubbles. In the tussle, his red-and-blue striped shirt had ripped, the fishbelly skin of his chest showing through a fist-size hole. He didn't resist as Kaz let go of his wrists, took hold of the tear in his shirt with both hands, and ripped it apart. The collar wouldn't give, and Kaz tugged it off over Soupy's ears in three hard jerks, then stood and twirled the shreds over his head like a lasso before flinging it down on Soupy and walking away. What astonished Evers, besides the inner wildness Kaz had tapped and the style with which he'd destroyed his opponent, was how fast it all happened. In total, it had taken maybe two minutes. The teachers still hadn't even made it outside.

When the kid disappeared a week later, Evers and his pals thought he must have run away. Soupy's mother thought differently. He liked to go on wildlife walks, she said. He was a dreamy boy, he might have gotten lost. There was a massive search of the nearby woods, including baying teams of bloodhounds brought from Boston. As Boy Scouts, Evers and his friends were in on it. They heard the commotion at the dam end of Marsden's Pond and came running. Later, when they saw the eyeless thing that rose dripping from the spillway, they would all wish they hadn't.

And now, thanks to God only knew what agency, here was Lester Embree at Tropicana Field, standing with the other fans watching the play at the plate. His fingers were mostly gone, but he still seemed to have his thumbs. His eyes and nose, too. Well, most of his nose. Lester was looking through the television screen at Dean Evers, just like Miss Nancy looking through her magic mirror on the old *Romper Room* show. "Romper, stomper, bomper, boo," Miss Nancy liked to chant in the way-back-when. "My magic mirror can see you."

Lester's pointing finger-stub, Lester's moving mouth. Saying what? Evers only had to watch it twice to be sure: *You murdered me.*

"Not true!" he yelled at the boy in the red-and-blue striped shirt, "Not true! *You fell in Marsden's! You fell in the pond! You fell in the pond and it was your own goddamned fault!*"

He turned off the TV and went to bed. He lay there awhile thrumming like a wire, then got up and took two Ambiens, washing them down with a healthy knock of scotch. The pill-and-booze combo killed the thrumming, at least, but he still lay wakeful, staring into the dark with eyes that felt as large and smooth as brass doorknobs. At three he turned the clock-radio around to face the wall. At five, as the first traces of dawn backlit the drapes, a comforting thought came to him. He wished he could share this comforting thought with Soupy Embree, but since he couldn't, he did the next best thing and spoke it aloud.

"If it were possible to go back in a time machine and change the stupid things some of us did in grammar school and junior high, Soups old buddy, that gadget would be booked up right into the twenty-third century."

Exactamundo. You couldn't blame kids. Grown-ups knew better, but kids were stupid by nature. Sometimes malevolent by nature too. He seemed to remember something about a girl in New Zealand who'd bludgeoned her best friend's mother to death with a brick. She'd hit the poor woman fifty times or more with that old brick, and when the girl was found guilty she went to jail for . . . what? Seven years? Five? Less? When she got out, she went to England and became an airline stewardess. Later she became a very popular mystery novelist. Who'd told him that story? Ellie, of course. El had been a great reader of mysteries, always trying—and often succeeding—in guessing whodunit.

"Soupy," he told his lightening bedroom, "you can't blame me. I plead diminished capacity." That actually made him smile.

As if it had just been waiting for this conclusion, another comforting thought arose. *I don't need to watch the game tonight. Nothing's forcing me to.*

That was finally enough to send him off. He woke shortly after noon, the first time he'd slept so late since college. In the kitchen he briefly considered the oatmeal, then fried himself three eggs in butter. He would have tossed in some bacon, if he'd had any. He did the next-best thing, adding it to the grocery list stuck to the fridge with a cucumber magnet.

"No game tonight for me," he told the empty condo, "Ah b'leeve Ah maht . . ."

He heard what his voice was doing and stopped, bewildered. It came to him that he might not be suffering from dementia or early-onset Alzheimer's; he might be having your ordinary everyday garden-variety nervous breakdown. That seemed a perfectly reasonable explanation for recent events, but knowledge was power. If you saw what was happening, you could stop it, right?

"I believe I might go out to a movie," he said in his own voice. Quietly. Reasonably. "That's all I meant to say."

In the end, he decided against a film. Although there were twenty screens in the immediate area, he could find nothing he wanted to watch on a single one of them. He went to the Publix instead, where he picked up a basketful of goodies (including a pound of the good thick-sliced pepper bacon Ellie loved). He started for the ten-items-or-less checkout lane, saw the girl at the register was wearing a Rays shirt with Matt Joyce's number 20 on the back, and diverted to one of the other lanes instead. That took longer, but he told himself he didn't mind. He also told himself he wasn't thinking about how someone would be singing the national anthem at the Trop right now. He'd picked up the new Harlan Coben in paperback, a little literary bacon to go with the literal variety. He'd read it tonight. Baseball couldn't match up to Coben's patented terror-in-the-burbs, not even when it was Jon Lester matched up against Matt Moore. How had he ever become interested in such a slow, boring sport to begin with?

He put away his groceries and settled onto the sofa. The Coben was terrific, and he got into it right away. Evers was so immersed that he didn't realize he'd picked up the TV remote, but when he got to the end of chapter six and decided to break for a small piece of Pepperidge Farm lemon cake, the gadget was right there in his hand.

Won't hurt to check the score, he thought, *Just a quick peek, and off it goes.*

The Rays were up one to nothing in the eighth, and Dewayne Staats was so excited he was burbling, "Don't want to talk about what's going on with Matt Moore tonight, folks—I'm old-school—but let's just say that the bases have been devoid of Crimson Hose."

No-hitter, Evers thought, *Moore's pitching a damn no-hitter and I've been missing it.*

Close-up on Moore. He was sweating, even in the Trop's constant 72 degrees, He went into his motion, the picture changed to the home plate shot, and there in the third row was Dean Evers's dead wife, wearing the same tennis whites she'd had on the day of her first stroke. He would have recognized that blue piping anywhere,

Ellie was deeply tanned, as she always was by this time of summer, and as was the case more often than not at the ballpark, she was ignoring the game entirely, poking at her iPhone instead. For an unfocused moment, Evers wondered who she was texting—someone here, or someone in the afterlife?—when, in his pocket, his cell phone buzzed.

She raised the phone to her ear and gave him a little wave.

Pick up, she mouthed, and pointed to her phone.

Evers shook his head no slowly.

His phone vibrated again, like a mild shock applied to his thigh.

"No," he said to the TV, and thought, logically: *She can just leave a message.*

Ellie shook her phone at him.

"This is wrong," he said. Because Ellie wasn't like Soupy Embree or Lennie Wheeler or Young Dr. Young. She loved him—of that Evers was sure—and he loved her. Forty-six years meant something, especially nowadays.

He searched her face. She seemed to be smiling, and while he didn't have a speech prepared, he guessed he did want to tell her how much he missed her, and what his days were like, and how he wished he was closer to Pat and Sue and the grandkids, because, really, there was no one else he could talk to.

He dug the phone from his pocket. Though he'd deactivated her account months ago, the number that came up was hers.

On TV, Moore was pacing behind the mound, juggling the rosin bag on the back of his pitching hand.

And then there she was, right behind David Ortiz, holding up her phone.

He pressed TALK.

"Hello?" he said.

"Finally," she said. "Why didn't you pick up?"

"I don't know. It's kind of weird, don't you think?"

"What's weird?"

"I don't know. You not being here and all."

"Dead, you mean. Me being dead."

"That."

"So you don't want to talk to me because I'm dead."

"No," he said. "I always want to talk to you." He smiled—at least, he thought he was smiling. He'd have to check the mirror to be sure, because his face felt frozen. "You're wanted, sweetheart, dead or alive."

"You're such a liar. That's one thing I always hated about you. And fucking Martha, of course. I wasn't a big fan of that either."

What could he say to that? Nothing. So he sat silent.

"Did you think I didn't know?" she said. "That's another thing I hated about you, thinking I didn't know what was going on. It was so obvious. A couple of times you came home still stinking of her perfume. Juicy Couture. Not the most subtle of scents. But then, you were never the most subtle guy, Dean."

"I miss you, EL."

"Okay, yes, I miss you too. That's not the point."

"I love you."

"Stop trying to press my buttons, all right? I need to do this. I didn't say anything before because I needed to keep everything together and make everything work. That's who I am. Or was, anyway. And I did. But you hurt me. You *cut* me."

"I'm sorr—"

"Please, Dean, I only have a couple minutes left, so for once in your life shut up and listen. You hurt me, and it wasn't just with Martha. And although I'm pretty sure Martha was the only one you slept with—"

That stung. "Of course she wa—"

"—don't expect any brownie points for that. You didn't have time to cheat on me with anyone outside the company because you were always there. Even when you were here you were there. I understood that, and maybe that was my fault for not sticking up for myself, but the one it really wasn't fair to was Patrick. You wonder why you never see him, it's because you were never there for him. You were always off in Denver or Seattle at some sales meeting or something. Selfishness is learned behavior, you know."

This criticism Evers had heard many times before, in many forms, and his attention waned. Moore had gone 3–2 on Papi. *Devoid*, Staats had said. Was Matt Moore really throwing a perfect game?

"You were always too worried about what you were doing, and not enough about the rest of us. You thought bringing home the bacon was enough."

I did, he almost told her. *I did bring home the bacon. Just tonight.*

"Dean? Are you hearing me? Do you understand what I'm telling you?"

"Yes," Evers said, just as the pitch from Moore caught the outside corner and the ump rang up Ortiz. "*Yes!*"

"I know that yes! God damn you, are you watching the stupid game?"

"Of course I'm watching the game." Though now it was a truck commercial. A grinning man—one who undoubtedly knew how to get things done—was driving through mud at a suicidal speed.

"I don't know why I called. You're hopeless."

"I'm not," Evers said. "I miss you."

"Jesus, why do I even bother? Forget it. Good-bye."

"Don't!" he said.

"I tried to be nice—that's the story of my life. I tried to be nice and look where it got me. People like you *eat* nice. Good-bye, Dean."

"I love you," he repeated, but she was gone, and when the game came back on, the woman with the sparkly top was in Ellie's seat. The woman with the sparkly top was a Tropicana Field regular. Sometimes the top was blue and sometimes it was green, but it was always sparkly. Probably so the folks at home could pick her out. As if she'd caught the thought, she waved. Evers waved back. "Yeah, bitch, I see you. You're on TV, bitch, good fucking job."

He got up and poured himself a scotch.

In the ninth Ellsbury snuck a seeing-eye single through the right side, and the crowd rose and applauded Moore for his effort. Evers turned the game off and sat before the dark screen, mulling what Ellie had said.

Unlike Soupy Embree's accusation, Ellie's was true. *Mostly true*, he amended, then changed it to *at least partly true*. She knew him better than anyone in the world—this world or any other—but she'd never been willing to give him the credit he deserved. He was, after all, the one who'd put groceries in the refrigerator all those years, some pretty high-grade bacon. He was also the one who'd *paid* for the refrigerator—a top-of-the-line Sub-Zero, thank you very much. He'd paid for her Audi. And her tennis club dues. And her massage therapist. And all the stuff she bought from the catalogs. And hey, let's not forget Patrick's college tuition! Evers had had to put together a jackleg combination of scholarships, loan packages, and shit summer jobs to get through school, but Patrick had gotten a full boat from his old man. The old man he was too busy to call these days.

She comes back from the dead, and why? To complain. And to do it on the goddamn iPhone I paid for.

He thought of an old saying and wished he'd quoted it to Ellie while he still had the chance: "Money can't buy happiness, but it allows one to endure unhappiness in relative comfort."

That might have shut her up.

The more he considered their life together—and there was nothing like talking to your dead spouse while you looked at her in a club seat to make you consider such things—the more he thought that while he hadn't been perfect, he'd still been all right. He did love her and Patrick, and had always tried to be kind to them. He'd worked hard to give them everything he never had, thinking he was doing the right thing. If it wasn't enough, there was nothing he could do about it now. As for the thing with Martha . . . some kinds of fucking were meaningless. Men understood that—*Kaz* certainly would have understood it— but women did not.

In bed, dropping into a blissful oblivion that was three parts Ambien and two parts scotch, it came to him that Ellie's rant was strangely freeing. Who else could they (whoever *they* were) send to bedevil him? Who could make him feel any worse? His mother? His father? He'd loved them, but not as he'd loved Ellie. Miss Pritchett? His uncle Elmer who used to tickle him till he wet his pants?

Snuggling deeper into the covers, Evers actually snickered at that. No, the worst had happened. And although there would be another great match-up tomorrow night at the Trop—Josh Beckett squaring off against James Shields— he didn't have to watch. His last thought was that from now on, he'd have more time to read. Lee Child, maybe. He'd been meaning to get to those Lee Child books.

But first he had the Harlan Coben to finish. He spent the afternoon lost in the green, pitiless suburbs. As the sun went down on another St. Petersburg Sunday, he was into the last fifty pages or so, and racing along. That was when his phone buzzed. He picked it up gingerly—the way a man might pick up a loaded mouse-trap—and looked at the readout. What he saw there was a relief. The call was from Kaz, and unless his old pal had suffered a fatal heart attack (not entirely out of the question; he was a good thirty pounds overweight), he was calling from Punta Gorda rather than the afterlife.

Still, Evers was cautious; given recent events, he had every reason to be. "Kaz, is that you?"

"Who the hell else would it be?" Kaz boomed. Evers winced and held the phone away from his ear. "Barack fucking Obama?"

Evers laughed feebly. "No, I just—"

"Fuckin' Dino Martino! You suck, buddy! Front-row seats, and you didn't even call me?"

From far away, Evers heard himself say: "I only had one ticket." He looked at his watch. Twenty past eight. It should have been the second inning by now— unless the Rays and Red Sox were the 8:00 Sunday-night game on ESPN.

He reached for the remote.

Kaz, meanwhile, was laughing. The way he'd laughed that day in the school-yard. It had been higher-pitched then, but otherwise it was just the same. *He* was just the same. It was a depressing thought. "Yeah, yeah, I'm just yankin' your ballsack. How's the view from there?"

"Great," Evers said, pushing the power button on the remote. Fox 13 was showing some old movie with Bruce Willis blowing things up. He punched 29 and ESPN came on. Shields was dealing to Dustin Pedroia, second in the Sox lineup. The game had just started.

I'm doomed to baseball, Evers thought.

"Dino? Earth to Dino Martino! You still there?"

"I'm here," he said, and turned up the volume. Pedroia flailed and missed. The crowd roared; those irritating cowbells the Rays fans favored clanged with maniacal fervor, "Pedie just struck out."

"No shit. I ain't blind, Stevie Wonder. The Rays Rooters are pumped up, huh?"

"Totally pumped," Evers said hollowly. "Great night for a ball game."

Now Adrian Gonzalez was stepping in. And there, sitting in the first row right behind the screen, doing a fair impersonation of a craggy old snowbird playing out his golden years in the Sunshine State, was Dean Patrick Evers.

He was wearing a ridiculous foam finger, and although he couldn't read it, not even in HD, he knew what it said: RAYS ARE #1. Evers at home stared at Evers behind home with the phone against his ear. Evers at the park stared back, holding the selfsame phone in the hand that wasn't wearing the foam finger. With a sense of outrage that not even his stunned amazement could completely smother, he saw that Ballpark Evers was wearing a Rays jersey. *Never,* he thought. *Those are traitor colors.*

"There you are!" Kaz shouted exultantly, "Shake me a wave, buddy!"

Evers at the ballpark raised the foam finger and waved it solemnly, like an oversize windshield wiper. Evers at home, on autopilot, did the same with his free hand.

"Love the shirt, Dino," Kaz said. "Seeing you in Rays colors is like seeing Doris Day topless." He snickered.

"I had to wear it," Evers said. "The guy who gave me the ticket insisted. Listen. I've gotta go. Want to grab a beer and a d—ohmygod, there it goes!"

Gonzo had launched a long drive, high and deep.

"Drink one for me!" Kaz shouted.

On Evers's expensive TV, Gonzalez was lumbering around the bases. As he watched, Evers suddenly understood what he had to do. There was only one way to put an end to this cosmic joke. On a Sunday night, downtown St. Pete would be deserted. If he took a taxi, he could be at the Trop by the end of the second inning. Maybe even sooner.

"Kaz?"

"Yeah, buddy?"

"We should either have been nicer to Lester Embree, or left him alone."

He pushed END before Kaz could reply. He turned off the TV. Then he went into his bedroom, rooted through the folded shirts in his bureau, and found his beloved Curt Schilling jersey, the one with the bloody sock on the front and WHY NOT US? on the back. Schilling had been The Man, afraid of nothing. When the Evers in the Rays shirt saw him in this one, he'd fade away like the bad dream he was and all of this would end.

Evers yanked the shirt on and called a cab. There was one nearby that had just dropped off a fare, and the streets were as deserted as Evers had expected. The cabbie had the game on the radio. The Sox were still batting in the top half of the second when he pulled up to the main gate.

"You'll have to settle for nosebleeds," the cabbie said. "Sox-Rays, that's a hot ticket."

"I've got one right behind home plate," Evers said. "Stop somewhere they've got the game on, you might see me. Look for the shirt with the bloody sock on it."

"I heard that fuckin' hoser's video game business went broke," the cabbie said as Evers handed him a ten. He looked, saw Evers still sitting in the backseat with the door open, and reluctantly made change. From it, Evers handed him a single rumpled simoleon.

"Guy with a front-row seat should be able to do better'n that for a tip," the cabbie grumbled.

"Guy with half a brain in his head should keep his mouth shut about the Big Schill," Evers said. "If he wants a better tip, that is." He slipped out, slammed the door and headed for the entrance.

"*Fuck you, Boston!*" the cabbie shouted.

Without turning around, Evers hoisted a middle finger—real, not foam.

The concourse with its palm trees lit like Christmas in Hawaii was all but empty, the sound of the crowd inside the stadium a hollow surf-boom. It was a sellout, the LED signs above the shuttered ticket windows bragged. There was only one window still open, all the way down at the end, the WILL CALL.

Yes, Evers thought, because they *will* call, won't they? He headed for it like a man on rails.

"Help you, sir?" the pretty ticket agent asked, and was that Juicy Couture she was wearing? Surely not. He remembered Martha saying, *It's my slut perfume. I only wear it for you.* She'd been willing to do things Ellie wouldn't dream of, things he remembered at all the wrong times.

"*Help* you, sir?"

"Sorry," Evers said. "Had a little senior moment there."

She smiled dutifully.

"Do you happen to have a ticket for Evers? Dean Evers?"

There was no hesitation, no thumbing through a whole box of envelopes, because there was only one left. It had his name on it. She slid it through the gap in the glass. "Enjoy the game."

"We'll see," Evers said.

He made for Gate A, opening the envelope and taking out the ticket. A piece of paper was clipped to it, just four words below the Rays logo: **COMPLIMENTS OF THE MANAGEMENT**. He strode briskly up the ramp and handed the ticket to a crusty usher who was standing there and watching as Elliot Johnson dug in against Josh Beckett. At the very least, the geezer was a good half century older than his employers. Like so many of his kind, he was in no hurry. It was one reason Evers no longer drove.

"Nice seat," the usher said, raising his eyebrows. "Just about the best in the house. And you show up late." He gave a disapproving head shake.

"I would have been here sooner," Evers said, "but my wife died."

The usher froze in the act of turning away, Evers's ticket in hand.

"Gotcha," Evers said, smiling and pointing a playful finger-gun. "That one never fails."

The usher didn't look amused. "Follow me, sir."

Down and down the steep steps they went. The usher was in worse shape than Evers, all wattle and liver spots, and by the time they reached the front row, Johnson was headed back to the dugout, a strikeout victim. Evers's seat was the only empty one—or not quite empty. Leaning against the back was a large blue foam finger that blasphemed: RAYS ARE #1.

My seat, Evers thought, and as he picked the offending finger up and sat down he saw, with only the slightest surprise, that he was no longer wearing his treasured Schilling jersey. Somewhere between the cab and this ridiculous, padded Captain Kirk perch, it had been replaced by a turquoise Rays shirt. And although he couldn't see the back, he knew what it said: MATT YOUNG.

"Young Matt Young," he said, a crack that his neighbors—neither of whom he recognized—pointedly ignored. He craned around, searching the section for

Ellie and Soupy Embree and Lennie Wheeler, but it was just a mix of anonymous Rays and Sox fans. He didn't even see the sparkly-top lady.

Between pitches, as he was twisted around trying to see behind him, the guy on his right tapped Evers's arm and pointed to the JumboTron just in time for him to catch a grotesquely magnified version of himself turning around.

"You missed yourself," the guy said.

"That's all right," Evers said. "I've been on TV enough lately."

Before Beckett could decide between his fastball and his slider, Evers's phone buzzed in his pocket.

Can't even watch the game in peace.

"Yello," he said.

"Who'm I talkin' to?" The voice of Chuckie Kazmierski was high and truculent, his I'm-ready-to-fight voice. Evers knew it well, had heard it often over the long arc of years stretching between Fairlawn Grammar and this seat at Tropicana Field, where the light was always dingy and the stars were never seen. "That you, Dino?"

"Who else? Bruce Willis?" Beckett missed low and away. The crowd rang their idiotic cowbells.

"Dino Martino, right?"

Jesus, Evers thought, *next he'll be saying who's on first and I'll be saying what's on second.*

"Yes, Kaz, the artist formerly known as Dean Patrick Evers. We ate paste together in the second grade, remember? Probably too much."

"It *is* you!" Kaz shouted, making Evers jerk the phone away from his ear. "I *told* that cop he was full of shit! Detective Kelly, my ass."

"What in hell are you talking about?"

"Some ass-knot pretending to be a cop's what I'm talkin' about. I knew it couldn't be real, he sounded too fuckin' official."

"Huh," Evers said, "An official official, imagine that."

"Guy tells me you're dead, so I go, if he's dead, how come I just talked to him on the phone? And the cop—the *so-called* cop—he goes, I think you're mistaken, sir. You must have talked to someone else. And *I* go, how come I just now saw him on TV at the Rays game? And this so-called cop goes, either you saw someone who looked like him or someone who looks like him is dead in his apartment. You believe this shit?"

Beckett bounced one off the plate. He was all over the place. The crowd was loving it. "If it wasn't a prank, I guess someone made a big mistake."

"Ya *think?*" Kaz gave his trademark laugh, low and raspy. "Especially since I'm talkin' to you right fuckin' now."

"You called to make sure I was still alive, huh?"

"Yeah." Now that he was settling down, Kaz seemed puzzled by this.

"Tell me something—if I'd turned out to be dead after all, would you have left a voice mail?"

"What? Jesus, I don't know." Kaz seemed more puzzled than ever, but that was nothing new. He'd always been puzzled. By events, by other people, probably by his own beating heart. Evers supposed that was part of why he'd so often been angry. Even when he wasn't angry, he was *ready* to be angry.

I'm speaking of him in the past tense, Evers realized.

"The guy I talked to said they found you at your place. Said you'd been dead for a while too."

The guy next to Evers nudged him again. "Lookin' good, buddy," he said.

On the JumboTron, shocking in its homely familiarity, was Evers's darkened bedroom. In the middle of the bed he'd shared with Ellie, the pillowtop king that was now too big for him, Evers lay still and pale, his eyes half-lidded, his lips purplish, his mouth a stiff rictus. Foam had dried like old spiderwebs on his chin.

When Evers turned to his seatmate, wanting to confirm what he was seeing, the seat beside him—the row, the section, the whole Tropicana Dome—was empty. And yet the players kept playing.

"They said you killed yourself."

"I didn't kill myself," Evers replied, and thought: *That damn expired Ambien. And maybe putting it with the scotch wasn't such a great idea. How long has it been? Since Friday night?*

"I know, it didn't sound like you."

"So, are you watching the game?"

"I turned it off. Fuckin' cop—that fuckin' ass-knot—upset me."

"Turn it on again," Evers said.

"Okay," Kaz said. "Lemme grab the remote."

"You know, we should have been nicer to Lester Embree."

"Water over the dam, old buddy. Or under the bridge. Or whatever the fuck it is."

"Maybe not. From now on, don't be so angry. Try to be nicer to people. Try to be nicer to everyone. Do that for me, will you, Kaz?"

"What the Christ is wrong with you? You sound like a fuckin' Hallmark card on Mother's Day."

"I suppose I do," Evers said. He found this a very sad idea, somehow. On the mound, Beckett was peering in for the sign.

"Hey, Dino! There you are! You sure don't *look* dead." Kaz gave out his old rusty cackle.

"I don't feel it."

"I was scared there for a minute," Kaz said. "Fuckin' crank yanker. Wonder how he got my number."

"Dunno," Evers said, surveying the empty park. Though of course he knew. After Ellie died, of the nine million people in Tampa-St. Pete, Kaz was the only person he could put down as an emergency contact. And that idea was sadder still.

"All right, buddy, I'll let you get back to the game. Maybe golf next week if it doesn't rain."

"We'll see," Evers said. "Stay cool, Kazzie, and—"

Kaz joined him then, and they chanted the last line together, as they had many, many times before: "*Don't let the bastards get you down!*"

That was it, it was over. He sensed things moving again, a flurry behind him, at the periphery of his vision. He looked around, phone in hand, and saw the spotted usher creakily leading Uncle Elmer and Aunt June down the stairs, and several girls he'd dated in high school, including the one who'd been sort of semiconscious—or maybe *unconscious* would be closer to the truth—when he'd had her. Behind them came Miss Pritchett with her hair down for once, and Mrs. Carlisle from the drugstore, and the Jansens, the elderly neighbors whose deposit bottles he'd stolen off their back porch. From the other side, as if it were a company outing, a second, equally ancient usher was filling in the rows at the top of the section with former Speedy employees, a number of them in their blue uniforms. He recognized Don Blanton, who'd been questioned during a child pornography investigation in the mid-nineties and had hung himself in his Malden garage. Evers remembered how shocked he'd been, both by the idea of someone he knew possibly being involved in kiddie porn and by Don's final action. He'd always liked the man, and hadn't wanted to let him go, but with that kind of accusation hanging over his head, what else could he do? The reputation of a company's employees was part of its bottom line.

He still had some battery left. What the hell, he thought. It was a big game. They were probably watching on the Cape.

"Hey, Dad," Pat answered.

"You watching the game?"

"The kids are. The grown-ups are playing cards."

Next to the first usher stood Lennie Wheeler's daughter, still in her black crepe and veil. She pointed like a dark spectre at Evers. She'd lost all her baby fat, and Evers wondered if that had happened before she died, or after.

"Go look at the game, son."

"Hang on," Pat said, followed by the screek of a chair. "Okay, I'm watching."

"Right behind home, in the front row."

"What am I looking at?"

Evers stood up behind the netting and waved his blue foam finger. "Do you see me?"

"No, where are you?"

Young Dr. Young hobbled down the steep stairs on his bad leg, using the seat backs to steady himself. On his smock, like a medal, was a coffee-colored splotch of dried blood.

"Do you see me now?" Evers took the phone from his ear and waved both arms over his head as if he was flagging a train. The grotesque finger nodded back and forth.

"No."

So, no.

Which was fine. Which was actually better.

"Be good, Patty," Evers said. "I love you."

He hit END as, all around the park, the sections were filling in. He couldn't see who'd come to spend eternity with him in peanut heaven or the far reaches of the outfield, but the premium seats were going fast. Here came the ushers with the shambling, rag-clad remnants of Soupy Embree, and then his mother, haggard after a double shift, and Lennie Wheeler in his pinstripe funeral suit and Grandfather Lincoln with his cane and Martha and Ellie and his mother and father and all the people he'd ever wronged in his life. As they filed into his row from both sides, he stuck his phone in his pocket and took his seat again, pulling off the foam finger as he did. He propped it on the now unoccupied seat to his left. Saving it for Kaz. Because he was sure Kaz would be joining them at some point, after seeing him on TV, and calling him. If Evers had learned anything about how this worked, it was that the two of them weren't done talking just yet.

A cheer erupted, and the rattle of cowbells. The Rays were still hitting. Down the right field line, though it was far too early, some loudmouth was exhorting the crowd to start the wave. As always when distracted from the action, Evers checked the scoreboard to catch up. It was only the third and Beckett had already thrown sixty pitches. The way things were looking, it was going to be a long game.

Karen Joy Fowler's lyrical and touching novel, *The Sweetheart Season*, brought together the national pastime and social change in 1940s America as it followed a barnstorming women's baseball team through a long Midwest summer of base hits, recipes and an awakening feminism. Fowler's *The Jane Austen Book Club* spent thirteen weeks on the *New York Times* bestsellers list and was a *New York Times* Notable Book. In the story reprinted here, a boy faces problems with bullies and with baseball before some unexpected help from friends in odd places helps him out.

The Further Adventures of the Invisible Man

⌒∾⌒

Karen Joy Fowler

MY MOTHER LIKES to refer to 1989 as the year I played baseball, as if she had nothing to do with it, as if nothing *she* did that year was worth noting. She has her un-amended way with too many of the facts of our lives, especially those occurring before I was born, about which there is little I can do. But this one is truly unfair. My baseball career was short, unpleasant, and largely her fault.

For purposes of calibration where my mother's stories are concerned, you should know that she used to say my father had been abducted by aliens. My mother and he made a pact after *Close Encounters of the Third Kind* that if one of them got the chance they should just go and the other would understand, so she figured right away that this is what had happened. He hadn't known I was coming yet or all bets would have been off, my mother said.

This was before *X-Files* gave alien abduction a bad name; even so my mother said we didn't need to go telling everyone. There'd be plenty of time for that when he returned, which he would be doing, of course. If he could. It might be tricky. If the aliens had faster-than-light spaceships, then he wouldn't be aging at the same rate as we; he might even be growing younger; no one knew for sure how these things worked. He might come back as a boy like me. Or it was entirely possible that he would have to transmutate his physical body into a beam of pure light in order to get back to us, which, honestly, wasn't going to do us a whole lot of good and he probably should just stay put. In any case, he wouldn't want us pining away, waiting for him—he would want us to get on with our lives. So that's what we were doing and none of this is about my father.

My mother worked as a secretary over at the college in the department of anthropology. Sometimes she referred to this job as her fieldwork. I could write a book, she would tell Tamara and me over dinner, I could write a book about that department that would call the whole theory of evolution into question. Tamara lived with us to help pay the rent. She looked like Theda Bara, though of course I didn't know that back then. She wore peasant blouses and ankle bracelets and rings in her ears. She slept in the big bedroom and worked behind the counter at Cafe Roma and sometimes sang on open mike night. She never did her dishes, but that was okay, my mom said. Tamara got enough of that at work and we couldn't afford not to be understanding. The dishes could be *my* job.

My other job was to go to school, which wasn't so easy in the sixth grade when this particular installment takes place. A lot of what made it hard was named Jeremy Campbell. You have to picture me, sitting in my first row desk, all hopeful attention. I just recently gave up my Inspector Gadget lunchbox for a nonpartisan brown bag. I'm trying to fit in. But that kid with the blond hair who could already be shaving, that's Jeremy Campbell. He's at the front of the room, so close I could touch him, giving his book report.

"But it's too late," Jeremy says, looking at me to be sure I know he's looking at me. "Every single person in that house is dead." He turns to Mrs. Gruber. "That's the end."

"I guess it would have to be," Mrs. Gruber says. "Are you sure this is a book you read? This isn't just some story you heard at summer camp?"

"*The Meathook Murders.*"

"Written by?"

Jeremy hesitates a moment. "King."

"Stephen King?"

"Stanley King."

"It's not on the recommended list."

Jeremy shakes his head sadly. "I can't explain that. It's the best book I ever read."

"All right," says Mrs. Gruber. "Take your seat, Jeremy."

On his way past my desk Jeremy deliberately knocks my books onto the floor. "Are you trying to trip me, Nathan?" he asks.

"Take your seat, Jeremy," Mrs. Gruber says.

"I'll talk to you later," Jeremy assures me.

* * *

After school, having no friends to speak of, I sometimes biked to my mom's office. The bike path between my school and hers took me past the Little League fields, the Mormon temple, some locally famous hybrid trees—a very messy half walnut–half elm created by Luther Burbank himself just to see if he could—and the university day care, where I once spent all day every day finger painting and was a much happier camper.

I came to a stop sign at the same time as a woman in a minivan. (Maybe this was the same day as Jeremy's book report, maybe not. I include it so you'll know the sort of town we live in.) Even though I came to a complete stop, even though I didn't know her from Adam, she rolled down her window to talk to me. "You should be wearing a helmet," she said. *That* kind of town. Someone had graffitied the words baseball spawns hate onto the Little League snack bar. This is a story about baseball, remember?

My mom's desk was in the same room as the faculty mailboxes. A busy place, but she liked that, she always liked to talk to people. On my way into the office I passed one of the other secretaries and two profs. By the time I got to my mom I'd been asked three times how school was and three times I'd said it was fine. There was a picture of me on her desk, taken when I was three and wearing a Batman shirt with the batwings stretched over my fat little three-year-old stomach, and also my most recent school picture, no matter how bad.

"Hey, cookie." My mom was always happy to see me; it's still one of the things I like best about her. "How was school?" I think she was pretty, but most kids think that about their moms; maybe she wasn't. Her hair was blond back then and cut extremely short, her eyes a light, light blue. She had a little snow globe on her desk only instead of a snow scene there was a miniature copy of the sphinx inside, and instead of snow there was gold glitter. I picked it up and shook it.

"Have you ever heard of a book called *The Meathook Murders?*" I asked. I was just making conversation. Mom's not much of a reader.

Sure enough, she hadn't. But it reminded her of a movie she'd seen and she started to tell me the plot, which took some time, being complicated and featuring nuns with hooks for hands. My mom went to Catholic school.

She kept forgetting bits of it and the whole time she was talking to me she was also typing a letter, up until the climax, which required both hands. My mom showed me how the sleeve of the habit fell so that you saw the hook, but only for a second, and then the nun said, "Are you here to confess?" just to get into the confessional where no one could see. And then it turned out not to be the nun with the hook, after all. It turned out to be the policeman, dressed in the wimple with a fake hook. He ended up stabbed with his own fake hook, which was, my mom assured me, a very satisfying conclusion.

Somewhere in the middle of her recitation Professor Knight came in to pick up his mail. Back in the fifth grade, during the Christmas concert, when we all had reindeer horns on our heads and jingle bells in our hands and our parents were there to see us, Bjorn Benson told me that Professor Knight was my father. "Everyone knows," Bjorn said. But Professor Knight had a daughter named Kate who was just a year older than me, and I'm betting she didn't know, nor his wife neither. Kate and I were at the same school then, where I could keep an eye on her. But by now she was at the junior high and I only saw her downtown sometimes. She was a skinny girl with cow eyes who sucked on her hair. "Stop staring at me" is about the only thing she ever said to me. She didn't *look* like my sister.

I kept meaning to ask my mom, but I kept chickening out. I wasn't ever really supposed to believe in the alien abduction story; it was just there to be something funny to say, but mainly to stop me asking anything outright. Which I certainly couldn't do then, not when she was working so hard to keep me distracted and entertained. Besides, Professor Knight didn't even glance our way; if he was my father I think he would've wanted to know how school was. But then I was suspicious all over again, because the moment he left, my mom started talking about my dad. The wonders he was seeing! The friends he was making! "On the planet Zandoor," she told me, "they only wish they had hooks for hands. Instead, they have herrings. Your dad could get stuck there a long time just dialing their phones for them."

She ran out of steam, all at once, her mouth sagging so she looked sad and tired. My response to this was complicated. I felt sorry for her, but it made me angry, too. I was just a kid, it didn't seem fair to make me see this. So I gave her the note Mrs. Gruber had said to take right home to her a couple of weeks ago. I was just being mean. I'd already read it. It said Mrs. Gruber wondered if I didn't need a male role model.

And then I was relieved that Mom didn't seem to mind. She crumpled the note and hooked it over her head into the wastebasket. "I've got a job to do, cup-cake," she said, so I went home and played *The Legend of Zelda* until dinnertime.

* * *

But she was more upset than she let on. Later that night Victor Wong dropped by, and I heard them talking. Victor worked in the computer department at Pacific Gas and Electric and was my mom's best friend. He was a thin-faced, delicate guy. I liked him a lot, maybe partly because he was the one man I knew for sure wasn't my dad—wrong race—and wasn't ever going to be my dad. He'd been coming around for a long time without it getting romantic. I always thought he liked Tamara though he never said so, even to my mom. If you believe her.

"Hey, don't look at me," Victor said when she brought up Mrs. Gruber's note. "I'm a heterosexual man and everyone who meets me assumes I'm gay. I'm a hopeless failure at both lifestyles."

"There's not a damn thing wrong with Nathan," my mom said, which was nice of her, especially since she didn't know I was listening. "He's a great kid. He's never given me a speck of trouble. Where does she get off?"

"Maybe the note wasn't aimed at Nathan. Maybe the note was aimed at you."

"I don't know what you're talking about."

"I think you do," Victor said. But I certainly didn't, although I spent a fair amount of time puzzling over it. I could make a better guess now. Apparently my mother used to flirt outrageously during PTA meetings in a way some people felt distracted from the business at hand. Or so Bjorn Benson says. He's still a font of information, but he's a CPA now. I doubt he'd lie.

"How you doing, Nathan?" Victor asked me later on his way to the bathroom. I was still playing *The Legend of Zelda*.

"I just need a magic sword," I told him.

"Who doesn't?" he said.

* * *

This brings us up to Saturday afternoon. The car wouldn't start; it put my mom in a very bad mood. She was always sure our mechanic was ripping her off. She had a date that evening, a fix-up from a friend, some guy named Michael she'd never even seen. So I left her getting ready and biked over to Bertilucci's Lumber and Drugs. My plan was to price a new game called *The Adventure of Link*. Even though I was such a great kid, and had never given her a speck of trouble, my mother had steadily refused to buy this game for me. I already spent too much time playing *The Legend of Zelda*, she said, as if getting me *The Adventure of Link* wouldn't solve that problem in a hot second. Anyway we couldn't afford it, especially not now that the car had to be repaired again.

Somewhere in the distance, a farmer was burning his fields. The sky to the south was painted with smoke and the whole town smelled sweetly of it. On my way to the store I passed the Yamaguchis'. Ms. Yamaguchi took self-defense with my mother and was very careful about gender-engendering toys. Her four-year-old son, Davey, was on the porch with his doll. As I biked by, he held the doll up, sighted along it. "Ack-ack-ack-ack," he said, picking me off cleanly.

I spent maybe fifteen minutes mooning over the video games. I wanted *The Adventure of Link* so bad I didn't even notice that Jeremy Campbell had come into the store, although if I'd looked into the shoplifting mirrors I could've seen him before he snuck up behind me. He put a hand on my shoulder and spun me around. He was with Diego Ruiz, a kid who'd never been anything but nice to me till this. "Come with me," Jeremy said.

We went to the front of the store where Mr. Bertilucci had temporarily abandoned the counter and Jeremy went around it and pulled the new copy of *Playboy* out from underneath. "Have you ever seen this before?" he asked me. He'd already flipped open the centerfold and he put it right on my face; I was actually breathing into her breasts, which was maybe all that kept me from hyperventilating.

"My mom says I have to get right home," I told him.

"Do pictures of naked women always make you think of your mom?" he asked. "Does your mom have tits like these?"

"I've seen his mom," Diego said. "No tits at all."

"Sad." Jeremy put an arm around me. "I'll tell you what," he said.

"Take this magazine out of the store for me"—he tucked it inside my jacket while he talked—"and I'll owe you one."

I would have offered to buy it, but I didn't have money and Mr. Bertilucci wouldn't have sold it to me if I did. I really didn't see how I had a choice in the matter so I zipped my jacket up, but then it occurred to me that if I was going to shoplift anyway I should get something I wanted, so I went back for *The Adventure of Link*.

Soon I was at the police department, talking with a cop named Officer Harper. I got my one phone call and caught my mom just as she and Michael were about to leave the house. Since my mom had no car she was forced to ask Michael to drive her to the police station. Since they were planning on a classy restaurant she arrived in her blue dress with dangly earrings in the shape of golden leaves, shoes with tiny straps, and heels that clicked when she walked, tea rose perfume on her neck. Michael had long hair and a Star Trek tie.

We all sat and watched a videotape of me sticking the game under my jacket. Apparently most theft occurred at the video games; it was the only part of the store televised. There was no footage at all of Jeremy, at least none that we saw. I was more scared of Jeremy than Officer Harper, so I kept my mouth shut. Officer Harper told my mom and Michael to call him Dusty.

"He's never done anything like this before, Dusty," my mom said. "He's a great kid."

Dusty had a stern look for me, a concerned one for my mother. "You and your husband," he began.

"I'm not her husband," Michael said.

"Where's his father?"

Apparently we weren't telling the police about the alien abduction. "He's not part of the picture," was all my mother would say about that. "Is there any other man taking an interest in him?" Dusty asked. He was looking at Michael.

"Christ." Michael blocked the look with his hands, waved them about. "This is our first date. This is me, meeting the kid for the first time. How do you do, Nathan."

"Don't kids with fathers ever shoplift?" my mother asked. She was looking so nice, but her voice had a tight-wound sound to it.

"I'm only asking because of the *Playboy*." Dusty had confiscated the magazine and inventoried it with the other officers. Now he put it, folded up discreetly, on the metal desk between us.

This was the first my mother had heard about the *Playboy*. I could see her taking it in and, unhappy as she already was, I could see it made an impact. "I do have a suggestion," Dusty said.

It was a terrible suggestion. Dusty coached a Little League team called the Tigers. He thought Mr. Bertilucci might not press charges if Dusty could tell him he'd be keeping a personal eye on me. "I don't like baseball," I said. I was very clear about this. I would rather have gone to jail.

"A whole team of ready-made friends," Dusty said encouragingly. You could see he was an athlete himself. He had big shoulders and a sunburned nose that he rubbed a lot. There were bowling trophies on the windowsill and a memo pad with golf jokes on the desk.

"And I suck at it."

"Maybe we can change that."

"Really suck."

My mother was looking at me, her eyes narrow, and her earrings swinging. "I think it's a wonderful idea." The words came out without her hardly opening her mouth. "We're so grateful to you, Dusty, for suggesting it."

So I was paroled to the Tigers. I was released into my mother's custody, and she wouldn't let me bike home by myself, and she was feeling bad about Michael's spoiled evening. So she hissed me into Michael's car, apologizing the whole time to him. She suggested that we could maybe all go to the miniature golf course together. Michael agreed, but it wasn't his idea, and he and my mom were still dressed for a first impression.

I couldn't have been more miserable. I was hoping hard that Michael would turn out to be a jerk so that I would only have ruined the date, and not the rest of my mother's life. I hated him the minute I saw him, but you can't go by that. I could pretty much be counted on to hate every guy my mom went out with. This was easy since they were all jerks.

My mom was so mad at me that she couldn't miss. By the time we got to the fourth hole she was already three strokes under par. The fourth hole was the castle.

"I still don't get what not having a father has to do with shoplifting." There was a perfect little thwock sound when she hit the ball. She was clicking along on her two-inch heels and she *owned* this golf course.

Michael had been holding his tongue, but this was about the eighth time she'd said this. "It's not my business," he offered.

"But . . ."

Michael banked the ball off the side of the castle door and it rolled all the way back to his feet. "I just don't think his father would be letting him off so easy."

"What does that mean?"

"It means, here he is. Two hours ago the police picked him up for shoplifting. Is he being punished? No. You take him out for a game of miniature golf."

"Oh, he's not having a good time," my mom said. She turned to me. "Are you?"

"No, ma'am," I assured her.

"He stole something. If that'd been me, my father would have made real sure it never happened again," Michael said. "With his belt he would have made sure." Another ball missed the opening by inches.

"I have raised this kid all by myself for eleven years," my mother said. She was below us now, on the second half of the hole, sinking her putt. "I've done a great job. This is a great kid."

I saw the glimmer of a chance. "Don't make me play baseball, Mom." I put my heart into my voice.

"You. Don't. Even. Speak to me," she answered.

By the time we got to the sixteenth hole, the anthill, we were really not getting along. "*Playboy!*" My mother was so far ahead there was no way for her to lose now. She'd forgotten about the dressed-up mousse in her hair, hair snot, she calls this. Sometime around hole seven she'd run her hand through it. Now it was sticking up in odd tufts. Of course, neither Michael nor I could tell her this even if we'd wanted to. She sank another ball. "I picketed the campus bookstore for carrying *Playboy*. Did you remember that, Nathan?"

I was hitting my balls too softly. I couldn't get them over the lip of the hole. Michael was hitting his balls too hard. They bounced into the hole and out again. He'd put his hair behind his ears, but it wouldn't stay there.

"There, you see . . ." Michael said.

"What?"

"Not that it's my business."

"Go ahead." My mom's voice was a wonder of nasty politeness. "Don't hold back."

"I just think a desire to look at *Playboy* magazine is pretty natural at his age. I think his father would understand that."

"I think *Playboy* promotes a degraded view of women. I think it's about power, not about sex. And I think Nathan knows how I feel."

Michael lined up his ball. He looked at the anthill, back down at his ball, looked at the anthill again. He took a little practice swing. "At a certain age, boys start to see breasts everywhere they look." He hit the ball too hard. "It's no big deal."

"I think that's six strokes," my mother said. "That would be your limit." She was snarling at him, her hair poking out of her head like pinfeathers.

His ears turned red. He snarled back. "It's not a real game."

"I think I've had six strokes, too," I said.

My mother retrieved her ball from the hole. "Don't *you* even speak to me."

* * *

Michael dropped us at home and we never saw him again. In my mind he lives forever, talking about breasts and taking that sad practice swing in his Star Trek tie. Because it was already midseason it took most of the next week to get me added to the Tigers' roster. Dusty let my mom know he was probably the only coach in town who could've accomplished it. His own son was the Tigers' top pitcher, a pleasant, pug-nosed kid named Ryan. Jeremy Campbell played third base.

My first game came on a Thursday night. So far I'd done nothing but strike out in practice and let ground balls go through my legs. While I was getting into my uniform my mom tossed a bag onto my bed. "What's this?" I asked. I opened it up. I was looking at something like a small white surgical mask, only rigid and with holes in it.

"Little something your coach said you might need," my mother told me.

"What is it?"

"An athletic cup."

"A *what?*"

"You wear it for protection."

I was starting to get it. What I was getting was horrifying. "I'm going to be hit in the balls? Is that what you're telling me?"

"Of course not."

"Then why am I wearing this?"

"So you don't have to worry even for a minute about it." Which of course I wasn't until this cup appeared. "I can show you how to wear it," my mom said. "On my hand."

"No!" I slammed the door. I couldn't get it comfortable, and I didn't know if this was because I wasn't wearing it right, or because it was just uncomfortable. In a million years I wouldn't ask my mother. I took it off and stowed it under the mattress.

Victor drove us to the game since we still didn't have a car. "It looks to me like your distributor got a bit wet," the mechanic had told my mom. "We could just dry it out, if that was all it was. But it looks to me like somebody just kept trying to start it and trying to start it until the starter burned out. Now your starter is shot and you're going to need a new battery too since it looks to me as if somebody tried to charge up the battery and thought they could just attach those jumper cables any which way. I wish you'd called us first thing when we could just have dried it out." He'd made my mom so mad she told him not to touch the car, but he'd let her leave it anyway, since we all knew she'd have to back down eventually.

So Victor drove us, and I tried to appeal to him. No way, I thought, could he have played baseball any better than I did. But he betrayed me, he was a scrappy little player, or so he chose to pretend. I've never yet met a grown man who'll admit he couldn't play ball. And then he added a second betrayal. "You watch too much television, Nathan." He had his arm stretched out comfortably across the seat back, driving with one hand. Nothing on his conscience at all. "This'll be good for you."

Tamara met us, since they all insisted on being in the stands for my debut. Because I was on the bench, I was practically sitting with them. I could hear them having a good time behind me, heading for the snack bar every couple of minutes, and I could have been having a good time too, except that I knew I had to go on the field eventually. Everyone plays, those were the stupid rules.

Ryan took the mound. A guy from the college was umping, a big, good-looking, long-armed cowboy of a guy named Chad. I heard my mom telling Tamara and Victor she thought he was cute and I was suddenly afraid she was going to like Little League way too much. Ryan warmed up and then the first batter stepped into the box. Ryan threw. "Strike!" Chad said.

"Good call, blue," my mother told him from the stands.

The other coach, a man with a red face, gray hair, and his ears sticking out on the outside of his baseball cap, called for a time-out. He spoke with Chad. "They're using an ineligible pitcher," he said. "We're filing a protest."

"You can talk to me," Dusty told him. "I'm right here. What the hell do you mean?"

"You pitched him Monday. All game. You can't use him again for four days."

Dusty counted on his fingers. "Monday, Tuesday, Wednesday, Thursday."

"You can't count Monday. You pitched him Monday."

"Did he pitch Monday?" Chad asked.

"Yes," Dusty said.

"Oh, you bet he did." The other coach pushed his hat back from his puffy, red face. "Thought I wouldn't notice?"

"I thought it was four days."

"Game goes to the Senators," Chad said.

"Wait. I'll pitch someone else," Dusty offered. "It was an honest mistake. Come on, he's only thrown a single pitch. The kids are all here to play. We'll start over."

"Not a chance." The other coach told the Senators to line up. "Shake their hands," he told them. "Give the Tigers a cheer. Let's show a little sportsmanship."

Back in the stands I could hear Victor saying how much better Little League would be if the kids made up the rules and didn't tell them to the parents.

Whenever the parents started to figure them out, Victor suggested, the kids could change them.

But I thought this had worked out perfectly. Chad was already picking up the bases. My mom called to him that he umped one hell of a game. "Don't give me such a hard time, lady," he said, but he was all smiling when he said it; he came over to talk to her. Dusty took the team out for ice cream. There was a white owl in the air and a cloud of moths around the streetlights. A breeze came in from the almond orchards. I was one happy ballplayer.

Of course they wouldn't all be like that. Sooner or later I could see I was going to be out in right field with the ball headed for my uncupped crotch, the game on the line, and Jeremy Campbell watching me from third.

* * *

On Friday my mother called and told the garage to go ahead and fix the car. This was a defeat and she took it as such. I didn't have another game until Monday, but I did have practice on Friday so I was not as happy as I could have been either. The practice field was on the way home from the garage so Mom drove by later after she'd picked up the car. The weather was hot and the team was just assembling. She stopped for a moment to watch and then the car wouldn't start. "Jesus Christ!" she said. She banged the horn once in frustration; it gave a startled caw.

Jeremy came biking in beside her. He started to pedal past, then swung around. "Pop the hood," he told her.

"I picked this car up from the garage about two minutes ago. I won't even tell you what I just paid that crook."

Jeremy lifted the hood. "Your ground strap came off." He did something I couldn't see; when my mom turned the key, it started right up.

"What a *wonderful* boy," she said to me. To him, "You're a wonderful boy."

"Forget it." Jeremy was all gracious modesty.

She took off then, engine churning like butter, and we'd just barely started passing the ball around when Dusty got called away on a 911. The assistant coach hadn't arrived yet, so Dusty told us all to go straight on home again. After Dusty left, Jeremy chased me into Putah Creek Park, where my bicycle skidded out from under me when I tried to make a fast, evasive turn. He threw my bike down into the creek gully. He left me lying on the ground, hating myself for being afraid to even stand up, thinking of ways I could kill him. I could run him through with a magic sword. I could hang him from a meathook. I could smother him with his own athletic cup. If I bashed his skull with a baseball bat, no one would ever suspect it was me.

The bank of the creek was steep. I slid all the way down it. Then I slipped in the mud trying to get myself and the bicycle out again. The creek was already covered with summer slime and I got slick, green, fish-smelling streaks of it on my pants. My shoes were ruined. The front wheel of the bike was bent and I had to carry it home, rolling it on the back tire.

This was a long, hard, hot walk. I loved my bicycle, but there were many, many moments when I considered just walking off and leaving it. I'd hit my knees and my hands on the pavement when I fell, and my injuries stung and throbbed while I was walking. I told my mother I'd fallen off the bike, which was certainly true, and she bought it, even though I'd never fallen off my bike before, and certainly not into the creek.

Tamara was singing at Cafe Roma that evening and my mother had mentioned it to Chad, so she was thinking he might show. It had her distracted and she didn't make the fuss over my injuries that I expected. She was busy borrowing clothes from Tamara and moussing up her hair. This was a good thing, I thought, fewer questions to deal with and it probably meant I was growing up. But the lack of attention made me even more miserable than I already was. It would have all been worthwhile if my injuries had kept me out of Monday's game, but they didn't.

When everyone had left the house I took a hammer to the athletic cup. I meant to prove the cup wasn't up to much, but I found out otherwise. The blows bounced off it without leaving a mark. To make sure the hammer wasn't defective I tested it on the floor in my room. I left a ding like a crescent in the linoleum inside my closet. I smashed up a bunch of old crayons and put a hole in the bedroom wall behind the bed. I took an apple I hadn't eaten at lunch outside and crushed it like an egg. I was more and more impressed with the cup. I just needed a whole suit of the stuff.

This was all about the same time Boston third baseman Wade Boggs went on national TV and told the world he was addicted to sex.

* * *

We had a game Monday against the Royals and, like a nightmare, suddenly, there we were, down by one run, two outs, sixth and final inning, with Bjorn Benson on first base and me at bat. So far I'd only connected with the ball once and that was a feeble foul. Jeremy came out to the box to give me a little pep talk. "This used to be a good team before you joined," he said. "But you suck. If you cost us this game you'll pay in ways you can't even imagine, faggot." He smelled of cigarettes, though no one in my town smoked; it was like a town ordinance. Jeremy spit into the dust beside my cleats. I turned to look at the stands and I saw my mother watching us.

Dusty came and took the bat out of my hand. He went to the umpire, who wasn't Chad. "Ryan batting for Nathan," he said. He sent me back to the bench. It took Ryan seven pitches to strike out, which is surely four more pitches than it would have taken me.

Our car wasn't working again and Victor had dropped us off, but he couldn't stay for the whole game, so my mom asked Dusty's wife, Linda, a pretty woman who wore lipstick even to the ballpark, for a ride home.

When we got in the car we were all quiet for a while. Dusty finally spoke. "You played a good game, Nathan. You too, Ryan."

Linda agreed. "It was a good game. Nothing to be ashamed of."

"Usually you can hit off Alex," Dusty said to Ryan. "I wonder what happened tonight."

"He didn't get to bed until late," Linda suggested. "Were you tired, honey?"

"I don't think Alex was pitching as fast as he usually does. I thought he was tiring. I thought you'd hit off him."

"That was a lot of pressure, putting him in then," Linda observed. "But usually he would have gotten a hit. Were you tired, honey?"

"One more pitch, we would have had him, right, Tigers?"

Ryan looked out the window and didn't say much. There was a song on the radio, "Believe It or Not," and his lips were moving as if he was singing along but I couldn't hear him.

They let us off and we went inside. Like Ryan, my mom had been quiet the whole way home. I went to clean up and then she called me into the kitchen. "Couple of things," she said. "First of all, you're scared of that boy. The one who fixed our car. Why?"

"Because he's scary?" I offered. "Because he's a huge, mean, cretinous freak who hates me?" I was relieved, but mortified that she knew. I was also surprised. It was too much to feel all at once. I made things worse by starting to cry, loudly, and with my shoulders shaking.

My mom put her arms around me and held me until I stopped. "I love you," she said. She kissed the top of my head.

"I love you, too."

"I loved you first." Her arms tightened on me. "So there's a rumor on the street that you don't want to play baseball anymore."

I pushed away to look at her face. She stuck out her tongue and crossed her eyes.

"You mean it?" I asked. "I can quit?"

"I'll call Dusty tonight and tell him he's short one little Tiger."

It turned out to be a little more complicated. My mom called Dusty, but Dusty said he needed to see me, said he needed to hear it from me. He'd made representations to Mr. Bertilucci, he reminded us. He didn't want those to have been false representations. He thought we owed it to him to listen to what he had to say. He asked us to come to the house.

My mom agreed. By now we had the car back again. My mother drove and on the way over she warned me about the good cop/bad cop routine she thought Dusty and Linda might be planning to pull. She promised she wouldn't leave me alone with Dusty and she was as good as her word even when Linda tried to entice her outside to show her where the new deck was going to go. Ryan had obviously made himself scarce.

We sat in the living room, which was done country style, white ruffles and blue-and-white checks. Someone, I'm guessing Linda, collected ceramic ducks. She stood at the kitchen door smiling nervously at us. The TV was on in the background, the local news with the affable local anchor. Dusty muted her to talk to me. "You haven't really given the team or yourself a chance," Dusty said. His face had a ruddy, healthy glow.

"I just don't like baseball."

"You don't like it because you think you're no good at it. Give yourself time to get better." He turned to my mother. "You shouldn't let him give up on himself."

"He's not giving up on himself. He's being himself."

"He was improving every game," Linda said.

"He never wanted to play. I made him."

Dusty leaned forward. "And I remember why you made him. You want that to happen again?"

"That's a separate issue."

"I don't think so," Dusty turned to me again. "Don't let yourself become one of the quitters, Nathan. Don't walk out on your team. The values you learn on the playing field, those are the values that make you a success in everything you do later in life."

"I never played on a team," my mom observed. "How ever do I manage to get through the day?"

It was a snotty comment. Really, she was the one who started it. Dusty was the one to go for the throat. "I'm sure his father wouldn't want him taught to be a quitter."

There was a long, slow, loud silence in the room. Then my mom was talking without moving her mouth again. "His father is none of your damn business."

"Would anyone like a cup of coffee?" Linda asked. Her sandals tapped anxiously as she started into the kitchen, then came back out again. "I made brownies! I hope everyone likes them with nuts!"

Neither my mom nor Dusty showed any sign of hearing her. Neither would take their eyes off the other. "He didn't quit on you, Dusty," my mom said. "You quit on him."

"What does that mean?"

"It was his turn to bat."

"That was okay with me," I pointed out. "I was really happy with that."

"That was a team decision," Dusty said. "That's just what I'm talking about. If you'd ever played on a team you wouldn't be questioning that decision."

My mother stood, taking me by the hand. "You run your team. Let me raise my kid," she said. And we left the house and one of us left it hopping mad. "On the planet Zandoor," she told me, "Little League is just for adults. Dusty wouldn't qualify. Of course it's not like Little League here. You try to design a glove that fits on a Zandoorian."

The other one of us was so happy he was floating. When we got home Victor, Tamara, and Chad were sitting together on our porch. "I'm not a baseball player anymore," I told them. I couldn't stop grinning about it.

"Way to go, champ," Tamara said. She put her arms around me. Her body was much softer than my mom's and her black hair fell over my face so I smelled her coconut shampoo. It was a perfect moment. I remember everything about it.

"What do you think of that?" my mom asked Chad. Through the curtain of Tamara's hair I watched him shrug. "If he doesn't like to play, why should he play?"

They were staring at each other. I thought he was a little young for her, besides being a fat jerk, but no one was asking me. "Saturday night," she told him, "there's a Take Back the Night march downtown. Victor, Tamara, and I are going. Do you want to come?"

Chad looked at Victor. "This is a test, isn't it?" he asked.

"You already passed the test," my mother said.

The next day she spotted Jeremy while she was dropping me at school. She waved him over and he actually came. "I'm so glad to see you," she told him. "I didn't thank you properly for helping with the car the other day. You were great. Where did you learn to do that?"

"My dad," Jeremy said.

"I'm going to call him up and thank him, too. Tell him what a great kid he has. And you should come to dinner. I owe you that much. Honestly, you'd be doing me a favor. I'm thinking of buying a new car, but I need someone knowledgeable advising me." She was laying it on so thick the air was hard to breathe.

Jeremy suggested a Mustang convertible, or maybe a Trans Am. He was walking away before she'd turn and see the look I was giving her. "That's wonderful," I said. "Jeremy Campbell is coming to dinner. That's a dream come true." I gathered up my homework, slammed the car door, stormed off. Then I came back. "And it won't work," I told her. "You don't know him like I do."

"Maybe not," my mom said. "But it's hard to dislike someone you've been good to, someone who's depending on you. It's an old women's trick. I think it's worth a try."

Let me just take a moment here to note that it did not work. Jeremy Campbell didn't even show up for the dinner my mom cooked specially for him. He did ease off for a bit until whatever it was about me that provoked him provoked him again. Not a thing worked with Jeremy until Mr. Campbell was laid off and the whole Campbell family finally had to move three states east. The last time I saw him was June of 1991. He was sitting on top of me, pinning my shoulders down with his knees, stuffing dried leaves into my mouth. He had an unhappy look on his face as if he didn't like it any more than I did, and that pissed me off more than anything.

Then he turned his head slightly and a beam of pure light came streaming through his ears, lighting them up, turning them into two bright red fungi at the sides of his head. It helped a little that he looked ridiculous, even though I was the only one in the right position to see. It's the picture I keep in my heart.

* * *

So that's the way it really was and don't let my mother tell you differently. Saturday turned out to be the night I won at *The Legend of Zelda*. I was alone in the house at the time. Mom and Tamara were off at their rally, marching down Second Street, carrying signs. The Playboy Bunny logo in a red circle with a red slash across its face. On my computer the theme played and the princess kissed the hero, again and again. These words appeared on the screen: *You have destroyed Ganon. Peace has returned to the country of Hyrule.*

And then the words vanished and were replaced with another message. *Do you wish to play again?*

What I wished was that I had *The Adventure of Link*. But before I could get bitter, the phone rang. "This is really embarrassing," my mom said. "There was a little trouble at the demonstration. We've been arrested."

"Arrested for what?" I asked.

"Assault. Mayhem. Crimes of a violent nature. None of the charges will stick. We were attacked by a group of nazi frat boys and I did nothing but defend myself. You know me. Only thing is, Dusty is in no mood to cut me any slack. I don't think I'm getting out tonight. What a vindictive bastard he's turned out to be!"

"Are you all right?"

"Oh, yeah. Hardly a scratch." There was a lot of noise in the background. I could just make out Tamara, she was singing that Merle Haggard song "Mama Tried." "There's a whole bunch of us here," my mother said. "It's the crime of the century. I might get my picture in the paper. Anyway, Victor wasn't arrested. You know Victor. So he's on his way to stay with you tonight. I just wanted you to hear from me yourself."

I didn't like to think of her spending the night in jail, even if it did sound like a slumber party over there. I could already hear Victor's car pulling up out front. I was glad he was staying; I wouldn't have liked to be alone all night. Sometime in the dark I'd have started thinking about nuns with hooks for hands. Now I could see him through the window and he was carrying a pizza. Good on Victor! "Just as long as you're all right," I told her.

"I must say you're being awfully nice about this," my mother said.

T. Coraghessan Boyle has published some two-dozen novels or collections and his stories regularly appear in such magazines as the *The New Yorker, The Atlantic, Esquire, The Paris Review, McSweeney's, Playboy, Harper's,* and *Granta*. He is the recipient of the PEN/Faulkner Prize for best novel of the year (for *World's End*); the PEN/Malamud Prize in the short story (for *T.C. Boyle Stories*); and the Prix Médicis Étranger for best foreign novel in France (for *The Tortilla Curtain*). In this story, Hector Quesadilla is an aging ballplayer and a man of large appetite. Hector knows that baseball can be cruel to its players as their ambitions outpace their fading skills. But on a most unusual day, Hector hopes that, for him, the game might go on forever.

The Hector Quesadilla Story

∽

T. Coraghessan Boyle

HE WAS NO JOLTIN' JOE, no Sultan of Swat, no Iron Man. For one thing, his feet hurt. And God knows no legendary immortal ever suffered so prosaic a complaint. He had shin splints too, and corns and ingrown toenails and hemorrhoids. Demons drove burning spikes into his tailbone each time he bent to loosen his shoelaces, his limbs were skewed so awkwardly that his elbows and knees might have been transposed and the once-proud knot of his *frijole*-fed belly had fallen like an avalanche. Worse: he was old. Old, old, old, the graybeard hobbling down the rough-hewn steps of the senate building, the ancient mariner chewing on his whiskers and stumbling in his socks. Though they listed his birthdate as 1942 in the program, there were those who knew better: it was way back in '54, during his rookie year for San Buitre, that he had taken Asunción to the altar, and even in those distant days, even in Mexico, twelve-year-olds didn't marry.

When he was younger—really young, nineteen, twenty, tearing up the Mexican League like a saint of the stick—his ears were so sensitive he could hear the soft rasping friction of the pitcher's fingers as he massaged the ball and dug in for a slider, fastball, or change-up. Now he could barely hear the umpire bawling the count in his ear. And his legs. How they ached, how they groaned and creaked and chattered, how they'd gone to fat! He ate too much, that was the problem. Ate prodigiously, ate mightily, ate as if there were a hidden thing inside him, a creature all of jaws with an infinite trailing ribbon of gut. *Huevos con chorizo* with beans, *tortillas, camarones* in red sauce, and a twelve-ounce steak for breakfast, the chicken in *mole* to steady him before afternoon games, a sea of beer to wash away the tension of the game and prepare his digestive machinery for the flaming *machaca*-and-pepper salad Asunción prepared for him in the blessed evenings of the home stand.

Five foot seven, one hundred eighty-nine and three-quarters pounds. Hector Hernán Jesús y María Quesadilla. Little Cheese, they called him. Cheese, Cheese, Cheesus, went up the cry as he stepped in to pinch-hit in some late-inning crisis, Cheese, Cheese, Cheesus, building to a roar until Chavez Ravine resounded as if with the holy name of the Saviour Himself when he stroked one of the clean line-drive singles that were his signature or laid down a bunt that stuck like a finger in jelly. When he fanned, when the bat went loose in the fat brown hands and he went down on one knee for support, they hissed and called him *Viejo.*

One more season, he tells himself, though he hasn't played regularly for nearly ten years and can barely trot to first after drawing a walk. One more. He tells Asunción too—One more, one more—as they sit in the gleaming kitchen of their house in Boyle Heights, he with his Carta Blanca, she with her mortar and pestle for grinding the golden, petrified kernels of maize into flour for the tortillas he eats like peanuts. *Una más,* she mocks. What do you want the Hall of Fame? Hang up your spikes, Hector.

He stares off into space, his mother's Indian features flattening his own as if the legend were true, as if she really had taken a spatula to him in the cradle, and then, dropping his thick lids as he takes a long slow swallow from the neck of the bottle, he says: Just the other day, driving home from the park, I saw a car on the freeway, a Mercedes with only two seats, a girl in it, her hair out back like a cloud, and you know what the license plate said? His eyes are open now, black as pitted olives. Do you? She doesn't. Cheese, he says. It said Cheese.

Then she reminds him that Hector Jr. will be twenty-nine next month and that Reina has four children of her own and another on the way. You're a grandfather, Hector—almost a great-grandfather, if your son ever settled down. A moment slides by, filled with the light of the sad, waning sun and the harsh Yucateco dialect of the radio announcer, *Hombres* on first and third, one down. *Abuelo,* she hisses, grinding stone against stone until it makes his teeth ache. Hang up your spikes, *abuelo.*

But he doesn't. He can't. He won't. He's no grandpa with hair the color of cigarette stains and a blanket over his knees, he's no toothless old gasser sunning himself in the park—he's a big-leaguer, proud wearer of the Dodger blue, wielder of stick and glove. How can he get old? The grass is always green, the lights always shining, no clocks or periods or halves or quarters, no punch-in and punch-out: this is the game that never ends. When the heavy hitters have fanned and the pitchers' arms gone sore, when there's no joy in Mudville, taxes are killing everybody, and the Russians are raising hell in Guatemala, when the manager paces the dugout like an attack dog, mind racing, searching high and low for the canny veteran to go in and do single combat, there he'll be—always, always, eternal as a monument—Hector Quesadilla, utility infielder with the .296 lifetime batting average and service with the Reds, Phils, Cubs, Royals, and L.A. Dodgers.

So he waits. Hangs on. Trots his aching legs round the outfield grass before the game, touches his toes ten agonizing times each morning, takes extra batting practice with the rookies and slumping millionaires. Sits. Watches. Massages his feet. Waits through the scourging road trips in the Midwest and along the East Coast, down to muggy Atlanta, across to stormy Wrigley, and up to frigid Candlestick, his gut clenched round an indigestible cud of meat-loaf and instant potatoes and wax beans, through the terrible night games with the alien lights in his eyes, waits at the end of the bench for a word from the manager, for a pat on the ass, a roar, a hiss, a chorus of cheers and catcalls, the marimba pulse of bat striking ball, and the sweet looping arc of the clean base hit.

And then comes a day, late in the season, the homeboys battling for the pennant with the big-stick Braves and the sneaking Jints, when he wakes from honeyed dreams in his own bed that's like an old friend with the sheets that smell of starch and soap and flowers, and feels the pain stripped from his body as if at the touch of a healer's fingertips. Usually he dreams nothing, the night a blank, an erasure, and opens his eyes on the agonies of the martyr strapped to a bed of nails. Then he limps to the toilet, makes a poor discolored water, rinses the dead taste from his mouth, and staggers to the kitchen table, where food, only food, can revive in him the interest in drawing another breath. He butters tortillas and folds them into his mouth, spoons up egg and melted jack cheese and *frijoles refritos* with the green *salsa*, lashes into his steak as if it were cut from the thigh of Kerensky, the Atlanta relief ace who'd twice that season caught him looking at a full-count fastball with men in scoring position. But not today. Today is different, a sainted day, a day on which sunshine sits in the windows like a gift of the Magi and the chatter of the starlings in the crapped-over palms across the street is a thing that approaches the divine music of the spheres. What can it be?

In the kitchen it hits him: *pozole* in a pot on the stove, *carnitas* in the saucepan, the table spread with sweetcakes, *buñuelos*, and the little marzipan *dulces* he could kill for. *Feliz cumpleaños*, Asunción pipes as he steps through the doorway. Her face is lit with the smile of her mother, her mother's mother, the line of gift givers descendant to the happy conquistadors and joyous Aztecs. A kiss, a *dulce*, and then a knock at the door and Reina, fat with life, throwing her arms around him while her children gobble up the table, the room, their grandfather, with eyes that swallow their faces. Happy birthday, Daddy, Reina says, and Franklin, her youngest, is handing him the gift.

And Hector Jr.?

But he doesn't have to fret about Hector Jr., his firstborn, the boy with these same great sad eyes who'd sat in the dugout in his Reds uniform when they lived in Cincy and worshiped the pudgy icon of his father until the parish priest had to straighten him out on his hagiography; Hector Jr., who studies English at USC and day and night writes his thesis on a poet his father has never heard of, because, here he is, walking in the front door with his mother's smile and a store-wrapped gift—a book, of course. Then Reina's children line up to kiss the *abuelo*—they'll be sitting in the box seats this afternoon—and suddenly he knows so much: he will play today, he will hit, oh yes, can there be a doubt? He sees it already. Kerensky, the son of a whore. Extra innings. Koerner or Manfredonia or Brooksie on third. The ball like an orange, a mango, a musk-melon, the clean swipe of the bat, the delirium of the crowd, and the gimpy *abuelo*, a big-leaguer still, doffing his cap and taking a tour of the bases in a stately trot, Sultan for a day.

Could things ever be so simple?

In the bottom of the ninth, with the score tied at 5 and Reina's kids full of Coke, hotdogs, peanuts, and ice cream and getting restless, with Asunción clutching her rosary as if she were drowning and Hector Jr.'s nose stuck in some book, Dupuy taps him to hit for the pitcher with two down and Fast Freddie Phelan on second. The eighth man in the lineup, Spider Martinez from Muchas Vacas, D. R., has just whiffed on three straight pitches, and Corcoran, the Braves' left-handed relief man, is all of a sudden pouring it on. Throughout the stadium a hush has fallen over the crowd, the torpor of suppertime, the game poised at apogee. Shadows are lengthening in the outfield, swallows flitting across the face of the scoreboard, here a fan drops into his beer, there a big mama gathers up her purse, her knitting, her shopping bags and parasol, and thinks of dinner. Hector sees it all. This is the moment of catharsis, the moment to take it out.

As Martinez slumps toward the dugout, Dupuy, a laconic, embittered man who keeps his suffering inside and drinks Gelusil like water, takes hold of Hector's arm. His eyes are red-rimmed and paunchy, doleful as a basset hound's. Bring the runner in, champ, he rasps. First pitch fake a bunt, then hit away. Watch Booger at third. Uh-huh, Hector mumbles, snapping his gum. Then he slides his bat from the rack—white ash, tape-wrapped grip, personally blessed by the archbishop of Guadalajara and his twenty-seven acolytes—and starts for the dugout steps, knowing the course of the next three minutes as surely as his blood knows the course of his veins. The familiar cry will go up—Cheese, Cheese, Cheesus—and he'll amble up to the batter's box, knocking imaginary dirt from his spikes, adjusting the straps of his golf gloves, tugging at his underwear, and fiddling with his batting helmet. His face will be impenetrable. Corcoran will work the ball in his glove, maybe tip back his cap for a little hair grease, and then give him a look of psychopathic hatred. Hector has seen it before. Me against you. My record, my career, my house, my family, my life, my mutual funds and beer distributorship against yours. He's been hit in the elbow, the knee, the groin, the head. Nothing fazes him. Nothing. Murmuring a prayer to Santa Griselda, patroness of the sun-blasted Sonoran village where he was born like a heat blister on his mother's womb, Hector Hernán Jesús y María Quesadilla will step into the batter's box, ready for anything.

But it's a game of infinite surprises.

Before Hector can set foot on the playing field, Corcoran suddenly doubles up in pain, Phelan goes slack at second, and the catcher and shortstop are hustling out to the mound, tailed an instant later by trainer and pitching coach. First thing Hector thinks is groin pull, then appendicitis, and finally, as Corcoran goes down on one knee, poison. He'd once seen a man shot in the gut at Obregon City, but the report had been loud as a thunderclap, and he hears nothing now but the enveloping hum of the crowd, Corcoran is rising shakily, the trainer and pitching coach supporting him while the catcher kicks meditatively in the dirt, and now Mueller, the Atlanta *cabeza*, is striding big-bellied out of the dugout, head down as if to be sure his feet are following orders. Halfway to the mound, Mueller flicks his right hand across his ear quick as a horse flicking its tail, and it's all she wrote for Corcoran.

Poised on the dugout steps like a bird dog, Hector waits, his eyes riveted on the bullpen. Please, he whispers, praying for the intercession of the Nino and pledging a hundred votary candles—at least, at least. Can it be?—yes, milk of my mother, yes—Kerensky himself strutting out onto the field like a fighting cock. Kerensky!

Come to the birthday boy, Kerensky, he murmurs, so certain he's going to put it in the stands he could point like the immeasurable Bambino. His tired old legs shuffle with impatience as Kerensky stalks across the field, and then he's turning to pick Asunción out of the crowd. She's on her feet now, Reina too, the kids come alive, beside her. And Hector Jr., the book forgotten, his face transfigured with the look of rapture he used to get when he was a boy sitting on the steps of the dugout. Hector can't help himself: he grins and gives them the thumbs-up sign.

Then, as Kerensky fires his warm-up smoke, the loudspeaker crackles and Hector emerges from the shadow of the dugout into the tapering golden shafts of the late-afternoon sun. That pitch, I want that one, he mutters, carrying his bat like a javelin and shooting a glare at Kerensky, but something's wrong here, the announcer's got it screwed up: BATTING FOR RARITAN, NUMBER 39, DAVE TOOL. What the—? And now somebody's tugging at his sleeve, and he's turning to gape with incomprehension at the freckle-faced batboy, Dave Tool striding out of the dugout with his big forty-two-ounce stick, Dupuy's face locked up like a vault, and the crowd, on its feet, chanting Tool, Tool, Tool! For a moment he just stands there, frozen with disbelief. Then Tool is brushing by him and the idiot of a batboy is leading him toward the dugout as if he were an old blind fisherman poised on the edge of the dock.

He feels as if his legs have been cut out from under him. Tool! Dupuy is yanking him for Tool? For what? So he can play the lefty-righty percentages like some chess head or something? Tool, of all people. Tool, with his thirty-five home runs a season and lifetime BA of .234; Tool, who's worn so many uniforms they had to expand the league to make room for him—what's he going to do? Raging, Hector flings down his bat and comes at Dupuy like a cat tossed in a bag. You crazy, you jerk, he sputters. I woulda hit him, I woulda won the game. I dreamed it. And then, his voice breaking: It's my birthday, for Christ's sake!

But Dupuy can't answer him, because on the first pitch Tool slams a real worm burner to short and the game is going into extra innings.

By seven o'clock, half the fans have given up and gone home. In the top of the fourteenth, when the visitors came up with a pair of runs on a two-out pinch-hit home run, there was a real exodus, but then the Dodgers struck back for two to knot it up again. Then it was three up and three down, regular as clockwork. Now, at the end of the nineteenth, with the score deadlocked at 7 all and the players dragging themselves around the field like gut-shot horses, Hector is beginning to think he may get a second chance after all. Especially the way Dupuy's been using up players like some crazy general on the Western Front, yanking pitchers, juggling his defense, throwing in pinch runners and pinch hitters until he's just about gone through the entire roster. Asunción is still there among the faithful, the foolish, and the self-deluded, fumbling with her rosary and mouthing prayers for Jesus Christ Our Lord, the Madonna, Hector, the home team, and her departed mother, in that order. Reina too, looking like the survivor of some disaster, Franklin and Alfredo asleep in their seats, the *niñitos* gone off somewhere—for Coke and dogs, maybe. And Hector Jr. looks like he's going to stick it out too, though he should be back in his closet writing about the mystical so-and-so and the way he illustrates his poems with gods and men and serpents. Watching him, Hector can feel his heart turn over.

In the bottom of the twentieth, with one down and Gilley on first—he's a starting pitcher but Dupuy sent him in to run for Manfredonia after Manfredonia jammed his ankle like a turkey and had to be helped off the field—Hector pushes himself up from the bench and ambles down to where Dupuy sits in the corner, contemplatively spitting a gout of tobacco juice and saliva into the drain at his feet, Let me hit, Bernard, come on, Hector says, easing down beside him.

Can't, comes the reply, and Dupuy never even raises his head. Can't risk it, champ. Look around you—and here the manager's voice quavers with uncertainty, with fear and despair and the dull edge of hopelessness—I got nobody left I hit you, I got to play you.

No, no, you don't understand—I'm going to win it, I swear.

And then the two of them, like old bankrupts on a bench in Miami Beach, look up to watch Phelan hit into a double play.

A buzz runs through the crowd when the Dodgers take the field for the top of the twenty-second. Though Phelan is limping, Thorkelsson's asleep on his feet, and Dorfman, fresh on the mound, is the only pitcher left on the roster, the moment is electric. One more inning and they tie the record set by the Mets and Giants back in '64, and then they're making history. Drunk, sober, and then drunk again, saturated with fats and nitrates and sugar, the crowd begins to come to life. Go, Dodgers! Eat shit! Yo Mama! Phelan's a bum!

Hector can feel it too. The rage and frustration that had consumed him back in the ninth are gone, replaced by a dawning sense of wonder—he could have won it then, yes, and against his nemesis Kerensky too—but the Nino and Santa Griselda have been saving him for something greater. He sees it now, knows it in his bones: he's going to be the hero of the longest game in history.

As if to bear him out Dorfman, the kid from Albuquerque, puts in a good inning, cutting the bushed Braves down in order. In the dugout, Doc Pusser, the team physician, is handing out the little green pills that keep your eyes open and Dupuy is blowing into a cup of coffee and staring morosely out at the playing field. Hector watches as Tool, who'd stayed in the game at first base, fans on three straight pitches, then he shoves in beside Dorfman and tells the kid he's looking good out there. With his big cornhusker's ears and nose like a tweezer, Dorfman could be a caricature of the green rookie. He says nothing. Hey, don't let it get to you, kid—I'm going to win this one for you. Next inning or maybe the inning after. Then he tells him how he saw it in a vision and how it's his birthday and the kid's going to get the victory, one of the biggest of all time. Twenty-four, twenty-five innings maybe.

Hector had heard of a game once in the Mexican League that took three days to play and went seventy-three innings, did Dorfman know that? It was down in Culiacán. Chito Mariti, the converted bullfighter, had finally ended it by dropping down dead of exhaustion in center field, allowing Sexto Silvestro, who'd broken his leg rounding third, to crawl home with the winning run. But Hector doesn't think this game will go that long. Dorfman sighs and extracts a bit of wax from his ear as Pantaleo, the third-string catcher, hits back to the pitcher to end the inning. I hope not, he says, uncoiling himself from the bench; my arm'd fall off.

Ten o'clock comes and goes. Dorfman's still in there, throwing breaking stuff and a little smoke at the Braves, who look as if they just stepped out of *The Night of the Living Dead*. The home team isn't doing much better. Dupuy's run through the whole team but for Hector, and three or four of the guys have been in there since two in the afternoon; the rest are a bunch of ginks and gimps who can barely stand up. Out in the stands, the fans look grim. The vendors ran out of beer an hour back, and they haven't had dogs or kraut or Coke or anything since eight-thirty.

In the bottom of the twenty-seventh Phelan goes berserk in the dugout and Dupuy has to pin him to the floor while Doc Pusser shoves something up his nose to calm him. Next inning the balls-and-strikes ump passes out cold, and Dorfman, who's beginning to look a little fagged, walks the first two batters but manages to weasel his way out of the inning without giving up the go-ahead run. Meanwhile, Thorkelsson has been dropping ice cubes down his trousers to keep awake, Martinez is smoking something suspicious in the can, and Ferenc Fortnoi, the third baseman, has begun talking to himself in a tortured Slovene dialect. For his part, Hector feels stronger and more alert as the game goes on. Though he hasn't had a bite since breakfast he feels impervious to the pangs of hunger, as if he were preparing himself, mortifying his flesh like a saint in the desert.

And then, in the top of the thirty-first, with half the fans asleep and the other half staring into nothingness like the inmates of the asylum of Our Lady of Guadalupe, where Hector had once visited his halfwit uncle when he was a boy, Pluto Morales cracks one down the first-base line and Tool flubs it. Right away it looks like trouble, because Chester Bubo is running around right field looking up at the sky like a birdwatcher while the ball snakes through the grass, caroms off his left foot, and coasts like silk to the edge of the warning track. Morales meanwhile is rounding second and coming on for third, running in slow motion, flat-footed and hump-backed, his face drained of color, arms flapping like the undersized wings of some big flightless bird. It's not even close. By the time Bubo can locate the ball, Morales is ten feet from the plate, pitching into a face-first slide that's at least three parts collapse, and that's it, the Braves are up by one. It looks black for the hometeam. But Dorfman, though his arm has begun to swell like a sausage, shows some grit, bears down, and retires the side to end the historic top of the unprecedented thirty-first inning.

Now, at long last, the hour has come. It'll be Bubo, Dorfman, and Tool for the Dodgers in their half of the inning, which means that Hector will hit for Dorfman. I been saving you, champ, Dupuy rasps, the empty Gelusil bottle clenched in his fist like a hand grenade. Go on in there, he murmurs, and his voice fades away to nothing as Bubo pops the first pitch up in back of the plate. Go on in there and do your stuff.

Sucking in his gut, Hector strides out onto the brightly lit field like a nineteen-year-old, the familiar cry in his ears, the haggard fans on their feet, a sickle moon sketched in overhead as if in some cartoon strip featuring drunken husbands and the milkman. Asunción looks as if she's been nailed to the cross, Reina wakes with a start and shakes the little ones into consciousness, and Hector Jr. staggers to his feet like a battered middleweight coming out for the fifteenth round. They're all watching him. The fans whose lives are like empty sacks, the wife who wants him home in front of the TV, his divorced daughter with the four kids and another on the way, his son, pride of his life, who reads for the doctor of philosophy while his crazy *padrecito* puts on a pair of long stockings and chases around after a little white ball like a case of arrested development. He'll show them. He'll show them some *cojones*, some true grit and desire: the game's not over yet.

On the mound for the Braves is Bo Brannerman, a big mustachioed machine of a man, normally a starter but pressed into desperate relief service tonight. A fine pitcher—Hector would be the first to admit it—but he just pitched two nights ago and he's worn thin as wire. Hector steps up to the plate, feeling legendary. He glances over at Tool in the on-deck circle, and then down at Booger, the third-base coach. All systems go. He cuts at the air twice and then watches Brannerman rear back and release the ball: strike one. Hector smiles. Why rush things? Give them a thrill. He watches a low outside slider that just about bounces to even the count, and then stands like a statue as Brannerman slices the corner of the plate for strike two. From the stands, a chant of *Viejo, Viejo*, and Asunción's piercing soprano, Hit him, Hector!

Hector has no worries, the moment eternal, replayed through games uncountable, with pitchers who were over the hill when he was a rookie with San Buitre, with pups like Brannerman, with big-leaguers and Hall of Famers. Here it comes, Hector, 92 MPH, the big gringo trying to throw it by you, the matchless wrists, the flawless swing, one terrific moment of suspended animation—and all of a sudden you're starring in your own movie.

How does it go? The ball cutting through the night sky like a comet, arching high over the center fielder's hapless scrambling form to slam off the wall while your legs churn up the base paths, you round first in a gallop, taking second, and heading for third . . . but wait, you spill hot coffee on your hand and you can't feel it, the demons apply the live wire to your tailbone, the legs give out and they cut you down at third while the stadium erupts in howls of execration and abuse and the *niñitos* break down, faces flooded with tears of humiliation. Hector Jr. turning his back in disgust and Asunción raging like a harpie, *Abuelo! Abuelo! Abuelo!*

Stunned, shrunken, humiliated, you stagger back to the dugout in a maelstrom of abuse, paper cups, flying spittle, your life a waste, the game a cheat, and then, crowning irony, that bum Tool, worthless all the way back to his washerwoman grandmother and the drunken muttering whey-faced tribe that gave him suck, stands tall like a giant and sends the first pitch out of the park to tie it. Oh, the pain. Flat feet, fire in your legs, your poor tired old heart skipping a beat in mortification. And now Dupuy, red in the face, shouting: The game could be over but for you, you crazy gimpy old beaner washout! You want to hide in your locker, bury yourself under the shower-room floor, but you have to watch as the next two men reach base and you pray with fervor that they'll score and put an end to your debasement. But no, Thorkelsson whiffs and the new inning dawns as inevitably as the new minute, the new hour, the new day, endless, implacable, world without end.

But wait, wait: who's going to pitch? Dorfman's out, there's nobody left, the astonishing thirty-second inning is marching across the scoreboard like an invading army, and suddenly Dupuy is standing over you—no, no, he's down on one knee, begging. Hector, he's saying, didn't you use to pitch down in Mexico when you were a kid, didn't I hear that someplace? Yes, you're saying, yes, but that was—

And then you're out on the mound, in command once again, elevated like some half-mad old king in a play, and throwing smoke. The first two batters go down on strikes and the fans are rabid with excitement, Asunción will raise a shrine, Hector Jr. worships you more than all the poets that ever lived, but can it be? You walk the next three and then give up the grand slam to little Tommy Oshimisi! Mother of God, will it never cease? But wait, wait, wait: here comes the bottom of the thirty-second and Brannerman's wild. He walks a couple, gets a couple out, somebody reaches on an infield single and the bases are loaded for you, Hector Quesadilla, stepping up to the plate now like the Iron Man himself. The wind-up, the delivery, the ball hanging there like a *piñata*, like a birthday gift, and then the stick flashes in your hands like an archangel's sword, and the game goes on forever.

One of science fiction's most respected writers, Kim Stanley Robinson has published fifteen novels and dozens of works of short fiction gathered into eight collections. He has won or been nominated often for all of science fiction's major awards, and his collection *The Martians* (1999) won the Locus Award for Best Collection. This story, a nominee for the short story category in that award, comes from that collection. The story is as much science-fictional as it is fantastic, but it is most certainly a strange and wonderful story of discovery, when a Terran working on a colonized Mars helps a troubled baseball player develop a new pitch that changes his life and the game as it's played on Mars.

Arthur Sternbach Brings the Curveball to Mars

Kim Stanley Robinson

HE WAS A TALL, skinny Martian kid, shy and stooping. Gangly as a puppy. Why they had him playing third base I have no idea. Then again they had me playing shortstop and I'm left-handed. And can't field grounders. But I'm American, so there I was. That's what learning a sport by video will do. Some things are so obvious people never think to mention them. Like never put a lefty at shortstop. But on Mars they were making it all new. Some people there had fallen in love with baseball, and ordered the equipment and rolled some fields, and off they went.

So there we were, me and this kid Gregor, butchering the left side of the infield. He looked so young I asked him how old he was, and he said eight and I thought Jeez you're not *that* young, but realized he meant Martian years of course, so he was about sixteen or seventeen, but he seemed younger. He had recently moved to Argyre from somewhere else, and was staying at the local house of his co-op with relatives or friends, I never got that straight, but he seemed pretty lonely to me. He never missed practice even though he was the worst of a terrible team, and clearly he got frustrated at all his errors and strikeouts. I used to wonder why he came out at all. And so shy; and that stoop; and the acne; and the tripping over his own feet, the blushing, the mumbling—he was a classic.

English wasn't his first language, either. It was Armenian, or Moravian, something like that. Something no one else spoke, anyway, except for an elderly couple in his co-op. So he mumbled what passes for English on Mars, and sometimes even used a translation box, but basically tried never to be in a situation where he had to speak. And made error after error. We must have made quite a sight— me about waist-high to him, and both of us letting grounders pass through us like we were a magic show. Or else knocking them down and chasing them around, then winging them past the first baseman. We very seldom made an out. It would have been conspicuous except everyone else was the same way. Baseball on Mars was a high-scoring game.

But beautiful anyway. It was like a dream, really. First of all the horizon, when you're on a flat plain like Argyre, is only three miles away rather than six. It's very noticeable to a Terran eye. Then their diamonds have just over normal-sized infields, but the outfields have to be huge. At my team's ballpark it was nine hundred feet to dead center, seven hundred down the lines. Standing at the plate the outfield fence was like a little green line off in the distance, under a purple sky, pretty near the horizon itself—what I'm telling you is that the baseball diamond about covered *the entire visible world*. It was so great.

They played with four outfielders, like in softball, and still the alleys between fielders were wide. And the air was about as thin as at Everest base camp, and the gravity itself only bats .380, so to speak. So when you hit the ball solid it flies like a golf ball hit by a big driver. Even as big as the fields were, there were still a number of home runs every game. Not many shutouts on Mars. Not till I got there, anyway.

I went there after I climbed Olympus Mons, to help them establish a new soil sciences institute. They had the sense not to try that by video. At first I climbed in the Charitums in my time off, but after I got hooked into baseball the game took up most of my spare time. Fine, I'll play I said when they asked me. But I won't coach. I don't like telling people what to do.

So I'd go out and start by doing soccer exercises with the rest of them, warming up all the muscles we would never use. Then Werner would start hitting infield practice, and Gregor and I would start flailing. We were like matadors. Occasionally we'd snag one and whale it over to first, and occasionally the first baseman, who was well over two meters tall and built like a tank, would catch our throws, and we'd slap our gloves together. Doing this day after day, Gregor got a little less shy with me, though not much. And I saw that he threw the ball pretty damned hard. His arm was as long as my whole body, and boneless it seemed, like something pulled off a squid, so loose-wristed that he got some real pop on the ball. Of course sometimes it would still be rising when it passed ten meters over the first baseman's head, but it was moving, no doubt about it. I began to see that maybe the reason he came out to play, beyond just being around people he didn't have to talk to, was the chance to throw things really hard. I saw, too, that he wasn't so much shy as he was surly. Or both.

Anyway our fielding was a joke. Hitting went a bit better. Gregor learned to chop down on the ball and hit grounders up the middle; it was pretty effective. And I began to get my timing together. Coming to it from years of slow-pitch softball, I had started by swinging at everything a week late, and between that and my shortstopping I'm sure my teammates figured they had gotten a defective American. And since they had a rule limiting each team to only two Terrans, no doubt they were disappointed by that. But slowly I adjusted my timing, and after that I hit pretty well. The thing was their pitchers had no breaking stuff. These big guys would rear back and throw as hard as they could, like Gregor, but it took everything in their power just to throw strikes. It was a little scary because they often threw right at you by accident. But if they got it down the pipe then all you had to do was time it.

And if you hit one, how the ball flew! Every time I connected it was like a miracle. It felt like you could put one into orbit if you hit it right, in fact that was one of their nicknames for a home run. Oh, that's orbital, they would say, watching one leave the park headed for the horizon. They had a little bell, like a ship's bell, attached to the backstop, and every time someone hit one out they would ring that bell while you rounded the bases. A very nice local custom.

So I enjoyed it. It's a beautiful game even when you're butchering it. My sorest muscles after practice were in my stomach from laughing so hard. I even began to have some success at short. When I caught balls going to my right I twirled around backward to throw to first or second. People were impressed though of course it was ridiculous. It was a case of the one-eyed man in the country of the blind. Not that they weren't good athletes, you understand, but none of them had played as kids, and so they had no baseball instincts. They just liked to play. And I could see why—out there on a green field as big as the world, under a purple sky, with the yellow-green balls flying around—it was beautiful. We had a good time.

I started to give a few tips to Gregor, too, though I had sworn to myself not to get into coaching. I don't like trying to tell people what to do. The game's too hard for that. But I'd be hitting flies to the outfielders, and it was hard not to tell them to watch the ball and run under it and then put the glove up and catch it, rather than run all the way with their arms stuck up like the Statue of Liberty's. Or when they took turns hitting flies (it's harder than it looks) giving them batting tips. And Gregor and I played catch all the time during warm-ups, so just watching me—and trying to throw to such a short target—he got better. He definitely threw hard. And I saw there was a whole lot of movement in his throws. They'd come tailing in to me every which way, no surprise given how loose-wristed he was. I had to look sharp or I'd miss. He was out of control, but he had potential.

And the truth was, our pitchers were bad. I loved the guys, but they couldn't throw strikes if you paid them. They'd regularly walk ten or twenty batters every game, and these were five-inning games. Werner would watch Thomas walk ten, then he'd take over in relief and walk ten more himself. Sometimes they'd go through this twice. Gregor and I would stand there while the other team's runners walked by as in a parade, or a line at the grocery store. When Werner went to the mound I'd stand by Gregor and say, You know Gregor, you could pitch better than these guys. You've got a good arm. And he would look at me horrified, muttering No no no no, not possible.

But then one time warming up he broke off a really mean curve and I caught it on my wrist. While I was rubbing it down I walked over to him. Did you see the way that ball curved? I said.

Yes, he said, looking away. I'm sorry.

Don't be sorry, That's called a curveball, Gregor. It can be a useful throw. You twisted your hand at the last moment and the ball came over the top of it, like this, see? Here, try it again.

So we slowly got into it. I was all-state in Connecticut my senior year in high school, and it was all from throwing junk—curve, slider, split-finger, change. I could see Gregor throwing most of those just by accident, but to keep from confusing him I just worked on a straight curve. I told him Just throw it to me like you did that first time.

I thought you weren't to coach us, he said.

I'm not coaching you! Just throw it like that. Then in the games throw it straight. As straight as possible.

He mumbled a bit at me in Moravian, and didn't look me in the eye. But he did it. And after a while he worked up a good curve. Of course the thinner air on Mars meant there was little for the balls to bite on. But I noticed that the blue dot balls they played with had higher stitching than the red dot balls. They played with both of them as if there was no difference, but there was. So I filed that away and kept working with Gregor.

We practiced a lot. I showed him how to throw from the stretch, figuring that a windup from Gregor was likely to end up in knots. And by midseason he threw a mean curve from the stretch. We had not mentioned this to anyone else. He was wild with it, but it hooked hard; I had to be really sharp to catch some of them. It made me better at shortstop, too. Although finally in one game, behind twenty to nothing as usual, a batter hit a towering pop fly and I took off running back on it, and the wind kept carrying it and I kept following it, until when I got it I was out there sprawled between our startled center fielders.

Maybe you should play outfield, Werner said.

I said Thank God.

So after that I played left center or right center, and I spent the games chasing line drives to the fence and throwing them back in to the cutoff man. Or more likely, standing there and watching the other team take their walks. I called in my usual chatter, and only then did I notice that no one on Mars ever yelled anything at these games. It was like playing in a league of deaf-mutes. I had to provide the chatter for the whole team from two hundred yards away in center field, including, of course, criticism of the plate umpires' calls. My view of the plate was miniaturized but I still did a better job than they did, and they knew it, too. It was fun. People would walk by and say, Hey there must be an American out there.

One day after one of our home losses, 28 to 12 I think it was, everyone went to get something to eat, and Gregor was just standing there looking off into the distance. You want to come along? I asked him, gesturing after the others, but he shook his head. He had to get back home and work. I was going back to work myself, so I walked with him into town, a place like you'd see in the Texas panhandle. I stopped outside his co-op, which was a big house or little apartment complex, I could never tell which was which on Mars. There he stood like a lamppost, and I was about to leave when an old woman came out and invited me in. Gregor had told her about me, she said in stiff English. So I was introduced to the people in the kitchen there, most of them incredibly tall. Gregor seemed really embarrassed, he didn't want me being there, so I left as soon as I could get away. The old woman had a husband, and they seemed like Gregor's grandparents. There was a young girl there, too, about his age, looking at both of us like a hawk. Gregor never met her eye.

Next time at practice, I said, Gregor, were those your grandparents?

Like my grandparents.

And that girl, who was she?

No answer.

Like a cousin or something?

Yes.

Gregor, what about your parents? Where are they?

He just shrugged and started throwing me the ball.

I got the impression they lived in another branch of his co-op somewhere else, but I never found out for sure. A lot of what I saw on Mars I liked—the way they run their businesses together in co-ops takes a lot of pressure off them, and they live pretty relaxed lives compared to us on Earth. But some of their parenting systems—kids brought up by groups, or by one parent, or whatever—I wasn't so sure about those. It makes for problems if you ask me. Bunch of teenage boys ready to slug somebody. Maybe that happens no matter what you do.

Anyway we finally got to the end of the season, and I was going to go back to Earth after it. Our team's record was three and fifteen, and we came in last place in the regular season standings. But they held a final weekend tournament for all the teams in the Argyre Basin, a bunch of three-inning games, as there were a lot to get through. Immediately we lost the first game and were in the losers' bracket. Then we were losing the next one, too, and all because of walks, mostly. Werner relieved Thomas for a time, then when that didn't work out Thomas went back to the mound to re-relieve Werner. When that happened I ran all the way in from center to join them on the mound. I said Look you guys, let Gregor pitch.

Gregor! they both said. No way!

He'll be even worse than us, Werner said.

How could he be? I said. You guys just walked eleven batters in a row. Night will fall before Gregor could do that.

So they agreed to it. They were both discouraged at that point, as you might expect. So I went over to Gregor and said Okay, Gregor, you give it a try now.

Oh no, no no no no no no no. He was pretty set against it. He glanced up into the stands where we had a couple hundred spectators, mostly friends and family and some curious passersby, and I saw then that his like grandparents and his girl something-or-other were up there watching. Gregor was getting more hangdog and sullen every second.

Come on, Gregor, I said, putting the ball in his glove. Tell you what, I'll catch you. It'll be just like warming up. Just keep throwing your curveball. And I dragged him over to the mound.

So Werner warmed him up while I went over and got on the catcher's gear, moving a box of blue dot balls to the front of the ump's supply area while I was at it. I could see Gregor was nervous, and so was I. I had never caught before, and he had never pitched, and bases were loaded and no one was out. It was an unusual baseball moment.

Finally I was geared up and I clanked on out to him. Don't worry about throwing too hard, I said. Just put the curveball right in my glove. Ignore the batter. I'll give you the sign before every pitch; two fingers for curve, one for fastball.

Fastball? he says.

That's where you throw the ball fast. Don't worry about that. We're just going to throw curves anyway.

And you said you weren't to coach, he said bitterly.

I'm not coaching, I said, I'm catching.

So I went back and got set behind the plate. Be looking for curveballs, I said to the ump. Curve ball? he said.

So we started up. Gregor stood crouched on the mound like a big praying mantis, red-faced and grim. He threw the first pitch right over our heads to the backstop. Two guys scored while I retrieved it, but I threw out the runner going from first to third. I went out to Gregor. Okay, I said, the bases are cleared and we got an out. Let's just throw now. Right into the glove. Just like last time, but lower.

So he did. He threw the ball at the batter, and the batter bailed, and the ball cut right down into my glove. The umpire was speechless. I turned around and showed him the ball in my glove. That was a strike, I told him.

Strike! he hollered. He grinned at me. That was a curveball, wasn't it.

Damn right it was.

Hey, the batter said. What was that?

We'll show you again, I said.

And after that Gregor began to mow them down. I kept putting down two fingers, and he kept throwing curveballs. By no means were they all strikes, but enough were to keep him from walking too many batters. All the balls were blue dot. The ump began to get into it.

And between two batters I looked behind me and saw that the entire crowd of spectators, and all the teams not playing at that moment, had congregated behind the backstop to watch Gregor pitch. No one on Mars had ever seen a curveball before, and now they were crammed back there to get the best view of it, gasping and chattering at every hook. The batter would bail or take a weak swing and then look back at the crowd with a big grin, as if to say: Did you see that? That was a curveball!

So we came back and won that game, and we kept Gregor pitching, and we won the next three games as well. The third game he threw exactly twenty-seven pitches, striking out all nine batters with three pitches each. Bob Feller once struck out all twenty-seven batters in a high school game; it was like that.

The crowd was loving it. Gregor's face was less red. He was standing straighter in the box. He still refused to look anywhere but at my glove, but his look of grim terror had shifted to one of ferocious concentration. He may have been skinny, but he was tall. Out there on the mound he began to look pretty damned formidable.

So we climbed back up into the winner's bracket, then into a semifinal. Crowds of people were coming up to Gregor between games to get him to sign their baseballs. Mostly he looked dazed, but at one point I saw him glance up at his co-op family in the stands and wave at them, with a brief smile.

How's your arm holding out? I asked him.

What do you mean? he said.

Okay, I said. Now look, I want to play outfield again this game. Can you pitch to Werner? Because there were a couple of Americans on the team we played next, Ernie and Caesar, who I suspected could hit a curve. I just had a hunch.

Gregor nodded, and I could see that as long as there was a glove to throw at, nothing else mattered. So I arranged it with Werner, and in the semi-finals I was back out in right-center field. We were playing under the lights by this time, the field like green velvet under a purple twilight sky. Looking in from center field it was all tiny, like something in a dream.

And it must have been a good hunch I had, because I made one catch charging in on a liner from Ernie, sliding to snag it, and then another running across the middle for what seemed like thirty seconds, before I got under a towering Texas leaguer from Caesar. Gregor even came up and congratulated me between innings.

And you know that old thing about how a good play in the field leads to a good at-bat. Already in the day's games I had hit well, but now in this semi-final I came up and hit a high fastball so solid it felt like I didn't hit it at all, and off it flew. Homerun over the center-field fence, out into the dusk. I lost sight of it before it came down.

Then in the finals I did it again in the first inning, back-to-back with Thomas— his to left, mine again to center. That was two in a row for me, and we were winning, and Gregor was mowing them down. So when I came up again the next inning I was feeling good, and people were calling out for another homer, and the other team's pitcher had a real determined look. He was a really big guy, as tall as Gregor but massive-chested as so many Martians are, and he reared back and threw the first one right at my head. Not on purpose, he was out of control. Then I barely fouled several pitches off, swinging very late, and dodging his inside heat, until it was a full count, and I was thinking to myself, Well heck, it doesn't really matter if you strike out here, at least you hit two in a row.

Then I heard Gregor shouting Come on, coach, you can do it! Hang in there! Keep your focus! All doing a passable imitation of me, I guess, as the rest of the team was laughing its head off. I suppose I had said all those things to them before, though of course it was just the stuff you always say automatically at a ball game, I never meant anything by it, I didn't even know people heard me. But I definitely heard Gregor, needling me, and I stepped back into the box thinking, Look I don't even like to coach, I played ten games at shortstop trying not to coach you guys, and I was so irritated I was barely aware of the pitch, but hammered it anyway out over the right field fence, higher and deeper even than my first two. Knee-high fastball, inside. As Ernie said to me afterward, You *drove* that baby. My teammates rang the little ship's bell all the way around the bases, and I slapped hands with every one of them on the way from third to home, feeling the grin on my face. Afterward I sat on the bench and felt the hit in my hands. I can still see it flying out.

So we were ahead 4–0 in the final inning, and the other team came up determined to catch us. Gregor was tiring at last, and he walked a couple, then hung a curve, and their big pitcher got into it and clocked it far over my head. Now I do okay charging liners, but the minute a ball is hit over me I'm totally lost. So I turned my back on this one and ran for the fence, figuring either it goes out or I collect it against the fence, but that I'd never see it again in the air. But running on Mars is so weird. You get going too fast and then you're pinwheeling along trying to keep from doing a faceplant. That's what I was doing when I saw the warning track, and looked back up and spotted the ball coming down, so I jumped, trying to jump straight up, you know, but I had a lot of momentum, and had completely forgotten about the gravity, so I shot up and caught the ball, amazing, but found myself *flying right over the fence.*

I came down and rolled in the dust and sand, and the ball stayed stuck in my glove. I hopped back over the fence holding the ball up to show everyone I had it. But they gave the other pitcher a home run anyway, because you have to stand inside the park when you catch one, it's a local rule. I didn't care. The whole point of playing games is to make you do things like that anyway. And it was good that the pitcher got one, too.

So we started up again and Gregor struck out the side, and we won the tournament. We were mobbed, Gregor especially. He was the hero of the hour. Everyone wanted him to sign something. He didn't say much, but he wasn't stooping either. He looked surprised. Afterward Werner took two balls and everyone signed them, to make some kind of trophies for Gregor and me. Later I saw half the names on my trophy were jokes, "Mickey Mantle" and other names like that. Gregor had written on it, "Hi, Coach Arnold, Regards, Greg." I have the ball still, on my desk at home.

Long before Jack Kerouac coined the term "Beat Generation" and went "on the road" with Neal Cassady to gather material for the famous book of the same name, he was a baseball fan. At thirteen, he invented a fantasy baseball board-game to play, using teams named after automobile brands and featuring statistics for each player that helped determine the outcome. "Ronnie on the Mound" was published in 1955 in *Esquire* magazine at the height of Kerouac's fame from the success of *On the Road*. The story was based on that early form of fantasy baseball from Kerouac's youth and is reflective of his athletic childhood, where he played several sports, and quite well, along with inventing fantasy versions of baseball players, teams and games.

Ronnie on the Mound

ᗡᗡ

Jack Kerouac

DURING INFIELD PRACTICE THE Chryslers are out on the field in their golden-yellow uniforms and the warm-up pitcher is little Theo K. Vance, bespectacled and scholarly, testing out his blazing fireball at catcher Babe Blagden, the veteran of more years in the league than he'd care to admit to any babe he tried to pick up last night in the Loop—it's a spring night in Chicago, the occasion a crucial game between the Chicago Chryslers (tied for the league lead with St. Louis at 21–11 all) and the Pittsburgh Plymouths, the usual door mats of the league now rejuvenated not only with a new manager, old Pie Tibbs, an all-time all-star great centerfielder and slugger, but with new additions like the kid outfielder Oboy Roy Turner, the steady rookie Leo Sawyer at short (son of veteran Vic Sawyer) and their new star pitcher Ronnie Melaney just up from the minors with a dazzling record and rumors of a blazing fast ball. It's May in the Loop town, the wind blows softly from the lake, with a shade of autumnal coolness in the air presaging the World Series excitement to come, even the lowly Plymouths at a 14-won and 18-lost record hoping to be up there by that time now that they have that new wild line-up—but it's just really another game, another night, the usual gathering, cigar smoke in the stands, hot dogs, the call of beer sellers, the latecoming fans, the kids yelling in the bleachers (Friday night) and the old umpire like W. C. Fields in black coat and bursting pants bending to brush the plate as on a thousand other occasions in his old spittoon life—but the thrill runs through the crowd to see the rookie making his debut on the big-league mound: Ronnie Melaney, nineteen, handsome, with dark eyes, pale skin, nervous hands, rubbing his hands down his green-striped trousers, kicking the mound, handling the rosin bag and eyeing the bright lamps all around the stadium, newspapermen in the press box leaning forward to report his showing. Old Frank "Pie" Tibbs is out there on the mound giving Ronnie last-minute pats on the pants. "Take it easy kid, these Chryslers can be beat just like the bushwallopers back home." "Thanks, Mr. Tibbs," gulps Ronnie as he takes a step off the mound and pretends to fiddle with his shoes as the umpire calls "Batter up" and the stands vibrate with the excitement of the opening pitch of the game. The first batter will be Lefty Murphree the new sensation, called a "sophomore," in his second year of play with the Chryslers, whose speed (16 doubles) and general .300 hitting has skyrocketed the Chryslers up to top tie position, a murderous hitter, second in the league also in stolen bases with 9 (behind the incomparable Pancho Villa of Los Angeles), a left-handed beauty, stepping in now with a delicate pinch at his cap tip and a knock on his spikes and a spit to the side, as the old umpire handles his bellywhomper and straightens it out and prepares to half squat to squint at that pitch and call 'em straight. Now Murphree is in the box leveling his bat around in easy aiming strokes and is the first big-leaguer to be looking down the slot at Ronnie Melaney.

The sign is for a fast ball. *Let 'em see it, boy!* thinks the catcher (antique Jake Guewa of thirty years on the very same Pittsburgh team—a hard, browned, seamy little man with guts of iron, a weak hitter but a clutch hitter, who maybe after six games hitless and arid can suddenly win a game with an unobtrusive single in the bottom of the ninth). "Come on Daddy Kid!" Ronnie dangles the ball from his strong right hand, nods, steps on the rubber, winds back and forth a little rock, throws up the left leg, comes around like a whip and balls one in straight at Murphree's strike zone and Murphree swings a mean white bat and the ball whistles past the umpire's crowned noggin for a bang-in foul strike into the screen and umpire J. C. Gwynn raises right hand and shouts "Streeike!" and the game is on and the crowd goes "Whooee!"

Old Jake Guewa takes a peak at the bench and Manager Pie Tibbs gives him the sign for a curve; Ronnie's curve is a good one with a hopper, many's the old seamed scout watched it from behind the screen in the Texas League. Ronnie nods and gulps, he likes to concentrate on his fast ball, but orders are orders. He winds back and forth as a gust of wind comes and ripples the flags around the stadium, someone whistles, someone hoots and the white pellet is seen flying home high in the night toward the tense Murphree—the umpire throws up his left arm, yells, "Ball one" and the crowd goes, "Oh, oh." Guewa has the ball where it exploded *plow* into his glove, holds it aloft as such, walks a few feet ahead of the plate, says something to Ronnie, who strains to listen and comes forward a few steps. Guewa fires it at him, hard, as if to wake him up, turns and goes back with the inestimable sorrow of the baseball catcher to squat and as if to sigh again behind that old plate and Murphree knocks the spikes with the bat (one and one is the count, the kid's first major-league count), grits his teeth, sets that foot back on the rubber and sees the sign for fast ball and says to himself, *I'll burn this guy right down!* and whams it around, wild and high again. "Ball Two!" "Hey!" yells the crowd. "He's wild!" "Throw the bum out!" "Where'd you get the bushman!" "Come on, kid, settle down!" "He's got fire in that ball but we better call the fire dee-part-ment": laughter, discussion, conversation between women about how cute he is, kids yelling with glee about nothing they can understand, a bottle breaking somewhere far back in the johns. Melaney is behind in the count and now he begins to sweat and takes the sign for sinker and nods gravely—he's afraid to look toward the bench where maybe now Manager Tibbs is frowning. Murphree strands in there, leveling the bat around, careful as a hawk, eyes right on Ronnie, chewing with no feeling. Ronnie winds up and delivers with his heart as big as a toad: strike down the middle which Murphree only glances at, because he's had his own orders to let this one go by—the ball has come in high, like a vision, but sunk in across the chest perfectly spotted, landing in old Guewa's glove like a shot of a gun, *plow!* "Yay!" yells a fan. "He'll make it! You'll be awright baby!" And now the count is two and two and Jake gives the sign for a fast ball, Ronnie steels himself, remembers the calm with which he used to deliver pitches like this on drowsy afternoons in Dallas and Fort Worth and even before that in the Sunset League in Arizona, and in a dream he lets go his next pitch, high, too high, just off, ball three! And now it's a full count.

Manager Pie Tibbs is staring anxiously toward the mound, trying to think what to order; finally he sends the sign to the catcher, curve ball, who transmits it to Ronnie, who gulps because a curve ball is harder to control—*But I'll make it true!* There is a silence now in the stadium, you can hear little clicks of teletypes up in the press box, and small familiar sounds like a distant car horn in the street, and the usual whistles and catcalls: "He's a bum left, let 'im have it!" "Another two-bagger, boy!" (These cries are from the Chrysler bench, from Hophead Deane the crazy first-baseman and from utility men like Ernie Shaw and veteran Johnny Keggs and kids like Phil Drayton the speed-boy pinch runner.) Ronnie winds up now and lets her go at Lefty Murphree, who's ready and raps the bat around and connects with a dead knock that signifies he's topped the ball and it bounces down in front of him and goes skittering straight at first-baseman Wade Hazard who just stands as if knock-kneed to let it pop into his glove and if he misses with the glove the knees'll stop it; it sticks in his glove and nonchalantly (almost spitting) he straightens up and trots to the first-base bag well ahead of the racing, smoky Murphree, out, and Murphree streaks across the bag a dead pigeon and Ronnie Melaney's first man up has grounded out to first.

But here comes mighty Herb Jangraw to the plate; a second ago he was kneeling and spitting with three bats between his big mitts, dreaming of something else, waiting for his turn, now here he comes for his licks and it's only the beginning of Ronnie Melaney's career in the world. The crowd lets out a yowl of joy to see the old-time great slugger in a slump this year, but still as explosive as ever potentially, a man who has hit home runs out of sight in every ball park in the league, six-foot-four, 210 pounds, a rangy body, mighty arms, a great, ragged, ruinous face—drinks cases of beer by himself, a big jaw, a big cud, a big splurt of brown tobacco juice on the green fresh grass, he doesn't care, hitches his mighty pants and steps in, also left-handed, but with an immense long 45-inch bat that puts the fear of God into Ronnie to see it. "Phew," says the kid—only one out and two to go, and then only one inning and eight to go, and then only one game and thirty, forty for the year, and then only one year and twenty to go (if lucky) and then death O Lord. Jake Guewa steps out a ways, winks at Ronnie, gives him the sign for a sinker, goes back and squats; the old umpire leans in, Ronnie toes the rubber, rocks, rocks one time extry, throws up the left leg and burns one down, twisting his wrist as hard as he can to make that sinker *sink* dear God or Jangraw'll golf it out of sight and Pittsburgh. He does golf it, hits it with a woodsy whack, it goes arcing weakly to the left, the third-baseman Joe Martin makes a leap but it means nothing, he knows he can't get it, he even lets his good glove go as a sign of *O well;* the glove sails up and the ball sails out to left field, where Oboy Roy scutters up to recover it and fires it to second at little Homer Landry, as Jangraw gallumps down to first and makes a halfhearted turn and goes back to stand on the bag with a single to left, arms akimbo and spitting brown juice and nodding as Wade Hazard makes a smiling remark at him and the first-base umpire yells some joke and the fans are buzzing and sitting down again. But what now? What with the next batter, the mighty Babe Blagden, one of the greatest hitters of all time and currently batting .323—in only 29 games he's had 31 hits and already delivered 8 homers (3 behind Jangraw) and catching up to the league leaders after he'd originally decided (in the spring) to give up active playing and be a coach, then persuaded to pinch hit, which he did with three home runs in a row or so, and so now back in the regular lineup and booming as good as ever.

Now Manager Pie Tibbs is stalking up and down before the bench with that familiar walk of his, well-known to two generations of baseball fans, that cat stalk, only now there are lines in his face and he has to decide weighty issues. The fans are jeering Ronnie, "It's only the beginning kiddo!" "Let's see that famous fast ball, Babe loves that fast ball!" "Beer! get me cold beer!" A cold sweat is on Ronnie's brow, he wipes it away like grease, he rubs his hands in the sand, on the rosin bag, something's wrong with his body juices—*I've gotta get outa this inning!* he prays—he gets the sign and gets ready to deliver.

It's a fast ball, fast as he can make it, to catch Blagden off balance; Babe is a right-hand powerhouse and swings with his wrists alone. He likes it and steps in with a short dusty push of his cleated foot and toothpicks the bat around and clacks it a weak popup into the air off the mound which Ronnie himself takes with a reassuring hand wave to the others. "I got it," he calls.

So Jangraw is left standing on first base and now there's two outs and can Ronnie make it? Babyface Kolek, the recent hot hitter of the league rewarded with cleanup spot on the Chryslers, is stepping in and the stands are in an uproar. Kolek is such a clever clutchhitter Manager Pie Tibbs is worried and comes out to the mound to talk to Ronnie; Pie is also worried about the kid's debut, his beginning inning will be so important in his development, besides who wants Jangraw sent around from first to score and put the Chryslers out ahead in the first inning.

"Boy, I want you to take it cagey with this Kiolex, he's a mean little bastat, let him have an assortment, start with a curve and keep it outside." "Yessir, Mr. Tibbs." "Lissen, kid, I don't have to come out here in the first inning, but I notice you're nervous . . . let old Jake tell you what to do now, aim straight." Ronnie, in a dream, toes the rubber, eyes Jangraw leading off first. Pie is back in the dugout, sitting, hunched, watching, Ronnie pumps fast and pours her in, at the lefthanded, squatting, keen-eyed Kolek, who lets it by his letters for a perfect strike. "Two more boy!" yells Jake Guewa, whanging the ball back, smarting Ronnie's hand. He pours another one in high, the count is even and still in the balance—"Just a few more pitches!" He sweats . . . now he pauses, wipes his hands, wishes for a drink of water, or a Coke, swallows, takes the sign for change-of-pace fast ball and again checks on big Jangraw on first, with Wade Hazard hovering behind him, both doing a little, slow, big-man hop. Ronnie turns his face from them and his arm responds, hard, whiplash, down-the-wrist twists, the ball sails home, sinks too far, low, for ball two—"What's the matter with me! Do I have to do everything in this world?" "Come on, kid!" yells the old third-base coach Pep McDill who's been with the Plymouths since the beginning of time, now a bow-legged pot-bellied old-timer with no real cares but plenty of sympathy, whom Ronnie as a kid had seen skittering around shortstop in Pittsburgh like a little rabbit. Sighing, Ronnie does the fast rock and comes in with his sinker, Kolek's eyes light up and he lunges for it, his right foot shows the cleated sole Ronnie sees the bat come around and blinks as it explodes hard and whistles over his head and into center field where Tommy Turner is running like a smooth hare to recover and whip it on down to third, after some difficulty, and even slow-footed Jangraw has made it to there on the long single and there are men on first and third and two out and things are tight.

O Lord, thinks Ronnie, *I'll get the boot sure, starting off like this!* Manager Pie Tibbs looks for the first time toward the bull pen in left field, this he's never done before. *That's the sign*, thinks Ronnie, his heart sinking. *Another boner and I'm out in the showers.* It will be K. L. Jordan facing him, bespectacled, bookkeeperish thin, but one of the most consistent hitters in baseball, currently whacking .307 in 32 games, with a slew of clutch hits to his credit, a dangerous man, the whole Chicago line-up packed with enthusiastic dynamite. Jake Guewa gives the sign for fast ball, Jordan's weakness; it will be a case of burn him down. Ronnie eyes the men on first and third one after the other, pauses, the whole game hinges on his action, and he blows her in and Jordan likes it and easily, with an expression of glint in his spectacles though there is unconcern on the face itself, and placks it down on the grass where again it rolls to Wade Hazard at first who leaps, startled to see it, and goes over a few feet and takes it in and trots a few feet to first and steps on the bag, sealing Ronnie's courage into the records—and Ronnie slowly walks off the mound, letting off a big sigh that can be seen deflating his chest from the farthest gloomiest seat in the upper deep center-field bleachers, and as he does he takes one side look of longing at his wife in the stands and she holds up her fingers in the sign of "All straight," and Ronnie is made.

Wilbur Schramm is most famous for being one of the critical founders of the scholarly study of communications and mass communications. In those fields his work is considered foundational and legendary. What is sometimes forgotten is that he got his start as a creative writer and even founded the famous Iowa Writers' Workshop at the University of Iowa in 1936. He won the O. Henry Prize for short fiction in 1942, and in 1944 he published this story in the *Saturday Evening Post*. Disarmingly witty and charming, "My Kingdom for Jones" can easily be read as a pointed satire on baseball's struggle to integrate the game in the 1940s.

My Kingdom for Jones

Wilbur Schramm

THE FIRST DAY JONES played third base for Brooklyn was like the day Galileo turned his telescope on the planets or Columbus sailed back to Spain. First, people said it couldn't be true; then they said things will never be the same.

Timothy McGuire, of the *Brooklyn Eagle*, told me how he felt the first time he saw Jones. He said that if a bird had stepped out of a cuckoo clock that day and asked him what time it was, he wouldn't have been surprised enough to blink an Irish eye. And still he knew that the whole future of baseball hung that day by a cotton thread.

Don't ask Judge Kenesaw Mountain Landis about this. He has never yet admitted publicly that Jones ever played for Brooklyn. He has good reason not to. But ask an old-time sports writer. Ask Tim McGuire.

It happened so long ago it was even before Mr. Roosevelt became President. It was a lazy Georgia spring afternoon, the first time McGuire and I saw Jones. There was a light-footed little breeze and just enough haze to keep the sun from burning. The air was full of fresh-cut grass, wisteria, fruit blossoms, and the ping of baseballs on well-oiled mitts. Everyone in Georgia knows that the only sensible thing to do on an afternoon like that is sleep. If you can't do that, if you are a baseball writer down from New York to cover Brooklyn's spring-training camp, you can stretch out on the grass and raise yourself every hour or so on one elbow to steal a glance at fielding practice. That was what we were doing— meanwhile amusing ourselves halfheartedly with a game involving small cubes and numbers—when we first saw Jones.

The *Times* wasn't there. Even in those days they were keeping their sports staff at home to study for Information Please. But four of us were down from the New York papers—the *World*, the *Herald*, Tim, and I. I can even remember what we were talking about.

I was asking the *World*, "How do they look to you?"

"Pitchers and no punch," the *World* said. "No big bats. No great fielders. No Honus Wagner. No Hal Chase. No Ty Cobb."

"No Tinker to Evers to Chance," said the *Herald*. "Seven come to Susy," he added soothingly, blowing on his hands.

"What's your angle today?" the *World* asked Tim.

Tim doesn't remember exactly how he answered. To the best of my knowledge, he merely said, "Ulk." It occurred to me that the *Brooklyn Eagle* was usually more eloquent than that, but the Southern weather must have slowed up my reaction.

The *World* said, "What?"

"There's a sorsh," Tim said in a weak, strangled sort of voice—"a horse . . . on third . . . base."

"Why don't they chase it off?" said the *Herald* impatiently. "Your dice."

"They don't. . . want to," Tim said in that funny voice.

I glanced up at Tim then. Now Tim, as you probably remember, was built from the same blueprints as a truck, with a magnificent red nose for a headlight. But when I looked at him, all the color was draining out of that nose slowly, from top to bottom, like turning off a gas mantle. I should estimate Tim was, at the moment, the whitest McGuire in four generations.

Then I looked over my shoulder to see where Tim was staring. He was the only one of us facing the ball diamond. I looked for some time. Then I tapped the *World* on the back.

"Pardon me," I asked politely, "do you notice anything unusual?"

"If you refer to my luck," said the *World*, "it's the same pitiful kind I've had since Christmas."

"Look at the infield," I suggested.

"Hey," said the *Herald*, "if you don't want the dice, give them to me."

"I know this can't be true," mused the *World*, "but I could swear I see a horse on third base."

The *Herald* climbed to his feet with some effort. He was built in the days when there was no shortage of materials.

"If the only way to get you guys to put your minds on this game is to chase that horse off the field," he said testily, "I'll do it myself."

He started toward the infield, rubbed his eyes, and fainted dead away.

"I had the queerest dream," he said, when we revived him. "I dreamed there was a horse playing third base. My God!" he shouted, glancing toward the diamond. "I'm still asleep!"

That is, word for word, what happened the first day Jones played third base for Brooklyn. Ask McGuire.

When we felt able, we hunted up the Brooklyn manager, who was a chunky, red-haired individual with a whisper like a foghorn. A foghorn with a Brooklyn accent. His name was Pop O'Donnell.

"I see you've noticed," Pop boomed defensively.

"What do you mean," the *Herald* said severely, "by not notifying us you had a horse playing third base?"

"I didn't guess you'd believe it," Pop said.

Pop was still a little bewildered himself. He said the horse had wandered on the field that morning during practice. Someone tried to chase it off by hitting a baseball toward it. The horse calmly opened its mouth and caught the ball. Nothing could be neater.

While they were still marveling over that, the horse galloped 30 yards and took a ball almost out of the hands of an outfielder who was poised for the catch. They said Willie Keeler couldn't have done it better. So they spent an hour hitting fungo flies—or, as some wit called them, horse flies—to the horse. Short ones, long ones, high ones, grass cutters, line drivers—it made no difference; the animal covered Dixie like the dew.

They tried the horse at second and short, but he was a little slow on the pivot when compared with men like Napoleon Lajoie. Then they tried him at third base and knew that was the right, the inevitable, place. He was a Great Wall of China. He was a flash of brown lightning. In fact, he covered half the shortstop's territory and two-thirds of left field, and even came behind the plate to help the catcher with foul tips. The catcher got pretty sore about it. He said that anybody who was going to steal his easy putouts would have to wear an umpire's uniform like the other thieves.

"Can he hit?" asked the *World*.

"See for yourself," Pop O'Donnell invited.

The Superbas—they hadn't begun calling them the Dodgers yet—were just starting batting practice. Nap Rucker was tossing them in with that beautiful, smooth motion of his, and the horse was at bat. He met the first ball on the nose and smashed it into left field. He laid down a bunt that waddled like a turtle along the base line. He sizzled a liner over second like a clothesline.

"What a story!" said the *World*.

"I wonder," said the *Herald*. "I wonder how good it is."

We stared at him.

"I wouldn't say it is quite as good as the sinking of the *Maine*, if you mean that," said Tim.

"I wonder how many people are going to believe it," said the *Herald*.

"I'll race you to the phone," Tim said.

Tim won. He admits he had a long start. Twenty minutes later he came back, walking slowly.

"I wish to announce," he said, "that I have been insulted by my editor and am no longer connected with the *Brooklyn Eagle*. If I can prove that I am sober tomorrow, they may hire me back," he added.

"You see what I mean," said the *Herald*.

We all filed telegraph stories about the horse. We swore that every word was true. We said it was a turning point in baseball. Two of us mentioned Columbus; and one, Galileo. In return, we got advice.

THESE TROUBLED TIMES, NEWSPAPERS NO SPACE FOR FICTION. EXPENSE ACCOUNT NO PROVISION DRUNKEN LEVITY, the *Herald's* wire read. The *World* read, ACCURACY, ACCURACY, ACCURACY, followed by three exclamation points, and signed "Joseph Pulitzer." CHARGING YOUR TELEGRAM RE BROOKLYN HORSE TO YOUR SALARY, my wire said. THAT'S A HORSE ON YOU!

Have you ever thought what you would do with a purple cow if you had one? I know. You would paint it over. We had a horse that could play third base, and all we could do was sit in the middle of Georgia and cuss our editors. I blame the editors. It is their fault that for the last 30 years you have had to go to smoking rooms or Pullman cars to hear about Jones.

But I don't blame them entirely, either. My first question would have been: How on earth can a horse possibly bat and throw? That's what the editors wondered. It's hard to explain. It's something you have to see to believe—like dogfish and political conventions.

And I've got to admit that the next morning we sat around and asked one another whether we really had seen a horse playing third base. Pop O'Donnell confessed that when he woke up he said to himself, "It must be shrimp that makes me dream about horses." Then all of us went down to the park, not really knowing whether we would see a horse there or not.

We asked Pop was he going to use the horse in games.

"I don't know," he thundered musingly. "I wonder. There are many angles. I don't know," he said, pulling at his chin.

That afternoon the Cubs, the world champs, came for an exhibition game. A chap from Pennsylvania—I forget his name—played third base for Brooklyn, and the horse grazed quietly beside the dugout. Going into the eighth, the Cubs were ahead, 2–0, and Three-Finger Brown was tying Brooklyn in knots. A curve would come over, then a fast one inside, and then the drop, and the Superbas would beat the air or hit puny little rollers to the infield, which Tinker or Evers would grab up and toss like a beanbag to Frank Chance. It was sickening. But in the eighth, Maloney got on base on an error, and Jordan walked. Then Lumley went down swinging, and Lewis watched perfect ones sail past him. The horse still was grazing over by the Brooklyn dugout.

"Put in the horse!" Frank Chance yelled. The Cubs laughed themselves sick.

Pop O'Donnell looked at Chance, and then at the horse, and back at Chance, as though he had made up his mind about something. "Go in there, son, and get a hit," he said. "Watch out for the curve." "Coive," Pop said.

The horse picked up a bat and cantered out to the plate.

"Pinch hitting for Batch," announced the umpire dreamily, "this horse." A second later he shook himself violently. "What am I saying?" he shouted.

On the Cubs' bench, every jaw had dropped somewhere around the owner's waist. Chance jumped to his feet, his face muscles worked like a coffee grinder, but nothing came out. It was the only time in baseball history, so far as I can find out, that Frank Chance was ever without words.

When he finally pulled himself together, he argued, with a good deal of punctuation, that there was no rule saying you could play a horse in the big leagues. Pop roared quietly that there was no rule saying you couldn't, either. They stood there nose to nose, Pop firing methodically like a cannon and Chance crackling like a machine gun. Chance gave up too easily. He was probably a little stunned. He said that he was used to seeing queer things in Brooklyn, anyway. Pop O'Donnell just smiled grimly.

Well, that was Jones' first game for Brooklyn. It could have been a reel out of a movie. There was that great infield—Steinfeldt, Tinker, Evers, and Chance—so precise, so much a machine that any ball hit on the ground was like an apple into a sorter. The infield was so famous that not many people remember Sheckard. Slagle, and Schulte in the outfield, but the teams of that day knew them. Behind the plate was Johnny Kling, who could rifle a ball to second like an 88-mm cannon. And on the mound stood Three-Finger Brown, whose drop faded away as though someone were pulling it back with a string.

Brown took a long time getting ready. His hand shook a little, and the first one he threw was 10 feet over Kling's head into the grandstand. Maloney and Jordan advanced to second and third. Brown threw the next one in the dirt. Then he calmed down, grooved one, and whistled a curve in around the withers.

"The glue works for you, Dobbin!" yelled Chance, feeling more like himself. Pop O'Donnell was mopping his forehead.

The next pitch came in fast, over the outside corner. The horse was waiting. He leaned into it. The ball whined all the way to the fence, Ted Williams was the only player I ever saw hit one like it. When Slagle finally got to the ball, the two runners had scored and the horse was on third. Brown's next pitch got a few yards away from Kling, and the horse stole home in a cloud of dust, all four feet flying. He got up, dusted himself off, looked at Chance, and gave a horselaugh.

If this sounds queer, remember that queerer things happen in Brooklyn every day.

"How do we write this one up?" asked the *Herald*. "We can't put just 'a horse' in the box score."

That was when the horse got his name. We named him Jones, after Jones, the caretaker who had left the gate open so he could wander onto the field. We wrote about "Horse" Jones.

Next day we all chuckled at a banner headline in one of the metropolitan papers. It read: JONES PUTS NEW KICK IN BROOKLYN.

Look in the old box scores. Jones got two hits off Rube Waddell of Philadelphia and three off Cy Young of Boston. He pounded Eddie Plank and Iron Man McGinnity and Wild Bill Donovan. He robbed Honus Wagner of a hit that would have been a double against any other third baseman in the league. On the base paths he was a bullet.

Our papers began to wire us, WHERE DOES JONES COME FROM? SEND BACKGROUND, HUMAN INTEREST, INTERVIEW. That was a harder assignment than New York knew. We decided by a gentlemen's agreement that Jones must have come from Kentucky and got his first experience in a Blue Grass league. That sounded reasonable enough. We said he was long-faced, long-legged, dark, a vegetarian, and a nonsmoker. That was true. We said he was a horse for work and ate like a horse. That was self-evident. Interviewing was a little harder.

Poor Pop O'Donnell for 10 years had wanted a third baseman who could hit hard enough to dent a cream puff. Now that he had one, he wasn't quite sure what to do with it. Purple-cow trouble. "Poiple," Pop would have said.

One of his first worries was paying for Jones. A strapping big farmer appeared at the clubhouse, saying he wanted either his horse or $50,000.

Pop excused himself, checked the team's bank balance, and then came back.

"What color is your horse?" he asked.

The farmer thought a minute. "Dapple gray," he said.

"Good afternoon, my man," Pop boomed unctuously, holding open the door. "That's a horse of another color." Jones was brown.

There were some audience incidents, too. Jonathan Daniels of Raleigh, North Carolina, told me that as a small boy that season he saw a whole row of elderly ladies bustle into their box seats, take one look toward third base, look questioningly at one another, twitter about the sun being hot, and walk out. Georgia police records show at least five people, cold sober, came to the ballpark and were afraid to drive their own cars home. The American medical journals of that year discovered a new psychoneurosis that they said was doubtless caused by a feeling of insecurity resulting from the replacement of the horse by the horseless carriage. It usually took the form of hallucination—the sensation of seeing a horse sitting in a baseball players' bench.

Perhaps that was the reason a famous pitcher, who shall here go nameless, came to town with his team, took one incredulous look at the Brooklyn fielding practice, and went to his manager, offering to pay a fine.

But the real trouble was about whether horses should be allowed to play baseball. After the first shock, teams were generally amused at the idea of playing against a horse. But after Jones had batted their star pitchers out of the box, they said the Humane Society ought to protect the poor Brooklyn horse.

The storm that brewed in the South that spring was like nothing except the storm that gathered in 1860. Every hotel that housed baseball players housed a potential civil war. The better orators argued that the right to play baseball should not be separated from the right to vote or the responsibility of fighting for one's country. The more practical ones said a few more horses like Jones and they wouldn't have any jobs left. Still others said that this was probably just another bureaucratic trick on the part of the Administration.

Even the Brooklyn players protested. A committee of them came to see ol' Pop O'Donnell. They said wasn't baseball a game for human beings? Pop said he had always had doubts as to whether some major-league players were human or not. They said touché, and this is all right so long as it is a one-horse business, so to speak. But if it goes on, before long won't a man have to grow two more legs and a tail before he can get in? They asked Pop how he would like to manage the Brooklyn Percherons, instead of the Brooklyn Superbas? They said, what would happen to baseball if it became a game for animals—say giraffes on one team, trained seals on a second, and monkeys on a third? They pointed out that monkeys had already got a foot in the door by being used to dodge baseballs in carnivals. How would Pop like to manage a team of monkeys called the Brooklyn Dodgers, they asked.

Pop said heaven help anyone who has to manage a team called the Brooklyn Dodgers. Then he pointed out that Brooklyn hadn't lost an exhibition game and that the horse was leading the league in batting with a solid .516. He asked whether they would rather have a World Series or a two-legged third baseman. They went on muttering.

But his chief worry was Jones himself.

"That horse hasn't got his mind on the game," he told us one night on the hotel veranda.

"Ah, Pop, it's just horseplay," said the *World*, winking.

"Nope, he hasn't got his heart in it," said Pop, his voice echoing lightly off the distant mountains. "He comes just in time for practice and runs the minute it's over. There's something on that horse's mind."

We laughed but had to admit that Jones was about the saddest horse we had ever seen. His eyes were just brown pools of liquid sorrow. His ears drooped. And still he hit well over .500 and covered third base like a rug.

One day he missed the game entirely. It was the day the Giants were in town, and 15,000 people were there to watch Jones bat against the great Matty. Brooklyn lost the game, and Pop O'Donnell almost lost his hair at the hands of the disappointed crowd.

"Who would have thought," Pop mused, in the clubhouse after the game, "that that (here some words are omitted) horse would turn out to be a prima donna? It's all right for a major-league ballplayer to act like a horse, but that horse is trying to act like a major-league ballplayer."

It was almost by accident that Tim and I found out what was really bothering Jones. We followed him one day when he left the ballpark. We followed him nearly two miles to a racetrack.

Jones stood beside the fence a long time, turning his head to watch the thoroughbreds gallop by on exercise runs and time trials. Then a little stable boy opened the gate for him.

"Po' ol' hoss," the boy said. "Yo' wants a little runnin'?"

"Happens every day," a groom explained to us. "This horse wanders here from God knows where and acts like he wants to run, and some boy rides him a while, bareback, pretending he's a racehorse."

Jones was like a different horse out there on the track; not drooping any more—ears up, eyes bright, tail like a plume. It was pitiful how much he wanted to look like a racehorse.

"That horse," Tim asked the groom, "is he any good for racing?"

"Not here, anyway," the groom said. "Might win a county-fair race or two."

He asked us whether we had any idea who owned the horse.

"Sir," said Tim, like Edwin M. Stanton, "that horse belongs to the ages."

"Well, mister," said the groom, "the ages had better get some different shoes on that horse. Why, you could hold a baseball in those shoes he has there."

"It's very clear," I said as we walked back, "what we have here is a badly frustrated horse."

"It's clear as beer," Tim said sadly.

That afternoon Jones hit a home run and absentmindedly trotted around the bases. As soon as the game was over, he disappeared in the direction of the racetrack. Tim looked at me and shook his head. Pop O'Donnell held his chin in his hands.

"I'll be boiled in oil," he said. "Berled in erl." Nothing cheered up poor Pop until someone came in with a story about the absentee owner of a big-league baseball club who had inherited the club along with the family fortune. This individual had just fired the manager of his baseball farm system because the farms had not turned out horses like Jones. "What are farms for if they don't raise horses?" the absentee owner had asked indignantly.

Jones was becoming a national problem second only to the Panama Canal and considerably more important than whether Mr. Taft got to be president. There were rumors that the Highlanders—people were just beginning to call them the Yankees—would withdraw and form a new league if Jones were allowed to play.

It was reported that a team of kangaroos from Australia was on its way to play a series of exhibition games in America, and Pres. Ban Johnson of the American League was quoted as saying that he would never have kangaroos in the American League because they were too likely to jump their contracts. There was talk of a constitutional amendment concerning horses in baseball.

The thing that impressed me, down there in the South, was that all this was putting the cart before the horse, so to speak. Jones simply didn't want to play baseball. He wanted to be a racehorse. I don't know why life is that way.

Jones made an unassisted triple play, and Ty Cobb accused Brooklyn of furnishing fire ladders to its infielders. He said that no third baseman could have caught the drive that started the play. At the end of the training season, Jones was batting .538 and fielding .997, had stolen 20 bases, and hit seven home runs. He was the greatest third baseman in the history of baseball and didn't want to be!

Joseph Pulitzer, William Randolph Hearst, Arthur Brisbane, and the rest of the bigshots got together and decided that if anyone didn't know by this time that Jones was a horse, the newspapers wouldn't tell him. He could find it out.

Folks seemed to find it out. People began gathering from all parts of the country to see Brooklyn open against the Giants—Matty against Jones. Even a tribe of Sioux Indians camped beside the Gowanus and had war dances on Flatbush Avenue, waiting for the park to open. And Pop O'Donnell kept his squad in the South as long as he could, laying plans to arrive in Brooklyn only on the morning of the opening game.

The wire said that night that 200,000 people had come to Brooklyn for the game, and 190,000 of them were in an ugly mood over the report that the League might not let Jones play. The governor of New York sent two regiments of the National Guard. The Giants were said to be caucusing to decide whether they would play against Jones. By game time, people were packed for six blocks, fighting to get into the park. The Sioux sent a young buck after their tomahawks, just in case.

Telephone poles a quarter of a mile from the field were selling for $100. Every baseball writer in the country was in the Brooklyn press box; the other teams played before cub reporters and society editors. Just before game time, I managed to push into Pop O'Donnell's little editorial office with the presidents of the two major leagues, the mayor of New York, a half dozen other reporters, and a delegation from the Giants.

"There's just one thing we want to know," the spokesman for the Giants was asking Pop, "Are you going to play Jones?"

"Gentlemen," said Pop in that soft-spoken, firm way of his that rattled window blinds, "our duty is to give the public what it wants. And the public wants Jones."

Like an echo, a chant began to rise from the bleachers; "We want Jones!"

"There is one other little thing," said Pop. "Jones has disappeared."

There were about 10 seconds of the awful silence that comes when your nerves are paralyzed but your mind keeps on thrashing.

"He got out of his boxcar somewhere between Georgia and Brooklyn," Pop said. "We don't know where. We're looking."

A Western Union boy dashed in. "Hold on!" said Pop. "This may be news!"

He tore open the envelope with a shaky hand. This message was from Norfolk, Virginia: HAVE FOUND ELEPHANT THAT CAN BALANCE MEDICINE BALL ON TRUNK, it read. WILL HE DO? If Pop had said what he said then into a telephone, it would have burned out all the insulators in New York.

Down at the field, the President of the United States himself was poised to throw out the first ball. "Is this Jones?" he asked. He was a little nearsighted.

"This is the mayor of New York," Pop said patiently. "Jones has gone. Run away."

The President's biographers disagree as to whether he said at that moment, "Oh, well, who would stay in Brooklyn if he could run?" or "I sympathize with you for having to change horses in midstream."

That was the saddest game ever covered by the entire press corps of the nation. Brooklyn was all thumbs in the field, all windmills at bat. There was no Jones to whistle hits into the outfield and make sensational stops at third. By the sixth inning, when they had to call the game with the score 18–1, the field was ankle deep in pop bottles, and the Sioux were waving their tomahawks and singing the scalp song.

You know the rest of the story. Brooklyn didn't win a game until the third week of the season, and no team ever tried a horse again, except a few dark horses every season. Pittsburgh, I believe, tried trained seals in the outfield. They were deadly at catching the ball but couldn't cover enough ground. San Francisco has an entire team of Seals, but I have never seen them play. Boston tried an octopus at second base but had to give him up. What happened to two rookies who disappeared trying to steal second base against Boston that spring is another subject baseball doesn't talk about.

There has been considerable speculation as to what happened to Jones.

Most of us believed the report that the Brooklyn players had unfastened the latch on the door of his boxcar, until Pop O'Donnell's *Confidential Memoirs* came out, admitting that he himself had taken the hinges off the door of his boxcar because he couldn't face the blame for making baseball a game for horses. But I have been a little confused since Tim McGuire came to me once and said he might as well confess. He couldn't stand to think of that horse standing wistfully beside the track, waiting for someone to let him pretend he was a racehorse. That haunted Tim. When he went down to the boxcar, he found the door unlatched and the hinges off, so he gave the door a little push outward. He judged it was the will of the majority.

And that is why baseball is played by men today instead of by horses. But don't think that the shadow of Jones doesn't still lie heavy on the game. Have you ever noticed how retiring, silent, and hangdog major-league ballplayers are, how they cringe before the umpire? They never know when another Jones may break away from a beer wagon, circus, or plow, wander through an unlocked gate, and begin batting .538 to their .290. The worry is terrible. You can see it in the crowds, too. That is why Brooklyn fans are so aloof and disinterested, why they never raise their voices above a whisper at Ebbets Field. They know perfectly well that this is only minor-league ball they are seeing, that horses could play it twice as well if they had a chance.

That is the secret we sportswriters have kept all these years: that is why we have never written about Jones. And the Brooklyn fans still try to keep it secret, but every once in a while the sorrow eats like lye into one of them until he can hold it back no longer, and then he sobs quietly and says, "Dem bums, if dey only had a little horse sense."

Louise Marley's background singing folk music and opera often informs her award-winning writing. Primarily a novelist, she also writes short fiction, including this splendid baseball story that offers a feminist perspective as it comments on Malamud's *The Natural* and talks about who and what and where you are in life, and how strange it can be sometimes to think about how you got there.

Diamond Girls

∽

Louise Marley

RICKY SAT ALONE IN her private locker room, turning a baseball in her elongated fingers. The pre-game had begun, and the speakers in the main locker room rattled with music and announcements and advertisements. She leaned forward, her elbows on her knees, and cradled the baseball in her palm. *Just another game*, she told herself. *It's a long season.*

But it wasn't true. Long season, sure. But this was no ordinary game.

Someone hammered on the door, and shouted, "Arendsen! Skip says to come over now."

"Coming," she called back. She stood, and stretched her arms over her head, her fingers ritually brushing the ceiling. She put the ball, her first major league game ball, back into its protective cube. Lew had saved it for her, gotten it signed.

She missed Lew. No one called a better game than he did, but he had retired at the end of last year, her rookie season, his bat worn out, his knees gone. It had been tough this season without him, a different catcher every rotation, a different attitude every game. She'd lost her last three starts. The sports columns had her on her way back to the minors after two of them, and they weren't far from the truth.

Her agent tried to shield her from the worst of Management's comments, but she knew her career was on the line. Three losses were a bad way for anyone to start a season. It was worse for Ricky Arendsen.

And now this. Skip had tried to warn her, in his bluff, half-articulate way. "Management took a risk on you," he had said this morning, shuffling through the scouting reports on Everett. "Not worth the grief if you aren't the best." She only nodded. She knew that already.

Now she closed her locker, and tucked her mitt under her arm. She left the cramped space that was hers, and walked around the corner to the other door. The official statement to the press said that Ricky Arendsen had a separate locker room for her own privacy, but Ricky—and everyone else—understood it was more complicated than just that. Maybe the guys didn't want a woman in their locker room. More likely, they didn't want her in their locker room.

It had been the same in high school, in college, in the minors. It didn't matter that she possessed a killer curve, a one-hundred-plus fastball, a splitter that made grown-up men wave their bats like beginning T-Ballers. What mattered, not to everyone, but to enough of them, was what she was, and how she got that way.

Ricky adjusted her cap, and pulled open the door with its vivid team logo.

The Skipper looked up when she came in, pointed to the bench in front of him. Raimundo grinned at her, and moved over to make room. He was catching her today, which was good. She felt a bit better when he was behind the plate. She didn't have to shake him off as often as she did Baker.

"Hey, Rick," he said as she eased herself onto the bench. He moved another couple of inches over to give her space. She nodded down at him. Raimundo was a good six inches shorter than she was, just clearing six feet four.

"Hey, Ray," she said. She quirked her lips and lifted her eyebrows, pretending a calm she didn't feel. "Place is crawling with reporters."

"Whatcha get, Newsmaker." He said it with sympathy, his forehead crinkling. "Yeah. I know."

Newsmaker was the least offensive of the many appellations attached to Ricky Arendsen when she came up to the show. The worst had been coined by a conservative preacher in a weekly newspaper column. The fans picked it up, shouting it whenever she took the mound. Lab Rat, Lab Rat, a one-two rhythm, a bit of doggerel that irritated her dreams.

She fiddled with the laces on her mitt, hooking them tight with the extra-long first joint of her finger, flexing the designer muscles of her wrists. She was a hell of a specimen, just as they said. Her thighs were smoothly muscled, perfectly jointed at the hip. Her calves were long and strong, her ankles like steel. Her eyesight was off the charts.

She wondered what Grace Everett's eyesight was like.

They were calling Everett "The Natural." No engineered virus, no stem cell modifications, no Lab Rat. Just a wiry, quick second baseman, a freckled girl with a stringy red ponytail and a wicked bat. In the minors they called her Gracie, or Little Red. Now, coming up against Ricky Arendsen, Grace Everett had become the Natural. No misunderstanding what that was about, no other way to interpret it. She was The Natural. Ricky wasn't.

"Okay, guys," the Skipper said. He stood in front of the chalkboard, where someone had scribbled the line-ups, a few names crossed out, substitutes chalked in. Some of the players were chowing down from the buffet, but Ricky never ate right before a game.

Skip nodded to her. "You okay, Rick?"

She gave him a thumbs-up, and pulled off her cap to scratch her scalp through her short scruff of brown hair.

"Good. So," the Skipper began. "Everybody. The main thing is, don't let it all get to you today, okay? Everett's just another ballplayer. Let's play it that way. Cool and calm."

Someone standing beside the row of open lockers snorted, "Yeah, Skip. That'll work."

The Skipper shot him a heated look. "I mean it," he growled. "No crap out there."

"Hey, Skip, it's not us," someone protested. "It's the fans. Worse than New York!"

Ricky hunched her shoulders. Ray murmured, "Easy, Rick."

"Yeah."

"It's a stunt," he added under his breath. "I hear they brought her up just to face you. She'll fan a few times, fall on her face, and go straight back to Triple-A."

Ricky turned her head without changing position. "Where'd you hear that?"

Ray shrugged. "Talk around the office."

"I don't know, Ray. Her stats are solid."

Ricky didn't want to think about Everett, about what this game must mean to her. She had to concentrate on her own problems. Three straight losses after her twelve-and-eight last year. If they sent her down, she'd never get called up again, not after all the stuff that happened last season. She needed a W today as much as she ever had in her life.

"Listen," the Skipper said. "Anybody's out of line, in the stands or on the field, Security throws 'em out of the park, okay?"

"If it's not too late," someone said from the back of the room. Ricky didn't need to turn to know who the grumbler was. Center field. Ditch Daniels, they called him, because he wore a ditch in the grass between left and right. Ditch had been struck by something when she was pitching her second game, a cup or a ball or something thrown from the outfield bleachers. He was touchy and hot-tempered on the best of days, and that really tipped him over. He never had a good word for her, not even when she came in on one day's rest to save the last game of the season, propelling the team into the playoffs. Ditch had memorized every one of the death threats she'd received since she came up. As if Ricky didn't remember them well enough without his quoting them word for word when he knew she could hear him.

"Look at it this way," the Skipper said finally. "The park's sold out, even the bleachers. For a regular season game. Management's happy, which is good news at contract time, right? Let's just get this one. Let Security worry about the nutcases."

The team grunted assent, and filed out of the locker room and up the ramp to the dugout. Ricky headed for the bullpen to warm up.

A solid wall of sound greeted her, defeating the announcer as he read the rosters. When Ricky trotted to the mound, tossed a few pitches to Ray, the volume dissipated, gradually, like a spent wave, leaving an electric silence in its wake. A familiar prickle crept across Ricky's shoulders and up under her cap, as if something were pointed at the back of her neck or between her shoulder blades. Jackie Robinson had felt the same thing, she supposed. Like a great big target. Sometimes Ricky felt as if the mound was a bull's-eye, with her smack in the center.

Ray gave the ump a nod, and the first batter, a leftie, stepped into the box, bat describing semi-circles above his shoulder. Ricky leaned forward, bent at the waist. She held the ball behind her back, turning it in the fingers of her left hand till she found just the right spot, the seams fitting perfectly between her fingers and her long, flexible thumb. Ray gave her the sign, curve down and in, and she nodded. She straightened. Her right leg lifted in the high kick, hands above her head. The wind-up. The throw. Strike one. Ragged cheers from the home town fans, half-hearted taunts from the visitors, and the game was underway.

The first two innings went hitless and scoreless on both sides, despite several long at-bats that went the full count, and a dozen or more foul balls. Ricky rested after the second, her warm-up jacket tugged up over her left arm, her chin on her chest.

Everett would come up in the third, batting eighth in the line-up. She'd hit over .300 in the minors, Ricky knew, but otherwise the scouts hadn't had much to say about her. No one had expected Little Red to be sent up, not now, not ever.

When the second ended, Ricky stood, and pulled the jacket off her arm. The crowd began to stir, a deep murmur rather than the usual calls and cheers. Camera flashes glimmered in the stadium like stars in a multi-colored sky.

The first hitter grounded to third, and the murmuring grew. Ricky turned her back on the mound, walked a little way toward second, bent to tighten a shoe lace. She caught some rosin on the way back. As she walked to the top, and started to dig her toes into the dirt, Everett moved into the box, swinging her bat with one hand, eyeing Ricky over her right shoulder. Her red ponytail swung between her shoulder blades. Matching red freckles dusted her nose and cheeks.

She deserved to be called The Natural, Ricky thought. There was nothing unusual about her physique, except that she looked strong, a little bigger than most women. But lots of women were big, lots of women were athletic. It took a special combination of speed and coordination and eyesight, as well as strength, to make a major-league ballplayer.

Ricky shook off Ray's first sign. He wanted to surprise the batter, try the curve instead of the fastball she expected. But Everett was a fastball hitter. Ricky wanted to see what she had.

Ray extended a forefinger. Fastball. Ricky nodded, straightened, kicked, wound, threw.

The crowd's murmur broke into shouts as the radar flashed a ninety-six, but it wasn't the speed of the pitch that made the difference. It was that little kick at the end, the tail. Ricky's long fingers could hold the seams right where she wanted them, and her fastball was almost impossible to hit.

Everett watched it go by with just a lift of her elbows, as if she thought it might be inside. It wasn't. Ricky stared at her opponent, and wondered if Everett felt like she did. Like a target. Like an outsider. Like no matter how well she played, it would never be enough.

Ray flashed the sign for the curve, and Ricky shook him off again. He tried the change-up, and she shook her head. She couldn't quite see his shrug before he extended the forefinger, but she was sure it was there. She didn't care. She wanted to play it this way.

Everett glanced at the third-base coach, and then faced her again. Ricky threw. Ninety-seven. Everett's bat never left her shoulder.

She backed out of the box, shaking her head, talking to herself. She put up a hand to ask for time. The ump gave it, and Ricky stepped off the mound to shake out her arms.

The next pitch was another fastball, but Ricky missed with it, just inside, brushing Everett's thighs so close her uniform rippled. A roar of fury erupted from the stands.

Ricky caught her breath at the sound. She had learned to tune out the jeers that greeted her trips to the mound, but this surge, when the fans thought she might have hit Everett, was staggering. Lew had talked her through it all the first few times, and by the end of her first season, she hardly heard the chants and catcalls. But this was different. She glanced up into the colorful mass of people, banners waving, hands in the air, hand-lettered signs dancing here and there. Were they hoping Everett would show her up, or hoping Everett would fail? Was there anyone out there just rooting for their favorite team, the way they used to?

She caught sight of a placard with her name on it, and beneath it a circle with "Jackie Robinson" inside, a black line crossing the circle. No Jackie Robinson, it meant to say. Ricky Arendsen is no Jackie Robinson. She'd seen it before.

Lew had told her to laugh it off. "They're right, anyway, kid," he had said. "You're no Jackie Robinson—you're bigger, faster, and stronger than he was. You'll show 'em."

Now Ray was jogging out to the mound, and she'd lost track of time. Not like her, to let anything interfere with her concentration.

"Hey, Rick," he said. The two of them turned their backs to the plate, and Ricky dropped her head to hear. "What's the matter? You got two strikes, one ball, you're ahead in the count. Nothing to worry about."

"Yeah, yeah, I know. I just . . ." She breathed deeply, adjusted her cap, and then shook her head. "I'm okay. Sorry, Ray."

"Let's go with the splitter now, okay? Quit messing around?"

She shook her head. "No. Fastball. I can get her. Let's do it."

He frowned, and tugged at his mask. "Well, Rick, you're the pitcher. Don't lose her though, or Skip will be pissed."

"I won't lose her."

Ray slapped her back with his mitt, and jogged back to the plate, pulling his mask down as he went.

* * *

Grace Everett chewed on her tongue, trying to get some moisture into her mouth as she faced Ricky Arendsen once again. Arendsen didn't look like someone whose career was in trouble. She looked unbeatable, her long form perfectly proportioned, her face calm, her eyes like steel. And the fastball!

Grace wished she'd taken the bubble gum someone had offered her. Her mouth felt like a desert. She stubbed her toe into the dirt, wiggled it, set her foot. She'd hit a ninety-five before, she reminded herself. Just the other day, down in Triple-A. Today was no different. Just another ballgame, the beginning of a long season . . .

But still, as she faced the Newsmaker, her heart pounded in her throat. She glanced up at the coach, and saw the signs. The splitter, he thought Arendsen would throw the splitter. It didn't seem right to Grace. She looked back at Arendsen, at the poker face, the forward-leaning posture, the hand hidden behind the back. Well, the coach was the coach, and this was her first game in the bigs. It was no time for independence. She lifted her bat from her shoulder, let it describe small, tight circles, watched Arendsen straighten, kick, wind, and throw.

Fastball! Again!

At least this time, Grace had a swing at it, but she was looking for the splitter, and the fastball surprised her. It smacked into the catcher's mitt before her bat crossed the plate. With a grunt and a gritting of her teeth, she turned and marched back to the dugout, her cheeks burning.

She didn't look at the coach, or her teammates. She didn't know them yet, didn't know what their expressions meant, what they might be thinking. Just thinking about their own at-bats, probably. She took off the batting helmet and picked up her mitt. She pulled her cap out of her belt as she trotted out to second base. Arendsen was walking in the other direction, to the home side, her lanky height making Grace feel like a half-pint. She pulled on her cap, and settled into her place between first and second.

So she struck out. Everybody struck out once in a while, right?

But you only get this chance, Gracie. This one chance. She sighed, and smacked her fist in her mitt. She knew they'd only brought her up to face Arendsen. Her Triple-A coach told her so.

"You're playing great, Little Red. None better. But it took guts for those guys to take Arendsen on. It's cost 'em plenty. Extra security, vandalism to the stadium, bad press. Only way they got through it was they made the play-offs. Our guys don't want to risk all that."

She had protested. "I'm hitting .326!"

"Yeah, but we're not the show, Gracie."

"So what, they're giving me one game, and that's it?"

"Depends, Red. You do well, get a couple hits, they might give you another shot."

"A couple hits? Against Ricky Arendsen? That's hardly fair."

"You're right. It's a stunt, is what it is, but I couldn't talk 'em out of it, Arendsen's a fastball pitcher, and you're a hell of a fastball hitter. And the boss is an old-fashioned guy. I think he wants to prove you can't do it, that The Natural can't cut it in the bigs."

Grace had pounded the cement floor with the heel of her spikes. "I hate that name. They only call me that because Arendsen—"

"Yeah, yeah, I know, kid. Tough breaks all around."

"And so what, the boss wants me out?"

The coach shrugged. "All I know is, he's been whining to the commissioner ever since Arendsen signed. Doesn't believe in women in baseball. Not in the majors."

Grace stood up, and fixed the coach with a direct stare. "Arendsen's a great ballplayer."

He stood up too, and grinned. "Damn straight, Gracie. And so are you."

* * *

Neither team scored until the bottom of the sixth, when Ray manufactured a run by stealing second and then scoring on Smitty's double. Ricky gave him the thumbs-up as she shrugged out of her warm-up jacket. He grinned, pulling on his chest protector and reversing his cap. As he pulled down his mask, he said, "Hold 'em now, Rick, okay?"

"Do my best."

Ricky knew her pitch count was already at eighty-four, but that didn't concern her. Among the gifts her mother's engineered virus had bestowed on her was stamina. In her first season she'd pitched five complete games, to the astonishment of the coaches and the envy of the rest of the pitching staff. Now, in the top of the seventh, she sent down the first batter on four pitches. She was beginning to breathe easier, feeling as if her season could turn around at last. The ump was giving her the called strikes, keeping the hitters honest, unlike the earlier games of the season. She didn't let the last batter of the inning rattle her, though he got a single and advanced to second on a fielder's choice, then stole third while she was dealing with their cleanup hitter. She eyed him before her last pitch. Ray flashed the splitter, and she nodded. It was her signature pitch, fast and smooth, toppling out of its trajectory just as it reached the plate. No one could read it, not even the umpire half the time.

This time the pitch was perfect. The hitter spun on his heels as he tried to adjust, but he was about an hour too late. Ricky grinned at Ray as they headed back to the dugout, feeling a burst of confidence. It felt like last year, with Lew. "Good work, Catch," she said as they stepped down into the shade and she folded her lengthy frame onto the bench. She pulled the warm-up over her arm.

Ray said, "Yeah. Some long at-bats, Rick, but you can get six more."

"Let's hope."

The Skipper glanced over at her. "How you holding up, Ricky?"

"Great, Skip."

He indicated the pitch counter with his chin. "You're at a hundred and three."

"I'm fine." She looked out across the field to the bullpen then, and saw that no one was up. She knew what would happen as her pitch count went up, into the eighth, into the ninth. A hundred and twenty. A hundred and thirty. The catcalls would grow louder, more frantic. Lab Rat, Lab Rat.

Had her mother known, when she was perfecting her virus? When she was injecting it into her own womb, targeting her unborn child's stem cells?

It could have failed, after all. Ricky Arendsen could have been some sort of monster. The others—the other experiments—had all had terrible problems. She was the only success, out of a dozen modified fetuses.

Involuntarily, Ricky glanced out at the infield, where The Natural danced between first and second. She wondered if Everett knew what it was like to be Ricky Arendsen. She might even have preferred to be like her, to have her genes modified within days after conception, her body engineered to be bigger, stronger, faster. If today was Everett's only chance at the bigs, her only shot . . . that was tough.

Ricky hunched her shoulders, and slid further down on her long, pliable spine. She didn't want to feel sorry for Grace Everett. She had to work hard enough not to be sorry for herself, not to be wounded by the nasty articles, the placards, the threatening letters.

It didn't matter now. Let them yell what they wanted. She would turn it off. Tune it out. Just six batters, and the whole season would turn around.

* * *

The rancor of the fans stunned Grace when she came out for her third at bat, at the top of the ninth. She read the sports columns, of course, like everyone else, but even those criers of doom hadn't prepared her for the insults that were shouted at Ricky Arendsen, for the hysterical screams of fans waving signs that said things like "Baseball, not biology." She'd spotted one that read, "Put the balls back in baseball," but Security had escorted the bearer of that one from the stadium before the first pitch. The din rose at her own appearance, rhythmic shouts of "The Natural, The Natural," at a volume that banged inside her helmet as if someone were beating it like a drum. There had to be supporters in the stands, people shouting encouragement for Ricky Arendsen, but Grace couldn't hear them. Hate had a stronger voice.

Something unwelcome and surprising twisted in her belly, and she recognized it as a surge of sympathy. She thrust it aside. Her team was down two to zip, ninth inning, one down, one on. And Grace's gut told her, in a cold voice, that this was it. Now or never.

And yet, if Ricky Arendsen weren't out there on the mound, she, Grace Everett, would still be riding the bus with the Triple-A team. No big league team ever gave a girl a chance before Arendsen. Ricky Arendsen stood alone on the mound, awash in antagonism, when all she wanted was to play ball.

Grace wanted to play ball, too. She swung her bat as she walked to the plate, trying to push away the useless thoughts. The coach was flashing her signs, and she nodded obediently, but it was a sham. No point now in sucking up. Her opportunity was slipping away. The coach didn't know what Ricky Arendsen was going to throw. Grace thought she just might.

It was because they were facing each other, she thought. Arendsen could get her with the splitter, that evil slicing arc that made veterans look like Little Leaguers. Or she could fool her with her change-up, that looped over the plate like a turtle on Valium. But Arendsen had thrown her nothing but fastballs. She wanted a test, head to head, the Lab Rat against The Natural. And she would do it again.

Grace dug in her toe, lifted her bat above her shoulder, flexed her thighs in her stance. Arendsen bent at the waist, nodded to the catcher, and went into her high kick, that incredible kick that made her look like a seven-foot ballet dancer.

Fastball. Grace swung, pivoting on her heels, the bat whistling. Miss.

She stepped out of the batter's box, and took a couple of swings. Arendsen circled the mound, bent to the rosin bag, stretched her shoulders. Grace saw the coach flashing signs at her, and she nodded again. He wore a glum look, and she knew he thought the game was already over. The runner took a long lead at first. Arendsen glanced at him from under her cap, but didn't bother with a throw. Her eyes came back to Grace, gleaming with determination across the sixty feet and six inches' distance. Grace paused at the edge of the batter's box. She felt the ump's questioning glance, but she was transfixed by Arendsen's gaze.

She knew all about the Newsmaker's stem cell modifications, her incredible speed, coordination, the flexibility in her hips and knees and shoulders. She knew her height was enhanced, her musculature, her vision.

But Ricky Arendsen's mother's patent had failed. The other recipients of the engineered virus had been failures. One child was born with a beautiful body and incredible strength, but with a brain that never matured. Another grew so fast in infancy that her bones deformed. One volunteer gave birth to twins who became implacable competitors—with each other. They had to be institutionalized when they were five.

Ricky Arendsen—and only Ricky Arendsen—had grown into a superb athlete, with a mind to match. But the gleam Grace saw in her eye was all hers. No virus had made her the competitor she was. She was a ballplayer. A gamer.

And so was Grace.

Grace's nerves vanished as if they never were. As if this was just another game, another ballpark, one in a long season. The din seemed to fade from her hearing as if someone had turned down the volume on a radio. She nodded to the umpire, glanced briefly at the coach, turned her face to Ricky Arendsen. She wanted—really wanted—that fastball.

The second pitch missed way outside, and Grace raised her eyebrows. Arendsen tiring? The catcher fell to his left, barely spearing the ball before it escaped to the wall. The runner dashed to second base. Scoring position.

Grace grinned, and lifted her bat, painting air circles. The coach stared at her, eyes hopeless. She watched Arendsen shake off her catcher's signs, one, two, three.

She'd thrown nothing but fastballs to Grace. But now it was the ninth inning, a runner on, only one away. Would she do it again? Grace dug her feet into the dirt, and eyed the pitcher.

The kick, the wind-up, Arendsen's impossibly long arms high over her head . . .

Time slowed, in that way it sometimes did, that way that let Grace Everett know the pitch that was coming was all hers. Great ballplayers, she knew, saw pitches differently, understood their speed and trajectory and spin in a way no ordinary mortal could. Grace didn't know if she had it in her to be a great ball-player, but once in a while she experienced that perfect moment of perception, that pinnacle of sight and sense and instinct. This pitch, turning seam over seam on its sixty-foot-six-inch path, was no fastball. Grace couldn't have said how she knew, but she knew. It was the splitter, Arendsen's famous, nasty pitch, that fell over the plate as if it had run into a wall.

Grace's heels braced, her gut tightened, her thighs flexed as she wheeled on that ball. She knew exactly where it would be. And she connected.

She felt the impact from her shoulders to her toes, that sweet, hard jolt that sent the baseball leaping for the infield, bouncing in the basepath, dodging the shortstop as if it had eyes.

Grace didn't watch it go. She knew. She tossed her bat away and dug for first base, head down to hide her grin.

As she approached first base, she looked up, and saw the coach waving her on. She spun on toward second, seeing Ditch Daniels scoop up the ball—her ball—and heave it toward home plate. She could hear the fans again, the shouts of dismay, the yells of approbation. She pulled up on second, panting, grinning. A double. An RBI. Whatever happened now, she'd had her chance, and it felt great. She felt like she had wings on her heels.

She flicked a quick glance at Arendsen.

Ricky Arendsen stood, baseball in hand, watching Grace. She lifted the baseball with a flick of her wrist. A salute. Then she pulled down her cap, and turned to face the next batter.

* * *

"You think I don't know what you're up to?" demanded the Skipper, glaring down at Ricky. She sat with her head back against the dugout wall, her cap tipped up, her legs stretched out to their full length.

"What, Skip?" she asked languidly.

"You wouldn't take Ray's calls, you wouldn't use the curve or the change. You just had to see if she could hit your fastball."

"I threw the splitter, Skip. She got lucky."

"Well, now the damned game is tied, and their closer's out there. We'll probably go into extra innings. You're already in trouble, Ricky! What did you think you were doing?"

She pulled her cap over her eyes. "Just playing ball, Skip. I'll get 'em next inning."

"You will not." He wheeled, and stamped away to the bullpen phone.

Ricky abruptly sat up. "Skip, no! Don't take me out. I'll get 'em, I promise."

He stopped, and glared back at her. "Oh, yeah? You know what your count is?"

"I'm fine. Look, I'm sorry." Ricky stood up, and went to stand beside the manager. "I just—" She shrugged. "I wanted to see what she's got. This may be the only day she gets."

"It's a fuckin' game, Rick," the Skip said with disgust. "It's not tea and crumpets."

She stiffened, and her cheeks flamed. "Come on. I get enough of that from the stands."

He hesitated, and then his stiff stance relaxed. "Yeah, yeah, I know, Rick. Sorry. It's been tough on you. It's tough every time you go out."

"I don't care about that, Skip, you know I don't. But let me have another inning."

He shrugged. "What the hell. It's early in the season." He pointed a thick finger at Ray, listening from the bench. "But remember, you pay attention to Ray's calls, okay? Your losses are mine, too, and the rest of the guys. No more grandstanding."

Ricky grinned at him, and touched the bill of her cap with her forefinger.

* * *

In the bottom of the ninth, Grace watched the closer mow down the batters in order, one, two, three. She hardly had to move her feet. In the tenth, Ricky

Arendsen was still pitching, unbelievably. Her shaky start seemed to have evaporated with Grace's double, and she, too, started mowing down batters.

In the dugout, the manager groaned, watching her. "She oughta be beat," he said. "There oughta be nothing left in that arm."

Somebody swore. "That's Arendsen for you."

Somebody else said, "Too bad we don't have our own Lab Rat."

Grace stiffened at that, but the player closest to her—the left fielder, a veteran who'd been one of her heroes when she was in high school—patted her shoulder. "We're doin' okay with Little Red, here," he said gruffly. "Game'd be over if it weren't for The Natural."

Two or three of the guys added their compliments. Grace blushed and ducked her head.

She didn't have another at-bat until the twelfth. They were still tied at two. Arendsen had settled into a rhythm, and since the ninth, no batter had looked at more than five pitches. There had been two hits, three guys on base, but no one scored. Arendsen's count was high, but it didn't seem to matter, to her or to her manager.

The fans seemed to have fallen into a rhythm, too. When Grace appeared in her batting helmet, the chant of "Natural, Natural," washed out across the field. The stands were still full. No one, it seemed, had left the ballpark. They'd bought tickets to see The Natural go against the Lab Rat, and they were getting their money's worth.

Arendsen had stopped trying to tempt her with the fastball. This time she threw a curve, a change, a splitter that missed outside, and then another change, that also missed outside.

Grace stepped out of the box to catch her breath. Two and two. She had that feeling in her gut again. One last chance.

She heaved a deep breath, and stepped back in. She lifted her bat, and met Ricky Arendsen's cool gaze across the expanse of grass and dirt.

Ricky rolled her left shoulder. Her arm, at last, was starting to tire. Heat ran from her shoulder to her elbow, and she felt the warmth in her ribs and in her wrist as well. When Ray flashed the sign for the splitter, she hesitated. He looked at her for a long moment, and then called time and trotted out to the mound, pushing up his mask as he went. She stepped down to meet him, and they turned their backs to the box.

"You okay?" Ray asked.

"Getting tired," she admitted.

"Wanta call in Baxter?"

Ricky glanced out to the bullpen, and saw that Baxter and one of the middle relievers were both up and throwing. She scratched her neck. "No," she said finally. "No, I want this one, this inning. Get this over with."

"Yeah. But you don't want to risk letting Everett get another hit."

Ricky looked back over her left shoulder, where Everett was swinging the bat and squinting out at them. Shadows stretched across the infield now, fingers of darkness pointing away from the setting sun. "What do you think, Ray? You think the splitter?"

"Yup."

She nodded, and he jogged back to the plate. She bent at the waist, then straightened. Everett's blue eyes glittered slightly as they met hers.

She lifted her right knee, high, and brought her hands above her head. She threw the splitter, but it got away from her. Chin music, they called it. It sure wasn't anywhere it was supposed to be. It didn't drop, but spun directly at Everett's face.

The rookie spun backward, landing on her butt in the dirt, her bat dropped, her helmet gone. The screams of the fans intensified, an eruption of rage.

Ray called time again, and sprinted to the mound. When he got there, Skip was there, too. Ricky turned her back, pulled off her cap to rub her fingers through her hair, and ducked her head to hear what the Skipper had to say.

* * *

They were shouting it now, Natural, Natural, against the screams of Lab Rat. But they were wrong, Grace reflected. This wasn't about modified genes, about great eyesight or elongated fingers or a designer skeleton. This was about desire.

Grace wanted it. She didn't want to walk, she didn't want to get on base by being struck by a pitch. She wanted a hit. She wanted to win, not because of Arendsen, not because it was her first day in the big leagues, not to prove The Natural could do it. She wanted to win because it was baseball, and she was in the game.

She lifted her bat to her shoulder, and met the Newsmaker's eyes once again. Ricky Arendsen straightened her shoulders, dropped her chin. She wasn't looking at her catcher now. She was looking at Grace.

Grace looked back. Her bat circled above her, and time slowed down.

It should have been something crafty, of course, another splitter, or the curve, or the change. But she knew in her bones the fastball was coming. She would have to anticipate, to be there before Arendsen was, to see it barreling toward her . . .

And she did. This time the crack of her bat made her wrists ache, drove her heels deep into the dirt around home plate. The ball exploded from her bat, a long, high arc that had nowhere to land except in the left field bleachers, far beyond the reach of the outfielder, into the outstretched hands of the fans. A roar greeted her as she jogged around the bases. Arendsen watched her, tossing a new ball in her hand, turning on the mound as she made her circuit.

Before she reached home, the manager was on the mound, and the catcher was on his way to join the conference. Grace touched the plate, and turned to the dugout, the chant following her. "Natural, Natural." The coach met her, grinning, and swatted her rear as she passed him.

Ricky said, "No, Skip. Just this inning."

"Hey, Rick, I gave you more time than I should have. You lost her."

Ricky stared down at him, her jaw clenching. "I didn't lose her. She hit the fastball. Just like she hit the splitter. There's a reason she hit over .300 in Triple-A."

Ray grunted, "True, Skip. It was a great pitch. They both were."

The Skipper glared at them both for a long moment, and Ricky saw movement over her shoulder as the umpire started out toward the mound to break it up. "Okay," the Skipper growled, half under his breath. "Okay. But this is it, Rick."

"Right. Thanks, Skip."

The last two outs were easy. One batter fanned on the curve, the other on the splitter. Ricky walked with deliberate slowness back to the dugout, letting the catcalls fall around her like warm rain. She stretched her arms, her shoulders, and reached for her batting helmet. It was the bottom of the order, and she was the bottom of the bottom. She had never hit .300, not even in high school. It didn't help that she made such a big strike zone.

Ditch Daniels singled to right. Ray came next, waging a long battle at the plate, but it ended with Ray flying out to short, not even advancing the runner. Williams, the third baseman, grounded to third. And then it was Ricky's turn.

The closer smirked at her, expecting an easy out, anticipating the W. Ditch poised just off first base. At second, Everett half-crouched, mitt at the ready for Ditch's steal attempt.

Whenever she came up to bat, Ricky thought of her father. Her mother, the doctor, the research scientist, had never forgiven him for encouraging Ricky's enthusiasm for athletics. When she decided baseball was her game, he spent hours lobbing balls to her, playing catch, and later, catching her first pitches.

When the virus failed, in every case except her daughter's, Ricky's mother hoped that Ricky's achievements would prove her right after all, validate her tireless, all-consuming endeavors. But Ricky's father—who had spent six years in the minor leagues in his youth—found her athletic ability his only consolation for what he regarded as betrayal by his wife. It was when the two of them divorced, and Ricky overheard their last bitter argument, that she learned her mother had injected herself with the engineered virus without telling her father. Ricky was already determined to be the first woman to play major league baseball. She felt no resentment, but her father never willingly spoke to her mother again.

What she remembered when she came to the plate was her dad laughing that as a hitter she made a great pitcher.

The closer's first pitch was a low strike, a neat fastball just at the knees. Ricky took an awkward swing, knowing it was in the zone, missing by at least two inches. The catcher threw hard to second, but Ditch was in there, standing up. Tying run in scoring position.

The next two pitches Ricky let go, seeing before they reached her that they would be outside, tumbling off to the catcher's left. The fourth pitch was a slider, the pitch Ricky hated the most. It came inside just at belt level, a nasty height for a batter with long arms. She bent back away from it, and the umpire called a second strike.

The closer tried to tempt her with the change, but Ricky knew by his stance, a slight hesitation at the release point, what he was throwing. It dropped too soon, bouncing right off the edge of the bag. Ditch was on it, tearing to third before the catcher had his mask off. Full count. Runner ninety feet away. A little spark of hope flickered in Ricky's belly, and she called time to eye the coach's signs and ponder what the next pitch might be.

As she stepped back in, she glanced out to the infield. Everett looked back, her cap pulled low, that skinny ponytail flopping over one shoulder. The infield was fully in shadow now. Game time.

Ricky lifted her bat, loosened her shoulders. Okay, she wasn't the hitter Everett was. But she could keep the game alive, get something. She eyed the closer. What would she throw, if she were on the mound and the game were on the line, the stands packed, the press box jammed? She wouldn't take a chance walking the batter, and facing the top of the lineup. She'd throw her very best pitch, and locate as if she were doing surgery. This guy didn't have a splitter, but he had a mean slider, if it didn't miss.

The pitch looked as if it would be outside, but she knew it wouldn't. It would turn, whip across the plate at the last moment, slide across the corner, jam her hands. She watched the pitch come, seeing it so clearly she could almost see the seams revolve. She thought of Everett, poised just beyond the infield. Okay, Gracie. Try this.

* * *

The din from the stands deafened Grace, and the tension in the ballpark electrified the short red hairs on her arms. Lab Rat, Lab Rat. Did they ever shout for Arendsen?

Arendsen slapped at the last pitch, and it spiked between Grace and the shortstop. The shortstop leaped to his left, but the ball bounced just beyond his reach. Grace launched herself like an arrow, arms extended, torso parallel to the ground. She hit with a mighty grunt, rolled, closed her mitt tight and hoped for the best.

As she bounced to her feet, the roar from the crowd had changed somehow. Cheers blurred the chant as Ricky Arendsen loped to first base. Ditch Daniels charged, head down, toward home. Grace opened her mitt, found the ball in it, seized it and threw.

The ball smacked into the catcher's mitt just one split second after Daniels crossed the plate. Ricky Arendsen, one foot on first base, grinned across the diamond. Tied again.

Chagrined, Grace ducked her head, brushing at the infield dirt on her uniform.

The next batter smacked a double into right field, and the closer, getting desperate, threw the next man four straight balls. The third man in the order hit a long, looping fly ball that dropped into left field, and Arendsen galloped easily into home to score the winning run.

It was over. Over for the night. Over for Grace.

Her feet felt like lead as she crossed the infield. She kept her eyes down, not wanting to look at the fans, to look up into the now-shadowed bleachers, at the flashing scoreboard with its garish ads and celebratory displays. It was over. Her big chance. She allowed herself one glance at Arendsen before she stepped down into the dugout.

Arendsen was surrounded by press, a microphone in her face, the lights of television cameras shining on her as she pulled off her batting helmet, pushed a hand through her hair. Someone ran out with an ice pack and wrapped it around her arm as she answered questions.

Grace paused. The Newsmaker, as if sensing her, looked up, past the clutch of reporters. Grace nodded to her, and touched two fingers to her cap. She hoped Arendsen understood that it was a gesture of respect. And of farewell. Surely Ricky Arendsen understood that Grace's moment had passed.

She made her leaden feet move then, down the steps, away from Arendsen's triumph.

"So, Ricky, the season's looking a lot better now, isn't it?"

Ricky nodded to the reporter, though she couldn't see him past the glare. "Yeah."

"Nice hit you got. Did that surprise you?"

Ricky laughed. "Yeah. Yeah, kind of a surprise. Wasn't very pretty."

"Hey, Rick." She turned her head, searching for the sportswriter. He grinned up at her, gestured toward the visitors' dugout. "Did you see the Na—um, did you see Everett's dive?"

"No. Was it good?"

"Fantastic. What did you think of them bringing her up to face you? Just a cheap trick?"

Ricky turned all the way around at that, putting her back to the television camera. "Why do you say that?"

"Well, you know, Ricky. Because you're the only woman in the big leagues."

Now Ricky recognized his face from the grainy photo at the head of his newspaper column. He had been the first to predict her own trip back to the minors. She squinted at him. "I'm not the only one," she said flatly. "Not now."

"Hey," he said, with a scornful laugh. "No way Everett's gonna stick after this loss. It was all about the novelty."

Ricky stared at him for a long moment, her jaw tight. He stared back, unabashed. Slowly, she swiveled back to look directly into the television cameras. "The girl can play. Hit, field, run. Management's nuts if they don't keep her. They deserve to lose."

She spun on her heel then, ducking her head as she moved down the dugout steps, on to her locker room. At the door she paused when she spotted the Skipper. "Hey, Skip. Anybody get Everett's ball for her? The homer?"

"Nah, it's gone," he said. "It'll show up on eBay tomorrow. We got the other one, though, the grounder."

"Get it for me, will you?"

* * *

Grace leaned against the outer wall of the locker room, arms folded, waiting for the men to finish so she could use the showers. Family members and friends of the players lounged about the door, talking with each other, obviously trying not to stare at her. The other ballplayers emerged, one by one, and the little crowd began to diminish. Grace slumped against the wall and closed her eyes.

"'Scuse me.'"

Grace opened her eyes, and shot upright.

It was Ricky Arendsen, still in her uniform, standing in front of her with a baseball in her left hand. She stuck out her right, and Grace could see those incredible fingers up close, the sculpted wrist, the powerful forearm. She said, "Ricky Arendsen."

"Oh!" Grace said, inadequately. "Oh. Wow. Ricky. Hey, it's great to meet you, really great." She put out her own hand, and shook Arendsen's.

"This is yours," Arendsen said, holding out the ball. "The homer's gone, but this was your infield hit. I signed it. Hope that was okay."

Grace took the ball and turned it in her hand. In blue ink, Arendsen had scrawled, "First hit in the bigs," and signed her name and the date. Grace felt her cheeks burn. "This is—this is so nice of you."

"Nah." Arendsen shrugged. "No problem."

A camera flashed, and they both looked up. Someone had snapped a picture of the two of them together.

"'Spose that'll be on eBay tomorrow, too," Arendsen said. "Do you think so?" Arendsen grinned. "Oh, yeah. First time we faced each other."

Grace made herself smile. "Probably the last, Ricky." Arendsen shook her head. "Nah. You'll be back, Gracie." She raised an impressive forefinger. "And I'm gonna get you on the splitter next time."

Grace's heart lifted. She said, laughing, "We'll just see about that."

Ricky Arendsen clapped her on the shoulder, and then turned and left, stopping once or twice to sign autographs. Grace went in for her shower, nodding to the security guys beside the door. Arendsen was right. She'd be back. She'd gotten her hits, made a good throw. If this team wouldn't have her, she'd get her agent to put her someplace else. She'd face Arendsen again, one way or another.

But she was going to watch out for that splitter.

Valerie Sayers is the author of six novels and her stories, essays, and reviews have appeared widely in publications like the *New York Times, Washington Post, Zoetrope, Ploughshares,* and *Prairie Schooner.* Her stories have been cited in *Best American Short Stories* and *Best American Essays* and she has won the Pushcart Prize for Fiction and received a National Endowment for the Arts literature fellowship. She is a professor of English and department chair at the University of Notre Dame. Here, she tells us of a woman who really knows the game and how to read the man at the plate. She can see what will happen next, almost every time.

How to Read a Man

Valerie Sayers

I REMEMBERED JUST HOW well I could read certain men in October, during the pennant races. I was following both leagues, the Yankees and the Mets, crazy in love with every man on the two rosters. I had a big crush on Bobby Valentine and a bigger one on Joe Torre. My father would have been appalled at me, rooting for two teams, *watching baseball like a girl.* Well, I'd sort it out come Series time: then the Yankees would be the only guys for me. Meanwhile, I had affection to spare.

I watched the first American League game on TV, a New York fan all alone in my rented house in Pinckney, South Carolina. I hadn't watched this much baseball in years: my ex-lover Diego, unlike every other Latin man I knew, hated the game and I'd forgotten how good I was at predicting what a batter would do. I noticed it first with Bernie Williams. I loved Bernie best of all the Yankees, the way he pleated his long body down like a squeezebox at the plate and cast that impassive eye on the pitcher. I'd never for a minute believed he was so sure of himself. He was scared out there, which was why he was good. He was the kind of guy who went all the way, deep down into a slump or out into the stratosphere of home-run heroics, and I'd always known which way it was going with him.

It wasn't just his face and it wasn't just his body: I put them together and I got myself a reading that was pretty accurate.

Exactly how accurate I hadn't realized till now. Diego was snuggling with his new honey somewhere in downtown Manhattan, so I didn't have to worry about his drifting off on the couch, sighing obnoxiously as the hours passed. At the end of nine innings, the score was tied and I was batting 1,000: I'd called every one of Bernie's at-bats. It wasn't some intuitive thing, either. I watched him from the time he came into the on-deck circle, ran a Geiger counter up and down his body, registered everything from the way he breathed through his nose to the precise angle of his shoulders. Ballplayers all have their stares down, but eyelash flutter is pretty well out of their control. Eyelashes were a big factor with Bernie.

I curled up on my rented couch, happy when the game went to extra innings. In the bottom of the tenth, Bernie looked centered: not driven or determined, just focused. He was sealed off from the game, on his own. His eyelashes were perfectly still. "Homer," I said, and off the ball went, on a trajectory that maybe now was my trajectory, too.

* * *

For the second game I called in Norm Fein, total Yankee fan, to witness what I could do. I was sleeping with Norm, every once in a while. So far it wasn't going very well. In August, when I got down to Pinckney and my new job at the university, there was a cocktail party in my honor and Norm Fein, who'd only been divorced a month, was my designated escort. I took one look at him—he was maybe forty, with straight graying blond hair down past his chin and a really creepy habit of throwing it back behind one ear, self-consciously—and I knew instantly that I couldn't stand him, and that one way or another I'd end up in bed with him. The first thing he said was, "What I like best about your film is how you bypass the pornography of the real and go straight to something so distanced and formal that we totally get it, that you're commenting on his integrity with the integrity of that unblinking camera."

Pornography of the real. He got it all out in one breath without even blushing. That was the sort of academic talk that drove me right up the bedroom wall, only then I climbed back down and found myself in bed with the guy. By then, though, he wasn't so creepy. He liked baseball. He had a sense of humor. He didn't do that hair-flinging thing so much once he got to know you.

And right now, I had to admit, I needed Norm Fein in my living room watching the playoffs with me. "Look," I said, "I'll make the prediction, you write it down.

Keep me honest. I know I can do Bernie, but tonight I want to go for Tino, too. And Paul O'Neill."

"What about Jeter?"

I always knew whether Derek Jeter was going to hit the ball. He might as well be holding a placard announcing his intentions. "Sure. But I need more time to get some of them. Knoblauch, for instance."

Norm sat on the old-lady couch that came with the house, making a scorecard with a straightedge and a lineup from *The New York Times*. I grew up fifty miles down the road and I found the house completely familiar—froofy chintz chairs with doilies on the arms, a rubber plant in the corner—but Norm looked itchy every time he walked onto the front porch. He was generally itchy in South Carolina: he was half Italian, half Jewish, and more than once he'd pointed out that Southerners like their Italians in pizza and their Jews in dry goods. Film studies, he said, they could do without entirely. On the phone he was all over me—sometimes he called three times a day—but in person he held back. Just now he sat a million miles away, on the edge of the couch, twitching, ready to flee.

Norm was itchy and I was lonely. I'd moved to New York when I was eighteen, a skinny girl in paint-splattered overalls fleeing a town full of beauty queens. Even then I had a serious love-hate relationship with the small-town South, so I must have been out of my middle-aged mind to come back this close to home, to take this gig all these years later no matter how much they were paying me. I was the distinguished visiting artist in the Theater and Film Department and I felt like a fraud. I'd only made three documentaries in my entire life, and the last one had accidentally, through no fault of my own, been paid a lot of attention at the Modern and then won Sundance. The high point of my artistic career. For years I'd thought of myself as a painter, and then I messed around some with video. Finally I managed to make a documentary about Diego, who would never forgive me for getting more out of the deal than he did. My career was back on track: I got a Guggenheim on my twenty-third try—I'm not kidding—and Diego consoled himself with an N.Y.U. student who was twenty years younger than his own daughter. I'm not kidding about that, either. After I kicked him out I landed this one-semester deal in Pinckney, where some investment banker had endowed an entire brand-new university that was hiring a sexy top-dollar faculty to match their postmod architecture. The younger painters with their Yale M.F.A.s went around talking about their *agendas* and the critical types wanted art to fit into their own narrow theories, like a coffin into its grave. You could avoid those people in New York, but here you couldn't hide.

At least Norm was a familiar guy. "Christ," he said. "Gotta call my bookie before this baby starts." He jumped up to call New York from the kitchen phone, and I trailed after to get us both a beer. One bottle would last him the whole game, which was another thing I admired about him. Diego used to put away a half-gallon not watching the game. I was with Diego for ten years, almost. He was a good guy, if baseball or women weren't involved. We'd moved past the time when we could have had a child and I'd been thinking that probably we'd get old together. We already were getting kind of old. Diego was sixty when he took up with the girl.

I was a month past fifty myself, but I still knew where to get a good haircut and I wasn't ashamed of my body, though maybe a forty-year-old guy was as far as I'd push it. The body wasn't good enough for Diego in the end. I was so unnerved by his betrayal that in one week I dyed my hair red and painted my toenails silver and got three more holes punched in my right ear. Thank God I remembered myself before I had my tongue pierced or a post drilled into my skull.

"Two thousand Yanks," I heard Norm say into the receiver.

"Two *thousand*?"

He hung up the phone. "Safer than I.B.M."

"I know they'll win. It's just a lot of money."

He picked up the phone again. "How much you in for?"

I shook my head no. I was used to living on nothing in New York, next to nothing if I actually sold a piece. One of the reasons I'd taken this job was to start a retirement fund like the rest of the world. Hanging out with Norm was a big enough risk for me.

We slurped our beer through the pregame and the first three innings. I predicted Williams, Jeter, O'Neill, and Martinez, so Norm could write it all down. I hadn't missed one of them, but he wasn't impressed.

"Look, the odds are with you. Three times out of four they're not going to hit the ball. And there's a whole country full of fans thinking they can tell what a guy's gonna do. Where'd you get the idea you were the one?"

I shrugged. I hadn't spent enough time with him to trust him with the story of my life. I grew up a Yankee fan in Due East, South Carolina, where Yankees of any stripe got run out of town. I was a shy little girl but I was sure about a couple of things. I knew I could draw what a person looked like, and I knew I was crazy for the Yankees no matter how that affected my already dubious social standing. I sat with my father and my brother to watch every game on network TV, and when my brother pretended he was Tony Kubek, dancing in pinstripes at shortstop, I didn't know whether it was my brother or Kubek I loved more. I read the standings and the stats, did imitations of Dizzy Dean and Peewee Reese calling the game. My dad drove us all the way from Due East to the Bronx, an eighteen-hour drive to watch three hours of baseball, and the usher found our seats the very instant Elston Howard, my favorite Yankee forever, hit a grand-slam home run. My father squeezed me so tight I couldn't breathe. I clung to his seersucker suit in Yankee Stadium and had a vision of my poor mother, home in South Carolina, baking pecan pies for the Garden Club.

Forty years later, I still hadn't joined the Garden Club and I still adored the Yanks. I was on another streak when Tino Martinez came up in the bottom of the fourth. By then Norm was watching me watching the game and, nearsighted as I was, I was leaning into the TV to get my reading. The woman I rented from had a little black-and-white that Norm liked to lament, but it had just the right contrast for what I wanted to see.

With Tino, I was beginning to think it was centered in the jaw. He looked cold at bat, but I'd seen him in interviews, a big softy with an easy grin. Right now his jaw floated, serene. "Extra base hit," I said, "maybe a triple. Wait. Home run."

Norm shook his head at my cockiness and Tino listed, fouling one off. "He's not hitting anything tonight. He'll be your undoing." Then we both watched Martinez whack the next high fastball into the upper deck.

Norm whistled low. "Maisie, you know what we could do with this peculiar gift of yours?"

"I have a suspicion you're talking about betting."

"No bookie's gonna touch it, but I could round up my boys. Twenty bucks a shot, can the man hit the ball. You could signal me somehow."

"Sorry, babe. I'm driving back on Sunday."

"New York for fall break? You got playoff tickets?"

"No tickets. I just need civilization."

"You don't want to drive all that way. You'll come back exhausted. Stick around, I'll treat you right."

"I thought you said everybody took off."

"They do." He sounded miserable. "Unless they have child support to cough up. Then they stick around Pinckney for the duration."

I'd forgotten he had children: I'd never seen them, though they lived in town. Was he hinting for a ride to New York? He sat morose, his lower lip jutting.

"All right," he said, "if you're not gonna be here at least tell me what you look for."

"I look for when they go Zen. When a guy goes deep into his own body."

"Holy shit, the distinguished visiting artist is talking about *the zone*."

"Oh hush up. Listen, this throwing problem of Knoblauch's, where you reckon that's coming from?" Chuck Knoblauch's arm had been spastic for weeks now and I almost couldn't bear to see him on-screen. He looked utterly confused in the infield, as panicked as Diego looked around the time my film took off.

"Knoblauch, Christ," said Norm. "I'm sitting on a gold mine."

"You're not sitting on anything, honey, but a rented couch."

In the bottom of the seventh, Knoblauch came to the plate with his face contorted: not a smirk, but close. He always grimaced through his at-bats, but this time he stretched his mouth out a hundred new ways and screwed his left eye tight into its socket. I could read him. I could see what the weeks of being off with his throwing arm had cost him, but I could see how fierce he was feeling, too. His features settled all at once, and so did his shoulders. "Extra base hit," I said. It was almost anticlimactic when he got the double, and now I was the one who felt a shiver of panic. I could read a stranger on a television screen, but I hadn't been able to read Diego, not after ten years of our failing side by side, ten years taking turns with adjunct teaching jobs and gallery rounds and all the humiliations of calling yourself an artist.

I stretched my feet out till my silver toenails caught the light. Knoblauch stood naked in front of millions of people who knew the worst about him and still he found the swing. It was the big act that made me crazy for ballplayers. What was wrong with me, that I hadn't been able to see that Diego was putting on a big act, too?

"Think about the Series, would you?" Norm was practically begging, but he hadn't moved any closer on the couch.

"I'm a not-for-profit."

"You're a goddess," Norm Fein said, and made me grin, but I couldn't meet his eye. There we sat, in the big old-fashioned living room of a white frame house in Pinckney, South Carolina, way too close to where my father taught me how to figure a batting average. A real Southern house, a small-town house, the traitor Yankees on the TV, a framed print of Fort Sumter over the mantel. I almost felt like I'd come home, but my father died years ago, my mother just before I kicked Diego out. There wasn't any family here.

Out of the corner of my eye, I watched Norm move to the farthest edge of the couch, his hair hanging down, his elbows on his jeans. We looked more like a couple of teenagers than we looked like professors. I had to stop being so hard-shelled. I had to crack a little, and not just for the guys on the screen. I probably should have asked Norm if he wanted to hitch a ride to New York.

* * *

I didn't ask him. On Saturday night we watched the Mets, down in the National League three games to zero. By then I was falling hard for them, and I could read most of the hitters. The Mets had a lot of veterans in the line-up, old guys who weren't going to roll over and play dead just because no team had ever come back to win after losing the first three. In my living room in Pinckney, batter after struggling batter morphed into Diego, staring down a muddy canvas, but somehow they stayed alive and won the game. Norm and I shrieked and toasted them and snuggled all night.

But on Sunday morning, I left for New York alone, and I was glad for the solitude. I planned to do the trip in one long sprint, the way my dad drove us to Yankee Stadium, and to let the Mets game carry me up the coast. They needed to nail three more in a row. If they lost this one, it was all over.

The game tied and stretched out to ten innings, company through North Carolina and Virginia. Eleven innings, twelve. I was alone and I was happy. On the Jersey Turnpike I began to think they might really win, and my old station wagon started slipping out of its lane. I was listening to the Mets but I was seeing Diego lying on my purple couch every time I watched a game, bored, mimicking the announcer.

The ballgame was still stalled at 2–2. Every ground ball, every strikeout was an omen. The Mets could pull this off. They were holding steady. Thirteen innings, fourteen. They could hang on and I could hang on. In the top of the fifteenth, the Braves pulled ahead by one and I almost sideswiped a truck. It couldn't end this way. They'd fought for fifteen innings. They couldn't lose now.

Only three outs left. The radio spat static. Shawon Dunston, one of the Mets I could read best, stepped into the batter's box. I pictured him, tall, broad-shouldered, *I'm an old man at this game and I don't give a shit what you think I'm about to do.* He dug in, worked the count to 3–2, and I saw two old men digging in, Diego the ghost-batter behind Dunston. If Shawon Dunston could make his move in the bottom of the fifteenth inning . . . Dunston hit his fifth foul ball. *He's been in there seven minutes now*, the announcer said, and the static cleared. *Eight minutes. That's gotta be getting close to the record.* Dunston fouled for the sixth time and I knew what I had to do: I coaxed him, the way I used to coax Diego through his depressions. "Stay with it, darlin'," I heard myself say. "You got it. Just a little deeper." I laughed out loud, alone in my big car, surrounded by big truckers, talking to a big ballplayer. Nine minutes in, Dunston hit the ball. I didn't breathe till the radio screamed *single*. I didn't need to see him on the screen: *We walk by faith and not by sight.*

I knew Dunston would steal, knew when he did that the Mets had it in their pockets. I was blissed out, listening to the rest of the game, and by the time I closed in on the Holland Tunnel and tuned in to the Yankees' third game, they'd widened their lead to 9–2. It was really beginning to look like a subway series now. I'd score a ticket for opening night—hey, I was a distinguished visiting professor, and for the first time in my life I could afford to look a scalper in the eye. The city would be on fire. I'd be back in Pinckney for the first day of classes after fall break. I'd get past this Diego thing.

* * *

It was close to midnight when I finally found a parking spot. Circling the block, I'd seen a light on in my loft. I had twelve hundred square feet right on Chambers, over a discount store, the third floor of a co-op I organized myself back in the days when nobody knew what a co-op was and nobody lived on Chambers Street.

The light on up there either meant that Diego had been there or that Diego was there right now. Either way, I was royally pissed. Not even two wins on the New Jersey Turnpike would be enough to calm me down if I walked in on him. But he wouldn't dare. Probably he just came by to get more of his stuff and left a lamp burning the way he left socks on the bathroom floor. I hoisted my suitcase out of the back of the car and wheeled it down the sidewalk, all the tension of fifteen innings, fifteen hours on the road, fifteen cups of coffee tight as a bungee cord in my shoulders and my neck. I made myself breathe to a count. I'd get upstairs, I'd call Norm Fein. He could take a joke in the middle of the night, when the Mets had kept it alive.

On the second-floor landing I heard, dimly, a television. I'd taken my keys back, so if Diego was in my loft it meant he'd copied them before he handed them over.

The television was playing when I opened the door. I sensed him over in the far corner, slumped down in my fattest, softest chair. I had to cross the entire space of the loft to look him in the eye. He'd come up with some charming excuse: he'd left his long filbert brush, he couldn't go on without it.

He sat in front of some postgame show, the tears rolling down his face. This was real familiar. Diego was depressed but he'd slit his wrists before he'd darken a shrink's door. He had no use for Prozac, either. Wine was his medicine: just now an empty liter of Concha y Toro sat on the floor beside him. He hadn't bothered with a glass. He was unshaven, and his hair looked like the Spanish moss I'd just left in South Carolina, curling at the back of his neck in damp gray tendrils.

I walked at a deliberate pace, like a manager heading out to the mound. He wouldn't look up. He was well practiced at the long holdout, but I'd just survived fifteen innings of baseball. I could wait. Finally he raised his hooded black eyes, mournful eyes, eyes I have to admit were better even than Bernie Williams's eyes. The whites were tinged with brown, and he had the lashes of a six-year-old boy, though at the moment they were crusted with yellow crud.

"What are you doing here," I said in a monotone, and knew he'd already got me behind in the count. "What are you doing watching baseball."

"I call the university, they say you're on fall break. I know you come here." He spoke English with the softest slur, his grammar flawless except for his reliance on the present tense. He was a present-tense kind of guy. "I know you want to see the game."

"Did you copy my key?"

He shook his head in sad denial. "Lily. She lets me in."

He was lying. Lily, my downstairs neighbor and oldest friend in New York, despised him. I scanned the room: big slick magazines, socks, wine bottles. He could have accomplished that much in a night or two: he was a slob but he was a clean slob, a compulsive duster and floor mopper. Every surface was shiny, though I'd been gone for two months.

"Get out." But he held me with the mournful eyes, stared me down. He was loose and relaxed in my comfy chair. His jaw floated.

"Maisie, we have ten years."

"Out."

"I go a little crazy, I see that. To throw away what we have? The tango lessons?"

"The tango lessons! You were carrying on like that for ten years." Hard to believe I'd let him get away with it for as long as I had. Middle age had made me a lot more forgiving. He was one of those guys who slept around, he just did: not a lot, but every once in a while, just to remind himself he was alive, I guess. He was short and stubby, but he was charming, and he had those hooded eyes: women came on to him right in front of me. I had no patience for a cheating man when I was younger, but Diego was transparent and guilty and I was a sucker for him. I knew he'd been fooling around when he came home and stroked my feet, cooked cazuela, stretched my canvases. He'd never confessed, he wasn't that kind of mean. We'd never had it out. This last time, though, was outrageous: he'd brought the woman, the girl, home. To my co-op.

And he must have wanted me to walk in on them, too. He was livid about the Modern. The two of them, Diego and this *child*, on the plank floor I'd stripped and varnished myself, inch by inch. The girl was skinny and muscular, with cropped brown hair streaked blue, and when she jumped up, I got the willies. She looked like me thirty years ago, before Diego even knew me. She had full cheeks and a wide mouth drained of color. Her nipples were like putty, like mine. The only difference was that this girl looked completely sure of herself and I'd been a mess, around men anyway. I had Diego packing by sundown.

And I hadn't seen him since, except for all the trips he made to pick up his stuff. He dawdled with moving out forever. He gave me a phone number, probably the girl's. I made myself throw it away. Now he had the nerve to do the sensitive crying thing? I pictured Scott Brosius, his father dying, steady at third base. Did the man ever once get weepy on camera? "Have some dignity, for God's sake."

Diego hung his head and looked like he was ninety. He had holes in the back of his T-shirt. A sixty-year-old man, older than my own father lived to be, in a pocked shirt. "Maisie," he said, "I have no dignity."

"Go home."

"I have no home but you."

I have no home but you. See what you can do with the present tense? I had to work to stoke my fury. "You were living here, weren't you?"

"Maisie." By now he whimpered: that was the only word for it.

I reached down for the empty wine bottle at my feet. "I don't care if you have to sleep in the park. You're out of here, buddy."

But he grabbed the bottle back and I realized it wasn't empty. The last drink still sloshed in the bottom. If he got drunker he'd pass out and I'd have to deal with him in the morning. I might weaken and let him stay. I hung on to the bottle and he tugged, a drunk's tug. Like two children, we fought for the bottle till it went flying from our hands and torpedoed into the TV. The screen and the bottle splintered together. The television died slowly, a beam of light disappearing into a black hole.

"How'm I supposed to watch the pennant races?" I heard myself wail. "For God's sake! We're on the verge of a subway series. I need to be able to see those guys. I have to read them on the screen."

"Maisie, you make no sense. I think you exhaust yourself in Carolina. You say it yourself, you never can go home again. Why do you go down there?"

"I go down there to see if I can pull my body and soul together, you cheating bastard. Get out!" I screamed like a banshee. "Out out out forever." I heard Lily stir downstairs, heard her door slam and her soft neighbor feet come padding bare on the stairwell to rescue me. From the man I was supposed to be living with for the rest of my life.

* * *

The Yankees were one game away from the World Series, but now I couldn't watch them, so I listened to them win the pennant on the radio, with Lily beside me. The two of us paced the space of my loft. Lily was a performance artist who didn't own a television, even though she was the one who convinced me to pick up a video camera in the first place, to document one of her street shows. She didn't like baseball either, but she was willing to endure it if I needed her.

After the way I coaxed Dunston on the New Jersey Turnpike, I thought maybe I really could predict what my guys would do by faith alone, but this time I was no good. I called a strikeout for Derek Jeter and he hit a two-run homer. "I can do it when I see them," I told Lily, but she wasn't listening. She was busy touching Diego's paintings on the walls, as if she'd be able to feel what was wrong with him that way.

He'd left three canvases, which meant he'd still be coming back. I'd never be rid of him, and every time I saw him I'd want to forgive him, or at least let him stay. "Penis paintings," Lily snorted. "The shining cock around which the universe revolves." They were really vegetables on cruciforms, but Lily was right, what else could he mean by eggplants and summer squash? The colors were gorgeous, sublime: I'd always been jealous of his colors. The eggplant was an acid green on a lavender cross.

And if Diego wanted to paint penis vegetables after all these years of painting women, why not? I'd watched him paint a female body for nine of the ten years we were together. He never had enough money for a model, but he didn't need a model anymore. He painted a woman just at the edge of aging, her breasts heaving down, her skin slack at the neck. He was painting me, but he was painting himself, too, his own slow decay.

He hadn't left any of the women, and I missed them, all that color and motion. Across the top of every painting he put a banner in Spanglish: *La zapata needs a new heel* or *The family está cansada*. Dealers kept telling him his work was stuck somewhere, only they couldn't figure out where. *A* he said, *I stick in a good place*. When he'd painted well, he turned on the stereo and gave me tango lessons. We were the same height, and his loose round belly punched up against mine. *Let go*, he used to whisper, *float*, and when I did let go I knew his every move before he made it. Perfect balance, what every artist goes for: form and content, body and soul, hip and heart.

I knew his body like I knew my own. For ten years I'd watched him stand in front of a canvas for an hour, jiggling the wax in his ear before he got to work. And then one day, I felt my arm moving with his, the same crazy thrill I got with the tango lessons. I knew precisely what he was going to do next. His strokes were my strokes. I picked up the camcorder. When he finally stabbed at the canvas, I followed his hand with my lens as if we *were* attached. We were attached. Every one of those Spanglish lines broke my heart.

Watching him on the Avid, I saw I had an interesting little formal piece that no one would give two shits about. I went back to work, set him up in the corner of the loft with one of his old friends, another Argentine guy who was going to slap paint on cloth till he died. They were both a little drunk, their accents thickening, and they did funny imitations of the dealers who'd stopped representing them. They did even funnier imitations of the clerks in an emergency room when they heard you didn't have insurance.

So I'd made another political piece, what I was getting known for, when what I'd started out with was sex. Once I wrote the grant proposal, once I spliced the two guys' talk, once I'd transferred video to film, once I'd spent that money and put that distance between Diego and me I showed it to a few people who showed it to a few people and there it was in the "Art and Capital" show: *Portrait of the Painter in a Frenzy*. I pointed out how well Diego's paintings would look surrounding a monitor, but painting was not, the curator told me, on the agenda.

Diego thought I should refuse the show. *Anyway you make us look like clowns in that movie*. No, I said, *No, let's don't give up now. They'll see your work, they'll find you*. But they didn't find him, not the galleries he wanted. He stopped painting his aging women and started painting vegetables, firm and fresh.

"Really," I said to Lily, when I caught her eye. "I can do it when I see their bodies. I can tell what they're going to do."

"Oh yeah?" Lily's performing name was Lily Pons, but her real name was Mary Ellen Dougherty. We met freshman year at Marymount Manhattan, both sent by our fathers to what they reckoned was the only safe school in New York City. We were the only two in the whole college who didn't own a headband or a pleated skirt. We'd outlasted each other's lovers, but Lily didn't have a clue what baseball was for. She tried to be a good sport, but she distrusted men, just about all of them, and Diego especially.

I, on the other hand, loved him still.

* * *

At least I still had a subway series to look forward to. By now the Yankees were the official American League champs and the Mets only had two more games to go. After the way they hung in for fifteen innings, there wasn't a doubt in my mind that they were going to the Series.

The Mets were down in Atlanta by then, trying to finish things off, and my TV was still busted. I talked Lily into coming with me to a dive on Chambers where a television sat high in the corner. I called every Met at-bat, but Lily was hardly listening. At the end of three innings, she plunked a five-dollar bill on the bar and asked if I'd mind . . .

I was alone with the three other customers, pale old men who looked like they lived in dark bars, and the bartender, who ran his fingers over his sparse black hair, Grecian formulaed and combed back like Joe Torre's.

Well, this was just great. When I ran away down South the university was shiny and new and unrecognizable and the loneliness was unbearable. When I came back to New York the bar was worn and old and familiar and the loneliness was unbearable. For years people had assumed that Lily and I were lovers, even when Diego was around. Nobody understood the impossibility: my dearest friend, and indifferent to baseball. At least Diego hated it.

I ordered a Jameson up—my dad's drink—and poured it down the hatch. I felt the wizened old man three stools away staring at me, and when I looked down from the game, another shot perched in front of me.

"Compliments of Frankie," the bartender mumbled. I raised my glass to the old man, his cap atop his head, and he sat up considerably higher. "Slainte," I said.

"Slainte." He saluted me. "Mets."

"Mets." The two shots on top of the beer toasted my cheeks and the tip of my nose. I wasn't a drinker—I'd nursed too many guys through their own troubles with the stuff—but I saw the attraction tonight. We all watched the game in silence as the Mets struggled on, Atlanta leading by five. I was strangely unconcerned. After what Dunston had done in the bottom of the fifteenth, I knew they could turn it around.

It was a relief to be in the company of men who never took their eyes from the screen. Finally, in the sixth, New York busted out with three runs and I bought a round for the house. We downed the shots in unison. Here was the closest I'd been to home in months, with strangers happy to watch the game. With four old men.

The Braves scored two more in the bottom of the inning, but I still knew what the Mets could do with sheer force of will. All evidence to the contrary notwithstanding, they'd fight their way back. I went to phone Norm Fein from the telephone on the wall and felt the old men watching me with the eyes in the backs of their heads.

I kept my own eyes on the TV, now playing ads, and thought I'd hear the same when Norm answered in South Carolina. But there was only chaos on his end of the wire: shrieks, giggles, little kids. A baby crying. A baby: *that* couldn't be his. He'd divorced his wife this very year.

"Sounds like you've got a crowd over. I won't keep you."

"Nah, just my kids. Only sounds like the Russian army."

"Normie—" A woman leaned close to the receiver. I could hear her smooch right over the wire. Normie. Normie, and a baby.

"Hang on, Maisie." He muffled the receiver. Frankie motioned for me to come back and watch the game. The ads had disappeared and Matt Franco was in to pinch hit. This could be it. Franco took the plate like Genghis Khan.

"Extra bases," I said to the bar.

"Jesus, Mary, and Joseph," Frankie said, "may this woman be right." He waved me over to come sit again.

"I'm back," Norm said. "That was just my ex leaving."

Just leaving, my ass. And wet-kissing him on the way out the door. Three kids, a baby: I saw the story whole. Norm had freaked, the usual midlife *get me out of here*. A lifetime job in a small town and a baby, too. His wife had let him divorce her but still called him Normie, still managed to distract him when the phone rang. I was rooting for her—*You go, don't let him stick you all alone with that baby*—but that made me the other woman on the end of the long-distance call.

"Extra base hit for Franco," I said, so at least Norm would remember what I could do.

"Yeah." I heard in his confusion that he hadn't even been watching the game. Hard to know what was more unforgivable, walking out on his wife after Baby Number Three or not watching the game. The Mets were on the verge of a subway series, playing their hearts out.

You'd think I could be sympathetic about the baby thing. I was the one who backed off when Diego, drunk, wept over the pleasures of parenthood. By then I was already past forty and my work habits were so strange: I painted by spotlights in the middle of the night, putzed around basement performing spaces. Would that be fair to some needy little baby? I had visions of myself crawling into P.T.A. meetings on arthritic legs. I told Diego I just couldn't have a child at this stage of the game.

"Gotta go," I said.

"Just do one more. I wanna tell the kids—"

"No. No, I can't."

I hung up the phone, and by the time I turned back to the screen Franco was crossing the plate. "Look what you missed," Frankie said, aggrieved.

Olerud was up. Oh, Olerud. I read somewhere that he rode the subway to the ballpark. The drink and the Mets had me soaked with love. Olerud looked like a college professor, like a brain surgeon, like the steady man my father'd been and had always had in mind for me. "Single," I said.

"Holy Mother of Christ," Frankie said, when the ball lined over to right field. "How do you do that each and every time?"

"Women," the bartender said. "Scary."

Now Mike Piazza hobbled up to the plate, an old man with all his injuries. Across the drunken space from bar to TV, I saw that he was hurting but maybe enjoying the martyr's role, too. I might have been watching Diego. I *was* watching Diego, and he was beckoning me to come tango with him. "Look at those arms," I said, when Piazza settled his bat. "Home run."

"You wish," Frankie said, but there it went, to right center, soaring.

Frankie grabbed my wrist and squeezed hard. "That's unbelievable." The Mets had tied the game at seven-all in the seventh. Piazza trotted across home plate, the weary glorious old warrior. You could hear the bellows and the cheers from bars all across lower Manhattan. You could hear them in Brooklyn. The old men twisted on their stools like schoolboys, punched out at one another, high-fived the bartender, beamed on me as if I were the one who'd hit the ball.

"Have you heard what she can do?" Frankie shouted. "We could make a fortune at this." Another shot appeared in front of me. Past drunk already, I swallowed the whiskey down and knew I wasn't just leaking love, going mushy over the wrong team, remembering the way my father and my brother watched the game. My eyes were on the screen but it was Diego I saw, his jowls sinking into his neck, his nose mapped with blood vessels, his arms flaccid, craving a baby. His fat eggplant, his bent summer squash. Now in his old age, when I thought I couldn't do it, he had to have another child, had to reproduce, that strange old biological urge in the face of his drooping body. Tears rolled down my jaw, but nobody noticed. They were all weeping, the four men in the bar right along with me, when the Braves tied it back.

* * *

Outside the loft building, his shoulder pressed against the gates of the discount store, Diego stood smoking, one hand holding up his eggplant painting. He hadn't even pulled it off the stretcher, which meant it was on its way to some other wall.

Unless I was hallucinating. I'd never been drunk enough to have visions, but right now it was hard to put one foot in front of the other. The way he watched me from a distance, impassive, made him look like somebody else, not the Diego who wept and begged the other night.

The sight of him sobered me up. I began to walk faster and then to skip a little. Suddenly I couldn't wait to reach him. I'd punished him long enough and I'd punished myself, too. I'd be sad again, every once in a while, because he'd cheat again, but I wouldn't be so sad as I'd been these last few months, hating him.

"Diego," I called, in case he couldn't recognize me, but he only drew his cigarette up for another pull. He looked like somebody in one of Lily's performance pieces. Was he trying to get me to really pity him? Well, I did pity him, but no more than I pitied myself. The Mets were weeping somewhere tonight and we might as well keep them company.

"Diego." I finally stopped, panting, in front of him. "The Mets lost."

"Good. You hate the Mets."

"I got to like them. It went eleven innings. Now there's no subway series."

"Just another way for those asshole investment bankers to spend their dough." He tossed his cigarette toward the gutter, but it landed a foot shy and smoldered.

I fingered a staple along the stretcher's edge and felt every thread of the canvas below. "Look," I said. "Will you bring this back upstairs now? Could we talk about stuff?" The future rolled out, hard but workable. Maybe he'd want to come see South Carolina.

But Diego said: "You make me look like a clown in that piece." I tried to read his face but saw only how calm it was.

"You never looked like a clown."

Diego stared up Chambers. I had no idea what expression that was in his face. Regret? Relief? Fury? He and his canvas were one body, waiting, leaning into something I couldn't imagine. "This one doesn't fit in the van before."

"What van?"

As if I really were hallucinating, not just Diego but the whole night, a beat-up white van chugged toward us and double-parked in front of my door. The girl at the wheel averted her eyes. This time she didn't look so much like me. Her left ear was laced with little safety pins, a dozen of them at least. She appeared to be about twelve. It was a wonder she could drive that truck around without getting pulled over for underage driving every fifteen feet.

"See you sometime," Diego said, and hoisted his painting. "Maybe at the MoMA, huh?" He didn't say it unkindly. He looked back and winked. He was sober and he knew where he was spending the night.

I turned my back to the van and fumbled with my keys. It would take me half an hour just to figure out which one went in the door. I didn't want the girl to see me weeping. Diego wouldn't mind, but the girl would hold that frame of me forever, would think she knew something about me just because of the way I stumbled and cried after the Mets lost the pennant.

I sniffled over my shoulder. Diego had finished loading the painting. He stood behind the van, one hand on the closed doors, waiting for me to look. I looked. He was wearing his black *Art & Anarchy* T-shirt. He was full of beans and he wanted me to know it.

I stuffed my keys in my pocket and extended my arm for a solo tango. That would be my goodbye to Diego: I would let him drive off remembering the dance lessons when I could predict his every move. Off I went, on my own, stretching across Chambers, dancing past the gated stores. Maybe I looked like a clown. For a minute I thought I might remember how to go deep into my own body, but I knew they were both watching me and really, it was only a big act. Sometimes you just have to go through the motions. I bent my knees like Bernie Williams. I settled my face like Chuck Knoblauch. I watched the van lurch past me.

Gardner Dozois is one of the most influential editors in science fiction and fantasy as longtime editor of the annual *The Year's Best Science Fiction*, which began in 1984 and continues today. He also served as editor of *Asimov's Science Fiction* magazine for twenty years. He has frequently won the Hugo Award for Best Professional Editor and has twice won the Nebula Award for Best Short Story. In this story he tells us of one of those frozen moments in baseball's past, like Bobby Thomson's home run, or Don Larsen's final pitch in his perfect World Series game, or Bill Mazeroski's Forbes Field home run. Or Karl Holzman's hanging curve.

The Hanging Curve

∞

Gardner Dozois

IT WAS A COOL October night in Philadelphia, with a wet wind coming off the river that occasionally shifted to bring in the yeasty spoiled-beer smell of the nearby refineries. Independence Stadium, the relatively new South Philly stadium that had been built to replace the old Veteran's Stadium, which still stood deserted a block or so away, was filled to capacity, and then some, with people standing in the aisles. It was the last game of a hard-fought and bitterly contested World Series between the New York Yankees and the Philadelphia Phillies, 3–2 in favor of the Phillies, the Yankees at bat with two out in the top of the ninth inning, and a man on third base. Eduardo Rivera was at bat for the Yankees against pitcher Karl Holzman, the Yankees' best slugger against the Phillies' best stopper, and Holzman had run a full count on Rivera, 3–2. Everything depended on the next pitch.

Holzman went into his slow, deliberate windup. Everybody in the stadium was leaning forward, everybody was holding their breath. Though there were almost ten thousand people in the stands, nobody was making a sound. Even the TV announcers were tense and silent. Hey, there it is! The *pitch*.

Some pundits later said that what was about to happen happened *because* the game was so tight, because so much was riding on the next pitch—that it was the psychic energy of the thousands of fans in the stands, the millions more in the viewing audience at home, every eye and every mind focused on that particular moment. That what happened was *caused by* the tension and the ever-tightening suspense felt by millions of people hanging on the outcome of that particular pitch . . .

And yet, in the more than a century and a half that people had been playing professional baseball, there had been many games as important as this one, many contests as closely fought, many situations as tense or tenser, with as much or more passion invested in the outcome—and yet what happened that night had never happened before, in any other game.

Holzman pitched. The ball left his hand, streaked toward the plate . . .

And then it froze.

The ball just *stopped*, inches from the plate, and hung there, motionless, in midair.

After a second of stunned surprise, Rivera stepped forward and took a mighty hack at the motionless ball. He broke his bat on it, sending splinters flying high. But the ball itself didn't move.

The catcher sat back on his butt with a thump, then, after a second, began to scoot backward, away from the plate, He was either praying or cursing in Spanish, perhaps both. Hurriedly, he crossed himself.

The home-plate umpire, Kellenburger, had been struck dumb with astonishment for a moment, but now he raised his hands to call time. He took his mask off and came a few steps closer to lean forward and peer at the ball, where it hung impossibly in midair.

The umpire was the first to actually touch the ball. Gingerly, he poked it with his finger, an act either very brave or very foolish, considering the circumstances. "It felt like a baseball," he later said, letting himself in for a great deal of comic ridicule by late-night talk show hosts, but it really wasn't that dumb a remark, again considering the circumstances. It certainly wasn't *acting* like a baseball.

He tried to scoop the ball out of the air. It wouldn't budge. When he took his hand away, there it still was, the ball, hanging motionless a few feet above home plate.

The fans in the stadium had been shocked into stunned silence for a few heartbeats. But now a buzzing whisper of reaction began to swell, soon growing into a waterfall roar. No one understood what had happened. But *something* had happened to stop the game at the most critical possible moment, and nobody liked it. Fistfights were already beginning to break out in the outfield bleachers.

Rivera had stepped forward to help Kellenburger tug at the ball, trying to muscle it down. They couldn't move it. Holzman, as puzzled as everyone else, walked in to see what in the world was going on, managers flew out of the dugouts, ready to protest *something*, although they weren't quite sure *what*. The rest of the umpires trotted in to take a look. Soon home plate was surrounded by almost everybody who was down on the ballfield, both dugouts emptying, all shouting, arguing, making suggestions, jostling to get a close look at the ball, which hung serenely in midair.

Within minutes, fights were breaking out on the field as well. The stadium cops were already having trouble trying to quell disturbances in the seats, where a full-fledged riot was brewing. They couldn't handle it. The fans began tearing up the seats, trampling each other in panicked or angry surges, pouring out on to the field to join in fistfights with the players. The city cops had to be called in, then more cops, then the riot squad, who set about forcibly closing the stadium, chasing the outraged fans out with tear gas and rubber bullets. Dozens of people were injured, some moderately seriously, but, by some other miracle, none were killed. Dozens of people were arrested, including some of the players and the manager of the Yankees. The stadium was seriously trashed. By the time the umpires got around to officially calling the game, it had become clear a long time before that World Series or no World Series, no game was going to be played in Independence Stadium that night, or, considering the damage that had been done to the bleachers, probably for many nights to come.

Finally, the last ambulance left, and the remaining players and grounds crew and assorted team personnel were herded out, still complaining and arguing. After a hurried conference between the police and the owners, the gates were locked behind them.

The ball still hung there, not moving. In the empty stadium, gleaming white under the lights, it somehow looked even more uncanny than it had with people swarming around it. Two cops were left behind to keep an eye on it, but the sight spooked them, and they stayed as far away from it as they could without leaving the infield, checking it every few minutes as the long night crept slowly past. But the ball didn't seem to be going anywhere.

Most of the riot had been covered live across the nation, of course, television cameras continued to roll as fans and players beat each other bloody, while the sportscasters provided hysterical commentary (and barricaded the doors of the press room). Reporters from local stations had been there within twenty minutes, but nobody knew quite how to handle the event that had sparked the riot in the first place; most ignored it, while others treated it as a Silly Season item. The reporters were back the next morning, though, some of them, anyway, as the owners and the grounds crew, more cops, the Commissioner of Baseball, and some Concerned City Hall Bigwigs went back into the stadium. In spite of the bright, grainy, mundane light of morning, which is supposed to chase all fancies away and dissolve all troubling fantasms, the ball was still frozen there in midair, motionless, exactly the same way it had been the night before. It looked even spookier though, more bewilderingly inexplicable, under the ordinary light of day than it had looked under the garish artificial lighting the night before. This was no trick of the eyes, no confusion of light and shadow. Although it *couldn't be*, the goddamn thing was *there*.

The grounds crew did everything that they could think of to get the ball to move, including tying a rope around it and having a dozen hefty men yank and heave and strain at it, their feet scrambling for purchase, as if they were playing tug-of-war with Mighty Joe Young and losing, but they could no more move the ball than Kellenburger had been able to the night before.

It was becoming clear that it might be a long time before another game could be played in Independence Stadium.

After two days of heated debate in the highest baseball circles, Yankee Stadium was borrowed to restage the potential final out of the series. Thousands of fans in the stadium (who had paid heretofore unheard-of prices for tickets) and millions of television viewers watched breathlessly as Holzman went into his windup and delivered the ball to the plate at a respectable ninety-five miles-per-hour. But nothing happened except that Rivera took a big swing at the ball and missed. No miracle. The ball thumped solidly into the catcher's mitt (who'd had to be threatened with heavy sanctions to get him to play, and who had a crucifix, a St. Christopher's medal, *and* an evil-eye-warding set of horns hung around his neck). Kellenburger, the home-plate umpire, pumped his fist and roared "You're out!" in a decisive, no-nonsense tone. And that was that. The Philadelphia Phillies had won the World Series.

The fans tore up the seats. Parts of New York City burned. The riots were still going on the following afternoon, as were riots in Philadelphia and (for no particular reason anyone could see; perhaps they were sympathy riots) in Cincinnati.

After another emergency session, the Commissioner announced that entire last game would be replayed in the interests of fairness. This time, the Yankees won, 7–5.

After more rioting, the Commissioner evoked special executive powers that no one was quite sure he had, and declared that the Series was a draw. This satisfied nobody, but eventually fans stopped burning down bits of various cities, and the situation quieted.

The bizarre result went into the record books, and baseball tried to put the whole thing behind it. In the larger world outside the insular universe of baseball, things weren't quite that simple.

Dozens of newspapers across the country had independently—and perhaps inevitably—come up with the headline HANGING CURVE BALL!!!, screamed across the front page in the largest type they could muster. A novelty song of the same name was in stores within four days of the Event, and available for download on some internet sites in two. Nobody knows for sure how long it took for the first Miracle Ball joke to appear, but they were certainly circulating widely by as early as the following morning, when the strange non-ending of the World Series was the hot topic of discussion in most of the workplaces and homes in America (and, indeed, around the world), even those homes where baseball had rarely—if ever—been discussed before.

Media hysteria about the Miracle Ball continued to build throughout the circus of replaying the World Series; outside of sports circles, where the talk tended to center around the dolorous effect all this was having on baseball, the focus was on the Miracle itself, and what it might—or might not—signify. Hundreds of conspiracy-oriented internet sites, of various degrees of lunacy, appeared almost overnight. Apocalyptic religious cults sprang up almost as fast as wacko internet sites. The Miracle was widely taken as a Sign that the Last Days were at hand, as nearly anything out of the ordinary had been, from an earthquake to Jesus's face on a taco, for the last thousand years. Within days, some people in California had sold their houses and all their worldly possessions and had begun walking barefoot toward Philadelphia.

After the Gates-of-Armageddon-are-gaping-wide theory, the second most popular theory, and the one with the most internet sites devoted to it was that Aliens had done it—although as nobody ever came up with an even remotely convincing reason *why* aliens would want to do this, that theory tended to run out of gas early, and never was as popular as the Apocalypse Now/Sign from the Lord theory. The respectable press tended to ridicule both of these theories (as well as the Sinister Government Conspiracy theory, a dark horse, but popular in places like Montana and Utah)—still, it was hard for even the most determined skeptic to deny that *something* was going on that no one could even begin to explain, something that defied the laws of physics as we thought we knew them, and more than one scientist, press-ganged into appearing on late-night talk shows or other Talking Head venues, burbled that if we could learn to understand the strange cosmic forces, whatever they were, that were making the Ball act as it was acting, whole new sciences would open up, and Mankind's technological expertise could be advanced a thousand years.

Up until this point, the government had been ignoring the whole thing, obviously not taking it seriously, but now, perhaps jolted into action by watching scientists on *The Tonight Show* enthuse about the wondrous new technologies that might be there for the taking, they made up for lost time (and gave a boost to the Sinister Government Conspiracy theory) by swooping down and seizing Independence Stadium, excluding all civilians from the property.

The city and the owners protested, then threatened to sue, but the feds smacked them with Eminent Domain and stood pat (eventually they would be placated by the offer to build a new stadium elsewhere in the city, at government expense; since you certainly couldn't play a game in Independence Stadium anyway, with *that* thing hanging in the air, the owners were not really all that hard to convince). Hordes of scientists and spooks from various alphabet-soup agencies swarmed over the playing field. A ring of soldiers surrounded the stadium day and night, military helicopters hovered constantly overhead to keep other helicopters with prying television cameras away, and when it occurred to somebody that this wouldn't be enough to frustrate spy satellites or high-flying spy planes, a huge tent enclosure was raised over the entire infield, hiding the Ball from sight.

Months went by, then years. No news about the Miracle Baseball was coming out of Independence Stadium, although by now a tent city had been raised in the surrounding parking lots to house the influx of government-employed scientists, who were kept in strict isolation. Occasionally, a fuss would be made in the media or a motion would be raised in Congress in protest of such stringent secrecy, but the government was keeping the lid down tight, in spite of wildfire rumors that scientists were conferring with UFO Aliens in there, or had opened a dimensional gateway to another universe.

The cultists, who had been refused admittance to Independence Stadium to venerate the Ball, when they'd arrived with blistered and bleeding feet from California several months after the Event, erected a tent city of their own across the street from the government's tent city, and could be seen keeping vigil day and night in all weathers, as if they expected God to pop his head out of the stadium to say hello at any moment, and didn't want to miss it. (They eventually filed suit against the government for interfering with their freedom to worship by refusing them access to the Ball, and the suit dragged through the courts for years, with no conclusive results.)

The lack of information coming out of Independence Stadium did nothing to discourage media speculation, of course. In fact, it was like pouring gasoline on a fire, and for several years it was difficult to turn on a television set at any time of the day or night without finding *somebody* saying *something* about the Miracle Ball, even if it was only on the PBS channels. Most of the players and officials who were down on the field When It Happened became minor media celebrities, and did the rounds of all the talk shows. Rivera, the batter who'd been at the plate that night, refused to talk about it, seeming bitter and angry about the whole thing—the joke was that Rivera was pissed because God had been scared to pitch to him—but Holzman, the pitcher, showed an unexpected philosophical bent—pitchers were all head-cases anyway, baseball fans told each other—and was a fixture on the talk show circuit for years, long after he'd retired from the game. "I'm not sure it proves the existence of God," he said one night. "You'd think that God would have better things to do. But it sure shows that there are forces at work in the universe we don't understand." Later, on another talk show, discussing the theory that heavenly intervention had kept his team from winning the Series, Holzman famously said, "I don't know, maybe God *is* a Yankees fan—but if He hates the Phillies all that much, wouldn't it have been a lot easier just to let Rivera get a *hit?*"

In the second year after the Event, a book, called *Schrödinger's Baseball* written by a young Harvard physicist, postulated the theory that those watching the game in the stadium that night had been so evenly split between Yankees fans wanting Rivera to get a hit and Phillies fans wanting him to strike out, the balance so exquisitely perfect between the two opposing pools of observers, that the quantum wave function had been unable to "decide" which way to collapse, and so had just frozen permanently into an indeterminate state, not resolving itself into *either* outcome. This was immediately derided as errant nonsense by other scientists, but the book became an international bestseller of epic proportions staying at the top of the lists for twenty months, and, although it had no plot at all, was later optioned for a (never made) Big Budget movie for a hefty seven-figure advance.

Eventually, more than four years later, after an election where public dislike of the Secret of Independence Stadium had played a decisive role, a new administration took charge and belatedly declared an Open Door policy, welcoming in civilian scientists, even those from other nations, and, of course, the media.

As soon became clear, they had little to lose. Nothing had changed in almost half a decade. The Ball still hung there in midair. Nothing could move it. Nothing could affect it. The government scientists had tried taking core samples, but no drill bit would bite. They'd tried dragging it away with tractor-hauled nets and with immense magnetic fields, and neither the brute-force nor the high-tech approach had worked. They'd measured it and surrounding space and the space above and below it with every instrument anybody could think of, and discovered nothing. They'd hit it with high-intensity laser beams, they'd tried crisping it with plasma and with flame-throwers, they'd shot hugely powerful bolts of electricity into it. Nothing had worked.

They'd learned nothing from the Ball, in spite of years of intensive, round-the-clock observation with every possible instrumentation, in spite of dozens of scientists working themselves into nervous exhaustion, mental breakdowns, and emotional collapse. No alien secrets. No heretofore unexpected forces of nature (none that they'd learned to identify and control, anyway). The Ball was just *there*. Who knew why? Or how?

More years of intensive investigation by scientists from around the world followed, but eventually, as years stretched into decades, even the scientists began to lose interest. Most ordinary people had lost interest long before, when the Miracle Ball resolutely refused to do anything else remarkable, or even moderately non-boring.

Baseball the sport did its best to pretend the whole thing had never happened. Game attendance had soared for a while, as people waited for the same thing to happen again, then, when it didn't, declined disastrously, falling to record lows. Several major-league franchises went out of business (although, oddly, sandlot and minor-league games were as popular as ever), and those who were lucky enough to survive did their best to see that the Ball was rarely mentioned in the sports pages.

Other seasons went into the record books, none tainted by the miraculous.

Forty more years went by.

Frederick Kellenburger had not been a young man even when he officiated at home plate during the Event. Now he was fabulously old, many decades into his retirement, and had chosen to spend the remaining few years of his life living in a crumbling old brownstone building in what remained of a South Philadelphia neighborhood, a couple of blocks from Independence Stadium. In the last few years, almost against his will, since he had spent decades resolutely trying to put the whole business behind him, he had become fascinated with the Event, with the Ball—in a mellow, non-obsessive kind of way, since he was of a calm, phlegmatic, even contemplative, temperament. He didn't expect to solve any mysteries, where so many others had failed. Still, he had nothing better to do with the residue of his life, and as almost everybody else who had been involved with the Event was dead by now, or else tucked away in nursing homes, it seemed appropriate somehow that someone who had been there from the start should keep an eye on the Ball.

He spent the long, sleepless nights of extreme old age on his newly acquired (only twenty years old) hobby studying the letters and journals of the Knights of St. John of twelfth-century Rhodes, a hobby that appealed to him in part just because it was so out of character for a retired baseball umpire, and an area in which, to everyone's surprise including his own—he had become an internationally recognized authority. Days, he would pick up a lightweight cloth folding chair, and hobble the few blocks to Independence Stadium, moving very, very slowly, like an ancient tortoise hitching itself along a beach in the Galapagos Islands. Hurry wasn't needed, even if he'd been capable of it. This neighborhood had been nearly deserted for years. There was no traffic, rarely anybody around. The slowly rising Atlantic lapped against the base of the immense Jersey Dike a few blocks to the east, and most of the buildings here were abandoned, boarded-up, falling down. Weeds grew through cracks in the middle of the street. For decades now, the city had been gradually, painfully, ponderously shifting itself to higher ground to the west, as had all the other cities of the slowly foundering East Coast, and few people were left in this neighborhood except squatters, refugees from Camden and Atlantic City who could afford nothing better, and a few stubborn South Philly Italians almost as old as he was, who'd been born here and were refusing to leave. No one paid any attention to an old man inching his way down the street. No one bothered him. It was oddly peaceful.

Independence Stadium itself was half-ruined, falling down, nearly abandoned. The tent cities were long gone. There was a towheaded, lazily smiling young boy with an old and probably non-functional assault rifle who was supposed to keep people out of the Stadium, but Kellenburger bribed him with a few small coins every few days, and he always winked and looked the other way. There were supposed to be cameras continuously running, focused on the Ball, part of an ongoing study funded by the University of Denver, recording everything just in case something ever happened, but the equipment had broken down long since, and nobody had seemed to notice, or care. The young guard never entered the Stadium, so, once inside, Kellenburger had the place pretty much to himself.

Inside, Kellenburger would set up his folding chair behind the faded outline of home plate, right where he used to stand to call the games, sit down in the dappled sunlight (the tent enclosing the infield had long since fallen down, leaving only a few metal girders and a few scraps of fabric that flapped lazily in the wind), and watch the Ball, which still hung motionless in the air, just as it had for almost fifty years now. He didn't expect to see anything, other than what had always been there to be seen. It was quiet inside the abandoned stadium, though, and peaceful. Bees buzzed by his ears, and birds flew in and out of the stadium, squabbling under the eaves, making their nests in amongst the broken seats, occasionally launching into liquid song. The air was thick with the rich smells of morning-glory and honeysuckle, which twined up around the ruined bleachers. Wildflowers had sprung up everywhere, and occasionally the tall grass in the outfield would rustle as some small unseen creature scurried through it. Kellenburger watched the Ball, his mind comfortably blank. Sometimes—more often than not, truth be told—he dozed, and nodded in the honeyed sunlight.

As chance would have it, he happened to be awake and watching when the Ball moved at last.

Without warning, the Ball suddenly shot forward across the plate, just as if Holzman had thrown it only a second before, rather than nearly half a century in the past. With no catcher there to intercept it, it shot past home plate, hit the back wall, bounced high in the air, fell back to Earth, bounced again, rolled away, and disappeared into the tall weeds near what had once been the dugout.

After a moment of silent surprise, Kellenburger rose stiffly to his feet. Ponderously, he shuffled forward, bent over as much as he could, tilted his head creakily this way and that, remembering the direction of the ball as it shot over the faded ghost of home plate, analyzing, judging angles. At last, slowly, he smiled.

"Strike!" he said, with satisfaction. "I *knew* it would be. You're out."

Then, without a backward look, without even a glance at where the famous Ball lay swallowed in the weeds, he picked up his folding chair, hoisted it to his shoulder, went out of the ruins of Independence Stadium, and, moving very slowly, shuffled home along the cracked and deserted street through the warm, bright, velvet air of spring.

John Kessel has published three novels, three short-story collections, and co-edited (with James Patrick Kelly) several influential anthologies on humanist fiction and slipstream fiction. He is a professor in the MFA program in creative writing at North Carolina State University and Director of Creative Writing at that university. In this story he explores a counterfactual intersection between politics and baseball, using a couple of baseball players engaged in a World Series struggle to muse about fathers and sons and strangely fat pitches.

The Franchise
∞

John Kessel

"Whoever wants to know the heart and mind of America had better learn baseball."

—Jacques Barzun

WHEN GEORGE HERBERT WALKER Bush strode into the batter's box to face the pitcher they called the Franchise, it was the bottom of the second, and the Senators were already a run behind.

But Killebrew had managed a bloop double down the rightfield line and two outs later still stood on second in the bright October sunlight, waiting to be driven in. The bleachers were crammed full of restless fans in colorful shirts. Far behind Killebrew, Griffith Stadium's green center-field wall zigzagged to avoid the towering oak in Mrs. Mahan's backyard, lending the stadium its crazy dimensions. They said the only players ever to homer into that tree were Mantle and Ruth. George imagined how the stadium would erupt if he did it, drove the first pitch right out of the old ball yard, putting the Senators ahead in the first game of the 1959 World Series. If wishes were horses, his father had told him more than once, then beggars would ride.

George stepped into the box, ground in his back foot, squinted at the pitcher. The first pitch, a fastball, so surprised him that he didn't get his bat off his shoulder. Belt high, it split the middle of the plate, but the umpire called, "Ball!"

"Ball?" Schmidt, the Giants' catcher, grumbled.

"You got a problem?" the umpire said.

"Me? I got no problem." Schmidt tossed the ball back to the pitcher, who shook his head in histrionic Latin American dismay, as if bemoaning the sins of the world that he'd seen only too much of since he'd left Havana eleven years before. "But the Franchise, he no like."

George ignored them and set himself for the next pitch. The big Cuban went into his herky-jerky windup, deceptively slow, then kicked and threw. George was barely into his swing when the ball thwacked into the catcher's glove. "Steerike one!" the umpire called.

He was going to have to get around faster. The next pitch was another fastball, outside and high, but George had already triggered before the release and missed it by a foot, twisting himself around so that he almost fell over.

Schmidt took the ball out of his glove, showed it to George, and threw it back to the mound.

The next was a curve, outside by an inch. Ball two.

The next, a fastball that somehow George managed to foul into the dirt.

The next, a fastball up under his chin that had him diving into the dirt himself. Ball three. Full count.

An expectant murmur rose in the crowd, then fell to a profound silence, the silence of a church, of heaven, of a lover's secret heart. Was his father among them, breathless, hoping? Thousands awaited the next pitch. Millions more watched on television. Killebrew took a three-step lead off second. The Giants made no attempt to hold him on. The chatter from the Senators' dugout lit up. "Come on, George Herbert Walker Bush, bear down! Come on, Professor, grit up!"

George set himself, weight on his back foot. He cocked his bat, squinted out at the pitcher. The vainglorious Latino gave him a piratical grin, shook off Schmidt's sign. George felt his shoulders tense. Calm, boy, calm, he told himself. You've been shot at, you've faced Prescott Bush across a dining-room table—this is nothing but baseball. But instead of calm he felt panic, and as the Franchise went into his windup his mind stood blank as a stone.

The ball started out right for his head. George jerked back in a desperate effort to get out of the way as the pitch, a curve of prodigious sweep, dropped through the heart of the plate. "Steerike!" the umpire called.

Instantly the scene changed from hushed expectation to sudden movement. The crowd groaned. The players relaxed and began jogging off the field. Killebrew kicked the dirt and walked back to the dugout to get his glove. The organist started up. Behind the big Chesterfield sign in right, the scorekeeper slid another goose egg onto the board for the Senators. Though the whole thing was similar to moments he had experienced more times than he would care to admit during his ten years in the minors, the simple volume of thirty thousand voices sighing in disappointment because he, George Herbert Walker Bush, had failed, left him standing stunned at the plate with the bat limp in his clammy hands. They didn't get thirty thousand fans in Chattanooga.

Schmidt flipped the ball toward the mound. As the Franchise jogged past him, he flashed George that superior smile. "A magnificent swing," he said.

George stumbled back to the dugout. Lemon, heading out to left, shook his head. "Nice try, Professor," the shortstop Consolo said.

"Pull your jock up and get out to first," said Lavagetto, the manager. He spat a stream of tobacco juice onto the sod next to the end of the dugout. "Senor Fidel Castro welcomes you to the bigs."

2

The Senators lost 7–1. Castro pitched nine innings, allowed four hits, struck out ten. George fanned three times. In the sixth, he let a low throw get by him; the runner ended up on third, and the Giants followed with four unearned runs.

In the locker room, his teammates avoided him. Nobody had played well, but George knew they had him pegged as a choker. Lavagetto came through with a few words of encouragement. "We'll get 'em tomorrow," he said. George expected the manager to yank him for somebody who at least wouldn't cost them runs on defense. When he left without saying anything, George was grateful to him for at least letting him go another night before benching him.

Barbara and the boys had been in the stands, but had gone home. They would be waiting for him. He didn't want to go. The place was empty by the time he walked out through the tunnels to the street. His head was filled with images from the game. Castro had toyed with him; he no doubt enjoyed humiliating the son of a U.S. senator. The Cuban's look of heavy-lidded disdain sparked an unaccustomed rage in George. It wasn't good sportsmanship. You played hard, and you won or lost, but you didn't rub the other guy's nose in it. That was bush league, and George, despite his unfortunate name, was anything but bush.

That George Bush should end up playing first base for the Washington Senators in the 1959 World Series was the result of as improbable a sequence of events as had ever conspired to make a man of a rich boy. The key moment had come on a May Saturday in 1948 when he had shaken the hand of Babe Ruth.

That May morning the Yale baseball team was to play Brown, but before the game a ceremony was held to honor Ruth, donating the manuscript of his autobiography to the university library. George, captain of the Yale squad, would accept the manuscript. As he stood before the microphone set up between the pitcher's mound and second base, he was stunned by the gulf between the pale hulk standing before him and the legend he represented. Ruth, only fifty-three on that spring morning, could hardly speak for the throat cancer that was killing him. He gasped out a few words, stooped over, rail thin, no longer the giant he had been in the twenties. George took his hand. It was dry and papery and brown as a leaf in fall. Through his grip George felt the contact with glorious history, with feats of heroism that would never be matched, with 714 home runs and 1,356 extra-base hits, with a lifetime slugging percentage of .690, with the called shot and the sixty-homer season and the 1927 Yankees and the curse of the Red Sox. An electricity surged up his arm and directly into his soul. Ruth had accomplished as much, in his way, as a man could accomplish in a life, more, even, George realized to his astonishment, than had his father, Prescott Bush. He stood there stunned, charged with an unexpected, unasked-for purpose.

He had seen death in the war, had tasted it in the blood that streamed from his forehead when he'd struck it against the tail of the TBM Avenger as he parachuted out of the flaming bomber over the Pacific in 1943. He had felt death's hot breath on his back as he frantically paddled the yellow rubber raft away from Chichi Jima against waves pushing him back into the arms of the Japanese, had felt death draw away and offered up a silent prayer when the conning tower of the U.S.S. *Finback* broke through the agitated seas to save him from a savage fate—to, he always knew, some higher purpose. He had imagined that purpose to be business or public service. Now he recognized that he had been seeing it through his father's eyes, that in fact his fate lay elsewhere. It lay between the chalk lines of a playing field, on the greensward of the infield, within the smells of pine tar and sawdust and chewing tobacco and liniment. He could feel it through the tendons of the fleshless hand of Babe Ruth that he held in his own at that very instant.

The day after he graduated from Yale he signed, for no bonus, with the Cleveland Indians. Ten years later, George had little to show for his bold choice. He wasn't the best first baseman you ever saw. Nobody ever stopped him on the street to ask for his autograph. He never made the Indians, got traded to the Browns. He hung on, bouncing up and down the farm systems of seventh and eighth-place teams. Every spring he went to Florida with high expectations, every April he started the season in Richmond, in Rochester, in Chattanooga. Just two months earlier he had considered packing it in and looking for another career. Then a series of miracles happened.

Chattanooga was the farm team for the Senators, who hadn't won a pennant since 1933. For fifteen years, under their notoriously cheap owner Clark Griffith, they'd been as bad as you could get. But in 1959 their young third baseman, Harmon Killebrew, hit forty-two home runs. Sluggers Jim Lemon and Roy Sievers had career years. A big Kansas boy named Bob Allison won rookie of the year in center field. Camilo Pascual won twenty-two games, struck out 215 men. A kid named Jim Kaat won seventeen. Everything broke right, including Mickey Mantle's leg. After hovering a couple of games over .500 through the All-Star break, the Senators got hot in August, won ninety games, and finished one ahead of the Yankees.

When, late in August, right fielder Albie Pearson got hurt, Lavagetto switched Sievers to right, and there was George Bush, thirty-five years old, starting at first base for the American League champions in the 1959 World Series against the New York Giants.

The Giants were heavy favorites. Who would bet against a team that fielded Willie Mays, Orlando Cepeda, Willie McCovey, Felipe Alou, and pitchers like Johnny Antonelli, the fireballer Toothpick Sam Jones, and the Franchise, Fidel Castro? If, prior to the series, you'd told George Herbert Walker Bush the Senators were doomed, he would not have disagreed with you. After game one he had no reason to think otherwise.

He stood outside the stadium looking for a cab, contemplating his series record—one game, 0 for 4, one error—when a pale old man in a loud sports coat spoke to him. "Just be glad you're here," the man said.

The man had watery blue eyes, a sharp face. He was thin enough to look ill. "I beg your pardon?"

"You're the fellow the Nats called up in September, right? Remember, even if you never play another inning, at least you were there. You felt the sun on your back, got dirt on your hands, saw the stands full of people from down on the field. Not many get even that much."

"The Franchise made me look pretty sick."

"You have to face him down."

"Easier said than done."

"Don't say—do."

"Who are you, old man?"

The man hesitated. "Name's Weaver. I'm a—a fan. Yes, I'm a baseball fan." He touched the brim of his hat and walked away.

George thought about it on the cab ride home. It did not make him feel much better. When he got back to the cheap furnished apartment they were renting, Barbara tried to console him.

"My father wasn't there, was he?" George said.

"No. But he called after the game. He wants to see you."

"Probably wants to give me a few tips on how to comport myself. Or maybe just gloat."

Bar came around behind his chair, rubbed his tired shoulders. George got up and switched on the television. While he waited for it to warm up, the silence stretched. He faced Barbara. She had put on a few pounds over the years, but he remembered the first time he'd seen her across the dance floor in the red dress. He was seventeen.

"What do you think he wants?"

"I don't know, George."

"I haven't seen him around in the last ten years. Have you?"

The TV had warmed up, and Prescott Bush's voice blared out from behind George. "I hope the baseball Senators win," he was saying. "They've had a better year than the Democratic ones."

George twisted down the volume, stared for a moment at his father's handsome face, then snapped it off. "Give me a drink," he told Barbara. He noticed the boys standing in the doorway, afraid. Barbara hesitated, poured a scotch and water.

"And don't stint on the scotch!" George yelled. He turned to Neil. "What are you looking at, you little weasel! Go to bed."

Barbara slammed down the glass so hard the scotch splashed the counter. "What's got into you, George? You're acting like a crazy man."

George took the half-empty glass from her hand. "My father's got into me, that's what. He got into me thirty years ago, and I can't get him out."

Barbara shot him a look in which disgust outweighed pity and went back to the boys' room. George slumped in the armchair, picked up a copy of *Look* and leafed through the pages. He stopped on a Gillette razor ad. Castro smiled out from the page, dark hair slicked back, chin sleek as a curveball, a devastating blonde leaning on his shoulder. "Look Sharp, Feel Sharp, *Be* Sharp," the ad told George.

Castro. What did he know about struggle? Yet that egomaniac lout was considered a hero, while he, George Herbert Walker Bush, who at twenty-four had been at the head of every list of the young men most likely to succeed, had accomplished precisely nothing.

People who didn't know any better had assumed that because of his background, money, and education he would grow to be one of the ones who told others what it was necessary for them to do, but George was coming to realize, with a surge of panic, that he was not special. His moment of communion with Babe Ruth had been a delusion, because Ruth was another type of man. Perhaps Ruth was used by the teams that bought and sold him, but inside Ruth was some compulsion that drove him to be larger than the uses to which he was put, so that in the end he deformed those uses, remade the game itself.

George, talented though he had seemed, had no such size. The vital force that had animated his grandfather George Herbert Walker, after whom he was named, the longing after mystery that had impelled the metaphysical poet George Herbert, after whom that grandfather had been named, had diminished into a trickle in George Herbert Walker Bush. No volcanic forces surged inside him. When he listened late in the night, all he could hear of his soul was a thin keening, a buzz like a bug trapped in a jar. *Let me go, let me go,* it whispered.

That old man at the ballpark was wrong. It was not enough, not nearly enough, just to be there. He wanted to be somebody. What good was it just to stand on first base in the World Series if you came away from it a laughingstock? To have your father call you not because you were a hero, but only to remind you once again what a failure you are.

"I'll be damned if I go see him," George muttered to the empty room.

3

President Nixon called Lavagetto in the middle of the night with a suggestion for the batting order in the second game. "Put Bush in the number-five slot," Nixon said.

Lavagetto wondered how he was supposed to tell the President of the United States that he was out of his mind. "Yessir, Mr. President."

"See, that way you get another right-handed batter at the top of the order."

Lavagetto considered pointing out to the president that the Giants were pitching a right-hander in game two. "Yessir, Mr. President," Lavagetto said. His wife was awake now, looking at him with irritation from her side of the bed. He put his hand over the mouthpiece and said, "Go to sleep."

"Who is it at this hour?"

"The President of the United States."

"Uh-huh."

Nixon had some observations about one-run strategies. Lavagetto agreed with him until he could get him off the line. He looked at his alarm clock. It was half past two.

Nixon had sounded full of manic energy. His voice dripped dogmatic assurance. He wondered if Nixon was a drinking man. Walter Winchell said that Eisenhower's death had shoved the veep into an office he was unprepared to hold.

Lavagetto shut off the light and lay back down, but he couldn't sleep. What about Bush? Damn Pearson for getting himself hurt. Bush should be down in the minors where he belonged. He looked to be cracking under the pressure like a ripe melon.

But maybe the guy could come through, prove himself. He was no kid. Lavagetto knew from personal experience the pressures of the Series, how the unexpected could turn on the swing of the bat. He recalled that fourth game of the '47 series, his double to right field that cost Floyd Bevens his no-hitter, and the game. Lavagetto had been a thirty-four-year-old utility infielder for the luckless Dodgers, an aging substitute playing out the string at the end of his career. In that whole season he'd hit only one other double. When he'd seen that ball twist past the right fielder, the joy had shot through his chest like lightning. The Dodger fans had gone crazy; his teammates had leapt all over him laughing and shouting and swearing like Durocher himself.

He remembered that, despite the miracle, the Dodgers had lost the Series to the Yankees in seven.

Lavagetto turned over. First in War, First in Peace, Last in the American League . . . that was the Washington Senators. He hoped young Kaat was getting more sleep than he was.

4

Tuesday afternoon, in front of a wild capacity crowd, young Jim Kaat pitched one of the best games by a rookie in the history of the Series. The twenty-year-old left-hander battled Toothpick Sam Jones pitch for pitch, inning for inning. Jones struggled with his control, walking six in the first seven innings, throwing two wild pitches. If it weren't for the overeagerness of the Senators, swinging at balls a foot out of the strike zone, they would surely have scored; instead they squandered opportunity after opportunity. The fans grew restless. They could see it happening, in sour expectation of disaster built up over twenty-five frustrated years: Kaat would pitch brilliantly, and it would be wasted because the Giants would score on some bloop single.

Through seven, the game stayed a scoreless tie. By some fluke George could not fathom, Lavagetto, instead of benching him, had moved him up in the batting order. Though he was still without a hit, he had been playing superior defense. In the seventh he snuffed a Giant uprising when he dove to snag a screamer off the bat of Schmidt for the third out, leaving runners at second and third.

Then, with two down in the top of the eighth, Cepeda singled. George moved in to hold him on. Kaat threw over a couple of times to keep the runner honest, with Cepeda trying to judge Kaat's move. Mays took a strike, then a ball. Cepeda edged a couple of strides away from first.

Kaat went into his stretch, paused, and whipped the ball to first, catching Cepeda leaning the wrong way. Picked off! But Cepeda, instead of diving back, took off for second. George whirled and threw hurriedly. The ball sailed over Consolo's head into left field, and Cepeda went to third. E-3.

Kaat was shaken. Mays hit a screamer between first and second. George dove, but it was by him, and Cepeda jogged home with the lead.

Kaat struck out McCovey, but the damage was done. "You bush-league clown!" a fan yelled. George's face burned. As he trotted off the field, from the Giants' dugout came Castro's shout: "A heroic play, Mr. Rabbit!"

George wanted to keep going through the dugout and into the clubhouse. On the bench his teammates were conspicuously silent. Consolo sat down next to him. "Shake it off," he said. "You're up this inning."

George grabbed his bat and moved to the end of the dugout. First up in the bottom of the eighth was Sievers. He got behind 0–2, battled back as Jones wasted a couple, then fouled off four straight strikes until he'd worked Jones for a walk. The organist played charge lines and the crowd started chanting. Lemon moved Sievers to second. Killebrew hit a drive that brought the people to their feet screaming before it curved just outside the left-field foul pole, then popped out to short. He threw down his bat and stalked back toward the dugout.

"C'mon, professor," Killebrew said as he passed Bush in the on-deck circle. "Give yourself a reason for being here."

Jones was a scary right-hander with one pitch: the heater. In his first three at-bats George had been overpowered; by the last, he'd managed a walk. This time he went up with a plan: he was going to take the first pitch, get ahead in the count, then drive the ball.

The first pitch was a fastball just high.

Make contact. Don't force it. Go with the pitch. The next was another fast-ball; George swung as soon as Jones let it go and sent a screaming line drive over the third baseman's head. The crowd roared, and he was halfway down the first-base line when the third-base umpire threw up his hands and yelled, "Foul ball!"

He caught his breath, picked up his bat, and returned to the box. Sievers jogged back to second. Schmidt, standing with his hands on his hips, didn't look at George. From the Giants' dugout George heard, "Kiss your luck good-bye, you effeminate rabbit! You rich man's table leavings! You are devoid of even the makings of guts!"

George stepped out of the box. Castro had come down the dugout to the near end and was leaning out, arms braced on the field, hurling his abuse purple faced. Rigney and the pitching coach had him by the shoulders, tugging him back. George turned away, feeling a cold fury in his belly.

He would show them all. He forgot to calculate, swept by rage. He set himself as far back in the box as possible. Jones took off his cap, wiped his forearm across his brow, and leaned over to check the signs. He shook off the first, then nodded and went into his windup.

As soon as he released George swung, and was caught completely off balance by a change-up. "Strike two, you shadow of a man!" Castro shouted. "Unnatural offspring of a snail and a worm! Strike two!"

Jones tempted him with an outside pitch; George didn't bite. The next was another high fastball; George started, then checked his swing. "Ball!" the home-plate ump called. Fidel booed. Schmidt argued, the ump shook his head. Full count.

George knew he should look for a particular pitch, in a particular part of the plate. After ten years of professional ball, this ought to be second nature, but Jones was so wild he didn't have a clue. George stepped out of the box, rubbed his hands on his pants. "Yes, wipe your sweaty hands, mama's boy! You have all the machismo of a bankbook!"

The rage came to his defense. He picked a decision out of the air, arbitrary as the breeze: fastball, outside.

Jones went into his windup. He threw his body forward, whipped his arm high over his shoulder. Fastball, outside. George swiveled his hips through the box, kept his head down, extended his arms. The contact of the bat with the ball was so slight he wasn't sure he'd hit it at all. A line drive down the right-field line, hooking as it rose, hooking, hooking . . . curling just inside the foul pole into the stands 320 feet away.

The fans exploded. George, feeling rubbery, jogged around first, toward second. Sievers pumped his fist as he rounded third; the Senators were up on their feet in the dugout shouting and slapping each other. Jones had his hands on his hips, head down and back to the plate. George rounded third and jogged across home, where he was met by Sievers, who slugged him in the shoulder, and the rest of his teammates in the dugout, who laughed and slapped his butt.

The crowd began to chant, "SEN-a-TOR, SEN-a-TOR." After a moment George realized they were chanting for him. He climbed out of the dugout again and tipped his hat, scanning the stands for Barbara and the boys. As he did he saw his father in the presidential box, leaning over to speak into the ear of the cheering President Nixon. He felt a rush of hope, ducked his head, and got back into the dugout.

Kaat held the Giants in the ninth, and the Senators won, 2–1.

In the locker room after the game, George's teammates whooped and slapped him on the back. Chuck Stobbs, the clubhouse comic, called him "the Bambino." For a while George hoped that his father might come down to congratulate him. Instead, for the first time in his career, reporters swarmed around him. They fired flashbulbs in salvoes. They pushed back their hats, flipped open their notebooks, and asked him questions.

"What's it feel like to win a big game like this?"

"I'm just glad to be here. I'm not one of these winning-is-everything guys."

"They're calling you the senator. Your father is a senator. How do you feel about that?"

"I guess we're both senators," George said. "He just got to Washington a little sooner than I did."

They liked that a lot. George felt the smile on his face like a frozen mask. For the first time in his life he was aware of the muscles it took to smile, as tense as if they were lifting a weight.

After the reporters left he showered. George wondered what his father had been whispering into the president's ear, while everyone around him cheered. Some sarcastic comment? Some irrelevant political advice?

When he got back to his locker, toweling himself dry, he found a note lying on the bench. He opened it eagerly. It read:

To the Effeminate Rabbit:
Even the rodent has his day. But not when the eagle pitches.
Sincerely,
Fidel Alejandro Castro Ruz

5

That Fidel Castro would go so far out of his way to insult George Herbert Walker Bush would come as no surprise to anyone who knew him. Early in Castro's first season in the majors, a veteran Phillies reliever, after watching Fidel warm up, approached the young Cuban. "Where did you get that curve?" he asked incredulously.

"From you," said Fidel. "That's why you don't have one."

But sparking his reaction to Bush was more than simple egotism. Fidel's antipathy grew from circumstances of background and character that made such animosity as inevitable as the rising of the sun in the east of Oriente province where he had been born thirty-two years before.

Like George Herbert Walker Bush, Fidel was the son of privilege, but a peculiarly Cuban form of privilege, as different from the blue-blooded Bush variety as the hot and breathless climate of Oriente was from chilly New England. Like Bush, Fidel endured a father as parsimonious with his warmth as those New England winters. Young Fidelito grew up well acquainted with the back of Angel Castro's hand, the jeers of classmates who tormented him and his brother Raul for their illegitimacy. Though Angel Castro owned two thousand acres and had risen from common sugarcane laborer to local caudillo, he did not possess the easy assurance of the rich of Havana, for whom Oriente was the Cuban equivalent of Alabama. The Castros were peasants. Fidel's father was illiterate, his mother a maid. No amount of money could erase Fidel's bastardy.

This history raged in Fidelito. Always in a fight, alternating boasts with moody silences, he longed for accomplishment in a fiery way that cast the longing of Bush to impress his own father into a sickly shadow. At boarding school in Santiago, he sought the praise of his teachers and admiration of his schoolmates. At Belen, Havana's exclusive Jesuit preparatory school, he became the champion athlete of all of Cuba. "El Loco Fidel" his classmates called him as, late into the night, at an outdoor court under a light swarming with insects, he would practice basketball shots until his feet were torn bloody and his head swam with forlorn images of the ball glancing off the iron rim.

At the University of Havana, between the scorching expanses of the baseball and basketball seasons, Fidel toiled over the scorching expanse of the law books. He sought triumph in student politics as he did in sports. In the evenings he met in tiny rooms with his comrades and talked about junk pitches and electoral strategy, about the reforms that were only a matter of time because the people's will could not be forever thwarted. They were on the side of history. Larger than even the largest of men, history would overpower anyone unless, like Fidel, he aligned himself with it so as not to be swept under by the tidal force of its inescapable currents.

In the spring of 1948, at the same time George Herbert Walker Bush was shaking the hand of Babe Ruth, these currents transformed Fidel's life. He was being scouted by several major league teams. In the university, he had gained control of his fastball and given birth to a curve of so monstrous an arc that Alex Pompez, the Giants' scout, reported that the well-spoken law student owned "a hook like Bo-Peep." More significantly, Pirates scout Howie Haak observed that Fidel "could throw and think at the same time."

Indeed Fidel could think, though no one could come close to guessing the content of his furious thought. A war between glory and doom raged within him. Fidel's fury to accomplish things threatened to keep him from accomplishing anything at all. He had made enemies. In the late forties, student groups punctuated elections for head of the law-school class with assassinations. Rival political gangs fought in the streets. Events conspired to drive Fidel toward a crisis. And so, on a single day in 1948, he abandoned his political aspirations, quit school, married his lover, the fair Mirta Diaz Balart, and signed a contract with the New York Giants.

It seemed a fortunate choice. In his rookie year he won fifteen games. After he took the Cy Young Award and was named MVP of the 1951 Series, the sportswriters dubbed him "the Franchise." This past season he had won twenty-nine. He earned, and squandered, a fortune. Controversy dogged him, politics would not let him go, the uniform of a baseball player at times felt much too small. His brother Raul was imprisoned when Batista overthrew the government to avoid defeat in the election of 1952. Fidel made friends among the expatriates in Miami. He protested U.S. policies. His alternative nickname became "the Mouth."

But all along Fidel knew his politics was mere pose. His spouting off to sports reporters did nothing compared to what money might do to help the guerrillas in the Sierra Maestra. Yet he had no money.

After the second game of the Series, instead of returning to the hotel Fidel took a cab down to the Mall. He needed to be alone. It was early evening when he got out at the Washington Monument. The sky beyond the Lincoln Memorial shone orange and purple. The air still held some of the sultry heat of summer, like an evening in Havana. But this was a different sort of capital. These North Americans liked to think of themselves as clean, rational men of law instead of passion, a land of Washingtons and Lincolns, but away from the public buildings it was still a southern city full of ex-slaves. Fidel looked down the Mall toward the bright Capitol, white and towering as a wedding cake, wondered what he might have become had he continued law school. At one time he had imagined himself the Washington of his own country, a liberating warrior. The true heir of Jose Marti, scholar, poet, and revolutionary. Like Marti, he admired the idealism of the United States, but like him he saw its dark side. Here at the Mall, however, you could almost forget about that in an atmosphere of bogus Greek democracy, of liberty and justice for all. You might even forget that this liberty could be bought and sold, a franchise purchasable for cold cash.

Fidel walked along the pool toward the Lincoln Memorial. The floodlights lit up the white columns, and inside shone upon the brooding figure of Lincoln. Despite his cynicism, Fidel was caught by the sight of it. He had been to Washington only once before, for the All Star Game in 1956. He remembered walking through Georgetown with Mirta on his arm, feeling tall and handsome, ignoring the scowl of the maître d' in the restaurant who clearly disapproved of two such dark ones in his establishment.

He'd triumphed but was not satisfied. He had forced others to admit his primacy through the power of his will. He had shown them, with his strong arm, the difference between right and wrong. He was the Franchise. He climbed up the steps into the Memorial, read the words of Lincoln's Second Inaugural address engraved on the wall. THE PROGRESS OF OUR ARMS UPON WHICH ALL ELSE CHIEFLY DEPENDS IS AS WELL KNOWN TO THE PUBLIC AS TO MYSELF . . . But he was still the crazy Cuban, taken little more seriously than Desi Arnaz, and the minute that *arm* that made him a useful commodity should begin to show signs of weakening—in that same minute he would be undone. IT MAY SEEM STRANGE THAT ANY MEN SHOULD DARE TO ASK A JUST GOD'S ASSISTANCE IN WRINGING THEIR BREAD FROM THE SIN OF OTHER MEN'S FACES BUT LET US JUDGE NOT THAT WE BE JUDGED.

Judge not? Perhaps Lincoln could manage it, but Fidel was a different sort of man.

In the secrecy of his mind Fidel could picture another world than the one he lived in. The marriage of love to Mirta had long since gone sour, torn apart by Fidel's lust for renown on the ball field and his lust for the astonishing women who fell like fruit from the trees into the laps of players such as he. More than once he felt grief over his faithlessness. He knew his solitude to be just punishment. That was the price of greatness, for, after all, greatness was a crime and deserved punishment.

Mirta was gone now, and their son with her. She worked for the hated Batista. He thought of Raul languishing in Batista's prison on the Isle of Pines. Batista, embraced by this United States that ran Latin America like a company store. Raul suffered for the people, while Fidel ate in four-star restaurants and slept with a different woman in every city, throwing away his youth, and the money he earned with it, on excrement.

He looked up into the great sad face of Lincoln. He turned from the monument to stare out across the Mall toward the gleaming white shaft of the Washington obelisk. It was full night now. Time to amend his life.

6

The headline in the *Post* the next morning read, SENATOR BUSH EVENS SERIES. The story mentioned that Prescott Bush had shown up in the sixth inning and sat beside Nixon in the presidential box. But nothing more.

Bar decided not to go up to New York for the middle games of the Series. George traveled with the team to the Roosevelt Hotel. The home run had done something for him. He felt a new confidence.

The game-three starters were the veteran southpaw Johnny Antonelli for the Giants and Pedro Ramos for the Senators. The echoes of the national anthem had hardly faded when Allison led off for the Senators with a home run into the short porch in left field. The Polo Grounds fell dead silent. The Senators scored three runs in the first; George did his part, hitting a change-up to right center for a double, scoring the third run of the inning.

In the bottom half of the first the Giants came right back, tying it up on Mays' three-run homer.

After that the Giants gradually wore Ramos down, scoring a single run in the third and two in the fifth. Lavagetto pulled him for a pinch hitter in the sixth with George on third and Consolo at first, two outs. But Aspromonte struck out, ending the inning.

Though Castro heckled George mercilessly throughout the game and the brash New York fans joined in, he played above himself. The Giants eventually won, 8–3, but George went three for five. Despite his miserable first game he was batting .307 for the Series. Down two games to one, the Washington players felt the loss, but had stopped calling him "George Herbert Walker Bush" and started calling him "the Senator."

7

Lavagetto had set an eleven o'clock curfew, but Billy Consolo persuaded George to go out on the town. The Hot Corner was a dive on Seventh Avenue with decent Italian food and cheap drinks. George ordered a club soda and tried to get into the mood. Ramos moaned about the plate umpire's strike zone, and Consolo changed the subject.

Consolo had been a bonus boy; in 1953 the Red Sox had signed him right out of high school for $50,000. He had never panned out. George wondered if Consolo's career had been any easier to take than his own. At least nobody had hung enough expectations on George for him to be called a flop.

Stobbs was telling a story. "So the Baseball Annie says to him, 'But will you respect me in the morning?' and the shortstop says, 'Oh baby, I'll respect you like crazy!'"

While the others were laughing, George headed for the men's room. Passing the bar, he saw, a corner booth, Fidel Castro talking to a couple of men in slick suits. Castro's eyes flicked over him but registered no recognition.

When George came out, the men in suits were in heated conversation with Castro. In the back of the room someone dropped a quarter into the jukebox, and Elvis Presley's silky "Money Honey" blared out. Bush had no use for rock and roll. He sat at the table, ignored his teammates' conversation and kept an eye on Castro. The Cuban was strenuously making some point, stabbing the tabletop with his index finger. After a minute George noticed that someone at the bar was watching them, too. It was the pale old man he had seen at Griffith Stadium.

On impulse, George went up to him. "Hello, old-timer. You really must be a fan, if you followed the Series up here. Can I buy you a drink?"

The man turned decisively from watching Castro, as if deliberately putting aside some thought. He seemed about to smile but did not. Small red splotches colored his face. "Buy me a ginger ale."

George ordered a ginger ale and another club soda and sat on the next stool. "Money honey, if you want to get along with me," Elvis sang.

The old man sipped his drink. "You had yourself a couple of good games," he said. "You're in the groove."

"I just got some lucky breaks."

"Don't kid me. I know how it feels when it's going right. You know just where the next pitch is going to be, and there it is. Somebody hits a line drive right at you, you throw out your glove and snag it without even thinking. You're in the groove."

"It comes from playing the game a long time."

The old man snorted. "Do you really believe this guff you spout? Or are you just trying to hide something?"

"What do you mean? I've spent ten years playing baseball."

"And you expect me to believe you still don't know anything about it? Experience doesn't explain the groove." The man looked as if he were watching something far away. "When you're in that groove you're not playing the game, the game is playing you."

"But you have to plan your moves."

The old man looked at him as if he were from Mars. "Do you plan your moves when you're making love to your wife?" He finished his ginger ale, took another look back at Castro, then left. Everyone, it seemed, knew what was wrong with him. George felt steamed. As if that wasn't enough, as soon as he returned to the table, Castro's pals left and the Cuban swaggered over to George, leaned into him, and blew cigar smoke into his face. "I know you, George Herbert Walker Bush," he said, "Sen-a-tor Rabbit. The rich man's son."

George pushed him away. "You know, I'm beginning to find your behavior darned unconscionable, compadre."

"I stand here quaking with fear," Castro said. He poked George in the chest. "Back home in Biran we had a pen for the pigs. The gate of this pen was in disrepair. But it is still a fact, Senator Rabbit, that the splintered wooden gate of that pigpen, squealing on its rusted hinges, swung better than you."

Consolo started to get up, but George put a hand on his arm. "Say, Billy, our Cuban friend here didn't by any chance help you pick out this restaurant tonight, did he?"

"What, are you crazy? Of course not."

"Too bad. I thought if he did, we could get some good Communist food here." The guys laughed. Castro leaned over.

"Very funny, Machismo Zero." His breath reeked of cigar smoke, rum, and garlic. "I guarantee that after tomorrow's game you will be even funnier."

8

Fidel had never felt sharper than he did during his warmups the afternoon of the fourth game. It was a cool fall day, partial overcast with a threat of rain, a breeze blowing out to right. The chill air only invigorated him. Never had his curve had more bite, his screwball more movement. His arm felt supple, his legs strong. As he strode in from the bullpen to the dugout, squinting out at the apartment buildings on Coogan's Bluff towering over the stands, a great cheer rose from the crowd.

Before the echoes of the national anthem had died he walked the first two batters, on eight pitches. The fans murmured. Schmidt came out to talk with him. "What's wrong?"

"Nothing is wrong," Fidel said, sending him back.

He retired Lemon on a pop fly and Killebrew on a fielder's choice. Bush came to the plate with two outs and men on first and second. The few Washington fans who had braved the Polo Grounds set up a chant: "SEN-a-TOR, SEN-a-TOR!"

Fidel studied Bush. Beneath Bush's bravado he could see panic in every motion of the body he wore like an ill-fitting suit. Fidel struck him out on three pitches.

Kralick held the Giants scoreless through three innings.

As the game progressed, Fidel's own personal game, the game of pitcher and batter, settled into a pattern. Fidel mowed down the batters after Bush in the order with predictable dispatch, but fell into trouble each time he faced the top of the order, getting just enough outs to bring Bush up with men on base and the game in the balance. He did this four times in the first seven innings.

Each time Bush struck out.

In the middle of the seventh, after Bush fanned to end the inning, Mays sat down next to Fidel on the bench. "What the hell do you think you're doing?"

Mays was the only player on the Giants whose stature rivaled that of the Franchise. Fidel, whose success came as much from craft as physical prowess, could not but admit that Mays was the most beautiful ballplayer he had ever seen. "I'm shutting out the Washington Senators in the fourth game of the World Series," Fidel said.

"What's this mickey mouse with Bush? You trying to make him look bad?"

"One does not have to try very hard."

"Well, cut it out—before you make a mistake with Killebrew or Sievers."

Fidel looked him dead in the eyes. "I do not make mistakes."

The Giants entered the ninth with a 3–0 lead. Fidel got two quick outs, then gave up a single to Sievers and walked Lemon and Killebrew to load the bases. Bush, at bat, represented the lead run. Schmidt called time and came out again. Rigney hurried out from the dugout, and Mays, to the astonishment of the crowd, came all the way in from center. "Yank him," he told Rigney.

Rigney looked exasperated. "Who's managing this team, Willie?"

"He's setting Bush up to be the goat."

Rigney looked at Fidel. Fidel looked at him. "Just strike him out," the manager said.

Fidel rubbed up the ball and threw three fastballs through the heart of the plate. Bush missed them all. By the last strike, the New York fans were screaming, rocking the Polo Grounds with a parody of the Washington chant: "Sen-a-TOR, Sen-a-TOR, BUSH, BUSH, BUSH!" and exploding into fits of laughter. The Giants led the series, 3–1.

9

George made the cabbie drop him off at the corner of Broadway and Pine, in front of the old Trinity Church. He walked down Wall Street through crowds of men in dark suits, past the Stock Exchange to the offices of Brown Brothers, Harriman. In the shadows of the buildings the fall air felt wintry. He had not been down here in more years than he cared to remember.

The secretary, Miss Goode, greeted him warmly; she still remembered him from his days at Yale. Despite Prescott Bush's move to the Senate, they still kept his inner office for him, and as George stood outside the door he heard a piano. His father was singing. He had a wonderful singing voice, of which he was too proud.

George entered. Prescott Bush sat at an upright piano, playing Gilbert and Sullivan:

> *Go, ye heroes, go to glory*
> *Though you die in combat gory.*
> *Ye shall live in song and story.*
> *Go to immortality!*

Still playing, he glanced over his shoulder at George, then turned back and finished the verse:

> *Go to death, and go to slaughter,*
> *Die, and every Cornish daughter*
> *With her tears your grave shall water.*
> *Go, ye heroes, go and die!*

George was all too familiar with his father's theatricality. Six feet, four inches tall, with thick salt-and-pepper hair and a handsome, craggy face, he carried off his Douglas Fairbanks imitation without any hint of self-consciousness. It was a quality George had tried to emulate his whole life.

Prescott adjusted the sheet music and swiveled his piano stool around. He waved at the sofa against the wall beneath his shelf of golfing trophies and photos of the Yale Glee Club. "Sit down, son. I'm glad you could make it. I know you must have a lot on your mind."

George remained standing. "What did you want to see me about?"

"Relax, George. This isn't the dentist's office."

"If it were, I would know what to expect."

"Well, one thing you can expect is to hear me tell you how proud I am."

"Proud? Did you see that game yesterday?"

Prescott Bush waved a hand. "Temporary setback. I'm sure you'll get them back this afternoon."

"Isn't it a little late for compliments?"

Prescott looked at him as calmly as if he were appraising some stock portfolio. His bushy eyebrows quirked a little higher. "George, I want you to sit down and shut up."

Despite himself, George sat. Prescott got up and paced to the window, looked down at the street, then started pacing again, his big hands knotted behind his back. George began to dread what was coming.

"George, I have been indulgent of you. Your entire life, despite my misgivings, I have treated you with kid gloves. You are not a stupid boy; at least your grades in school suggested you weren't. You've got that Phi Beta Kappa key, too—which only goes to show you what they are worth." He held himself very erect. "How old are you now?"

"Thirty-five."

Prescott shook his head. "Thirty-five? Lord. At *thirty-five* you show no more sense than you did at seventeen, when you told me that you intended to enlist in the Navy. Despite the fact, that the secretary of war himself, God-forbid-me, *Franklin D. Roosevelt*'s secretary of war, had just told the graduating class that you, the cream of the nation's youth, could best serve your country by going to college instead of getting shot up on some Pacific Island."

He strolled over to the piano, flipped pensively through the sheet music on top. "I remember saying to myself that day that maybe you knew something I didn't. You were young. I recalled my own recklessness in the first war. God knew we needed to lick the Japanese. But that didn't mean a boy of your parts and prospects should do the fighting. I prayed you'd survive and that by the time you came back you'd have grown some sense." Prescott closed the folder of music and faced him.

George, as he had many times before, instead of looking into his father's eyes looked at a point beyond his left ear. At the moment, just past that ear he could see half of a framed photograph of one of his father's singing groups. Probably the Silver Dollar Quartet. He could not make out the face of the man on the end of the photo. Some notable businessman, no doubt. A man who sat on four boards of directors making decisions that could topple the economies of six banana republics while he went to the club to shoot eight-handicap golf. Someone like Prescott Bush.

"When you chose this baseball career," his father said, "I finally realized you had serious problems facing reality. I would think the dismal history of your involvement in this sport might have taught you something. Now, by the grace of God and sheer luck you find yourself, on the verge of your middle years, in the spotlight. I can't imagine how it happened. But I know one thing: you must take advantage of this situation. You must seize the brass ring before the carousel stops. As soon as the Series is over, I want you to take up a career in politics."

George stopped looking at the photo. His father's eyes were on his. "Politics? But, Dad, I thought I could become a coach."

"A coach?"

"A coach. I don't know anything about politics. I'm a baseball player. Nobody is going to elect a baseball player."

Prescott Bush stepped closer. He made a fist, beginning to be carried away by his own rhetoric. "Twenty years ago, maybe, you would be right. But, George, times are changing. People want an attractive face. They want somebody famous. It doesn't matter so much on what they've done before. Look at Eisenhower. He had no experience of government. The only reason he got elected was because he was a war hero. Now you're a war hero, or at least we can dress you up into a reasonable facsimile of one. You're Yale educated, a brainy boy. You've got breeding and class. You're not bad looking. And thanks to this children's game, you're famous—for the next two weeks, anyway. So after the Series we strike while the iron's hot. You retire from baseball. File for Congress on the Republican ticket in the third Connecticut district."

"But I don't even live in Connecticut."

"Don't be contrary, George. You're a baseball player; you live on the road. Your last stable residence before you took up this, this—baseball—was New Haven. I've held an apartment there for years in your name. That's good enough for the people we're going to convince."

His father towered over him. George got up, retreated toward the window. "But I don't know anything about politics!"

"So? You'll learn. Despite the fact I've been against your playing baseball, I have to say that it will work well for you. It's the national game. Every kid in the country wants to be a ballplayer, most of the adults do, too. It's hard enough for people from our class to overcome the prejudice against money, George. Baseball gives you the common touch. Why, you'll probably be the only Republican in the Congress ever to have showered with a Negro. On a regular basis, I mean."

"I don't even like politics."

"George, there are only two kinds of people in the world, the employers and the employees. You were born and bred to the former. I will not allow you to persist in degrading yourself into one of the latter."

"Dad, really, I appreciate your trying to look out for me. Don't get me wrong, gratitude's my middle name. But I love baseball. There's some big opportunities there, I think. Down in Chattanooga I made some friends. I think I can be a good coach, and eventually I'll wear a manager's uniform."

Prescott Bush stared at him. George remembered that look when he'd forgotten to tie off the sailboat one summer up in Kennebunkport. He began to wilt. Eventually his father shook his head. "It comes to me at last that you do not possess the wits that God gave a Newfoundland retriever."

George felt his face flush. He looked away. "You're just jealous because I did what you never had the guts to do. What about you and your golf? You, you— dilettante! I'm going to be a manager!"

"George, if I want to I can step into that outer office, pick up the telephone, and in fifteen minutes set in motion a chain of events that will guarantee you won't get a job mopping toilets in the clubhouse."

George retreated to the window. "You think you can run my life? You just want me to be another appendage of Senator Bush. Well, you can forget it! I'm not your boy anymore."

"You'd rather spend the rest of your life letting men like this Communist Castro make a fool of you?"

George caught himself before he could completely lose his temper. Feeling hopeless, he drummed his knuckles on the window sill, staring down into the narrow street. Down below them brokers and bankers hustled from meeting to meeting trying to make a buck. He might have been one of them. Would his father have been any happier?

He turned. "Dad, you don't know anything. Try for once to understand. I've never been so alive as I've been for moments—just moments out of eleven years—on the ball field. It's truly American."

"I agree with you, George—it's as American as General Motors. Baseball is a product. You players are the assembly-line workers who make it. But you refuse to understand that, and that's your undoing. Time eats you up, and you end up in the dustbin, a wasted husk."

George felt the helpless fury again. "Dad, you've got to—"

"Are you going to tell me I *have to* do something, George?" Prescott Bush sat back down at the piano, tried a few notes. He peeked over his shoulder at George, unsmiling, and began again to sing:

Go and do your best endeavor,
And before all links we sever,
We will say farewell for ever
Go to glory and the grave!

"For your foes are fierce and ruthless,
False, unmerciful and truthless.
Young and tender, old and toothless,
All in vain their mercy crave.

George stalked out of the room, through the secretary's office, and down the corridor toward the elevators. It was all he could do to keep from punching his fist through the rosewood paneling. He felt his pulse thrumming in his temples, slowing as he waited for the dilatory elevator to arrive, rage turning to depression.

Riding down he remembered something his mother had said to him twenty years before. He'd been one of the best tennis players at the River Club in Kennebunkport. One summer, in front of the whole family, he lost a championship match. He knew he'd let them down, and tried to explain to his mother that he'd only been off his game.

"You don't have a game," she'd said.

The elevator let him out into the lobby. On Seventh Avenue, he stepped into a bar and ordered a beer. On the TV in the corner, sound turned low, an announcer was going over the highlights of the Series. The TV switched to an image of some play in the field. George heard a reference to "Senator Bush," but he couldn't tell which one of them they were talking about.

10

A few of the pitchers, including Camilo Pascual, the young right hander who was to start game five, were the only others in the clubhouse when George showed up. The tone was grim. Nobody wanted to talk about how their season might be over in a few hours. Instead they talked fishing.

Pascual was nervous; George was keyed tighter than a Christmas toy. Ten years of obscurity, and now hero one day, goat the next. The memory of his teammates' hollow words of encouragement as he'd slumped back into the dugout each time Castro struck him out made George want to crawl into his locker and hide. The supercilious brown bastard. What kind of man would go out of his way to humiliate him?

Stobbs sauntered in, whistling. He crouched into a batting stance, swung an imaginary Louisville Slugger through Kralick's head, then watched it sail out into the imaginary bleachers. "Hey, guys, I got an idea," he said. "If we get the lead today, let's call time out."

But they didn't get the lead. By the top of the second, they were down 3–0. Pascual, on the verge of being yanked, settled down. The score stayed frozen through six. The Senators finally got to Jones in the seventh when Allison doubled and Killebrew hit a towering home run into the bullpen in left center: 3–2, Giants. Meanwhile the Senators' shaky relief pitching held as the Giants stranded runners in the sixth and eighth and hit three double plays.

By the top of the ninth the Giants still clung to the 3–2 lead, three outs away from winning the Series, and the rowdy New York fans were gearing up for a celebration. The Senator dugout was grim, but they had the heart of the order up: Sievers, Lemon, Killebrew. Between them they had hit ninety-four home runs that season. They had also struck out almost three hundred times.

Rigney went out to talk to Jones, then left him in, though he had Stu Miller up and throwing in the bullpen. Sievers took the first pitch for a strike, fouled off the second, and went down swinging at a high fastball. The crowd roared.

Lemon went into the hole 0–2, worked the count even, and grounded out to second.

The crowd, on their feet, chanted continuously now. Fans pounded on the dugout roof, and the din was deafening. Killebrew stepped into the batter's box, and George moved up to the on-deck circle. On one knee in the dirt, he bowed his head and prayed that Killer would get on base.

"He's praying!" Castro shouted from the Giants' dugout. "Well might you pray, Sen-a-tor Bush!"

Killebrew called time and spat toward the Giants. The crowd screamed abuse at him. He stepped back into the box. Jones went into his windup. Killebrew took a tremendous cut and missed. The next pitch was a change-up that Killebrew mistimed and slammed five hundred feet down the left-field line into the upper deck—foul. The crowd quieted. Jones stepped off the mound, wiped his brow, shook off a couple of signs, and threw another fastball that Killebrew slapped into right for a single.

That was it for Jones. Rigney called in Miller. Lavagetto came out and spoke to George. "All right. He won't try anything tricky. Look for the fastball."

George nodded, and Lavagetto bounced back into the dugout. "Come on, George Herbert Walker Bush!" Consolo called. George tried to ignore the crowd and the Giants' heckling, while Miller warmed up. His stomach was tied into twelve knots. He avoided looking into the box seats where he knew his father sat. Politics. What the blazes did he want with politics?

Finally, Miller was ready. "Play ball!" the ump yelled. George stepped into the box.

He didn't wait. The first pitch was a fastball. He turned on it, made contact, but got too far under it. The ball soared out into left, a high, lazy fly. George slammed down his bat and, heart sinking, legged it out. The crowd cheered, and Alou circled back to make the catch. George was rounding first, his head down, when he heard a stunned groan from fifty thousand throats at once. He looked up to see Alou slam his glove to the ground. Miller, on the mound, did the same. The Senators' dugout was leaping insanity. Somehow, the ball had carried far enough to drop into the overhanging upper deck, 250 feet away. Home run. Senators lead, 4–3.

"Lucky bastard!" Castro shouted as Bush rounded third. Stobbs shut them down in the ninth, and the Senators won.

11

SENATOR BUSH SAVES WASHINGTON! the headlines screamed. MAKES CASTRO SEE RED. They were comparing it to the 1923 Series, held in these same Polo Grounds, where Casey Stengel, a thirty-two-year-old outfielder who'd spent twelve years in the majors without doing anything that might cause anyone to remember him, batted .417 and hit home runs to win two games.

Reporters stuck to him like flies on sugar. The pressure of released humiliation loosened George's tongue. "I know Castro's type," he said, snarling what he hoped was a good imitation of a manly snarl. "At the wedding he's the bride, at the funeral he's the dead person. You know, the corpse. That kind of poor sportsmanship just burns me up. But I've been around. He can't get my goat because of where I've got it in the guts department."

The papers ate it up. Smart money had said the Series would never go back to Washington. Now they were on the train to Griffith Stadium, and if the Senators were going to lose, at least the home fans would have the pleasure of going through the agony in person.

Game six was a slugfest. Five homers: McCovey, Mays, Cepeda for the Giants; Naragon and Lemon for the Senators. Kaat and Antonelli were both knocked out early. The lead changed back and forth three times.

George hit three singles, a sacrifice fly, and drew a walk. He scored twice. The Senators came from behind to win, 10–8. In the ninth, George sprained his ankle sliding into third. It was all he could do to hobble into the locker room after the game.

"It doesn't hurt," George told the reporters. "Bar always says, and she knows me better than anybody, go ahead and ask around, 'You're the game one, George.' Not the gamy one, mind you!" He laughed, smiled a crooked smile.

"A man's gotta do what a man's gotta do," he told them. "That strong but silent type of thing. My father said so."

12

Fonseca waited until Fidel emerged into the twilight outside the Fifth Street stadium exit. As Fonseca approached, his hand on the slick automatic in his overcoat pocket, his mind cast back to their political years in Havana, where young men such as they, determined to seek prominence, would be as likely to face the barrel of a pistol as an electoral challenge. Ah, nostalgia.

"Pretty funny, that *Sen*-a-TOR Bush," Fonseca said. He shoved Fidel back toward the exit. Nobody was around.

If Fidel was scared, a slight narrowing of his eyes was the only sign. "What is this about?"

"Not a thing. Raul says hello."

"Hello to Raul."

"Mirta says hello, too."

"You haven't spoken to her." Fidel took a cigar from his mohair jacket, fished a knife from a pocket, trimmed off the end, and lit it with a battered Zippo. "She doesn't speak with exiled radicals. Or mobsters."

Fonseca was impressed by the performance. "Are you going to do this job, finally?"

"I can only do my half. One cannot make a sow look like a ballet dancer."

"It is not apparent to our friends that you're doing your half."

"Tell them I am truly frightened, Luis." He blew a plume of smoke. It was dark now, almost full night. "Meanwhile, I am hungry. Let me buy you a Washington dinner."

The attitude was all too typical of Fidel, and Fonseca was sick of it. He had fallen under Fidel's spell back in the university, thought him some sort of great man. In 1948, his self-regard could be justified as necessary boldness. But when the head of the National Sports Directory was shot dead in the street, Fonseca had not been the only one to think Fidel was the killer. It was a gesture of suicidal machismo of the sort that Fidel admired. Gunmen scoured the streets for them. While Fonseca hid in a series of airless apartments, Fidel got a quick tryout with the Giants, married Mirta, and abandoned Havana, leaving Fonseca and their friends to deal with the consequences.

"If you don't take care, Fidel, our friends will buy you a Washington grave."

"They are not my friends—or yours."

"No, they aren't. But this was our choice, and you have to go through with it." Fonseca watched a beat cop stop at the corner, then turn away down the street. He moved closer, stuck the pistol into Fidel's ribs. "You know, Fidel, I have a strong desire to shoot you right now. Who cares about the World Series? It would be pleasant just to see you bleed."

The tip of Fidel's cigar glowed in the dark. "This Bush would be no hero then."

"But I would be."

"You would be a traitor."

Fonseca laughed. "Don't say that word again. It evokes too many memories." He plucked the cigar from Fidel's hand, threw it onto the sidewalk. "Athletes should not smoke."

He pulled the gun back, drew his hand from his overcoat, and crossed the street.

13

The night before, the Russians announced they had shot down U.S. spy plane over the Soviet Union. A pack of lies, President Nixon said. No such planes existed.

Meanwhile, on the clubhouse radio, a feverish announcer was discussing strategy for game seven. A flock of telegrams had arrived to urge the Senators on. Tacked on the bulletin board in the locker room, they gave pathetic glimpses into the hearts of the thousands who had for years tied their sense of well-being to the fate of a punk team like the Senators.

Show those racially polluted commie-symps what Americans stand for.

My eight year old son, crippled by polio, sits up in his wheel chair so that he can watch the games on TV.

Jesus Christ, creator of the heavens and earth, is with you.

As George laced up his spikes over his aching ankle in preparation for the game, thinking about facing Castro one last time, it came to him that he was terrified.

In the last week, he had entered an atmosphere he had not lived in since Yale. He was a hero. People had expectations of him. He was admired and courted. If he had received any respect before, it was the respect given to someone who refused to quit when every indication shouted he ought to try something else. He did not have the braggadocio of a Castro. Yet here, miraculously, he was shining.

Except he *knew* that Castro was better than he was, and he *knew* that anybody who really knew the game knew it, too. He knew that this week was a fluke, a strange conjunction of the stars that had knocked him into the "groove," as the old man in the bar had said. It could evaporate at any instant. It could already have evaporated.

Lavagetto and Mr. Griffith came in and turned off the radio. "Okay, boys," Lavagetto said. "People in this city been waiting a long time for this game. A lot of you been waiting your whole careers for it, and you younger ones might not get a lot of chances to play in the seventh game of the World Series. Nobody gave us a chance to be here today, but here we are. Let's make the most of it, go out there and kick the blazes out of them, then come back in and drink some champagne!"

The team whooped and headed out to the field. Coming up the tunnel, the sound of cleats scraping damp concrete, the smell of stale beer and mildew, Bush could see a sliver of the bright grass and white baselines, the outfield fence and crowds in the bleachers, sunlight so bright it hurt his eyes. When the team climbed the dugout steps onto the field, a great roar rose from the throats of the thirty thousand fans. He had never heard anything so beautiful, or frightening. The concentrated focus of their hope swelled George's chest with unnamable emotion, brought tears to his eyes, and he ducked his head and slammed his fist into his worn first baseman's glove.

The teams lined up on the first- and third-base lines for the National Anthem. The fans began cheering even before the last line of the song faded away, and George jogged to first, stepping on the bag for good luck. His ankle twinged; his whole leg felt hot. Ramos finished his warmups, the umpire yelled "Play ball!" and they began.

Ramos sent the Giants down in order in the top of the first. In the home half Castro gave up a single to Allison, who advanced to third on a single by Lemon. Killebrew walked. Bush came up with bases loaded, one out. He managed a fly ball to right, and Allison beat the throw to the plate. Castro struck out Bertoia to end the inning. 1–0, Senators.

Ramos retired the Giants in order in the second. In the third, Lemon homered to make it 2–0.

Castro had terrific stuff, but seemed to be struggling with his control. Or else he was playing games again. By the fourth inning he had seven strikeouts to go along with the two runs he'd given up. He shook off pitch after pitch, and Schmidt went out to argue with him. Rigney talked to him in the dugout, and the big Cuban waved his arms as if emphatically arguing his case.

Schmidt homered for the Giants in the fourth, but Ramos was able to get out of the inning without further damage. Senators, 2–1.

In the bottom of the fourth, George came up with a man on first. Castro struck him out on a high fastball that George missed by a foot.

In the Giants' fifth, Spencer doubled off the wall in right. Alou singled him home to tie the game, and one out later, Mays launched a triple over Allison's head into the deepest corner of center field, just shy of the crazy wall protecting Mrs. Mahan's backyard. Giants up, 3–2. The crowd groaned. As he walked out to the mound, Lavagetto was already calling for a left-hander to face McCovey. Ramos kicked the dirt, handed him the ball, and headed to the showers, and Stobbs came on to pitch to McCovey. He got McCovey on a grounder to George at first, and Davenport on a pop fly.

The Senators failed to score in the bottom of the fifth and sixth, but in the seventh George, limping for real now, doubled in Killer to tie the game, and was driven home, wincing as he forced weight down on his ankle, on a single by Naragon. Senators 4–3. The crowd roared.

Rigney came out to talk to Castro, but Castro convinced him to let him stay in. He'd struck out twelve already, and the Giants' bullpen was depleted after the free-for-all in game six.

The score stayed that way through the eighth. By the top of the ninth the crowd was going wild in the expectation of a world championship. Lavagetto had pulled Stobbs, who sat next to Bush in his warmup jacket, and put in the right-hander Hyde, who'd led the team in saves.

The Giants mounted another rally. On the first pitch, Spencer laid a bunt down the first-base line. Hyde stumbled coming off the mound, and George, taken completely by surprise, couldn't get to it on his bad foot. He got up limping, and the trainer came out to ask him if he could play. George was damned if he would let it end so pitifully, and shook him off. Alou grounded to first, Spencer advancing. Cepeda battled the count full, then walked.

Mays stepped into the box. Hyde picked up the rosin bag, walked off the mound, and rubbed up the ball. George could see he was sweating. He stepped back onto the rubber, took the sign, and threw a high fastball that Mays hit four hundred feet, high into the bleachers in left. The Giants leapt out of the dugout, slapping Mays on the back, congratulating each other. The fans tore their clothing in despair, slumped into their seats, cursed and moaned. The proper order had been restored to the universe. George looked over at Castro, who sat in the dugout impassively. Lavagetto came out to talk to Hyde; the crowd booed when the manager left him in, but Hyde managed to get them out of the inning without further damage. As the Senators left the field, the organist tried to stir the crowd, but despair had settled over them like a lead blanket. Giants, 6–4.

In the dugout, Lavagetto tried to get them up for the inning. "This is it, gentlemen. Time to prove we belong here."

Allison had his bat out and was ready to go to work before the umpire had finished sweeping off the plate. Castro threw three warmups and waved him into the box. When Allison lined a single between short and third, the crowd cheered and rose to their feet. Sievers, swinging for the fences, hit a nubbler to the mound, a sure double play. Castro pounced on it in good time, but fumbled the ball, double-clutched, and settled for the out at first. The fans cheered.

Rigney came out to talk it over. He and Schmidt stayed on the mound a long time, Castro gesturing wildly, insisting he wasn't tired. He had struck out the side in the eighth.

Rigney left him in, and Castro rewarded him by striking out Lemon for his seventeenth of the game, a new World Series record. Two down. Killebrew was up. The fans hovered on the brink of nervous collapse. The Senators were torturing them; they were going to drag this out to the last fatal out, not give them a clean killing or a swan-dive fade—no, they would hold out the chance of victory to the last moment, then crush them dead.

Castro rubbed up the ball, checked Allison over his shoulder, shook off a couple of Schmidt's signs, and threw. He got Killebrew in an 0–2 hole, then threw four straight balls to walk him. The crowd noise reached a frenzy.

And so, as he stepped to the plate in the bottom of the ninth, two outs, George Herbert Walker Bush represented the winning run, the potential end to twenty-seven years of Washington frustration, the apotheosis of his life in baseball, or the ignominious end of it. Castro had him set up again, to be the glorious goat for the entire Series. His ankle throbbed. "Cmon, Senator!" Lavagetto shouted. "Make me a genius!"

Castro leaned forward, shook off Schmidt's call, shook off another. He went into his windup, then paused, ball hidden in his glove, staring soberly at George— not mocking, not angry, certainly not intimidated—as if he were looking down from a reconnaissance plane flying high above the ballpark. George tried not to imagine what he was thinking.

Then Castro lifted his knee, strode forward, and threw a fat hanging curve, the sweetest, dopiest, laziest pitch he had thrown all day. George swung. As he did, he felt the last remaining strength of the dying Babe Ruth course down his arms. The ball kissed off the sweet spot of the bat and soared, pure and white as a six-year-old's prayer, into the left-field bleachers.

The stands exploded. Fans boiled onto the field even before George touched second. Allison did a kind of hopping balletic dance around the bases ahead of him, a cross between Nureyev and a man on a pogo stick. The Senators ran out of the dugout and bear-hugged George as he staggered around third; like a broken-field runner he struggled through the fans toward home. A weeping fat man in a plaid shirt, face contorted by ecstasy, blocked his way to the plate, and it was all he could do to keep from knocking him over.

As his teammates pulled him toward the dugout, he caught a glimpse over his shoulder of the Franchise standing on the mound, watching the melee and George at the center of it with an inscrutable expression on his face. Then George was pulled back into the maelstrom and surrendered to his bemused joy.

14

Long after everyone had left and the clubhouse was deserted, Fidel dressed, and instead of leaving walked back out to the field. The stadium was dark, but in the light of the moon he could make out the trampled infield and the obliterated base paths. He stood on the mound and looked around at the empty stands. He was about to leave when someone called him from the dugout. "Beautiful, isn't it?" Fidel approached. It was a thin man in his sixties. He wore a sporty coat and a white dress shirt open at the collar. "Yes?" Fidel asked.

"The field is beautiful."

Fidel sat next to him on the bench. They stared across the diamond. The wind rustled the trees beyond the outfield walls. "Some people think so," Fidel said.

"I thought we might have a talk," the man said. "I've been waiting around the ballpark before the last few games trying to get hold of you."

"I don't think we have anything to talk about, Mr . . ."

"Weaver. Buck Weaver."

"Mr. Weaver. I don't know you, and you don't know me."

The man came close to smiling. "I know about winning the World Series. And losing it. I was on the winning team in 1917, and the losing one in 1919."

"You would not be kidding me, old man?"

"No. For a long time after the second one, I couldn't face a ball park. Especially during the Series. I might have gone to quite a few, but I couldn't make myself do it. Now I go to the games every chance I get."

"You still enjoy baseball."

"I love the game. It reminds me of where my body is buried." As he said all of this the man kept smiling, as if it were a funny story he was telling, and a punch line waited in the near future.

"You should quit teasing me, old man," Fidel said. "You're still alive."

"To all outward indications I'm alive, most of the year now. For a long time I was dead the year round. Eventually I was dead only during the summer, and now it's come down to just the Series."

"You are the mysterious one. Why do you not simply tell me what you want with me?"

"I want to know why you did what you just did."

"What did I do?"

"You threw the game."

Fidel watched him. "You cannot prove that."

"I don't have to prove it. I know it, though."

"How do you know it?"

"Because I've seen it done before."

From somewhere in his boyhood, Fidel recalled the name now. Buck Weaver. The 1919 Series. "The Black Sox. You were one of them."

That appeared to be the punch line. The man smiled. His eyes were set in painful nets of wrinkles. "I was never one of them. But I knew about it, and that was enough for that bastard Landis to kick me out of the game."

"What does that have to do with me?"

"At first I wanted to stop you. Now I just want to know why you did it. Are you so blind to what you've got that you could throw it away? You're not a fool. Why?"

"I have my reasons, old man. Eighty thousand dollars, for one."

"You don't need the money."

"My brother in prison does. The people in my home do."

"Don't give me that. You don't really care about them."

Fidel let the moment stretch, listening to the rustling of the wind through the trees, the traffic in the distant street. "No? Well, perhaps. Perhaps I did it just because I could. Because the game betrayed me, because I wanted to show it is as corrupt as the *mierda* around it. It's not any different from the world. You know how it works. How every team has two black ballplayers—the star and the star's roommate." He laughed. "It's not a religion, and this place"— he gestured at Griffith Stadium looming in the night before them—"is not a cathedral."

"I thought that way, when I was angry," Weaver said. "I was a young man. I didn't know how much it meant to me until they took it away."

"Old man, you would have lost it regardless. How old were you? Twenty-five? Thirty? In ten years it would have been taken from you anyway, and you'd be in the same place you are now."

"But I'd have my honor. I wouldn't be a disgrace."

"That's only what other people say. Why should you let their ignorance affect who you are?"

"Brave words. But I've lived it. You haven't—yet." Plainly upset, Weaver walked out onto the field to stand at third base. He crouched; he looked in toward the plate. After a while he straightened, a frail old man, and called in toward Fidel: "When I was twenty-five, I stood out here; I thought I had hold of a baseball in my hand. It turned out it had hold of me."

He came back and stood at the top of the dugout steps. "Don't worry, I'm not going to tell. I didn't then, and I won't now."

Weaver left, and Fidel sat in the dugout.

15

They used the photo of George's painfully shy, crooked smile, a photograph taken in the locker room after he'd been named MVP of the 1959 World Series, on his first campaign poster.

In front of the photographers and reporters, George was greeted by Mr. Griffith. And his father. Prescott Bush wore a political smile as broad as his experience of what was necessary to impress the world. He put his arm around his son's shoulders, and although George was a tall man, it was apparent that his father was still a taller one.

"I'm proud of you, son," Prescott said, in a voice loud enough to be heard by everyone. "You've shown the power of decency and persistence in the face of hollow boasts."

Guys were spraying champagne, running around with their hair sticky and their shirts off, whooping and shouting and slapping each other on the back. Even his father's presence couldn't entirely deflect George's satisfaction. He had done it. Proved himself for once and for all. He wished Bar and the boys could be there. He wanted to shout in the streets, to stay up all night, be pursued by beautiful women. He sat in front of his locker and patiently answered the reporters' questions at length, repeatedly. Only gradually did the furor settle down. George glanced across the room to the brightly lit corner where Prescott was talking, oil camera, with a television reporter.

It was clear that his father was setting him up for this planned political career. It infuriated him that he assumed he could control George so easily, but at the same time George felt confused about what he really wanted for himself. As he sat there in the diminishing chaos, Lavagetto came over and sat down beside him. The manager was still high from the victory.

"I don't believe it!" Lavagetto said. "I thought he was crazy, but old Tricky Dick must have known something I didn't!"

"What do you mean?"

"Mean?—nothing. Just that the President called after the first game and told me to bat you behind Killebrew. I thought he was crazy. But it paid off."

George remembered Prescott Bush whispering into Nixon's ear. He felt a crushing weight on his chest. He stared over at his father in the TV lights, not hearing Lavagetto.

But as he watched, he wondered. If his father had indeed fixed the Series, then everything he'd accomplished came to nothing. But his father was an honorable man. Besides, Nixon was noted for his sports obsession, full of fantasies because he hadn't succeeded himself. His calling Lavagetto was the kind of thing he would do anyway. Winning had been too hard for it to be a setup. No, Castro had wanted to humiliate George, and George had stood up to him.

The reporter finished talking to his father; the TV lights snapped off. George thanked Lavagetto for the faith the manager had shown in him, and limped over to Prescott Bush.

"Feeling pretty good, George?"

"It was a miracle we won. I played above myself."

"Now, don't take what I said back in New York so much to heart. You proved yourself equal to the challenge, that's what." Prescott lowered his voice. "Have you thought any more about the proposition I put to you?"

George looked his father in the eye. If Prescott Bush felt any discomfort, there was no trace of it in his patrician's gaze.

"I guess maybe I've played enough baseball," George said.

His father put his hand on George's shoulder; it felt like a burden. George shrugged it off and headed for the showers.

Many years later, as he faced the Washington press corps in the East Room of the White House, George Herbert Walker Bush was to remember that distant afternoon, in the ninth inning of the seventh game of the World Series, when he'd stood in the batter's box against the Franchise. He had not known then what he now understood: that, like his father, he would do anything to win.

Max Apple's stories and essays have appeared in the *Atlantic Monthly, Harper's, Esquire* and *Best American* Stories, and he has published two collections, two books of non-fiction and two novels. He has received grants from the National Endowment for the Humanities, the National Endowment for the Arts, and the Guggenheim Foundation. He taught creative writing at Rice University for nearly thirty years and now teaches creative writing at the University of Pennsylvania. Apple is known for his quiet satire and sharp wit. In this story he reduces Fidel Castro and Cuba's troubled relationship with the United States to a few pitches and some dubious diplomacy on a makeshift baseball diamond in Oriente Province.

Understanding Alvarado

∞

Max Apple

I

CASTRO THOUGHT IT WAS no accident that Achilles "Archie" Alvarado held the world record for being hit in the head by a pitched ball.

"Because he was a hero even then," Fidel said, "because he stood like a hero with his neck proudly over the plate."

When people asked Mrs. Alvarado what she thought of her husband's career, she said, "Chisox okay, the rest of the league stinks. Archie, he liked to play every day, bench him and his knees ached, his fingers swelled, his tongue forgot English. He would say, 'Estelle, let's split, let's scram, *vámonos a* Cuba. What we owe to Chisox?'

"I'd calm him down. 'Arch,' I'd say, 'Arch, Chisox have been plenty good to us. Paid five gees more than Tribe, first-class hotels, white roomies on the road, good press.'

"'Estelle,' he would say, 'I can't take it no more. They got me down to clubbing in the pinch and only against southpaws. They cut Chico Carrasquel and Sammy Esposito and Cactus Bob Kuzava. What we owe to Chisox?'

"When it got like that, I would say, 'Talk to Zloto,' and Zloto would say, 'Man, you Latinos sure are hotheads. I once got nine hits in a row for the Birds, was

Rookie of the Year for the Bosox. I have the largest hands in either league and what do you think I do? I sit on the bench and spit-shine my street shoes. Look there, you can see your greasy black mug in 'em.' Zloto always knew how to handle Alvarado."

Zloto came to Havana, showed Fidel his hands, talked about the '50s. Fidel said, "They took our good men and put them in Yankee uniforms, in Bosox, Chisox, Dodgers, Birds. They took our manhood, Zloto. They took our Achilles and called him Archie. Hector Gonzalez they called Ramrod, Jesus Ortiz they made a Jayo. They treated Cuban manhood like a bowl of chicos and ricos. Yes, we have no bananas but we got vine-ripened Latinos who play good ball all year, stick their heads over the plate, and wait for the Revolution. Fidel Castro gave it to them. It was three and two on me in Camagüey around November 1960. There were less than two dozen of us. Batista had all roads blocked and there was hardly enough ammunition left to kill some rabbits. He could have starved us out but he got greedy, he wanted the quick inning. When I saw that he was coming in with his best stuff with his dark one out over the middle, I said to Che and to Francisco Muñiz, 'Habana for Christmas,' and I lined his fascist pitch up his capitalist ass."

"I'm not impressed," Zloto said. "When I heard about the Bay of Pigs I said to myself, 'Let's wipe those oinks right off the face of the earth.' You took Cuba, our best farm property, and went Commie with it. You took our best arms, Castro, our speed and our curve-ball artists. You dried up our Cuban diamonds."

"Zloto, Zloto," Fidel said. "Look at this picture of your buddy, 'Archie' Alvarado, Don't you like him better as 'Achilles'? Look at his uniform, look at his AK 47 rifle."

"I liked him better when he was number twenty-three and used a thirty-six-inch Hillerich and Bradsby Louisville Slugger to pound out line drives in Comiskey Park."

"There's no more Comiskey Park," Fidel said. "No more Grace, no more Chuck Comiskey to come down after a tough extra-inning loss and buy a drink for the whole clubhouse. No more free Bulova watches. The Chisox are run by an insurance company now. You punch a time clock before batting practice and they charge for overtime in the whirlpool bath."

"That's goddamn pinko propaganda," Zloto said.

"You've been outta the game, big Victor," Fidel said. "You've been sitting too long out in Arizona being a dental assistant. You haven't been on the old diamonds, now AstroTurfed, closed to the sun, and air-conditioned. You have not seen the bleachers go to two-fifty. While you've been in Arizona the world changed, Zloto. Look at our Achilles, four fractured skulls, thirteen years in the big time. Played all over the outfield, played first and played third. A lifetime mark of two ninety-nine and RBIs in the thousands. He never got an Achilles day from Chisox, Bosox, Tribe, or Birds. When he came home Fidel made him a day, made him a reservist colonel. I did this because Achilles Alvarado is not chickenshit. You, Zloto, know this better than anyone.

"Achilles said to me the first time we met, 'Fidel, the big time is over for Archie Alvarado, but send me to the cane fields, give me a machete, and I'll prove that Alvarado has enough arm left to do something for Cuba.' A hero, this Achilles 'Archie' Alvarado, but they sent him back to us a broken-down, used-up pinch hitter with no eye, no arm, and no speed.

"'Achilles, Archie,' I said, 'the Revolution was not made for Chisox, Bosox, Bengals, and Birds. We didn't take Habana for chicos and ricos. Cuba Libre doesn't give a flying fuck for RBIs. The clutch hit is every minute here, baby brother. Cuba loves you for your Cuban heart. I'll make you a colonel, a starter in the only game that counts. Your batting average will be counted in lives saved, in people educated, fed, and protected from capitalist exploitation.'"

"Cut the shit, Fidel," Zloto said. 'I'm here because Archie will be eligible for his pension in September. He'll pull in a thousand a month for the rest of his days. That'll buy a lot of bananas down here, won't it?

"You may think that you understand Alvarado, Fidel, but I knew the man for eight years, roomed with him on the Chisox and the Bosox. I've seen him high, seen him in slumps you wouldn't believe. I've seen him in the dugout after being picked off first in a crucial situation. You wouldn't know what that's like, Castro. I'm talking about a man who has just met a fast ball and stroked it over the infield. He has made the wide turn at first and watched the rosin of his footprint settle around the bag. He has thrown off the batting helmet and pulled the soft, longbilled cap from his hip pocket. The coach has slapped his ass and twenty, thirty, maybe forty thousand Chisox fans start stomping their feet while the organ plays 'Charge,' and then he is picked off in a flash, caught scratching his crotch a foot from the bag. And it's all over. You hear eighty thousand feet stop stomping. The first baseman snickers behind his glove; even the ump smiles. I've seen Alvarado at times like that cry like a baby. He'd throw a towel over his head and say, 'Zloto, I'm a no-good dummy. Good hit and no head. We coulda won it all here in the top of the ninth. That Yankee pitcher is good for shit. My dumbass move ruined the Chisox chances.' He would sit in front of his locker taking it real hard until the GM or even Chuck Comiskey himself would come down and say, 'Archie, it's just one game that you blew with a dumb move. We're still in it, still in the thick of the race. You'll help these Sox plenty during the rest of the year. Now take your shower and get your ass over to a Mexican restaurant.' The Alvarado that I knew, Castro, that Alvarado could come back the next afternoon, sometimes the next inning, and change the complexion of a game."

Fidel laughed and lit a cigar. "Zloto, you've been away too long. The Archie you knew, this man went out of style with saddle shoes and hula hoops. Since the days you're talking about when Alvarado cried over a pick-off play, since then Che and Muñiz are dead and two Kennedys assassinated. There have been wars in the Far East and Middle East and in Bangladesh. There have been campus shootings, a revolution of the Red Guard, an ouster of Khrushchev, a fascist massacre in Indonesia, two revolutions in Uruguay, fourteen additions to the U.N. There has been détente and Watergate and a Washington-Peking understanding and where have you been, Zloto? You've been in Tucson, Arizona, reading the newspaper on Sunday and cleaning teeth. Even dental techniques have changed. Look at your fluorides and your gum brushing method."

"All right, boys," Mrs. Alvarado said, "enough is enough. What are we going to prove anyway by reminiscing about the good old days? Zloto means well. He came here as a friend. Twelve grand a year for life is not small potatoes to Archie and me. In the Windy City or in Beantown we could live in a nice integrated neighborhood on that kind of money and pick up a little extra by giving autographs at Chevy dealerships. Fidel, you know that Archie always wanted to stay in the game. In one interview he told Bill Fuller of the *Sun-Times* that he wanted to manage the Chisox someday. They didn't want any black Cuban managers in the American League, not then. But, like you say, Fidel, a lot of water has gone under the bridge since those last days when Archie was catching slivers for the Bosox, Chisox, and Birds. These days, there might even be some kind of front-office job to round off that pension. Who knows, it might be more than he made twenty years ago when he led the league in RBIs."

Castro said, "Estelle, apart from all ideological arguments, you are just dreaming. Achilles was never a U.S. citizen. After a dozen years as one of Castro's colonels, do you really think Uncle Sam is going to say, 'C'mon up here, Archie, take a front-office job and rake in the cash'? Do you really think America works that way, Estelle? I know Zloto thinks that, but you've been down here all this time, don't you understand capitalist exploitation by now?"

Estelle said, "Fidel, I'm not saying that we are going to give up the ideals of the Revolution and I'm not deluded by the easy capitalist life. I am thinking about only getting what's coming to us. Alvarado put in the time, he should get the pension."

"That's the whole reason I took a week off to come down here," Zloto said. "The commissioner called me up—he heard we were buddies—and said, 'Zloto, you might be in a position to do your old friend Alvarado some good, that is if you're willing to travel.' The commissioner absolutely guaranteed that Archie would get his pension if he came back up and established residence. The commissioner of baseball is not about to start mailing monthly checks through the Swiss embassy, and I don't blame him. The commissioner is not even saying you have to stay permanently in the U.S. He is just saying, 'Come up, get an apartment, make a few guest appearances, an interview or two, and then do whatever the hell you want.'"

Fidel said, "Yes, go up to America and tell them how mean Fidel is, how bad the sugar crop was, and how poor and hungry we Cubans are. Tell them what they want to hear and they'll pension you off. The Achilles I know would swallow poison before he'd kowtow to the memory of John Foster Dulles that way. They sent an Archie back home, but Cuba Libre reminded him he was really an Achilles."

"Fidel, let's not get sentimental," Mrs. Alvarado said. "Let's talk turkey. We want the twelve grand a year, right?"

"Right, but only because it is the fruit of Achilles' own labor."

"Okay, in order to get the money we have to go back."

"I could take it up in the United Nations, I could put the pressure on. Kissinger is very shaky in Latin America. He knows we all know that he doesn't give a fuck about any country except Venezuela. I could do it through Waldheim, and nobody would have to know. Then we could threaten to go public if they hold out on what's coming to him."

Zloto said, "America doesn't hold out on anybody, Castro. Ask Joe Stalin's daughter if you don't believe me. You guys are batting your heads against the wall by hating us. There's nothing to hate. We want a square deal for everyone. In this case too. As for Kissinger, he might carry some weight with the Arabs, but the commissioner of baseball cannot be pressured. That damned fool Alvarado should have become a citizen while he was playing in the States. I didn't know he wasn't a citizen. It was just crazy not to become one. Every other Latin does."

"But our Achilles, he was always different," Castro said. "He always knew that the Chisox, Bosox, Birds, and Braves didn't own the real thing. The real Achilles Alvarado was in Camagüey with me, in Bolivia with Che, with Mao on the Long March."

"The real Achilles was just too lazy to do things right," Mrs. Alvarado said. "He didn't want to fill out complicated papers, so he stayed an alien. As long as he had a job, it didn't matter."

"Zloto," Fidel said, "you one-time Rookie of the Year, now a fat, tooth-cleaning capitalist, you want to settle this the way Achilles would settle this? I mean why should we bring in Kissinger and Waldheim and everyone else? I say if a man believes in the Revolution, what's a pension to him? You think I couldn't have been a Wall Street lawyer? And what about our Doctor Che? You don't think he would have made a big pension in the AMA? I say our Achilles has recovered his Cuban manhood. He won't want to go back. Estelle does not speak for him."

"Fidel is right," she said. "I do not speak for Archie Alvarado, only write his English for him."

"If Estelle wants to go back and be exploited, let her go. Do you want those television announcers calling you Mrs. Archie again as if you had stepped from the squares of a comic strip? Does the wife of a colonel in the Cuban Army sound like a comic-strip girl to you, Zloto?"

"Fidel," Estelle said, "don't forget the issue is not so large. Only a trip to the Windy City or Beantown, maybe less than two weeks in all."

"You are forgetting," Fidel said, "what happened to Kid Gavilan when he went back to see an eye surgeon in New York. They put his picture in *Sepia* and in the *National Enquirer*, the news services showed him with his bulging eye being hugged by a smooth-faced Sugar Ray Robinson. They wanted it to seem like this: here are two retired Negro fighters. One is a tap dancer in Las Vegas, the other has for ten years been working in the cane fields of Castro's Cuba. Look at how healthy the American Negro is. His teeth are white as ever, his step lithe in Stetson shoes, while our Kid Gavilan, once of the bolo punch that decked all welterweights, our Kid stumbles through the clinics of New York in worker's boots and his eye bulges from the excesses of the Revolution. They degraded the Kid and the Revolution and they sent him home with a red, white, and blue eye patch. That's how they treated Kid Gavilan, and they'll do the same to Achilles Alvarado."

"Well, goddamn," Zloto said, "I've had enough talk. I want to see Alvarado; whether he wants to do it is up to him."

"That," Castro said, "is typical bourgeois thinking. You would alienate the man from his fellows, let him think that his decision is personal and lonely, that it represents only the whims of an Alvarado and does not speak for the larger aspirations of all Cubans, and all exploited peoples. The wants of an Alvarado are the wants of the people. He is not a Richard Nixon to hide out in Camp David surrounded by bodyguards while generals all over the world are ready to press the buttons of annihilation."

"No more bullshit, I want to see Alvarado."

Estelle said, "He is in Oriente Province on maneuvers with the army. He will be gone for . . . for how long, Fidel?"

"Achilles Alvarado's unit is scheduled for six months in Oriente. I could bring him back to see you, Zloto, but we don't operate that way. A man's duty to his country comes before all else."

"Then I'm going up to see him and deliver the commissioner's letter. I don't trust anybody else around here to do it for me."

"We'll all go," Fidel said. "In Cuba Libre, no man goes it alone."

II: On Maneuvers in Oriente Province

The Ninth Infantry Unit of the Cuban Army is on spring maneuvers. Oriente is lush and hilly. There are villages every few miles in which happy farmers drink dark beer brewed with local hops. The Ninth Army bivouacs all over the province and assembles each morning at six a.m. to the sound of the bugle. The soldiers eat a leisurely breakfast and plan the next day's march. By two p.m., they are set up somewhere and ready for an afternoon of recreation. Colonel Alvarado is the only member of the Ninth Infantry with major-league experience, but there are a few older men who have played professional baseball in the minor leagues. Because there is no adequate protective equipment, army regulations prohibit hardball, but the Ninth Infantry plays fast-pitch softball, which is almost as grueling.

When Fidel, Zloto, and Estelle drive up to the Ninth Army's makeshift diamond, it is the seventh inning of a four-four game between the Reds and Whites. A former pitcher from Iowa City in the Three I League is on the mound for the Reds. Colonel Alvarado, without face guard or chest protector, is the umpire behind the plate. His head, as in the old days, seems extremely vulnerable as it bobs behind the waving bat just inches from the arc of a powerful swing. He counts on luck and fast reflexes to save him from foul tips that could crush his Adam's apple.

When the jeep pulls up, Reds and Whites come to immediate attention, then raise their caps in an "Olé" for Fidel.

"These are liberated men, Zloto. The army does not own their lives. When their duties are completed they can do as they wish. We have no bedchecks, no passes, nobody is AWOL. If a man has a reason to leave, he tells his officer and he leaves. With us, it is an honor to be a soldier."

When Zloto spots Alvarado behind the plate he runs toward him and hugs his old friend. He rubs Alvarado's woolly black head with his oversize hands. Estelle is next to embrace her husband, a short businesslike kiss, and then Fidel embraces the umpire as enthusiastically as Zloto did. An army photographer catches the look of the umpire surprised by embraces from an old friend, a wife, and a Prime Minister in the seventh inning of a close game.

"Men of the Revolution." Fidel has advanced to the pitcher's mound, the highest ground. The congregated Reds and Whites gather around the makeshift infield. "Men of the Revolution, we are gathered here to test the resolve of your umpire, Colonel Alvarado. The Revolution is tested in many ways. This time it is the usual thing, the capitalist lure of money. Yet it is no simple issue. It is money that rightfully belongs to Colonel Alvarado, but they would degrade him by forcing him to claim it. To come there so that the capitalist press can say, 'Look what the Revolution has done to one of the stars of the fifties. Look at his stooped, arthritic back, his gnarled hands, from years in the cane fields.' They never cared about his inadequate English when they used him, but now they will laugh at his accent and his paltry vocabulary. When they ask him about Cuba, he will stumble and they will deride us all with the smiles of their golden teeth.

"The commissioner of baseball has sent us this behemoth, the Polish-American veteran of eleven campaigns in the American League, Victor Zloto, who some of you may remember as Rookie of the Year in 1945. This Zloto is not an evil man, he is only a capitalist tool. They use his friendship for the colonel as a bait. Zloto speaks for free enterprise. He has two cars, a boat, and his own home. His province is represented by their hero of the right, Barry Goldwater, who wanted to bomb Hanoi to pieces. Zloto wants the colonel to come back, to go through the necessary charade to claim his rightful pension, and then return to us if he wishes. Mrs. Alvarado shares this view. I say no Cuban man should become a pawn for even one hour."

"What does the colonel say?" someone yells from the infield. "Does the colonel want to go back?"

The umpire is standing behind Castro. He is holding his wife's hand while Zloto's long arm encircles both of them. Castro turns to his colonel. "What do you say, Achilles Alvarado?"

Zloto says, "It's twelve grand a year, Archie, and all you have to do is show up just once. If you want to stay, you can. I know you don't like being a two-bit umpire and colonel down here. I know you don't give a shit about revolutions and things like that."

Castro says, "The colonel is thinking about his long career with the Chisox, Bosox, Tribe, and Birds. He is thinking about his four fractured skulls. He justifiably wants that pension. And I, his Prime Minister and his friend, I want him to have that pension, too. Believe me, soldiers, I want this long-suffering victim of exploitation to recover a small part of what they owe to him and to all victims of racism and oppression."

Colonel Alvarado grips tightly his wife's small hand. He looks down and kicks up clouds of dust with his army boots. He is silent. Zloto says, "It's not fair to do this, Castro. You damn well know it. You get him up here in front of the army and make a speech so it will look like he's a traitor if he puts in his pension claim. You staged all this because you are afraid that in a fair choice Archie would listen to reason just like Estelle did. You can bet that I'm going to tell the commissioner how you put Archie on the spot out here. I'm going to tell him that Archie is a softball umpire. This is worse than Joe Louis being a wrestling referee."

"Think fast, Yankee," one of the ballplayers yells as he lobs a softball at Zloto's perspiring face. The big first baseman's hand closes over the ball as if it were a large mushroom. He tosses it to Castro. "I wish we could play it out, Fidel, just you and I, like a world series or a one-on-one basketball game. I wish all political stuff could work out like baseball, with everybody where they belong at the end of the season and only one champion of the world."

"Of course, you would like that, Zloto, so long as you Yankee capitalists were the champions."

"The best team would win. If you have the material and the management, you win; it's that simple."

"Not as simple as you are, Zloto. But why should we stand here and argue political philosophy? We are interrupting a game, no? You have accused Fidel of not giving Alvarado a fair opportunity. I will do this with you, Zloto, if Achilles agrees, I will do this. Fidel will pitch to you. If you get a clean hit, you can take Alvarado back on the first plane. If not, Alvarado stays. It will be more than fair. This gives you a great advantage. A former big leaguer against an out-of-shape Prime Minister. My best pitch should be cake for you. You can go back and tell the commissioner that you got a hit off Castro. Barry Goldwater will kiss your fingertips for that."

Zloto smiles. "You're on, Castro, if it's okay with Archie and Estelle." Colonel Alvarado still eyes the soft dirt; he shrugs his shoulders. Castro says, "Do you think this is a just experience for you, Achilles Alvarado? This is like a medieval tournament, with you as the prize. This smacks of capitalism. But this once, Fidel will do it if you agree that your fate shall be so decided."

"What's all this about fate and justice," Estelle says. She takes the ball from Castro. "Archie had eleven brothers and sisters and hardly a good meal until he came up to the Chisox. He cracked his wrist in an all-star game and that cost him maybe four or five years in the big leagues because the bones didn't heal right. It's a mean, impersonal world with everything always up for grabs. Alvarado knows it, and he accepts it. He is a religious man." She throws the ball to her Prime Minister. "Get it over with."

The teams take their places, with Castro replacing the Three I League pitcher. Zloto removes his jacket, shirt, and necktie. He is six five and weighs over 250. His chest hairs are gray, but he swings three bats smoothly in a windmill motion as he loosens his muscles. Castro warms up with the catcher. The Prime Minister has a surprisingly good motion, more sidearm than underhand. The ball comes in and sinks to a right-handed batter like Zloto. Colonel Alvarado takes his place behind home plate, which is a large army canteen.

"Achilles Alvarado," says Castro, "you wish to be the umpire in this contest?"

"Why not?" Zloto says. "It's his pension, let him call the balls and strikes. If it's a walk or an error, we'll take it over. Otherwise, a hit I win, an out you win."

"Play ball!" the umpire says. Castro winds up twice, and his first pitch is so far outside that the catcher diving across the plate cannot even lay his glove on the ball. Fidel stamps his foot.

"Ball one," says the umpire.

The infield is alive with chatter: "The old dark one, Fidel," they are yelling. "Relax, pitcher, this ox is an easy out, he can't see your stuff, there's eight of us behind you, Fidel, let him hit."

Zloto grins at the Prime Minister. "Put it down the middle, Mr. Pink, I dare you."

Fidel winds and delivers. Zloto's big hands swing the bat so fast that the catcher doesn't have a chance to blink. He has connected and the ball soars a hundred feet over the head of the left fielder who watches with astonishment the descending arc of the power-driven ball.

"Foul ball," says the umpire, eyeing the stretched clothesline which ended far short of where Zloto's fly ball dropped.

The power hitter grins again. "When I straighten one out, Castro, I'm gonna hit it clear out of Cuba. I never played in a little country before."

Castro removes his green army cap and runs his stubby fingers through his hair. He turns his back to the batter and looks toward his outfield. With a tired motion he orders his center fielder to move toward left center, then he signals all three outfielders to move deeper, Estelle Alvarado stands in foul territory down the first-base line, almost in the spot of her complimentary box seat at the Chisox home games.

Zloto is measuring the outside corner of the canteen with a calm, deliberate swing. He does not take his eyes off the pitcher. Castro winds and delivers another wild one, high and inside. Zloto leans away but the ball nicks his bat and dribbles into foul territory, where Estelle picks it up and throws it back to Castro.

"One ball, two strikes," says the umpire.

"Lucky again, Castro," the batter calls out, "but it only takes one, that's all I need from you."

The Prime Minister and the aging Rookie of the Year eye one another across the sixty feet from mound to plate. Castro rubs the imagined gloss from the ball and pulls at his army socks. With the tip of a thin Cuban softball bat, Zloto knocks the dirt from the soles of his Florsheim shoes. The infielders have grown silent. Castro looks again at his outfield and behind it at the green and gentle hills of Oriente Province. He winds and delivers a low, fast ball.

"Strike three," says the umpire. Zloto keeps his bat cocked. Estelle Alvarado rushes to her husband. She is crying hysterically. Fidel runs in at top speed to embrace both Alvarados at home plate. Zloto drops the bat. "It was a fair call, Archie," he says to the umpire. "I got caught looking."

"Like Uncle Sam," Castro says as the soldiers stream in yelling, "Fidel, Fidel, the strike-out artist." Castro waves his arms for silence.

"Not Fidel, men, but Achilles Alvarado, a hero of the Cuban people. A light for the Third World."

"Third World for Alvarado. Third strike for Zloto," an infielder shouts as the Ninth Army raises Fidel, Achilles, and Estelle to their shoulders in a joyful march down the first-base line. The Prime Minister, the umpire, and the lady gleam in the sun like captured weapons.

Zloto has put on his shirt and tie. He looks now like a businessman, tired after a long day at a convention. Fidel is jubilant among his men. The umpire tips his cap to the army and calms his wife, still tearful atop the bobbing shoulders of the Cuban Ninth.

"Alvarado," Estelle says, "you honest ump, you Latin patriot, you veteran of many a clutch situation. Are you happy, you fractured skull?"

"Actually," Alvarado whispers in her ear, "the pitch was a little inside. But what the hell, it's only a game."

Bruce McAllister taught literature and writing at the University of Redlands in Southern California for twenty-four years, and helped establish and direct the Creative Writing Program. He was the Edith R. White Distinguished Professor of Literature and Writing from 1990 to 1995. Known primarily for his short stories, McAllister has published several dozen short stories in a variety of mainstream and genre magazines and he has been a finalist for both the Nebula and Hugo awards. Here, as others in this collection have done, he takes a counterfactual look at a Fidel Castro who in this story is a famous, if fading, baseball player, and one who must wrestle with his dreams in any of several ways as he talks with another Cuban star about life in America and life back home.

The Southpaw

∽

Bruce McAllister

Eventually New York Giants' scout Alex Pompez got the authorization from their front office to offer Castro a contract. After several days of deliberation with friends, family, and some of his professors, Castro turned down the offer. The Giants' officials were stunned. "No one had ever turned us down from Latin America before," recalled Pompez. "Castro said no, but in his very polite way. He was really a very nice kid. . . ."

—J. David Truby, *Sports History*, November 1988

FIDEL STANDS ON THE pitcher's mound, dazed. For an instant he doesn't know where he is. It *is* a pitcher's mound. It *is* a baseball diamond, and there is a woman—the woman he loves—out there in the stands with her beautiful blonde hair and her very American name waving to him, because she loves him, too. It is *July*. He is sure of this. It is '51 or '52. He cannot remember which. But the crowd is as big as ever and he can smell the leather of his glove, and he knows he is playing baseball—the way, as a child in the sugarcane fields of Oriente Province, he always dreamed he might.

* * *

His fastball is a problem, but he throws one anyway, it breaks wide and the ump calls the ball. He throws a curve this time, a *fine* one, and it's a strike—the third. He grins at Westrum, his catcher, his friend. The next batter's up. Fidel feels an itching on his face and reaches up to scratch it. It feels like the beginning of a beard, but that can't be. You keep a clean face in baseball. He tried to tell his father that, in Oriente, the last time he went home, but the old man, as always, had just argued.

He delivers another curve—with *great* control—and smiles when the ball drops off the table and Sterling swings like an idiot. He muscles up on the pitch, blows the batter down with a heater, but Williams gets a double off the next slider, Miller clears the bases with a triple, and they bring Wilhelm in to relieve him at last. The final score is 9 to 4, just like the oddsmakers predicted, and that great centerfielder Mays still won't look at him in the lockers.

* * *

Nancy—her name is Nancy—is waiting for him at the back entrance when he's in his street clothes again, the flowered shirt and the white ducks he likes best, and she looks wonderful. She's chewing gum, which drives him crazy, but her skin is like a dream—like moonlight on the Mulano—and he kisses her hard, feeling her tongue between his lips. When they pull away she says: "I really like the way you walked that Negro in the fifth."

He smiles at her. He loves her so much it hurts. She doesn't know a damn thing about the game and nothing about Cuba, but she's doing her best and she loves him, too. "I do it for *you, chica*," he tells her. "I *always* do it for you."

That night he dreams he's in the mountains of the Sierra Maestra, at a place called La Playa. He has no idea why he's here. He's never dreamt this dream before. He's lying on the ground with a rifle in his hand. He's wearing the fatigues a soldier wears, and doesn't understand why—who the two men lying beside him are, what it means. The clothes he's wearing are rough. His face itches like hell.

When he wakes, she is beside him. The sheet has fallen away from her back, which is to him, and her ass—which is so beautiful, which any man would find beautiful—is there for him and him alone to see. *How can anything be more real than this? How can I be dreaming of such things?* He can hear a song fading but does not know it. There is a bay—a bay with naval ships—and the song is fading away.

Guantanamera . . . the voice was singing.

Yo soy un hombre sincero, it sang.

I am a truthful man.

Why, Fidel wonders, was it singing this?

* * *

After the game with the Cardinals on Saturday, when he pitches six innings before they bring Wilhelm in to relieve him and end up a little better than the oddsmakers had it, a kid comes up to him and wants his autograph. The kid is dark, like the children he played with on the *finca* his father owns—the ones that worked with their families during the cane harvest and sat beside him in the country school at Marcana between harvests. He knows this boy is Cuban, too.

"*Señor?*" the kid asks, holding up a baseball card. "*Por favor?*"

Fidel doesn't understand. It is a baseball card, sure. But whose? He takes it and sees himself. No one has told him—no one has told him there is a card with his face on it, something else he has always dreamed of. He remembers now. He has been playing for the Giants—this is his first year. The offer was a good one, with a five thousand dollar bonus for signing. Now he's on a baseball card. He tries to read it, but the words are small, Nancy has his glasses and he must squint. The words fill him with awe.

It says nothing about his fastball, and he is grateful. He smiles at the boy, whose eyes are on him. The father hands him a pen. "What's your name, *hijo?*" he asks. "Raul," the boys says. "*Me llamo Raul.*" *To Raul*, he writes. He writes it across his own face because that is where the room is. It is harder than hell writing on a card this small and he must kneel down, writing it on his knee. *May your dreams come true*, he also writes, putting it across his jersey now. He wants to write *And may your fastball be better than mine*, but there isn't any room. He gives the card back and returns the pen. The boy thanks him. The father nods, grinning. Fidel grins back. "*Muy guapo*," Fidel tells him. The man keeps nodding. "I mean it," Fidel says.

* * *

He dreams of a cane field near Allegria del Oio, to the north, of soldiers moving through the cane. He can't breathe. He is lying on the ground, he can't move, can't breathe. He's holding something in his hand—but what? None of it makes sense. There isn't any war in Cuba. Life in Cuba is peaceful, he knows. Fulgencio Batista, the President, is running it, and running it well. After Pirontes, how could he not? Relations with the United States are good. Who could possibly be hiding in the Sierra Maestra? Who could be lying in the cane with rifles in their hands, hiding from soldiers and singing a song about a *truthful man*?

After they have made love, after she has asked him to take her from behind first, then from the front, where they can see each other, after they've reached their most beautiful moment together, he tells her about his dream and she says: "Dreams aren't supposed to make sense, honey."

He can't believe she is a waitress. He cannot, even for a moment, believe that anyone this beautiful, this American in so many ways, is only a waitress. He wants her to stop working. He would rather have her watch television all day in the apartment or shop for nice clothes for herself than walk around in such a dull uniform. But she's going to keep working, she tells him, until he gets his new contract. She *wants* to, she says.

He doesn't have the heart to tell her that he is probably not going to be renewed, that he's probably going to be sent back to work on his strength, which has been getting worse, not better, and how once you go back down it is so very hard to return. Durocher, that crazy man, may love having him, a left-handed Cuban, on his team, may have brought him up just for that, but that just isn't enough now.

He loves her too much to scare her, and there's always a chance—isn't there?—that his fastball will get better, that his arm will become as strong as it needs to be.

All he really needs, he knows, is a break—like the one Koslo got in the Series, Durocher's surprise starter who got to go all the way in that first great game with the Yankees, when they really had them by the balls. His arm would feel the pride, would be strong from it, and maybe then Mays and Irvin would look at him in the fucking lockers.

* * *

Nancy loves the *I Love Lucy* television show. Because she does, on her birthday he buys her a new Zenith television set—a big one. One with an antenna big enough to make the picture better. Someday there will be television sets with *colored* pictures—everyone says so—and he knows he'll buy her one of those, too, when the stores have them. On her days off she watches the show, and every chance he gets he watches it with her. She tells him: "I wish I had red hair like Lucy. Would you like that?" He looks at the black-and-white picture on the television set and does his best to imagine Lucy's hair *in color*. *Sure*, he thinks. *Red hair is amazing. But so is blonde.* "If you want," he says, "but I like your blonde hair, *chica.* You look like an angel to me. You fill this room with light—just like an angel." He wants to sound like a poet; he has always wanted to sound like a poet. He wants never to lose the magic of their lives, and this is possible in America, is it not? Not to lose what you have, what you have dreamed of? If she wants red hair, okay, but not if it's because she thinks she isn't beautiful without it. "You're beautiful, *chica.* You're the most beautiful woman I have ever known," he tells her, and then a face—a woman with dark hair, in the ugly green fatigues a soldier wears—comes to him. He doesn't know her. He doesn't know why this face has come to him, when he is with the woman he loves.

He closes his eyes and the face, like the song, fades.

They watch *I Love Lucy* and *Your Show of Shows* and *You Bet Your Life* and the next week, too—like a date, there in their own living room on the big Zenith he has bought for her birthday—they watch Lucy and her best friend Ethel work on Lucy's crazy plans to get what she wants out of life. They laugh at all the trouble Lucy gets herself into only because she wants to be taken seriously, and also wants to be a good wife. *Is this the struggle of all American women?* he wonders. To be taken seriously, but to be a good wife, too?

Nancy isn't laughing, and he knows that look. She isn't happy. Like Lucy, she wants something but isn't sure she can have it. She still wants that *red hair,* he knows. She wants red hair the same way he has always wanted to play pro ball, because in America all things are possible, and so you dream about them, and you aren't happy unless you get them. The tenderness he feels for her suddenly brings tears to his eyes, and he hides them by looking away.

Now she is laughing. She has lost herself again in the television show. She is watching Lucy do her crazy things while Ricky, that amazing drummer—that Cuban dancer all American women are in love with—doesn't know what she's up to, though when he finds out he will indeed forgive her, because he loves her. This is American, too, Fidel knows.

* * *

The Cuban phones him three days later. The man says only, "I would like the opportunity to meet with you, *Señor.* Would this be possible?" When Fidel asks what it is about, the man says, "Our country."

"Cuba?" Fidel asks.

"Yes," the man tells him. "I ask only for an hour of your time—at the very most."

Fidel feels an uneasiness begin, but says, "Yes." *Why not?* This man is a fellow Cuban, another son of Cuba and Martí, so why should he not? If there is something happening in Cuba that he should know about, what is an hour of his time?

They meet at the coffee shop where Nancy works. Nancy serves them and smiles at them both. The man begins to talk. He is not direct. He talks of many things, but not important ones. The uneasiness grows. What is wrong? What is so wrong in Cuba that a man contacts him like this, talks around things and does not get to the point? "What are you trying to say?" Fidel says.

"Things are happening now," the man says.

"What things?"

"People are not happy, *Señor.*"

"What people?"

"The farmers and workers," the man says, and Fidel understands at last.

"You are a *communist,*" he says to the man.

"No. I am not," the man answers. "I am a son of Cuba, like you. I am simply *concerned*. And I happen to represent others who are concerned, others who feel that you, a son of Cuba—a celebrity in both countries—might wish to know about these things, to consider them."

"I am a baseball player," Fidel says at last. "I know nothing of politics. We have a president in Cuba and a president in the United States. Except for an American war in Asia, I am not aware of any problems."

The man is quiet for a moment. "Yes," he says, "you are in America now, and you are playing baseball, and so you might not be in a position to hear about things at home, would you agree?"

That is true, Fidel thinks. *A baseball player would not, would he. . . .*

"There is a movement in Oriente Province, your own province," the man tells him, "a movement that is growing. The current administration in Havana is not happy with it, but I must emphasize to you that it is a movement of *the sons of Cuba*, men who are tired of the manner in which Cuba remains a child in the shadow of North America—a child not allowed to grow up, to know what it is like to be a man, to build a life from hard work, to have a family, to feel the pride a *man* should feel. . . ."

The man is looking at him, and Fidel looks away.

"The United States is a good country," Fidel says.

"Yes, I know. It has been good to Cubans like you, *Señor*. But, if you will forgive me, it has not been as good to everyone. Those who work on the *fincas*, in the cities, those who work for a few *kilos* a day to serve the wealthy tourists who come to Havana to play. . . ."

He knows what the man is saying. He knows he is lucky. He remembers the boys and girls from the cane fields and knows where they are now. They do not play on baseball fields in New York. They do not play on tennis courts in California. They do not run hotels in Miami. And only a few will ever have careers in boxing. He knows what the man is saying, and he feels the shame.

He sighs at last. "What is the United States doing that is so wrong? Please, I would like to know. . . ."

* * *

When the man is gone, Fidel sits for a while in the booth with its red upholstery. Nancy comes to give him the check, to smile at him, and to purse her lips in a kiss in his direction, so that he will do the same. When he does not, she frowns just like Lucy—as if to say *What's wrong, Ricky?* He gives her what smile he can, so that she will not think he no longer loves her.

He hasn't felt this way since he was a child, he realizes, as he walks from the coffee shop to the blue Chevrolet in the parking lot—since the days he would argue with his father at home and his father would shout, not wanting to hear what he had to say. His father, with that wonderful beard of his, had come from Spain, the poorest part, had begun his life as a soldier sent to fight in Cuba, had become a brickmaster who bought a little land here and there, until eventually he was a *land owner*, a man of the *finca*, a man who had made a life for himself out of *nothing*, who did not want to hear about the poor children his son played with. And why should he? *You should not be playing with them!* his father would shout.

No son wants his father angry with him, Fidel knows.

Even the thought of *love*—even the thought of love of a woman like Nancy, or a fine baseball card with his picture on it—cannot make the feelings go away as he drives toward the Polo Grounds and the double-header.

* * *

That night he dreams that someone—he himself or someone else—has set fire to his father's cane fields. He wakes from the dream in a sweat. And yet his father was *there*—in the dream. Standing beside the flames and nodding, as if everything were okay, as if he had given his permission. When he falls asleep again, he dreams of a prison on an island of pine trees, a ship that almost sinks, of soldiers asleep (or *dead*) lying beside him under the *paja* of dried cane leaves.

* * *

After the game with Brooklyn on Sunday, when he pitches six innings before they call in Hutchinson, he doesn't take Nancy out for black beans or steak. She isn't angry. He goes to bed early. He dreams of the mountains again, and then, right before he wakes, of that same ship, the one full of the soldiers he knew . . . before they died.

* * *

It takes him three weeks to get through to Desi Arnaz. He tries calling the studio where the show is filmed, and then the company that makes the show. He writes two letters, certain that neither will get through. When he sends a telegram, it says simply, "A fellow son of Cuba would like to meet with you."

The answer takes four weeks. Arnaz, who lives in a valley north of Hollywood, California, will meet with him if he can be in Los Angeles on the thirteenth of September at ten in the morning. A driver will be sent to his hotel.

Nancy wants to go, and for a moment he almost says *yes*. Yet he knows what it will be like: He, full of feelings he hasn't felt in so long, needing to talk to a fellow son of Cuba; she, wanting to have fun in the city she has always dreamed of. It would be worse to take her with him, would it not? Worse than telling her *no?* "But *why?*" she asks. She is hurt. He has made a dream come true for her for a moment—the chance to go to Hollywood, maybe even to meet Lucille Ball herself—only to take it away. What has she done? Her body sags, older, and he is afraid: *What am I doing? What am I doing to us?* Suddenly he is angry at the man for telling him about Cuba, for making him feel what he feels, for making him hurt the woman he loves. And for making him *afraid*. "*Señor* Arnaz is a busy man, *chica*," he tells her gently. "His wife is a busy woman. I will be speaking to him for no more than an hour and then I will come home. It is *political* business. *Cuban* business. If I were going to Hollywood for fun, you would be the only one I would take. But I am not going for fun. I would not be able to have fun without you. Can you understand?"

She does not speak, and when she does, she says: *Maybe another time.* She says: *I understand.* This should make him happy, but it does not. Even this depresses him—that she understands, that she is willing to wait for something that may never come again. *Everything is falling apart*, he feels. *Everything is becoming something else—*

A darkness.

* * *

The night before he leaves for Hollywood, he dreams he is high up in an airplane, looking down at an island. It is Cuba. Below him he can see things he does not understand. Below, in black and white—like photographs—are buildings, are trucks covered with palm fronds and bushes, things that look like long, thin bullets. He is holding something in his hand—a glove, a camera, a favorite rifle with a telescope on top—but he cannot see it. He is looking down.

Everything is quiet . . . as if the whole world were waiting.

* * *

The chauffeur sent by Arnaz takes him from the ancient hotel on Hollywood Boulevard to the Valley, which is over the hills, to a gate, which the driver gets out and opens. At the end of a long driveway stands Lucy and Desi's house, which looks not unlike a *hacienda*. Arnaz is waiting in the hallway for him—with a smile and a manly handshake—and they sit down immediately in a bright white room full of windows and light. A servant brings them drinks—a rum for Fidel and a lemonade for Desi. Lucy does not appear. She is pregnant—everyone knows this—and besides, she is very involved in her Hollywood projects. She will not appear, he knows now. He will not even be able to ask her for an autograph to take back to Nancy.

But he can see the portrait of Lucy—that famous painting by that famous American painter—on the wall above them, in the light. *In color* her hair is indeed remarkable. "I have heard many great things about you, *Señor* Castro," Arnaz says suddenly. He is wearing gabardine slacks, is thinner than Fidel imagined. "I was the only boy in Cuba never to play baseball, I am certain, but I follow the sport avidly—especially when one of its players is a son of Cuba and boasts your gifts."

"*Muchas gracias,*" Fidel says. He is uncomfortable, sitting with the man he has seen so many times on television, and knows he should not be. They are both Cubans. They are both important men. "If I may say so, *Señor* Arnaz, you are the most famous Cuban in America and my girlfriend and I are but two of the many, many fans you and your wife have in both countries. . . ."

It is not what he wanted to say. Arnaz smiles, saying nothing. He is waiting. He is waiting to hear the reason Fidel has come.

He has rehearsed this many times and yet the rehearsals mean nothing. It is like his fastball. All the practice in the world means nothing. He must simply find the courage to say what he has come to say:

"Thank you for agreeing to meet with me, *Señor*. I have asked for this meeting because I am concerned about our country. . . ."

He waits. The face of Arnaz does not change. The smile is there. The eyes look at him respectfully, just as the eyes of the Cuban in the coffee shop looked at him.

And then Arnaz says, "I see," and the smile changes.

Fidel is unable to breathe. All he can see is the frown, faint but there. All he can do, holding his breath, is wonder what it means: *Disappointment,* because Arnaz imagined something different—a Hollywood project, a *baseball* Hollywood project, an event for charity with baseball players and Hollywood people . . . for the poor of Cuba perhaps?

Or is it *anger?*

"To what do you refer?" Arnaz asks, his voice different now. *I do not imagine this,* Fidel tells himself. *It is real. The warmth is gone. . . .*

Even the room looks darker now, Lucy's portrait on the wall, dimmer. Fidel takes a breath, exhales, and begins again: "I cannot be sure of the details myself, *Señor*. That is why I wished to see you. Perhaps you know more than I." He takes another breath, exhales it, too, and smells suddenly the cane fields of Oriente, their sweetness, and sweet rain. "We are both celebrities, *Señor* Arnaz—myself to a much lesser degree, to be sure—and I believe that celebrities like you and I hold unusual positions in our two countries. We are Cubans, yes, but we are not *ordinary* Cubans. We are famous in two countries and have the power, I believe, and even—if I may be so bold—the responsibility as well, to know what is happening in Cuba, to speak publicly, even to influence matters between those two countries . . . for the sake of the sons and daughters of Martí. . . ."

Arnaz waits.

"Have you," Fidel goes on quickly, "heard of a movement in Oriente Province, in the Sierra Maestro, or of any general unrest in our country, *Señor?* Word of such matters has reached me recently through a fellow Cuban whose credentials I have no reason to question and who I do *not* believe is a communist."

Arnaz looks at him and the silence goes on and on. When the little Cuban finally speaks, it is like wind through pine trees near a sea, like years of walls there. "Forgive me for what I am about to say, *Señor* Castro, but like many men in your profession, you are very naïve. You hear a rumor and from it imagine a *revolution.* You hear the name of José Martí invoked by those who would invoke any name to suit their purposes and from this suddenly imagine that it is your duty to become *involved.*

"It would hurt you seriously, *Señor* Castro," Arnaz continues, "were word of this concern of yours—of our meeting and your very words to me today—to become public. Were that to happen, I assure you, you would find yourself in an unfavorable public light, one that would have consequences for you professionally for many, many years, for your family in Cuba, for your girlfriend here. I will not mention your visit to anyone. I trust you will do the same."

Arnaz is getting up. "I would also suggest, *Señor* Castro, that you leave matters of the kind you have been so concerned with to the politicians, to our presidents in Washington and Havana, who have wisdom in such things."

Fidel is nodding, rising, too. He can feel the heat of the shame on his face. They are at the door. The chauffeur is standing by the limousine. Arnaz is telling him goodbye, wishing him good luck and a fine baseball season. The gracious smile is there, the manly handshake somehow, and now the limousine is carrying him back down the driveway toward the gate.

The despair that fills him is vast, as vast as the uncleared forests beyond the sugarcane and tobacco fields of Oriente Province, lifting only when the limousine is free of the gate and he can think of Nancy again—her face, her hair—and can realize that, *yes*, she would look good with red hair, that indeed he would like her hair to be such an amazing red.

The publication of *The Martian Chronicles* in 1950 established Ray Bradbury as one of the great visionaries of fantastic fiction. Author of some six hundred short stories and more than thirty books, including *Dandelion Wine, The Illustrated Man, I Sing the Body Electric,* and that great classic, *Fahrenheit 451,* Bradbury received many major mainstream literary awards like the PEN Center USA West Lifetime Achievement Award, while also receiving the World Fantasy Award for Lifetime Achievement and the Grand Master Award from the Science Fiction Writers of America. Here, Bradbury blends two great classics together in a poem that uses the dark violence of Herman Melville's *Moby Dick* to deconstruct and reimagine the great baseball classic, "Casey at the Bat," by Ernest Lawrence Thayer.

Ahab at the Helm
ॐ

Ray Bradbury

With apologies to Herman Melville and the illustrious author of Casey at the Bat, *Ernest Lawrence Thayer.*

It looked extremely rocky for the Melville nine that day,
The score stood at two lowerings, with one lowering yet to play,
And when Fedallah died and rose, and others did the same,
A pallor wreathed the features of the patrons of this Game.

A straggling few downed-oars to go, leaving behind the rest,
With that hope which springs eternal from the blind dark human breast.
They prayed that Captain Ahab's rage would thrust, strike, overwhelm!
They'd wager "Death to Moby!" with old Ahab at the helm.

But Flask preceded Ahab, and likewise so did Stubb,
And the former was a midget, while the latter was a nub.
Behold! the stricken multitudes in silence pent did swoon,
For when, oh when would Ahab rise to hurl his dread harpoon?!

First Flask let drive a gaffing hook. The wonderment of all!
Then much-despised Stubb's right arm brought blood and bile and gall!
But when the mist had lifted. Ishmael saw what had occurred:
Flask stood safe in the second boat, while Stubb clutched to the third.

Then from the gladdened whaling-men went up a joyous yell,
It bounded from the tidal hills and echoed in the dell,
It struck upon the soaring wave, shook Pequod's mast and keel,
For Ahab, mighty Ahab, was advancing with his steel.

There was ease in Ahab's manner as he stepped into his place,
There was pride in Ahab's bearing and a smile on Ahab's face;
The cheers, the wildest shoutings, did not him overwhelm,
No man in all that crowd could doubt, 'twas Ahab at the helm.

Four dozen eyes fixed on him as he coiled the hempen rope,
Two dozen tongues applauded as he raised his steel, their hope.
And while the writhing Moby ground the whale-boats with his hip,
Defiance gleamed from Ahab's eye, a sneer curled Ahab's lip.

And now the white-fleshed monster came a-hurtling through the air,
While Ahab stood despising it in haughty grandeur there!
Close by the sturdy harpooner the Whale unheeded sped—
"That ain't my style," said Ahab.
"Strike! Strike!" Good Starbuck said.

From the longboats black with sailors there uprose a sullen roar,
Like the beating of mad storm waves on a stern and distant shore:
"Kill Starbuck! Kill the First Mate!" shouted someone of the band.
And it's likely they'd have done so had not Ahab raised his hand.

With a smile of Christian charity great Ahab's visage shone,
He stilled the rising tumult and he bade the Chase go on.
He signalled to the White Whale, and again old Moby flew.
But still Ahab ignored it. Ishmael cried, "Strike! Strike, man!" too.

"Fraud!" yelled the rebel sailors, and sea-echoes answered, "Fraud!"
But one scornful glance from Ahab and his audience was awed.

They saw his face grow pale and cold, they saw his muscles strain,
And they knew that Ahab's fury would not pass that Whale again.

The sneer is gone from Ahab's lips, his teeth are clenched in hate,
He pounds with cruel violence his harpoon upon his pate,
And now old Moby gathers power, and now he lets it go.
And now the air is shattered by the force of Ahab's blow!

Oh, somewhere on the Seven Seas, the sun is shining bright,
The hornpipe plays yet somewhere and somewhere hearts are light;
And somewhere teachers laugh and sing, and somewhere scholars shout,
But there is no joy in Melville—mighty Ahab has Struck Out.

Robert Coover is a major literary voice as a novelist and writer. He has published a dozen novels and dozens of shorter works for publications like *Harper's* and the *New Yorker,* and his novel, *The Universal Baseball Association, Inc., J. Henry Waugh, Prop.* is one of the cornerstones of modern baseball fantasy. In this story, Coover gives us a pitcher trapped inside a poem that only he seems to understand, and in that understanding he gives vent to sharp satire about baseball scholars, literary criticism, poetry, and the national pastime. As McDuff notes, there's always something richly ludicrous about extremity. And wonderfully so.

McDuff on the Mound

∽

Robert Coover

IT WASN'T MUCH, a feeble blooper over second, call it luck, but it was enough to shake McDuff. He stepped weakly off the left side of the pitcher's mound, relieved to see his catcher Gus take the job of moving down behind the slow runner to back up the throw in to first. Fat Flynn galloped around the bag toward second, crouched apelike on the basepath, waggled his arms, then bounded back to first as the throw came in from short center. McDuff felt lightheaded. Flynn's soft blooper had provoked a total vision that iced his blood. Because the next batter up now was Blake: oh yes, man, it was all too clear. "Today's my day," McDuff told himself, as though taking on the cares of the world. He tucked his glove in his armpit briefly, wiped the sweat from his brow, resettled his cap, thrust his hand back into his glove.

Gus jogged over to the mound before going back behind the plate, running splaylegged around the catcher's guard that padded his belly. McDuff took the toss from first, over Gus's head, stood staring dismally at Flynn, now edging flatfooted away from the bag, his hands making floppy loosewristed swirls at the cuffs of his Mudville knickers. Gus spat, glanced back over his shoulder at first, then squinted up at McDuff. "Whatsa matter, kid?"

McDuff shrugged, licked his dry lips. "I don't know, Gus. I tried to get him." He watched Flynn taunt, flapping his hands like donkey ears, thumbing his nose.

The hoodoo. Rubbing it in. Did he know? He must. "I really tried." He remembered this nightmare, running around basepaths, unable to stop.

Gus grinned, though, ignoring the obvious: "Nuts, the bum was lucky. C'mon, kid, ya got this game in ya back pocket!" He punched McDuff lightly in the ribs with his stiff platter of a mitt, spat in encouragement, and joggled away in a widelegged trot toward home plate, head cocked warily toward first, where Flynn bounced insolently and made insulting noises. Settling then into his crouch, and before pulling his mask down, Gus jerked his head at the approaching batter and winked out at McDuff. Turkey Blake. Blake the cake. Nothing to it. A joke. Maybe Gus is innocent, McDuff thought. Maybe not.

Now, in truth, McDuff was not, by any standard but his own, in real trouble. Here it was, the bottom of the ninth, two away, one more out and the game was over, and he had a fat two-run lead going for him. A lot of the hometown Mudville fans had even given it up for lost and had started shuffling indifferently toward the exits. Or was their shuffle a studied shuffle and itself a cunning taunt? A mocking rite like Flynn's buffoonery at first? Had they shuffled back there in the shadows just to make Flynn's fluke hit sting more? It was more than McDuff could grasp, so he scratched his armpits and tried to get his mind off it. Now, anyway, they were all shuffling back. And did they grin as they shuffled? Too far away to tell. But they probably did, goddamn them. You're making it all up, he said. But he didn't convince himself. And there was Blake. Blake the Turkey. Of course.

Blake was the league clown, the butt. Slopeshouldered, potbellied, broad-rumped, bandylegged. And a long goiter-studded neck with a small flat head on top, overlarge cap down around the ears. They called him "Turkey," Blake the Turkey. The fans cheered him with a gobbling noise. And that's just what they did now as he stepped up: gobbled and gobbled. McDuff could hardly believe he had been brought to this end, that it was happening to him, even though he had known that sooner or later it must. Blake had three bats. He gave them a swing and went right off his feet. Gobble gobble gobble. Then he got up, picked out two bats, chose one, tossed the other one away, but as though by mistake, hung on to it, went sailing with it into the bat racks. Splintering crash. Mess of broken bats. Gobble gobble. McDuff, in desperation, pegged the ball to first, but Flynn was sitting on the bag, holding his quaking paunch, didn't even run when the ball got away from the first baseman, just made gobbling noises.

Vaguely, McDuff had seen it coming, but he'd figured on trouble from Cooney and Burroughs right off. A four-to-two lead, last inning, four batters between him and Casey, two tough ones and two fools, it was all falling into place: get the two tying runs on base, then two outs, and bring Casey up. So he'd worked like a bastard on those two guys, trying to head it off. Should've known better, should've seen that would have been too easy, too pat, too painless. McDuff, a practical man with both feet on the ground, had always tried to figure the odds, and that's where he'd gone wrong. But would things have been different if Cooney and Burroughs had hit him? Not substantially maybe, there'd still be much the same situation and Casey yet to face. But the stage wouldn't have been just right, and maybe, because of that, somehow, he'd have got out of it.

Cooney, tall, lean, one of the best percentage hitters in the business: by all odds, see, it should have been him. That's what McDuff had thought, so when he'd sucked old Cooney into pulling into an inside curve and grounding out, third to first, he was really convinced he'd got himself over the hump. Even if Burroughs should hit him, it was only a matter of getting Flynn and Blake out, and they never gave anybody any trouble. And Burroughs *didn't* hit him! Big barrelchested man with a bat no one else in the league could even lift—some said it weighed half a ton—and he'd wasted all that power on a cheap floater, sent it dribbling to the mound and McDuff himself had tossed him out. Hot damn! he'd cried. Waiting for fat Flynn to enter the batter's box, he'd even caught himself giggling. And then that unbelievable blooper. And—*bling!*—the light.

McDuff glared now at Blake, wincing painfully as though to say: get serious, man! Blake was trying to knock the dirt out of his cleats. But each time he lifted his foot, he lost his balance and toppled over. Gobble gobble gobble. Finally, there on the ground, teetering on his broad rump, he took a healthy swing with the bat at his foot. There was a bang like a firecracker going off, smoke, and the shoe sailed into the stands. Turkey Blake hobbled around in mock pain (or real pain: who could tell and what did it matter? McDuff's pain was real), trying to grasp his stockinged foot, now smoking faintly, but he was too round in the midriff, too short in the arms, to reach it. Gobble gobble gobble. Someone tossed the shoe back and it hit him in the head: bonk! Blake toppled stiffly backwards, his short bandy legs up in the air as though he were dead. Gobble gob—

McDuff, impatient, even embittered, for he felt the injury of it, went into his stretch. Blake leaped up, grabbed a bat from the mad heap, came hopping, waddling, bounding, however the hell it was he moved, up to the plate to take his place. It turned out that the bat he'd picked up was one he'd broken in his earlier act. It was only about six inches long, the rest hanging from it as though by a thread. McDuff felt himself at the edge of tears. The crowd gobbled on, obscenely, delightedly. Blake took a preparatory backswing, and the dangling end of the bat arced around and hit him on the back of the head with a hollow exaggerated clunk. He fell across the plate. Even the umpire now was emitting frantic gobbling sounds and holding his trembling sides. Flynn the fat baserunner called time-out and came huffing and puffing in from first to resuscitate his teammate. McDuff, feeling all the strength go out of him, slumped despairingly off the mound. He picked up the rosin bag and played with it, an old nervous habit that now did not relieve him.

His catcher Gus came out. "Gobble gobble," he said.

McDuff winced in hurt. "Gus, for God's sake, cut that out!" he cried. Jesus, they were all against him!

Gus laughed. "Whatsa matter, kid? These guys buggin' ya?" He glanced back toward the plate, where Flynn was practicing artificial respiration on Blake's assend, sitting on Blake's small head. "It's all in the game, buddy. Don't forget: gobble and the world gobbles with ya! Yak yak!" McDuff bit his lip. Past happy Gus, he could see Flynn listening to Blake's butt for a breath of life.

"Play baseball and you play with yourself," McDuff said sourly, completing Gus's impromptu aphorism.

"Yeah, you *got* it, kid!" howled Gus, jabbing McDuff in the ribs with his mitt, then rolling back onto the grass in front of the mound, holding his sides, giddy tears springing from his eyes, tobacco juice oozing out his cheeks.

There was a loud moist sound at the plate, like air escaping a toy balloon, and it was greeted by huzzahs and imitative noises from the stands. Flynn jumped up, lifted one of Blake's feet high in the air in triumph, and planted his fallen baseball cap in the clown's crotch, making Blake a parody of Blake, were such a thing absurdly possible. Cheers and courteous gobbling. Blake popped up out of the dust, swung at Flynn, hit the ump instead.

"Why don't they knock it off?" McDuff complained.

"Whaddaya mean?" asked Gus, now sober at his side.

"Why don't they just bring on Casey now and let me get it over with? Why do they have to push my nose in it first?"

"Casey!" Gus laughed loosely. "Never happen, kid. Blake puts on a big show, but he'd never hit you, baby, take it from old Gus. You'll get him and the game's over. Nothin' to it." Gus winked reassuringly, but McDuff didn't believe it. He no longer believed Gus was so goddamn innocent either.

Flynn was bounding now, in his apelike fashion, toward first base, but Blake had a grip on his suspenders. Flynn's short fat legs kept churning away and the dust rose, but he was getting nowhere. Then Blake let go—*whap!*—and Flynn blimped nonstop out to deep right field. Gobble gobble gobble. While

Flynn was cavorting back in toward first, Blake, unable to find his own hat, stole the umpire's. It completely covered his small flat head, down to the goiter, and Blake staggered around blind, bumping into things. Gobble. The ump grabbed up Blake's cap from where it had fallen and planted it defiantly on his own head. A couple gallons of water flooded out and drenched him. Gobble. Blake tripped over home plate and crashed facefirst to the dirt again. The hat fell off. Gobble. The umpire took off his shoes and poured the water out. A fish jumped out of one of them. Gobble. Blake spied his own hat on the umpire's soggy head and went for it. Gobble. The ump relinquished it willingly, in exchange for his own. The ump was wary now, however, and inspected the hat carefully before putting it back on his head. He turned it inside out, thumped it, ran his finger around the lining. Satisfied at last, he put the hat on his head and a couple gallons of water flooded out on him. Gobble boggle, said the crowd, and the umpire said: "PLAY BALL!"

Flynn was more or less on first, Blake in the box, the broken bat over his shoulder. McDuff glanced over toward the empty batter-up circle, then toward the Mudville dugout. Casey had not come out. Casey's style. And why should he? After all, Blake hadn't had a hit all season. Maybe in all history. He was a joke. McDuff considered walking Blake and getting it over with. Or was there any hope of that: of "getting it over with"? Anyway, maybe that's just what they wanted him to do, maybe it was how they meant to break him. No, he was a man meant to play this game, McDuff was, and play it, by God, he would. He stretched, glanced at first, studied Gus's signal, glared at Turkey Blake. The broken end of the bat hung down Blake's sunken back and tapped his bulbous rump. He twitched as though shooing a fly, finally turned around to see who or what was back there, feigned great surprise at finding no one. Gobble gobble. He resumed his batter's stance. McDuff protested the broken bat on the grounds it was a distraction and a danger to the other players. The umpire grumbled, consulted his rulebook. Gus showed shock. He came out to the mound and asked: "Why make it any easier for him, kid?"

"I'm not, Gus. I'm making it easier for myself." That seemed true, but McDuff knew Gus wouldn't like it.

"You are nuts, kid. Lemme tell ya. Plain nuts. I don't folla ya at all!" Blake was still trying to find out who or what was behind him. He poised very still, then spun around—the bat swung and cracked his nose: loud honking noise, chirping of birds, as Blake staggered around behind home plate holding his nose and splattering catsup all around. Gobble gobble gobble. Gus watched and grinned.

"I mean a guy who can't hit with a good bat might get lucky with a broken one," McDuff said. He didn't mean that at all, but he knew Gus would like it better.

"Oh, I getcha." Gus spat pensively. "Yeah, ya right." The old catcher went back to the plate, showed the ump the proper ruling, and the umpire ordered Blake to get a new bat. Gus was effective like that when he wanted to be. Why not all the time then? It made McDuff wonder.

Blake returned to the plate dragging Burroughs' half-ton bat behind him. He tried to get it on his shoulder, grunted, strained, but he couldn't even get the end of it off the ground. He sat down under it, then tried to stand. Steam whistled out his nose and ears and a great wrenching sound was heard, but the bat stayed where it was. While the happy crowd once more lifted its humiliating chorus, Flynn called time-out and came waddling in from first to help. The umpire, too, lent a hand. Together, they got it up about as high as Blake's knees, then had to drop it. Exaggerated thud. Blake yelped, hobbled around grotesquely, pointing down at the one foot still shoed. The toe of it began to swell. The seams of the shoe split. A red bubble emerged, expanded threateningly: the size of a plum, a crimson baseball, grapefruit, volleyball, a red pumpkin. Larger and larger it grew. Soon it was nearly as big as Blake himself. Everyone held his ears. The umpire crawled down behind Flynn and then Flynn tried to crawl behind the umpire. It stretched, quivered. Strained. Flynn dashed over, and reaching into Blake's behind, seemed to pull something out. Sound of a cork popping from a bottle. The red balloon-like thing collapsed with a sigh. Laughter and relieved gobbling. Blake bent over to inspect his toe. Enormous explosion, blackening Blake's face. Screams and laughter.

Then Burroughs himself came out and lifted the half-ton bat onto Blake's shoulder for him. What shoulder he had collapsed and the bat slid off, upending Blake momentarily, so Burroughs next set it on Blake's head. The head was flat and, though precariously, held it. Burroughs lifted Blake up and set him, bat on head, in the batter's box. Blake under his burden could not turn his head to see McDuff's pitch. He just crossed his eyes and looked up at the bat. Gus crouched and signaled. McDuff, through bitter sweaty tears, saw that Flynn was still not back on first, but he didn't care. He stretched, kicked, pitched. Blake leaned forward. McDuff couldn't tell if he hit the ball with the bat or his head. But hit it he did, as McDuff knew he would. It looked like an easy pop-up to the mound, and McDuff, almost unbelieving, waited for it. But what he caught was only the cover of the ball. The ball itself was out of sight far beyond the mowed grass of left-center field, way back in the high weeds of the neighboring acreage.

McDuff, watching then for Casey to emerge from the Mudville dugout, failed at first to notice the hubbub going on around the plate. It seemed that the ump had called the hit a homerun, and Gus was arguing that there were no official limits to the Mudville outfield and thus no automatic homers. "You mean," the umpire cried, "if someone knocked the ball clean to Gehenny, it still wouldn't be considered outa the park? I can't believe that!" Gus and the umpire fought over the rulebook, trying to find the right page. The three outfielders were all out there in the next acreage, nearly out of sight, hunting for the ball in the tall grass. "I can't believe that!" the umpire bellowed, and tore pages from the rulebook in his haste. Flynn and Blake now clowned with chocolate pies and waterpistols.

"Listen," said McDuff irritably, "whether it's an automatic homerun or not, they still have to run the bases, so why don't they just do that, and then it won't matter."

Gus's head snapped up from his search in the rulebook like he'd been stabbed. He glared fiercely at McDuff, grabbed his arm, pushed him roughly back toward the mound. "Whatsa matter with you?" he growled.

"Lissen! I ain't runnin' off nowheres I ain't got to!" Flynn hollered, sitting down on a three-legged stool which Blake was pulling out from under him. "If it's automatic, I'll by gum walk my last mile at my own dadblame ease, thank ya, ma'am!" He sprawled.

"Of *course* it ain't automatic," Gus was whispering to McDuff. "You know that as well as I do, Mac. If we can just get that ball in from the outfield while they're screwin' around, we'll tag *both* of 'em for good measure and get outa this friggin' game!"

McDuff knew this was impossible, he even believed that Gus was pulling his leg, yet, goddamn it, he couldn't help but share Gus's hopes. Why not? Anyway, he had to try. He turned to the shortstop and sent him out there with orders: *"Go bring that ball in!"*

The rulebook was shot. Pages everywhere, some tumbling along the ground, others blowing in the wind like confetti. The umpire, on hands and knees, was trying to put it all back together again. Gus held up a page, winked at McDuff, stuffed the page in his back pocket. Flynn and Blake used other pages to light cigars that kept blowing up in their faces. That does it, thought McDuff.

He looked out onto the horizon and saw the shortstop and the outfielders jumping up and down, holding something aloft. And then the shortstop started running in. Yet, so distant was he, he seemed not to be moving.

At home plate, the umpire had somehow discovered the page in Gus's back pocket, and he was saying: "I just can't believe it!" He read it aloud: " 'Mudville's field is open-ended. Nothing is automatic here, in spite of appearances. A ball driven even unto Gehenna is not necessarily a homerun. In short, anything can happen in Mudville, even though most things are highly improbable. Blake, for example, has never had a hit, nor has Casey yet struck out.' And et cetera!" The crowd dutifully applauded the reading of the rulebook. The umpire shook his head. "All the way to Gehenny!" he muttered.

The baserunners, meanwhile, had taken off, and Turkey Blake was flapping around third on his way home, when he suddenly noticed that fat Flynn, who should be preceding him, was still grunting and groaning down the basepath toward first.

The shortstop was running in from the next acreage with the ball.

Blake galloped around the bases in reverse, meeting Flynn head-on with a resounding thud at first. Dazed, Flynn headed back toward home, but Blake set him aright on the route to second, pushed him on with kicks and swats, threw firecrackers at his feet. The fans chanted: "*Go! Go! Go!*"

The shortstop had reached the mowed edge of the outfield. McDuff hustled back off the mound, moved toward short to receive the throw, excitement grabbing at him in spite of himself.

Flynn fell in front of second, and Blake rolled over him. Blake jumped up and stood on Flynn's head. Honking noise. Flynn somersaulted and kicked Blake in the teeth. Musical chimes.

The shortstop was running in from deep left-center. "*Throw it!*" McDuff screamed, but the shortstop didn't seem to hear him. He ran, holding the ball high like a torch.

Flynn had Blake in a crushing bear-hug at second base, while Blake was clipping Flynn's suspenders. Blake stamped on Flynn's feet—sound of wood being crushed to pulp—and Flynn yowled, let go. Blake produced an enormous rocket. Flynn in a funk fled toward third, but his pants fell down, and he tripped.

The shortstop was still running in from the outfield. McDuff was shouting himself hoarse, but the guy wouldn't throw the goddamn ball. McDuff's heart was pounding and he was angry at finding himself so caught up in it all.

Flynn had pulled up his pants and Blake was chasing him with the rocket. They crashed into McDuff. He felt trampled and heard hooting and gobbling sounds. When the dust had cleared, McDuff found himself wearing Flynn's pants, ten sizes too large for him, and Blake's cap, ten sizes too small, and holding a gigantic rocket whose fuse was lit. Flynn, in the confusion, had gone to second and Blake to third. The fuse burned to the end, there was a little pop, the end of the rocket opened, and a little bird flew out.

The shortstop was running in, eyes rolled back, tongue lolling, drenched in sweat, holding the ball aloft.

Flynn and Blake discovered their error, that they'd ended up on the wrong bases, came running toward each other again. McDuff, foreseeing the inevitable, stepped aside to allow them to collide. Instead, they pulled up short and exchanged niceties.

"After *you*," said Blake, bowing deeply.

"No, no, dear fellow," insisted Flynn with an answering bow, "after *you!*"

The shortstop stumbled and fell, crawled ahead.

Flynn and Blake were waltzing around and around, saying things like "Age before beauty!" and "Be my guest!" and "Hope springs eternal in the human breast!", wound up with a chorus of "Take Me Out to the Ballgame!" with all the fans in the stands joining in.

The shortstop staggered to his feet, plunged, gasping, forward.

The umpire came out and made McDuff give Flynn his pants back. He took Blake's cap off McDuff's head, looked at it suspiciously, held it over his own head, and was promptly drenched by a couple gallons of water that came flooding out.

McDuff felt someone hanging limply on his elbow. It was the shortstop. Feebly, but proudly, he held up the baseball. Blake, of course, was safe on second, and Flynn was hugging third. The trouble is, thought McDuff, you mustn't get taken in. You mustn't think you've got a chance. That's when they really kill you. "All right," he said to Blake and Flynn, his voice choking up and sounding all too much like a turkey's squawk, "screw you guys!" They grinned blankly and there was a last dying ripple of mocking gobbling in the stands. Then: silence. Into it, McDuff dropped Blake's giant rocket. No matter what he might have hoped, it didn't go off. Then he turned to face the Man.

And now, it was true about the holler that came from the maddened thousands, true about how it thundered on the mountaintop and recoiled upon the flat, and so on. And it was true about Casey's manner, the maddening composure with which he came out to take his turn at bat. Or was that so, was it true at that? McDuff, mouth dry, mind awhirl, could not pin down his doubt. "Quit!" he said, but he couldn't, he knew, not till the side was out.

And Casey: who *was* Casey? A Hero, to be sure. A Giant. A figure of grace and power, yes, but wasn't he more than that? He was tall and mighty (omnipotent, some claimed, though perhaps, like all fans, they'd got a bit carried away), with a great moustache and a merry knowing twinkle in his eye. Was he, as had been suggested, the One True Thing? McDuff shook to watch him. He was ageless, older than Mudville certainly, though Mudville claimed him as their own. Some believed that "Casey" was a transliteration of the initials "K. C." and stood for King Christ. Others, of a similar but simpler school, opted for King Corn, while another group believed it to be a barbarism for Krishna. Some, rightly observing that "case" meant "event," pursued this reasoning back to its primitive root, "to fall," and thus saw in Casey (for a case was also a container) the whole history and condition of man, a history perhaps as yet incomplete. On the other hand, a case was also an oddity, was it not, and a medical patient, and maybe, said some, mighty Casey was the sickest of them all. Yet a case was an example, argued others, plight, the actual state of things, thus a metaphysical example, they cried—while a good many thought all such mystification was so much crap, and Casey was simply a good ballplayer. Certainly, it was true, he could belt the hell out of a baseball. All the way to Gehenny, as the umpire liked to put it. Anyway, McDuff knew none of this. He only knew that here he was, that here was Casey, and the stage was set. He didn't need to know the rest. Just that was enough to shake any man.

Gus walked out to talk to McDuff, while the first baseman covered home plate. Gus kept a nervous eye on Flynn and Blake. "How the hell'd you let that bum hit ya, Mac?"

"Listen, I'm gonna walk Casey," McDuff said. Gus looked pained. "Firstbase is open, Gus. It's playing percentages."

"You and ya goddamn percentages!" snorted Gus. "Ya dumb or somethin', kid? Dontcha know this guy's secret?" Gus wasn't innocent, after all. Maybe nobody was.

"Yeah, I know it, Gus." McDuff sighed, swallowed. Knew all along he'd never walk him. Just stalling.

"Well, then, *kill* him, kid! You can do it! It's the only way!" Gus punctuated his peptalk with stiff jabs to McDuff's ribs. At the plate, Casey, responding to the thunderous ovation, lightly doffed his hat. They were tearing the stands down.

"But all these people, Gus—"

"Don't let the noise fool ya. It's the way they want it, kid."

Casey reached down, bat in his armpit, picked up a handfull of dust, rubbed it on his hands, then wiped his hands on his shirt. Every motion brought on a new burst of enraptured veneration.

McDuff licked his dry lips, ground the baseball into his hip. "Do you really think?"

"Take it from old Gus," said his catcher gently. "They're all leanin' on ya." Gus clapped him on the shoulder, cast a professional glance over toward third, then jogged splaylegged back to the plate, motioning the man there back to first.

Gus crouched, spat, lowered his mask; Casey swung his bat in short choppy cuts to loosen up; the umpire hovered. McDuff stretched, looked back at Blake on second, Flynn on third. Must be getting dark. Couldn't see their faces. They stood on the bags like totems. Okay, thought McDuff, I'll leave it up to Casey. I'm just not gonna sweat it (though in fact he had not stopped sweating, and even now it was cold in his armpits and trickling down his back). What's another ballgame? Let him take it or leave it. And without further wind-up, he served Casey a nice fat pitch gently down the slot, a little outside to give Casey plenty of room to swing.

Casey ignored it, stepped back out of the box, flicked a gnat off his bat.

"*Strike one!*" the umpire said.

Bottles and pillows flew and angry voices stirred the troubled air. The masses rose within the shadows of the stands, and maybe they'd have leapt the fences, had not Casey raised his hand. A charitable smile, a tip of the cap, a twirl of the great moustache. For the people, a pacifying gesture with a couple mighty fingers; for the umpire, an apologetic nod. And for McDuff: a strange sly smile and flick of the bat, as though to say . . . everything. McDuff read whole books into it, and knew he wasn't far from wrong.

This is it, Case, said McDuff to himself. We're here. And he fingered the rosin bag and wiped the sweat and pretended he gave a damn about the runners on second and third and stretched and lifted his left leg, then came down on it easily and offered Casey the sweetest, fattest, purest pitch he'd ever shown a man. Not even in batting practice had he ever given a hitter more to swing at.

Casey only smiled.

And the umpire said: "*Strike two!*"

The crowd let loose a terrible wrathful roar, and the umpire cowed as gunfire cracked and whined, and a great darkness rose up and all the faces fell in shadows, and even Gus had lost his smile, nor did he wink at McDuff.

But Casey drew himself up with a mighty intake of breath, turned on the crowd as fierce as a tiger, ordered the umpire to stand like a man, and then even, with the sudden hush that fell, the sun came out again. And Casey's muscles rippled as he exercised the bat, and Casey's teeth were clenched as he tugged upon his hat, and Casey's brows were darkened as he gazed out on McDuff, and now the fun was done because Casey'd had enough.

McDuff, on the other hand, hadn't felt better all day. Now that the preliminaries were over, now that he'd done all he could do and it was on him, now that everybody else had got serious, McDuff suddenly found it was all just a gas and he couldn't give a damn. You're getting delirious, he cautioned himself, but his caution did no good. He giggled furtively: there's always something richly ludicrous about extremity, he decided. He stepped up on the rubber, went right into his stretch. Didn't bother looking at second and third: irrelevant now. And it was so ironically simple: all he had to do was put it down the middle. With a lot of stuff, of course, but he had the stuff. He nearly laughed out loud. He reared back, kicking high with his left, then hurtled forward, sent the ball humming like a shot right down the middle.

Casey's mighty cut split the air in two—*WHEEEEP!*—and when the vacuum filled, there was a terrible thunderclap, and some saw light, and some screamed, and rain fell on the world.

Casey, in the dirt, stared in openjawed wonderment at his bat.

Gus plucked the ball gingerly out of his mitt, fingered it unbelievingly.

Flynn and Blake stood as though forever rooted at third and second, static parts of a final fieldwide tableau.

And forget what Gus said. No one cheered McDuff in Mudville when he struck Casey out.

Rod Serling had already won two Emmy Awards when he turned to science fiction and fantasy with *The Twilight Zone*, but it is with that show that he is most closely linked and it won him another Emmy. Serling wrote ninety-two scripts for *The Twilight Zone*, and one of the most famous of those is "The Mighty Casey," which starts with one of the best known names in baseball literature and then inverts it to feature a pitcher for the Brooklyn Dodgers who struggles with his growing sense of humanity. Serling later rewrote the script as a short story and included it in his *Stories from the Twilight Zone*, and it is that short-story adaptation that is included here.

The Mighty Casey

∞

Rod Serling

THERE IS A LARGE, extremely decrepit stadium overgrown by weeds and high grass that is called, whenever it is referred to (which is seldom nowadays), Tebbet's Field, and it lies in a borough of New York known as Brooklyn. Many years ago it was a baseball stadium housing a ball club known as the Brooklyn Dodgers, a major league baseball team then a part of the National League. Tebbet's Field today, as we've already mentioned, houses nothing but memories, a few ghosts and tier after tier of decaying wooden seats and cracked concrete floors. In its vast, gaunt emptiness nothing stirs except the high grass of what once was an infield and an outfield, in addition to a wind that whistles through the screen behind home plate and howls up to the rafters of the overhang of the grandstand.

This was one helluva place in its day, and in its day, the Brooklyn Dodgers was one rip-roaring ball club. In the last several years of its existence, however, it was referred to by most of the ticket-buying, turnstile-passers of Flatbush Avenue as "the shlumpfs!" This arose from the fact that for five years running the Brooklyn Dodgers were something less than spectacular. In their last year as members of the National League, they won exactly forty-nine ball games. And by mid-August of that campaign a "crowd" at Tebbet's Field was considered to be any ticket-buying group of more than eighty-six customers.

After the campaign of that year, the team dropped out of the league. It was an unlamented, unheralded event, pointing up the fact that baseball fans have a penchant for winners and a short memory for losers. The paying customers proved more willing to travel uptown to the Polo Grounds to see the Giants, or crosstown to Yankee Stadium to see the Yankees, or downtown to any movie theater or bowling alley than to watch the Brooklyn Dodgers stumble around in the basement of the league season after season. This is also commentative on the forgetfulness of baseball enthusiasts, since there are probably only a handful who recollect that for a wondrous month and a half, the Brooklyn Dodgers were a most unusual ball club that last season. They didn't start out as an unusual ball club. They started out as shlumpfs, as any Dodger fan can articulately and colorfully tell you. But for one month and one-half they were one helluva club. Principally because of a certain person on the team roster.

It all began this way. Once upon a time a most unusual event happened on the way over to the ball park. This unusual event was a left-hander named Casey!

It was tryout day for the Brooklyn Dodgers, and Mouth McGarry, the manager of the club, stood in the dugout, one foot on the parapet, both hands shoved deep into his hip pockets, his jaw hanging several inches below his upper lip. "Tryout days" depressed Mouth McGarry more than the standing of his ball club, which was depressing enough as it stood, or lay—which would be more apt, since they were now in last place, just thirty-one games out of first. Behind him, sitting on a bench, was Bertram Beasley, the general manager of the ball club. Beasley was a little man whose face looked like an X ray of an ulcer. His eyes were sunk deep into his little head, and his little head was sunk deep in between two narrow shoulder blades. Each time he looked up to survey McGarry, and beyond him, several gentlemen in baseball uniforms, he heaved a deep sigh and saw to it that his head sank just a few inches deeper into his shoulder blades. The sigh Bertram Beasley heaved was the only respectable heave going on within a radius of three hundred feet of home plate. The three pitchers that scout Maxwell Jenkins had sent over turned out to be pitchers in name only. One of them, as a matter of fact, had looked so familiar that McGarry swore he'd seen him pitch in the 1911 World Series. As it turned out, McGarry had been mistaken. It was not he who had pitched in the 1911 World Series but his nephew.

Out on the field McGarry watched the current crop of tryouts and kept massaging his heart. Reading left to right they were a tall, skinny kid with three-inch-thick glasses; a seventeen-year-old fat boy who weighed about two hundred and eighty pounds and stood five feet two; a giant, hulking farm boy who had taken off his spike shoes; and the aforementioned "pitcher," who obviously had dyed his hair black, but it was not a fast color and the hot summer sun was sending black liquid down both sides of his face. The four men were in the process of doing calisthenics. They were all out of step except the aging pitcher, who was no longer doing calisthenics. He had simply sat down and was fanning himself with his mitt.

Beasley rose from the bench in the dugout and walked over to McGarry. Mouth turned to look at him.

"Grand-looking boys!"

"Who were you expecting?" Beasley said, sticking a cigar in his mouth. "The All-Stars? You stick out a tryout sign for a last division club"—he pointed to the group doing the calisthenics—"and this is the material you usually round up." He felt a surge of anger as he stared into the broken-nosed face of Mouth McGarry. "Maybe if you were any kind of a manager, McGarry, you'd be able to whip stuff like this into shape."

McGarry stared at him like a scientist looking through a microscope at a bug. "I couldn't whip stuff like that into shape," he said, "if they were eggs and I was an electric mixer. You're the general manager of the club. Why don't you give me some ballplayers?"

"You'd know what to do with them?" Beasley asked. "Twenty games out of fourth place and the only big average we've got is a manager with the widest mouth in either league. Maybe you'd better get reminded that when the Brooklyn Dodgers win one game we gotta call it a streak! Buddy boy," he said menacingly, "when contract time comes around, *you* don't have to." His cigar went out and he took out a match and lit it. Then he looked up toward home plate, where a pitcher was warming up. "How's Fletcher doing?" he asked.

"Are you kidding?" Mouth spat thirty-seven feet off to the left. "Last week he pitched four innings and allowed only six runs. That makes him our most valuable player of the month!"

The dugout phone rang and Beasley went over to pick it up. "Dugout," he said into the receiver. "What? Who?" He cupped his hand over the phone and looked over at Mouth. "You wanta look at a pitcher?" he asked.

"Are you kidding?" Mouth answered.

Beasley talked back into the phone. "Send him down," he said. He hung up the receiver and walked back over to Mouth. "He's a lefty," he announced.

"Lefty, Shmefty," Mouth said. "If he's got more than one arm and less than four—he's for us!" He cupped his hands over his mouth and yelled out toward the field. "Hey, Monk!"

The catcher behind home plate rose from his squat and looked back over toward the dugout. "Yeah?"

"Fletcher can quit now," Mouth called to him. "I've got a new boy coming down. Catch him for a while."

"Check," the catcher said. Then he turned toward the pitcher. "Okay, Fletch. Go shower up."

Beasley walked back over to sit on the bench in the dugout. "You got the lineup for tonight?" he asked the manager.

"Working on it," Mouth said.

"Who starts?"

"You mean pitcher? I just feel them one by one. Whoever's warm goes to the mound." He spat again and put his foot back up on the parapet, staring out at the field. Once again he yelled out toward his ballplayers. "Chavez, stop already with the calisthenics."

He watched disgustedly as the three men stopped jumping up and down and the old man sitting on the ground looked relieved. Chavez thumbed them off the field and turned back toward the bench and shrugged a what-the-hell-can-I-do-with-things-like-this kind of shrug.

Mouth took out a handkerchief and wiped his face. He walked up the steps of the dugout and saw the sign sticking in the ground which read: "Brooklyn Dodgers—tryouts today." He pulled back his right foot and followed through with a vicious kick, which sent the sign skittering along the ground. Then he went over to the third-base line, picked up a piece of grass, and chewed it thoughtfully. Beasley left the dugout to join McGarry. He kneeled down alongside of him and picked up another piece of grass and began to chew. They knelt and lunched together until McGarry spit out his piece of grass and glared at Beasley.

"You know something, Beasley?" he inquired. "We are so deep in the cellar that our roster now includes an infield, an outfield and a furnace! And you know whose fault that is?"

Beasley spit out his own piece of grass and said, "You tell me!"

"It ain't mine," McGarry said defensively. "It just happens to be my luck to wind up with a baseball organization whose farm system consists of two silos and a McCormick reaper. The only thing I get sent up to me each spring is a wheat crop."

"McGarry," Beasley stated definitely, "if you had material, would you really know what to do with it? You ain't no Joe McCarthy. You ain't one half Joe McCarthy."

"Go die, will you," McGarry said. He turned back to stare down the third-base line at nothing in particular. He was unaware of the cherubic little white-haired man who had just entered the dugout. Beasley *did* see him and stared wide-eyed. The little old man came up behind Mouth and cleared his throat.

"Mr. McGarry?" he said. "I am Dr. Stillman. I called about your trying out a pitcher."

Mouth turned slowly to look at him, screwed up his face in distaste. "All right! What's the gag? What about it, Grampa? Did this muttonhead put you up to it?" He turned to Beasley. "This is the pitcher, huh? Big joke. Yak, yak, yak. Big joke."

Dr. Stillman smiled benignly. "Oh, I'm not a pitcher," he said, "though I've thrown baseballs in my time. Of course, that was before the war."

"Yeah," Mouth interjected. "Which war? The Civil War? You don't look old enough to have spent the winter at Valley Forge." Then he glared at him intently. "Come to think of it—was it really as cold as they say?"

Stillman laughed gently. "You really have a sense of humor, Mr. McGarry." Then he turned and pointed toward the dugout. "Here's Casey now," he said.

Mouth turned to look expectantly over the little old man's shoulder. Casey was coming out of the dugout. From cleats to the button on top of his makeshift baseball cap there was a frame roughly six feet, six inches high. The hands at his sides were the dimensions of two good-sized cantaloupes. His shoulders, McGarry thought to himself, made Primo Carnero look like the "before" in a Charles Atlas ad. In short, Casey was long. He was also broad. And in addition, he was one of the most powerful men either McGarry or Beasley had ever seen. He carried himself with the kind of agile grace that bespeaks an athlete, and the only jarring note in the whole picture was a face that should have been handsome, but wasn't, simply because it had no spark, no emotion, no expression of any sort at all. It was just a face. Nice teeth, thin lips, good straight nose, deep-set blue eyes, a shock of sandy hair that hung out from under his baseball cap. But it was a face, McGarry thought, that looked as if it had been painted on.

"You're the lefty, huh?" McGarry said. "All right." He pointed toward the home plate. "You see that guy with the great big mitt on? He's what's known as a catcher. His name is Monk. Throw a few into him."

"Thanks very much, Mr. McGarry," Casey said dully.

He went toward home plate. Even the voice, McGarry thought. Even the voice. Dead. Spiritless. McGarry picked up another long piece of grass and headed back to the dugout, followed by Beasley and the little old man, who looked like something out of Charles Dickens. In the dugout, McGarry assumed his familiar pose of one foot on the parapet, both fists in his hip pockets. Beasley left the dugout to return to his office, which was his custom on days the team didn't play. He would lock himself in his room and add up attendance figures, then look through the want ads of *The New York Times*. Just Stillman and Mouth McGarry stood in the dugout now, and the elderly little man watched everything with wide, fluttering eyes, like a kid on a tour through a fireworks factory. McGarry turned to him.

"You his father?"

"Casey's?" Stillman asked. "Oh, no. He has no father. I guess you'd call me his—well, kind of his creator." Dr. Stillman's words went past McGarry the way the super-chief goes by a water tank. "That a fact?" he asked rhetorically. "How old is he?"

"How old is he?" Stillman repeated. He thought for a moment. "Well, that's a little difficult to say."

Mouth looked over toward the empty bench with a see-the-kind-of-idiocy-I-have-to-put-up-with kind of look. "That's a little difficult to say," he mimicked fiercely.

Stillman hurriedly tried to explain. "What I mean is," he said, "it's hard to be chronological when discussing Casey's age. Because he's only been in existence for three weeks. What I mean is—he has the physique and mind of roughly a twenty-two-year-old, but in terms of how long he's been here—the answer to that would be about three weeks."

The words had poured out of Dr. Stillman's mouth, and McGarry had blinked through the whole speech.

"Would you mind going over that again?" he asked.

"Not at all," Dr. Stillman said kindly. "It's really not too difficult. You see, I made Casey. I built him." He smiled a big, beatific smile. "Casey's a robot," he said. The old man took a folded and creased document from his vest pocket and held it out to Mouth. "These are the blueprints I worked from," he said.

Mouth swatted the papers out of the old man's hand and dug his gnarled knuckles into the sides of his head. That goddamn Beasley. There were no depths to which that son of a bitch wouldn't go to make his life miserable. He had to gulp several times before he could bring himself to speak to the old man, and when finally words came, the voice didn't sound like his at all.

"Old friend." His voice came out in a wheeze. "Kind, sweet old man. Gentle grandfather, with the kind eyes, I am very happy that he's a robot. Of course, that's what he is." He patted Stillman's cheek. "That's just what he is, a nice robot." Then there was a sob in his voice as he glared up at the roof of the dugout. "Beasley, you crummy son of a bitch!" A robot yet. This fruity old man and that miserable ball club and the world all tumbling down and it just never ended and it never got any better. A robot!

Dr. Stillman scurried after Mouth, who had walked up the steps of the dugout and out onto the field. He paused along the third-base line and began to chew grass again. Over his shoulder Casey was throwing pitches into the catcher at home plate, but Mouth didn't even notice him.

"I dunno," he said to nobody in particular. "I don't even know what I'm *doing* in baseball."

He looked uninterested as Casey threw a curve ball that broke sharply just a foot out in front of home plate and then shrieked into the catcher's mitt like a small, circular, white express train.

"That Beasley," Mouth said to the ground. "That guy's got as much right in the front office as I've got in the Alabama State Senate. This guy is nothing, that's all. Simply a nothing. He was born a nothing. He's a nothing now!"

On the mound Casey wound up again and threw a hook that screamed in toward home plate, swerved briefly to the left, shot back to the right, and then landed in the catcher's mitt exactly where it had been placed as a target. Monk stared at the ball wide-eyed and then toward the young pitcher on the mound. He examined the ball, shook his head, then threw it back to him, shaking his head slowly from side to side.

Meanwhile Mouth continued his daily analysis of the situation to a smiling Dr. Stillman and an empty grandstand. "I've had bum teams before," he was saying. "Real bad outfits. But this one!" He spat out the piece of grass. "These guys make Abner Doubleday a criminal! You know where I got my last pitcher? He was mowing the infield and I discovered that he was the only guy on the club who could reach home plate from the pitcher's mound on less than two bounces. He is now ensconced as my number two starter. That's exactly where he's ensconced!"

He looked out again at Casey to see him throw a straight fast ball that landed in Monk's glove and sent smoke rising from home plate. Monk whipped off the glove and held his hand agonizedly. When the pain subsided he stared at the young pitcher disbelievingly. It was then and only then that picture and sound began to register in Mouth McGarry's mind. He suddenly thought about the last two pitches that he'd seen and his eyebrows shot up like elevators. Monk approached him, holding his injured hand.

"You see him?" Monk asked in an incredulous voice. "That kid? He picks up where Feller left off, I swear to God! He's got a curve, hook, knuckler, slider, and a fastball that almost went through my palm! He's got control like he uses radar. This is the best pitcher I ever caught in my life, Mouth!"

Mouth McGarry stood there as if mesmerized, staring at Casey, who was walking slowly away from the mound. Monk tucked his catcher's mitt under his arm and started toward the dugout.

"I swear," he said as he walked, "I never seen anything like it. Fantastic. He pitches *like nothing human!*"

Mouth McGarry and Dr. Stillman looked at one another. Dr. Stillman's quiet blue eyes looked knowing, and Mouth McGarry chewed furiously down the length of a piece of grass, his last bite taking in a quarter inch of his forefinger. He blew on it, waved it in the air and stuck it in his mouth as he turned toward Stillman, his voice shaking with excitement.

"Look, Grampa," Mouth said, "I want that boy! Understand? I'll have a contract drawn up inside of fifteen minutes. And don't give me no tough talk either! You brought him here on a tryout and that gives us first option."

"He's a robot, you know," Stillman began quietly.

Mouth grabbed him and spoke through clenched teeth. "Grampa," he said in a quiet fury, "don't ever say that to nobody! We'll just keep that in the family here." Then suddenly remembering, he looked around wildly for the blueprint, picked it up from the ground and shoved it in his shirt pocket. He saw Stillman looking at him.

"Would that be honest?" Stillman said, rubbing his jaw.

Mouth pinched his cheek and said, "You sweet old guy, you're looking at a desperate man. And if the baseball commissioner ever found out I was using a machine—I'd be dead. D-E-D! Dead, you know?" Mouth's face brightened into a grimace that vaguely brought to mind a smile when he saw Casey approaching. "I like your stuff, kid," Mouth said to him. "Now you go into the locker room and change your clothes." He turned to Stillman. "He wears clothes, don't he?"

"Oh, by all means," Stillman answered.

"Good," Mouth said, satisfied. "Then we'll go up to Beasley's office and sign the contract." He looked at the tall pitcher standing there and shook his head. "If you could pitch once a week like I just seen you pitch, the only thing that stands between us and a pennant is if your battery goes dead or you rust in the rain! As of right now, Mr. Casey—you're the number-one pitcher of the Brooklyn Dodgers!"

Stillman smiled happily and Casey just looked impassive, no expression, no emotion, neither satisfied nor dissatisfied. He just stood there. Mouth hurried back to the dugout, took the steps three at a time and grabbed the phone.

"General Manager's office," he screamed into it. "Yeah!" In a moment he heard Beasley's voice. "Beasley?" he said. "Listen, Beasley, I want you to draw up a contract. It's for that left-hander. His name is Casey. That's right. Not just good, Beasley. Fantastic. Now you draw up that contract in a hurry." There was an angry murmur at the other end of the line. "Who do you think I'm giving orders to?" Mouth demanded. He slammed the phone down, then turned to look out toward the field.

Stillman and Casey were heading toward the dugout. Mouth rubbed his jaw pensively. Robot-shmobot, he said to himself. He's got a curve, knuckler, fast ball, slider, change of pace and—hallelujah—he's got two arms!

He picked up one of Bertram Beasley's cigars off the ground, smoothed out the pleats and shoved it into his mouth happily. For the first time in many long and bleak months Mouth McGarry had visions of a National League pennant fluttering across his mind. So must John McGraw have felt when he got his first look at Walter Johnson, or Muller Higgins when George Herman Ruth came to him from the Boston Red Socks. And McGarry's palpitations were surely not unlike those of Marse Joseph McCarthy when a skinny Italian kid named DiMaggio ambled out into center field for the first time. Such was the bonfire of hope that was kindled in Mouth McGarry's chest as he looked at the blankfaced, giant left-hander walking toward him, carrying on his massive shoulders, albeit invisibly, the fortunes of the Brooklyn Dodgers and Mrs. McGarry's son, Mouth!

* * *

It was a night game against St. Louis forty-eight hours later. The dressing room of the Brooklyn Dodgers was full of noise, clattering cleats, slammed locker doors, the plaintive protests of Bertram Beasley, who was accusing the trainer of using too much liniment (at seventy-nine cents a bottle), and the deep, bullfrog profanity of Mouth McGarry, who was all over the room, on every bench, in every corner, and in every head of hair.

"You sure he's got the signals down, Monk?" he asked his catcher for the fourteenth time.

Monk's eyes went up toward the ceiling and he said tiredly, "Yeah, boss. He knows them."

Mouth walked over to the pitcher, who was just tying up his shoes. "Casey," he said urgently, wiping the sweat from his forehead, "if you forget them signals—you call time and bring Monk out to you, you understand? I don't want no cross-ups." He took out a large handkerchief and mopped his brow, then he pulled out a pill from his side pocket and plopped it into his mouth. "And above all," he cautioned his young pitcher, "—don't be nervous!"

Casey looked up at him puzzled. "Nervous?" he asked.

Stillman, who had just entered the room, walked over to them smiling. "Nervous, Casey," he explained, "ill at ease. As if one of your electrodes were—"

Mouth drowned him out loudly, "You know 'nervous,' Casey! Like as if there's two outs in the ninth, you're one up, and you're pitchin' against DiMaggio and he comes up to the plate lookin' intent!"

Casey stared at him deadpan. "That wouldn't make me nervous. I don't know anyone named DiMaggio."

"He don't know anyone named DiMaggio," Monk explained seriously to Mouth McGarry.

"I heard 'im," Mouth screamed at him. "I heard 'im!" He turned to the rest of the players, looked at his watch, then bellowed out, "All right, you guys, let's get going!"

Monk took Casey's arm and pulled him off the bench and then out the door. The room resounded with the clattering cleats on concrete floor as the players left the room for the dugout above. Mouth McGarry stood alone in the middle of the room and felt a dampness settle all over him. He pulled out a sopping wet handkerchief and wiped his head again.

"This humidity," he said plaintively to Dr. Stillman, who sat on the bench surveying him, "is killing me. I've never felt such dampness—I swear to God!"

Stillman looked down at Mouth's feet. McGarry was standing with one foot in a bucket of water.

"Mr. McGarry." He pointed to the bucket.

Mouth lifted up his foot sheepishly and shook it. Then he took out his bottle of pills again, popped two of them in his mouth, gulped them down, and pointed apologetically to his stomach. "Nerves," he said. "Terrible nerves. I don't sleep at night. I keep seeing pennants before my eyes. Great big, red-white-and-blue pennants. All I can think about is knocking off the Giants and then taking four straight from the Yanks in the World Series." He sighed deeply. "But for that matter," he continued, "I'd like to knock off the Phillies and the Cards, too. Or the Braves or Cincinnati." A forlorn note crept into his voice now. "Or anybody, when you come down to it!"

Dr. Stillman smiled at him. "I think Casey will come through for you, Mr. McGarry."

Mouth looked at the small white-haired man. "What have you got riding on this?" he asked. "What's your percentage?"

"You mean with Casey?" Stillman said. "Just scientific, that's all. Purely experimental. I think that Casey is a superman of a sort and I'd like that proved. Once I built a home economist. Marvelous cook. I gained forty-six pounds before I had to dismantle her. Now with Casey's skills, his strength and his accuracy, I realized he'd be a baseball pitcher. But in order to prove my point I had to have him pitch in competition. Also, as an acid test, I had to have him pitch with absolutely the worst ball team I could find."

"That's very nice of you, Dr. Stillman," Mouth said. "I appreciate it."

"Don't mention it. Now shall we go out on the field?"

Mouth opened the door for him. "After you," he said.

Dr. Stillman went out and Mouth was about to follow him when he stopped dead, one eyebrow raised. "Wait a minute, dammit," he shouted. "The worst?" He started out after the old man. "You should have seen the Phillies in 1903!" he yelled after him.

An umpire screamed, "Play ball!" and the third baseman took a throw from the catcher, then, rubbing up the ball, he carried it over to Casey on the mound, noticing in a subconscious section of his mind that this kid with the long arms and the vast shoulders had about as much spirit as a lady of questionable virtue on a Sunday morning after a long Saturday night. A few moments later, the third baseman cared very little about the lack of animation on Casey's features. This feeling was shared by some fourteen thousand fans, who watched the left-hander look dully in for a sign, then throw a sidearm fast ball that left them gasping and sent the entire dugout of the St. Louis Cardinals to their feet in amazement.

There are fast balls and fast balls, but nothing remotely resembling the white streak that shot out of Casey's left hand, almost invisibly, toward the plate, had ever been witnessed. A similar thought ran through the mind of the St. Louis batter as he blinked at the sound of the ball hitting the catcher's mitt and took a moment to realize that the pitch had been made and he had never laid eyes on it.

This particular St. Louis batter was the first of twenty-five men to face Casey that evening. Eighteen of them struck out and only two of them managed to get to first base, one on a fluke single that was misjudged over first base. By the sixth inning most of the people in the stadium were on their feet, aware that they were seeing something special in the tall left-hander on the mound. And by the ninth inning, when Brooklyn had won its first game in three weeks by a score of two to nothing, the stadium was in a frenzy.

There was also a frenzy of a sort in the Brooklyn dugout. The corners of Mouth McGarry's mouth tilted slightly upward in a grimace that the old team trainer explained later to a couple of mystified ballplayers was a "smile." Mouth hadn't been seen to smile in the past six years.

Bertram Beasley celebrated the event by passing out three brand-new cigars and one slightly used one (to McGarry). But the notable thing about the Brooklyn dugout and later the locker room was that the ball team suddenly looked different. In the space of about two and a half hours, it had changed from some slogging, lead-footed, aging second-raters to a snappy, heads-up, confident-looking crew of ballplayers who had a preoccupation with winning. The locker room resounded with laughter and horseplay, excited shouting drifted out from the showers. All this in a room that for the past three years had been as loud and comical as a funeral parlor.

While wet towels sailed across the room and cleated shoes banged against locker doors, one man remained silent. This was the pitcher named Casey. He surveyed the commotion around him with a mild interest, but was principally concerned with unlacing his shoes. The only emotion he displayed was when Doc Barstow, the team trainer, started to massage his arm. He jumped up abruptly and yanked the arm away, leaving Barstow puzzled. Later on Barstow confided to Mouth McGarry that the kid's arm felt like a piece of tube steel. McGarry gulped, smiled nervously and asked Doc how his wife had been feeling. All this happened on the night of July 1.

* * *

Three weeks later the Brooklyn Dodgers had moved from the cellar to fifth place in the National League. They had won twenty-three games in a row, seven of them delivered on a platter by one left-handed pitcher named Casey. Two of his ball games were no-hitters, and his earned-run average was by far the lowest not only in either League, but in the history of baseball. His name was on every tongue in the nation, his picture on every sports page, and contracts had already been signed so that he would be appearing on cereal boxes before the month was out. And as in life itself, winning begot winning. Even without Casey, the Dodgers were becoming a feared and formidable ball club. Weak and ineffectual bat-slappers, who had never hit more than .200 in their lives, were becoming Babe Ruths. Other pitchers who had either been too green or too decrepit were beginning to win ball games along with Casey. And there was a spirit now—an aggressiveness, a drive, that separated the boys from the pennant-winners and the Brooklyn Dodgers were potentially the latter. They looked it and they played it.

Mouth McGarry was now described as "that master strategist" and "a top field general" and, frequently, "the winningest manager of the year" in sports columns that had previously referred to him as "that cement-headed oaf who handles a ball club like a bull would handle a shrimp cocktail." The team was drawing more customers in single games than they'd garnered in months at a time during previous seasons. And the most delightful thing to contemplate was the fact that Casey, who had begun it all, looked absolutely invulnerable to fatigue, impervious to harm, and totally beyond the normal hazards of pitchers. He had no stiff arms, no sore elbows, no lapses of control, no nothing. He pitched like a machine and while it was mildly disconcerting, it was really no great concern that he also walked, talked, and acted like a machine. There was no question about it. The Dodgers would have been in first place by mid-August at the very latest, if a shortstop on the Philadelphia Phillies had not hit a line ball directly at Casey on the mound, which caught him just a few inches above his left eye.

The dull, sickening thud was the shot heard all around the borough, and if anyone had clocked Mouth McGarry's run from the dugout to the mound, where his ace left-hander was now sprawled face downward, two guys named Landy and Bannister would have been left in eclipse. Bertram Beasley, in his box seat in the grand-stand, simply chewed off one quarter of his cigar and swallowed it, then fell off his seat in a dead faint.

The players grouped around Casey, and Doc Barstow motioned for a stretcher. McGarry grabbed his arm and whispered at him as if already they were in the presence of the dead.

"Will he pull through, Doc? Will he make it?"

The team doctor looked grim. "I think we'd better get him to a hospital. Let's see what they say about him there."

Half the team provided an escort for the stretcher as it moved slowly off the field. It looked like a funeral cortege behind a recently deceased head of state, with Mouth McGarry as the principal mourner. It was only then that he remembered to motion into the bull pen for a new pitcher, an eager young towhead out of the Southern Association League who had just been called up.

The kid ambled toward the mound. It was obvious that at this moment he wished he were back in Memphis, Tennessee, sorting black-eyed peas. He took the ball from the second baseman, rubbed it up, then reached down for the rosin bag. He rubbed his hands with the bag, then rubbed the ball, then rubbed the bag, then put down the ball, wound up and threw the rosin bag. As it turned out, that was his best pitch of the evening. Shortly thereafter he walked six men in a row and hit one man in the head. Luckily, it was a hot-dog vendor in the bleachers, so that no harm was done in terms of moving any of the men on base. This was taken care of by his next pitch to the number-four batter on the Philadelphia Phillies squad, who swung with leisurely grace at what the kid from Memphis referred to as his fast ball, and sent it on a seven-hundred-foot-trip over the center-field fence, which took care of the men on the bases. The final score was thirteen to nothing in favor of the Phillies, but Mouth McGarry didn't even wait until the last out. With two outs in the ninth, he and Beasley ran out of the park and grabbed a cab. Beasley handed the driver a quarter and said, "Never mind the cops. Get to the hospital."

The hackie looked at the quarter, then back toward Beasley and said, "This better be a rare mint, or I'll see to it that you have your baby in the cab!"

They arrived at the hospital twelve minutes later and pushed their way through a lobby full of reporters to get to an elevator and up to the floor where Casey had been taken for observation. They arrived in his room during the last stages of the examination. A nurse shushed them as they barged into the room.

"Boobie," McGarry gushed, racing toward the bed. The doctor took off his stethoscope and hung it around his neck. "You the father?" he asked Mouth.

"The father," McGarry chortled. "I'm closer than any father."

He noticed now for the first time that Dr. Stillman was sitting quietly in the corner of the room, looking like a kindly old owl full of wisdom hidden under his feathers.

"Well, gentlemen, there's no fracture that I can see," the doctor announced professionally. "No concussion. Reflexes seem normal—"

Beasley exhaled, sounding like a strong north wind. "I can breathe again," he told everyone.

"All I could think of," Mouth said, "was there goes Casey! There goes the pennant! There goes the Series!" He shook his head forlornly, "And there goes my career."

The doctor picked up Casey's wrist and began to feel for the pulse. "Yes, Mr. Casey," he smiled benevolently down into the expressionless face and unblinking eyes, "I think you're in good shape. I'll tell you, though, when I heard how the ball hit you in the temple I wondered to myself how—"

The doctor stopped talking. His fingers compulsively moved around the wrist. His eyes went wide. After a moment he opened up Casey's pajamas and sent now shaking fingers running over the chest area. After a moment he stood up, took out a handkerchief and wiped his face.

"What's the matter?" Mouth asked nervously. "What's wrong?"

The doctor sat down in a chair. "There's nothing wrong," he said softly. "Not a thing wrong. Everything's fine. It's just that—"

"Just that what?" Beasley asked.

The doctor pointed a finger toward the bed. "It is just that this man doesn't have any pulse. No heartbeat." Then he looked up toward the ceiling. "This man," he said in a strained voice, "this man isn't alive."

There was absolute silence in the room, marred only by the slump of Beasley's body as he slid quietly to the floor. No one paid any attention to him. It was Dr. Stillman who finally spoke.

"Mr. McGarry," he said in a quiet, firm voice, "I do believe it'll have to come out now."

Beasley opened his eyes. "All right, you son of a bitch, McGarry. What are you trying to pull off?"

Mouth looked around the room as if searching for an extra bed. He looked ill. "Beasley," he said plaintively, "you ain't gonna like this. But it was Casey or it was nothing. God, what a pitcher! And he was the only baseball player I ever managed who didn't eat nothing." Stillman cleared his throat and spoke to the doctor. "I think you should know before you go any further that Casey has no pulse or heartbeat. . . because he hasn't any heart. He's a robot."

There was the sound of another slump as Bertram Beasley fell back unconscious. This time he didn't move.

"A *what?*" the doctor asked incredulously.

"That's right," Stillman said. "A robot."

The doctor stared at Casey on the bed, who stared right back at him. "Are you sure?" the doctor asked in a hushed voice.

"Oh, by all means. I built him."

The doctor slowly removed his coat and then took off his tie. He marched toward the bed with his eyes strangely wide and bright. "Casey," he announced, "get up and strip. Hear me? Get up and strip."

Casey got up and stripped and twenty minutes later the doctor had opened the window and was leaning out breathing in the evening air. Then he turned, removed his stethoscope from around his neck, and put it in his black bag. He took the blood pressure equipment from the nightstand and added it to the bag. He made a mental note to check the X rays as soon as they came out, but knew this would be gratuitous because it was all very, very evident. The man on the bed wasn't a man at all. He was one helluva specimen, but a man he wasn't! The doctor lit a cigarette and looked across the room.

"Under the circumstances," he said, "I'm afraid I must notify the baseball commissioner. That's the only ethical procedure."

"What do you have to be ethical about it for?" McGarry challenged him. "What the hell are you—a Giant fan?" The doctor didn't answer. He took the twenty or thirty sheets of paper that he'd been making notes on and rammed them in his pocket. He mentally ran down the list of medical societies and organizations that would have to be informed of this. He also devised the opening three or four paragraphs to a monumental paper he'd write for a medical journal on the first mechanical man. He was in for a busy time. He carried his black bag to the door, smiled, and went out, wondering just how the American Medical Association would react to this one. The only sound left in the room was Beasley's groaning, until McGarry walked over to Casey on the bed.

"Casey," he said forlornly, "would you move over?"

The Daily Mirror had it first because one of the interns in the maternity ward was really a leg man for them. But the two wire services picked it up twenty minutes later, and by six the following morning the whole world knew about Casey—the mechanical man. Several scientists were en route from Europe, and Dr. Stillman and Casey were beleaguered in a New York hotel room by an army of photographers and reporters. Three missile men at Cape Canaveral sent up a fabulous rocket that hit the moon deadeye, only to discover that the feat made page twelve of the afternoon editions because the first eleven pages were devoted exclusively to a meeting to be held by the commissioner of baseball, who had announced he would make a decision on the Casey case by suppertime.

At four thirty that afternoon the commissioner sat behind his desk, drumming on it with the end of a pencil. A secretary brought him in a folder filled with papers, and in the brief moment of the office door opening, he could see the mob of reporters out in the corridor.

"What about the reporters?" the secretary asked him.

Mouth McGarry, sitting in a chair close to the desk, made a suggestion at this point as to what might be done to the reporters or, more specifically, what they could do to themselves. The secretary looked shocked and left the room. The commissioner leaned back in his chair.

"You understand, McGarry," he said, "that I'm going to have to put this out for publication. Casey must definitely be suspended."

Bertram Beasley, sitting on a couch across the room, made a little sound deep in his throat, but stayed conscious.

"Why?" Mouth demanded noisily.

The commissioner pounded a fist on the desk top. "Because he's a robot, goddamn it," he said for the twelfth time that hour.

Mouth spread out his palms. "So he's a robot," he said simply.

Once again the commissioner picked up a large manual. "Article six, Section two, the Baseball Code," he said pontifically. "I quote: 'A team should consist of nine men,' end of quote. Men, understand, McGarry? Nine *men*. Not robots."

Beasley's voice was a thin little noise from the couch. "Commissioner," he said weakly. "To all intents and purposes—he *is* human." Then he looked across the room at the tall pitcher, who stood in the shadows practically unnoticed. "Casey, talk to him. Tell him about yourself."

Casey swallowed. "What—what should I say," he asked hesitantly.

"See," Mouth shouted. "He talks as good as me. And he's a whole helluva lot smarter than most of the muttonheads I got on my ball team!"

The commissioner's fist pounded on the desk. "*He is not human!*"

Again the weak voice of desperation from the couch. "How human do you want him?" the general manager asked. "He's got arms, legs, a face. He talks—"

"And no heart," the commissioner shouted. "He doesn't even own a heart. How could he be human without a heart?"

McGarry's voice absolutely dripped with unassailable logic and fundamental truth. "Beasley don't have a heart neither," he said, "and he owns forty per cent of the club."

The commissioner pushed the papers away from him and put the flat of his hands down on the desk. This was a gesture of finality, and it fitted perfectly the judicial tone of his voice. "That's it, gentlemen," he announced. "He doesn't have a heart. That means he isn't human, and that's a clear violation of the baseball code. Therefore, he doesn't play."

The door opened and Dr. Stillman walked quietly into the room in time to hear the last words of this proclamation. He waved at Casey, who waved back. Then he turned to the commissioner.

"Mr. Commissioner," he said.

The commissioner stopped halfway to his feet and looked at the old man. "Now what?" he asked tiredly.

Stillman walked over to the desk. "Supposing," he asked, "we gave him a heart? If that essentially is the only thing that makes him different from the norm, I believe I could operate and supply him with a mechanical heart."

"That's thinking!" McGarry shrieked into the room.

Beasley inched forward on the couch and took out a cigar. The commissioner sat back and looked very, very thoughtful. "This is irregular. This is highly irregular." Then he picked up the telephone and asked to speak to the examining physician who had sent in the report in the first place. "Doctor," he asked, "relative to the Casey matter, if he were to be given a mechanical heart—would you classify him as—what I mean is—would you call him a—" Then he held the phone close to his face, nodding into it. "Thank you very much, Doctor."

The commissioner looked across the room at Casey. He drummed on the desk top with the pencil, puckered up his lips, and made smacking sounds inside his mouth. McGarry took out his bottle of pills and plopped three of them into his mouth.

"All right," the commissioner announced. "*With* a heart, I'll give him a temporary okay, until the League meeting in November. Then we'll have to take it up again. The other clubs are gonna scream bloody murder!"

Beasley struggled to his feet. The look of massive relief on his face shone like a beacon. "It's all settled then," he said. "Casey here needs an accreditation as being human, and this requires a simple—" He stopped, looking over toward Stillman. "Simple?" he asked.

"Relatively," Stillman answered.

Beasley nodded. "A simple operation having to do with a mechanical heart." He walked across the room to the door and opened it. The reporters, milling around, stopped talking instantly. "Gentlemen," Beasley called out to them, "you may quote me."

The reporters made a beeline for the door and within a moment had filled up the room.

"You may quote me, gentlemen," Beasley repeated when the room was quiet once again. "The mighty Casey will be back in the lineup within forty-eight hours." He threw another questioning look at Stillman. "Forty-eight hours?"

"About," Stillman answered quietly.

Questions shot around the room like bolts of lightning, and for the next few moments McGarry, Beasley, and Casey were inundated by notebooks and cigarette smoke. Then the room started to empty. Mouth McGarry took a position close to the desk, stuck a cigar in his mouth, lit it, took a deep drag and held it out away from his body, gently flicking ashes on the floor.

"Gentlemen," he announced, "as manager of the Brooklyn Dodgers, I want to tell you, and since I was the man who discovered Casey—"

The reporters rapidly left the room, followed by the commissioner and his secretary, followed by Casey and Stillman.

"It behooves me to tell you, gentlemen," Mouth continued, wetting his lips over the word "behooves" and wondering to himself where he got the word. "It behooves me to make mention of the fact that the Brooklyn Dodgers are the team to beat. We've got the speed, the stamina," he recollected now the Pat O'Brien speech in the Knute Rockne picture—"the vim, the vigor, the vitality—"

He was unaware of the door slamming shut and unaware that Bertram Beasley was the only other man in the room. "And with this kind of stuff," he continued, in the Knute Rockne voice, "the National League pennant and the World Series and—"

"McGarry," Beasley yelled at him.

Mouth started as if suddenly waking from a dream.

Beasley rose from the couch. "Why don't you drop dead?" He walked out of the room, leaving Mouth all by himself, wondering how Pat O'Brien wound up that speech in the locker room during the halftime of that vital Army–Notre Dame game.

How either McGarry or Bertram Beasley got through the next twenty-odd hours was a point of conjecture with both of them. Mouth emptied his bottle of nerve pills and spent a sleepless night pacing his hotel-room floor. Beasley could recall only brief moments of consciousness between swoons that occurred every time the phone rang.

The following night the team was dressing in the locker room. They were playing the first of a five-game series against the New York Giants, and McGarry had already devised nine different batteries, then torn them all up. He now sat on a bench surveying his absolutely silent ballplayers. There was not a sound. At intervals each pair of eyes would turn toward the phone on the wall. Beasley had already phoned Dr. Stillman's residence seven times that evening and received no answer. He was on the phone now, talking to the long-distance operator in New Jersey.

"Yeah," Beasley said into the phone. "Yeah, well, thank you very much, operator."

Mouth and the rest of the players waited expectantly. "Well?" Mouth asked. "How is he?"

Beasley shook his head. "I don't know. The operator still can't get an answer."

Monk, the big catcher, rose from the bench. "Maybe he's right in the middle of the operation," he suggested.

Mouth whirled around at him, glaring. "So he's in the middle of the operation! Whatsa matter, he can't use one hand to pick up a phone?" He loafed up at the clock on the wall, then jutted his jaw fiercely, his eyes scanning the bench. "We can't wait no longer," he announced. "I got to turn in a battery. Corrigan," he said, pointing toward one of the players, "you'll pitch tonight. And now the rest of you guys!" He stuck his hands in his back pockets and paced back and forth in front of them in a rather stylized imitation of Pat O'Brien.

"All right, you guys," he said grimly. "All right, you guys!" He stopped pacing and pointed toward the door. "That's the enemy out there," he said, his voice quivering a little. "That's the New York Giants." He spoke the words as if they were synonymous with a social disease. "And while we're out there playing tonight"—again his voice quivered—"there's a big fellah named Casey lying on a table, struggling to stay alive."

Tears shone in Monk's eyes as the big catcher got a mental picture of a courageous kid lying on a hospital table. Gippy Resnick, the third baseman, sniffed and then honked into a handkerchief as a little knot of sentiment tightened up his throat. Bertram Beasley let out a sob as he thought about what the attendance record was, six weeks B.C.—before Casey—and did some more projecting on what it would be without Casey. Mouth McGarry walked back and forth before the line of players.

"I know," he said, his voice tight and strained. "I know that his last words before that knife went into his chest were—'Go up there, Dodgers, and win one for the big guy!'"

The last words of this speech were choked by the tears that rolled down McGarry's face and the sob that caught in his own chest.

The street door to the locker room opened and Dr. Stillman came in, followed by Casey. But all the players were watching Mouth McGarry, who had now moved into his big finale scene.

"I want to tell you something, guys! From now on"—he sniffed loudly—"from now on there's gonna be a ghost in that dugout. Every time you pick up a bat, look over to where Casey used to sit—because he's gonna be there in spirit rooting for us, cheering for us, yellin', 'Go Dodgers, go!'"—McGarry turned and looked at Casey, who was smiling at him. Mouth nodded perfunctorily. "Hello there, Casey," he said and turned back to the team. "Now I'm gonna tell you something else about that big guy. This fellah has a heart. Not a real heart, maybe, but this fellah that's lyin' there with a hole in his chest—"

Mouth's lower jaw dropped seven inches, as he turned very slowly to look at Casey. He had no chance to say anything, however, because the team had pushed him aside as they rushed toward the hero, shaking his hand, pounding him on the back, pulling, grabbing, shouting at him. Mouth spent a moment recovering and then screamed, "All right, knock it off! Let's have quiet! Quiet! QUIET!" He pulled players away from Casey and finally stood in front of the big pitcher. "Well?" he asked.

Stillman smiled. "Go ahead, Casey. Tell him."

It was then that everyone in the room noticed Casey's face. He was smiling. It was a big smile. A broad smile. An enveloping smile. It went across his face and up and down. It shone in his eyes. "Listen, Mr. McGarry," he said proudly. He pointed a thumb at his chest and Mouth put his ear there. He could hear the steady tick, tick, tick.

Mouth stepped back and shouted excitedly. "You got a heart!"

There was a chorus of delighted exclamation and comment from all the players and Beasley, poised for a faint, decided against it.

"And look at that smile," Stillman said over the shouting. "That's the one thing I couldn't get him to do before—smile!"

Casey threw his arm around the old man. "It's wonderful. It's just wonderful. Now I feel—I feel—like—togetherness!"

The team roared their approval and Bertram Beasley mounted a rubbing-table, cupping his hands like a megaphone, and shouted, "All right, Dodgers, out on the field. Let's go, team. Casey starts tonight. The new Casey!"

The team thundered out onto the field, pushing Mouth McGarry out of the way and blotting out the first part of the speech which had begun, "All right, you guys, with vim, vigor and vital—" He never got to finish the speech because Monk, Resnick, and a utility infielder had carried him with their momentum out the door and up to the dugout.

When Casey's name was announced as the starter for the Dodgers that night the crowd let out a roar that dwarfed any thunder ever heard in or around the environs of New York City. And when Casey stepped out on the field and headed toward the mound, fifty-seven thousand eight hundred and thirty-three people stood up and applauded as one, and it was only the second baseman who, as he carried the ball over to the pitcher, noticed that there were tears in Casey's eyes and an expression on his face that made him pause. True, he'd never seen *any* expression on Casey's face before, but this one made him stop and look over his shoulder as he went back to his base.

The umpire shouted, "Play ball," and the Dodgers began the running stream of chatter that always prefaced the first pitch. Monk, behind the plate, made a signal and then held up his glove as a target. Start with a fast ball, he thought. Let them know what they're up against, jar them a little bit. Confuse them. Unnerve them. That was the way Monk planned his strategy behind the plate. Not that much strategy was needed when Casey was on the mound, but it was always good to show the big guns first. Casey nodded, went into his windup and threw. Twelve seconds later a woman in a third-floor apartment three blocks away had her bedroom window smashed by a baseball that had traveled in the neighborhood of seven hundred feet out of Tebbet's Field.

Meanwhile, back at the field, the crowd just sat there silently as the lead-off batter of the New York Giants ambled around the base path heading home to the out-stretched hands of several fellow Giants greeting him after his lead-off home run.

Mouth McGarry at this moment felt that he would never again suffer a stab of depression such as the one that now intruded into his head. He would recall later that his premonition was quite erroneous. He would feel stabs of depressions in innings number two, three and four that would make that first stab of depression seem like the after-effect of a Miltown tablet. That's how bad it got forty-five minutes later, when Casey had allowed nine hits, had walked six men, had thrown two wild pitches, and had muffed a pop fly to the mound, which, McGarry roared to the bench around him, "could have been caught by a palsied Civil War veteran who lost an arm at Gettysburg."

In the seventh inning Mouth McGarry took his fifth walk over to the mound and this time didn't return to the bench till he'd motioned to the bullpen for Casey's relief—a very eager kid, albeit a nervous one, who chewed tobacco going to the mound and got violently sick as he crossed the third-base line because he'd swallowed a piece. Coughing hard, he arrived at the mound and took the ball from Mouth McGarry. Casey solemnly shoved his mitt into his hip pocket and took the long walk back toward the showers.

At ten minutes to midnight the locker room had been emptied. All the players save Casey had gone back to the hotel. Bertram Beasley had left earlier—on a stretcher in the sixth inning. In the locker room were a baseball manager who produced odd grunts from deep within his throat and kept shaking his head back and forth—and a kindly white-haired old man who built robots. Casey came out of the shower, wrapped in a towel. He smiled gently at Mouth and then went over to his locker, where he proceeded to dress.

"Well?" Mouth shouted at him. "Well? One minute he's three Lefty Groves, the next minute he's the cousin to every New York Giant who ever lived. He's a tanker. He's a nothing. All right—you wanna tell me, Casey? You wanna explain? You might start by telling me how one man can throw nine pitched balls and give up four singles, two doubles, a triple and two home runs!"

The question remained unanswered. Stillman looked toward Casey and said very softly, "Shall I tell him?"

Casey nodded apologetically.

Stillman turned toward McGarry. "Casey has a heart," he said quietly.

Mouth fumed. "So? Casey has a heart! So I know he's gotta heart! So this ain't news, Prof! Tell me something that is!"

"The thing is," Casey said in his first speech over three sentences since McGarry had met him. "The thing is, Mr. McGarry, I just couldn't strike out those poor fellahs. I didn't have it in me to do that—to hurt their feelings. I felt—I felt compassion!" He looked toward Stillman as if for confirmation.

Stillman nodded. "That's what he's got, Mr. McGarry. Compassion. See how he smiles?"

Casey grinned obediently and most happily, and Stillman returned his smile. "You see, Mr. McGarry," Stillman continued. "You give a person a heart—particularly someone like Casey, who hasn't been around long enough to understand things like competitiveness or drive or ego. Well"—he shrugged—"that's what happens."

Mouth sat down on the bench, unscrewed the bottle of pills and found it was empty. He threw the bottle over his shoulder. "That's what happens to *him*," he said. "Shall I tell you what happens to me? I go back to being a manager of nine gleeps so old that I gotta rub them down with formaldehyde and revive them in between innings." He suddenly had a thought and looked up at Casey. "Casey," he asked, "don't you feel any of that compassion for the Brooklyn Dodgers?"

Casey smiled back at him. "I'm sorry, Mr. McGarry," he said. "It's just that I can't strike out fellahs. I can't bring myself to hurt their careers. Dr. Stillman thinks I should go into social work now. I'd like to help people. Right, Dr. Stillman?"

"That's right, Casey," Stillman answered.

"Are you going?" Casey asked McGarry as he saw the manager head for the door.

Mouth nodded.

"Well good-bye, Mr. McGarry," Casey said. "And thank you for everything."

Mouth turned to him. The grin on his face was that of dying humanity all over the world. "Don't mention it," he said.

He sighed deeply and walked out to the warm August evening that awaited him and the black headlines on a newspaper stand just outside the stadium that said "I told you so" at him, even though the lettering spelled out, "Casey Shelled from Mound." A reporter stood on the corner, a guy McGarry knew slightly.

"What about it, McGarry?" the reporter asked. "What do you do for pitchers now?"

Mouth looked at him dully. "I dunno," he sighed. "I just feel them one by one and whoever's warm—"

He walked past the reporter and disappeared into the night, a broken-nosed man with sagging shoulders who thought he heard the rustle of pennants in the night air, and then realized it was three shirts on a clothesline that stretched across two of the adjoining buildings.

Harry Turtledove is the acknowledged master of the alternate-history story, whether told at novel length or in the shorter forms. Winner of the HOMer Award, the Sidewise Award for Best Alternate History and the Hugo Award for best novella, he is a frequent nominee for those and other science fiction and fantasy awards. He is the author of several dozen novels and collections, and dozens more short stories. Dr. Turtledove holds a PhD in Byzantine History. In this story, Turtledove wonders what life might have been like if George Herman Ruth's life had gone a little differently.

The House that George Built

Harry Turtledove

PUFFING SLIGHTLY, HENRY LOUIS MENCKEN paused outside of George's Restaurant. He'd walked a little more than a mile from the redbrick house on Hollins Street to the corner of Eutaw and Lombard. Along with masonry, walking was the only kind of exercise he cared for. Tennis and golf and other so-called diversions were to him nothing but a waste of time. He wished his wind were better, but he'd turned sixty the summer before. He carried more weight than he had as a younger man. Most of the parts still worked most of the time. At his age, who could hope for better than that?

He chuckled as his gloved hand fell toward the latch. Every tavern in Baltimore seemed to style itself a restaurant. Maybe that was the Germanic influence. A proud German himself, Mencken wouldn't have been surprised.

His breath smoked. It was cold out here this February afternoon. The chuckle cut off abruptly. Because he was a proud German, he'd severed his ties with the *Sun* papers a couple of weeks before, just as he had back in 1915. Like Wilson a generation before him, Roosevelt II was bound and determined to bring the United States into a stupid war on England's side. Mencken had spent his working life taking swipes at idiots in America. Somehow, they always ended up running the country just when you most wished they wouldn't.

The odors of beer and hot meat and tobacco smoke greeted him when he stepped inside. Mencken nodded happily as he pulled a cigar from an inside pocket of his overcoat and got it going. You could walk into a tavern in Berlin or Hong Kong or Rio de Janeiro or San Francisco and it would smell the same way. Some things didn't, and shouldn't, change.

"Hey, buddy! How ya doin'?" called the big man behind the bar. He had to go six-two, maybe six-three, and at least two hundred fifty pounds. He had a moon face, a wide mouth, a broad, flat nose, and a thick shock of dark brown hair just starting to go gray: he was about fifteen years younger than the journalist. He never remembered Mencken's name, though Mencken was a regular. But, as far as Mencken could see, the big man never remembered anybody's name.

"I'm fine, George. How are you?" Mencken answered, settling himself on a stool. He took off the gloves, stuck them in his pocket, and then shed the overcoat.

"Who, me? I'm okay. What'll it be today?" George said.

"Let me have a glass of Blatz, why don't you?"

"Comin' up." George worked the tap left-handed. He was a southpaw in most things, though Mencken had noticed that he wrote with his right hand. He slid the glass across the bar. "Here y'go."

Mencken gave him a quarter. "Much obliged, publican."

"Publican?" George shook his head. "You got me wrong, pal. I voted for FDR all three times."

Mencken had voted for Roosevelt II once, and regretted it ever after. But if arguing politics with a bartender wasn't a waste of time, he didn't know what would be. He sipped the beer, sucking foam from his upper lip as he set the glass down.

Halfway along the bar, two cops were working on beers of their own and demolishing big plates of braised short ribs. One of them was saying, "So the dumb S.O.B tried to run away from me, y'know? I got him in the back of the head with my espantoon"—he patted the billy club on his belt—"and after that he didn't feel like runnin' no more."

"That's how you do it," the other policeman agreed. "You gotta fill out all kindsa papers if you shoot somebody, but not if you give him the old espantoon. It's just part of a day's work, like."

Hearing the familiar Baltimore word made Mencken smile. He took a longer pull from his glass, then raised his eyes to the big plaque on the wall behind the bar. Mounted on it were a baseball, a bat, and a small, old-fashioned glove. He caught the bartender's eye and pointed to the bat. "There's your espantoon, eh, George?"

"Damn straight," George said proudly. Then he raised a quizzical eyebrow. "Never heard before you was a baseball fan."

He might not remember Mencken's name, but he knew who he was. "I used to be, back in the Nineties," Mencken answered. "I could give you chapter and verse—hell's bells, I could give you word and syllable—about the old Orioles. Do you know, the very first thing I ever had in print was a poem about how ratty and faded the 1894 pennant looked by 1896. The very first thing, in the *Baltimore American*."

"Them was the National League Orioles," George said. "Not the International League Orioles, like I played for."

"Yes, I know." Mencken didn't tell the bartender that for the past thirty years and more he'd found baseball a dismal game. He did add, "Everybody in Baltimore knows for whom George Ruth played." As any native would have, he pronounced the city's name *Baltm'r*.

And he told the truth. People in Baltimore did recall their hometown hero. No doubt baseball aficionados in places like Syracuse and Jersey City and even Kansas City remembered his name, too. He'd played in the high minors for many years, mostly for the Orioles, and done splendidly both as a pitcher and as a part-time outfielder and first baseman.

Did they remember him in Philadelphia? In Boston? In New York, where you needed to go if you wanted to get remembered in a big way? No and no and no, and he'd played, briefly and not too well, in both Philly and Boston. Did they remember him in Mobile and in Madison, in Colorado Springs and in Wichita, in Yakima and in Fresno, in all the two-bit towns where being remembered constituted fame? They did not. And it wasn't as if they'd forgotten him, either. They'd simply never heard of him. That was what stopping one rung shy of the top of the ladder did for you—and to you.

But this was Baltimore. Here, George Ruth was a hometown hero in his hometown. A superannuated hometown hero, but nevertheless . . . Mencken pointed to the bat on the plaque again. "Is that the one you used to hit the I Told You So Homer?" he asked.

He hadn't been a baseball fan these past two-thirds of his life. But he was a Baltimorean. He knew the story, or enough of it. In the 1922 Little World Series—or was it 1921? or 1923?—the Kansas City pitcher facing Ruth knocked him down with a fastball. Ruth got up, dusted himself off, and announced to all and sundry that he'd hit the next one out of the park. He didn't. The Blues' hurler knocked him down again, almost performing a craniotomy on him in the process.

He got to his feet once more . . . and blasted the next pitch not only out of Oriole Park but through a plate glass window in a building across the street on the fly. As he toured the bases, he loudly and profanely embellished on the theme of *I told you so.*

A famous home run—in Baltimore. One the older fans in Kansas City shuddered to remember. A homer nobody anywhere else cared about.

Ruth turned to eye the shillelagh. He was an ugly bruiser, though you'd have to own a death wish to tell him so. Now he morosely shook his head. "Nah. That winter, some guy said he'd give me forty bucks for it, so I sold the son of a gun. You'd best believe I did. I needed the jack."

"I know the feeling," Mencken said. "Most of us do at one time or another— at one time *and* another, more likely."

"Boy, you got that right." George Ruth assumed the expression of an overweight Mask of Tragedy. Then he said, "How's about you buy me a drink?"

"How's about I do?" Mencken said agreeably. He fished another quarter from his trouser pocket and set it on the bar. Ruth dropped it into the cash box. The silver clinked sweetly.

Ruth gave himself his—or rather, Mencken's—money's worth, and then some. In a mixing glass, he built a Tom Collins the size of a young lake. Lemon juice, sugar syrup, ice cubes (which clinked on a note different from the coins'), and enough gin to put every *pukka sahib* in India under the table. So much gin, Mencken laughed out loud. Ruth decorated the drink with not only the usual cherry but a couple of orange slices as well.

And then, as Mencken's eyes widened behind his round-lensed spectacles, Ruth proceeded to pour it down his throat. All of it—the fruit salad, the ice cubes, the works. His Adam's apple bobbed a couple of times, but that was as much hesitation as he gave. A pipe big enough to manage that . . . Mencken would have thought the Public Works Department needed to lay it down the middle of the street. But no.

"Not too bad. No, sirree," Ruth said. And damned if he didn't fix himself another Collins just as preposterous as the first one. He drank it the same way, too. Everything went down the hatch. He put the empty mixing glass down on the bar. "Boy, that hits the spot."

Both cops were staring at him. So was Mencken. He'd done some serious boozing in his day, and seen more than he'd done. But he'd never witnessed anything to match this. He waited for Ruth to fall over, but the man behind the bar might have been drinking Coca-Cola. He'd been a minor-league ballplayer, but he was a major-league toper.

"My hat's off to you, George," one of the policemen said, and doffed his high-crowned, shiny-brimmed cap.

"Mine, too, by God!" Mencken lifted his own lid in salute. "You just put a big dent in this week's profits."

"Nahh." Ruth shook his head. "I was thirsty, that's all—thirsty and pissed off, know what I mean?" How he could have absorbed that much gin without showing it Mencken couldn't imagine, but he had.

"Pissed off about what?" the journalist asked, as he was surely meant to do.

"That cocksucker Rasin. Carroll Wilson Chickenshit Rasin." Here was a name Ruth remembered, all right: remembered and despised. "You know who that rotten prick was?"

Nobody who hadn't lived in Baltimore for a long time would have, but Mencken nodded. "Politico—Democrat—back around the time of the last war. Had a pretty fair pile of cash, too, if I remember straight."

"Yeah, that's him, all right," Ruth agreed. "Lousy four-flushing cocksucker."

"What did he ever do to you?" Mencken had trouble envisioning circles in which both Rasin and Ruth would have traveled a generation earlier.

"Back in 1914, Jack Dunn of the Orioles, he signed me to a contract. Signed me out of St. Mary's Industrial School, way the hell over at the west end of town."

"All right." If Mencken had ever heard of George Ruth's baseball beginnings, they'd slipped his mind. "But what's that got to do with Carroll Rasin?" He wondered if the gin was scrambling Ruth's brains. That the big palooka could still stand up and talk straight struck him as the closest thing to a miracle God had doled out lately. Wherever the ex-ballplayer had bought his liver, Mencken wanted to shop there, too.

"Rasin talked about putting a Federal League team in town. The Baltimore Terrapins, he was gonna call 'em. And when Dunn heard about that, he damn near shit. The Federal League, it was a major league, like." Ruth paused to light a cigar: a cheroot that, with Mencken's, thickened the fug in the air. After a couple of irate puffs, Ruth went on, "The International League, that was minor-league ball. With the Terrapins in town, the Orioles wouldn't've drawn flies."

Mencken remembered the Federal League only vaguely. Had Ruth not reminded him of it, he probably wouldn't have remembered it at all. He'd long since outgrown his fandom by 1914. "So what's that got to do with you?" he asked. "And while you're at it, how about another beer?"

"Sure thing." Ruth took back the glass, but waited to see money before working the tap again. As he gave Mencken the refill, he growled, "What's it got to do with me? I'll tell you what. If the Orioles ain't drawin' flies, Dunn ain't makin' any dough. How's he supposed to keep the Orioles goin'? Hell, how's he supposed to eat?"

"How?" Mencken lobbed another question down the middle.

"You sell your players, that's how. Weren't no farm teams in those days." Ruth's lip curled so scornfully, the cigar threatened to fall out. "Nah, none o' that crap. The minor-league owners was out for themselves, same as the guys in the bigs. An' they got cash by sellin' contracts. I had people innarested in me, too, let me tell you I did. Connie Mack of the Athaletics, he was innarested, only he didn't have no money himself then, neither. The Red Sox, they was innarested. And Cincinnati, they was makin' noises like they wanted me."

He reminded Mencken of an aging chorus girl, all crow's-feet and extra chins, going on about the hot sports who'd drunk champagne from her slipper back in the day. The bloom went off a baseball player just about as fast. It was a cruel way to try to make a living. "So why didn't you sign with one of them, then?" he asked.

Ruth snorted angrily—he'd missed something. "I couldn't. Fuckin' Dunn held my contract. Unless he turned me loose, I had to play for him or nobody. And that no good piece of shit of a Rasin crapped out on me. Turned out he didn't have the moolah, or maybe didn't wanna spend the moolah, to get into the Federal League after all. The Milwaukee Creams was the last franchise instead. The Creams! Ain't that a crappy name for a team? And Dunn made a go of it here after all. I was stuck, is what I was. Fuckin' stuck."

Now that Mencken thought about it, fragments of the war between the upstart league and its established rivals came back to him. "Why didn't you join the Federal League yourself? Plenty of players did."

The man behind the bar threw his hands in the air, a gesture of extravagant disgust. "I couldn't even do that, Goddamn it to fucking hell. When Dunn got me out of St. Mary's, I was a whole hot week past my nineteenth birthday. Deal he made with the holy fathers said he was my legal guardian till I turned twenty-one. I couldn't sign nothin' without him givin' the okay. An' by my twenty-first birthday, goddamn Federal League was dead as shoe leather. I got screwed, an' I didn't even get kissed."

"You did all right for yourself," Mencken said, reasonable—perhaps obnoxiously reasonable—as usual. "You played your game at the highest level. You played for years and years at the next highest level. When you couldn't play any more, you had enough under the mattress to let you get this place, and it's not half bad, either."

"It's all in the breaks, all dumb fuckin' luck," Ruth said. "If Dunn had to sell me to the bigs when I was a kid, who knows what I coulda done? I was thirty years old by the time they changed the rules so he couldn't keep me forever no more. I already had the start of my bay window, and my elbow was shot to shit. I didn't say nothin' about that—otherwise, nobody woulda bought me. But Jesus Christ, if I'd made the majors when I was nineteen, twenty years old, I coulda been Buzz Arlett."

Every Broadway chorine thought she could start in a show. Every pug thought he could have been a champ. And every halfway decent ballplayer thought he could have been Buzz Arlett. Even a nonfan like Mencken knew his name. Back in the Twenties, people said they were two of the handful of Americans who needed no press agent. He came to Brooklyn from the Pacific Coast League in 1922. He belted home runs from both sides of the plate. He pitched every once in a while, too. And he turned the Dodgers into the powerhouse they'd been ever since. He made people forget about the Black Sox scandal that had hovered over the game since it broke at the end of the 1920 season. They called him the man who saved baseball. They called Ebbets Field the House That Buzz Built. And the owners smiled all the way to the bank.

Trying to be gentle with a man he rather liked, Mencken said, "Do you really think so? Guys like that come along once in a blue moon."

Ruth thrust out his jaw. "I coulda, if I'd had the chance. Even when I got up to Philly, that dumbshit Fletcher who was runnin' the team, he kept me pitchin' an' wouldn't let me play the field. There I was, tryin' to get by with junk from my bad flipper in the Baker Bowl, for Chrissakes. It ain't even a long piss down the right-field line there. Fuck, I hit six homers there myself. For a while, that was a record for a pitcher. But they said anybody could do it there. An' I got hit pretty hard myself, so after a season and a half they sold me to the Red Sox."

"That was one of the teams that wanted you way back when, you said," Mencken remarked.

"You was listenin'! Son of a bitch!" Ruth beamed at him. "Here, have one on me." He drew another Blatz and set it in front of Mencken. The journalist finished his second one and got to work on the bonus. Ruth went on, "But when the Sox wanted me, they was good. Time I got to 'em, they stunk worse'n the Phils. They pitched me a little, played me in the outfield and at first a little, an' sat me on the bench a lot. I didn't light the world on fire, so after the season they sold me down to Syracuse. 'Cept for a month at the end of '32 with the Browns"—he shuddered at some dark memory—"I never made it back to the bigs again. But I coulda been hot stuff if fuckin' Rasin came through with the cash."

A line from Gray's "Elegy" went through Mencken's mind: *Some mute inglorious Milton here may rest.* A mute (or even a loudmouthed) inglorious Arlett tending bar in Baltimore? Mencken snorted. Not likely! He knew why that line occurred to him now. He'd mocked it years before: *There are no mute, inglorious Miltons, save in the imaginations of poets. The one sound test of a Milton is that he functions as a Milton.*

Mencken poured down the rest of the beer and got up from his stool. "Thank you kindly, George. I expect I'll be back again before long."

"Any time, buddy. Thanks for lettin' me bend your ear." George Ruth chuckled. "This line o' work, usually it goes the other way around."

"I believe *that*." Mencken put on his overcoat and gloves, then walked out into the night. Half an hour—not even—and he'd be back at the house that faced on Union Square.

Ray Gonzalez is an award-winning poet, editor and writer. He is the author of ten books of poetry and several collections of essays and short fiction, and also the editor of a dozen anthologies. He specializes in poetry, creative nonfiction, flash fiction and prose poetry. He teaches in the English and Creative Writing departments at the University of Minnesota. In this compact and literate story he toys with time, history, baseballs and baseball, giving us a collapsed novel's worth of storytelling.

Baseball

∽

Ray Gonzalez

THE HOME RUN BALL rose over right field and disappeared before it started its downward arc. The right fielder backed to the warning path, but there was no ball to catch. He stood dazed as the roar of the crowd turned to confusion. Thousands of fans were on their feet for the home run. But, where was it? The hitter, a national hero who led the league in home runs, slowed to a hesitant jog as he rounded first base. The first and second basemen stood at their positions, one of them removing his cap from his head as he searched the night sky for the ball. The hitter nodded to the closest umpire, as if asking permission to keep running the bases, though he kept going. Managers, coaches, and players from both benches came out of the dugout. Unable to lower their heads from searching for the ball, some of the players stumbled over each other in front of the dugouts. The manager of the team at bat waved to his batter to keep running. The opposing manager ran toward one of the umpires. There was no ball, just the memory of the loud whack as the player's bat met the ball and sent it rocketing toward the right field bleachers. The ball's rapid trajectory was the last thing anyone recalled before it vanished. Thousands of witnesses amplified their stunned silence with a magnetic restlessness. With two men on base, the home run would give the visiting team a 3–2 lead in the first game of the World Series. It was the bottom half of the sixth inning. Where was the ball? As the hitter, his mouth agape, rounded third and headed home, the right fielder ran as fast as he could toward the second base umpire. With his confused manager joining him, both men screamed at the umpire to do something. The right fielder claimed the ball had not been hit hard enough for a home run. He screamed that he was in position to catch it when it vanished. His manager yelled that the three runs should not count because there was no ball hit out of the park. The opposing manager was welcoming his hero at home plate. He was not going to argue with anybody, even though he had no idea what had happened to the ball. In his book, it was a home run and the ball's speed and height made that obvious to the entire stadium before it disappeared. The beleaguered umpire at second base walked toward the umpire at first. He was surrounded by angry players and one red-faced manager. The first base umpire was coming to his defense when, suddenly, the ball appeared in the night sky. It fell where the right fielder was previously standing and settled in the warning path. Thousands of spectators saw it and both teams saw it. They pointed, screamed, and waved, but it was too late. The bases had been run, the three men had scored, and it would be ruled an inside-the-park home run. The last thing reported in the sports pages of every major newspaper was the right fielder running from the umpire he had been attacking, to the ball in the right field corner. He picked it out of the dirt and stared at it. What was not reported was his surprise at how old and yellow the baseball was. The stitches were coming off, and the ball was slightly warped. Some balls looked like that after a good hit, but this one was different. He threw it to the cut-off man at second, who also noticed how old the ball was. He picked it out of his glove and handed it to the umpire who was recovering from being attacked. When the umpire realized he had not seen this brand of baseball since his dirt lot days in the fifties, he tucked it into his coat pocket. The home plate umpire threw out another ball. When the papers carried the story, the second base umpire was surprised no sports writer asked him about the ball. Maybe it was because the home team won by a score of 5–3, three more runs coming on base hits. After the game, the umpire took his coat off in the umpire's dressing room and searched the pockets, but couldn't find the antique ball.

Ron Carlson is the author of six story collections and six novels, most recently *Return to Oakpine*. His fiction has appeared in *Esquire*, *Harper's*, *The New Yorker*, *GQ*, and many other magazines and journals and has been selected for *The Best American Short Stories*, *The O. Henry Prize Series*, *The Pushcart Prize Anthology*, *The Norton Anthology of Short Fiction* and dozens of other anthologies. He is the Director of the Graduate Program in Fiction at the University of California, Irvine. In this touching and comic story, Carlson uses small-town baseball to explore the acceptance of the Other, telling the story through the naive eye of a farm-boy ballplayer who's just glad to be playing the game for as long as he can.

My Last Season with the Owls

∽

Ron Carlson

DEVLIN IS A VAMPIRE and Coleman is also a vampire, but there are no two guys in the whole Mid-Prairie League who can turn a sweeter double play at second base, one of them on a knee or flat out on the infield with the other leaping over the slide and throwing from his place in the air. If records were kept in this league, and they're going to be next year, they'd have the record twice. As is, every player on all seven teams in the Mid-Prairie League knows that to hit it on the ground up our middle is going to about retire the side. They're good, and for little guys they can hit.

There may be one other vampire on the team, but no one's sure. No one's exactly sure about Devlin and Coleman; it's what they call an open secret. I mean, they're vampires, but none of us has really talked about it. At batting practice, I've talked to both of them. I asked Devlin when he learned to hit left (meaning how long has he been a vampire), and he said that he decided in high school to learn because there were all those farm boy right-handers. I asked Coleman if he was going to try for the River League (meaning is it hard being a vampire, is there a future in it), and he told me that it was a long shot, that league, but he'd take what he could get.

You'd think two vampires on a baseball team in the Midwest would hang out together, but they really don't. They don't sit together on the bus or room together and they're not even from the same towns. But still. I don't care. What I care about is taking the grounder off the line at third and throwing across to Coleman and knowing for perfect sure that he'll make the play. What I care about is that when Devlin hits in front of me that he gets on and steals second, so that I'm not the dummy every night who hits into the double play.

Coach Kaiser doesn't care about what the guys do off the field as long as they show up and play their hearts out. Everybody has something, he has said in our team meetings, and he's right. Our right fielder, Benito Porch, who can run like a demon, has full blown diabetes, and Kaiser has to check before every pitch that he hasn't gone face down in the bunchgrass. It has happened. Harry Whisper is our best pitcher and he's only got three fingers on his business hand. He can be a pain when he wins, arrogant, and he says some things. Like he said that he had the finger removed on purpose so he could throw his drop ball, a pitch that wins games—for the team. He always says *for the team*. If you look at him sideways, he adds: *You want to see it. I kept it. I've got it back at the farm in a jar.* He does not have it in a jar. Some skunk ate it the same day he tore it off in a cornfield in a mistake with a combine. And then there's Mikel Antenna who had our team name OWLS picked off the back of his jersey and replaced with his name in big satin letters. *I like to hear my name*, he told me. *It helps me at the plate and it doesn't hurt with the scouts either.* He is kidding himself about the scouts, but I'm not going to correct him after he's altered his shirt that way.

Here are the steps from Mid-Prairie to the Big Leagues: you'd get called to the River League up in Illinois. They have one scout total, a hard drinking guy name of Fergus Finity who is on like a permanent DUI and arrives by bus most times. The backseat of his car, Coach Kaiser told me, has got more tickets in it than player notes. The one night last season he was coming to see us play the Hawks out in the village of Toil, he spent the night in jail or so they said. He never showed up, but that didn't prevent Mikel Antenna from playing his heart out, strutting around, showing his back to two men he thought were the scouts. They were surprised when he went out to where they sat by third base after the game and asked them how they liked it. They said they'd liked it fine, though it had been hard to see because the lights in Toil are old streetlights hung too low. He smiled at them, chewing his gum, waiting, and then he found out they were the vacuum truck drivers waiting for the park to clear so they could clear the septic tanks. Still, there's hope. From the River League, if you make it, you try for the Ice League, so called because it is up on the North Dakota border and half of the teams are from Canada. It looks like a tough league, and almost all the guys there have full beards, none of these designer goatees you see in Triple A. From the Ice League, you'd go into the Outskirts Association which plays all over. They've got an airplane that will seat most of any team, and there have been, so far three guys, all infielders, go on to play in that league with the Bucket Vikings and the LaFluge Pioneers both of whom play one game a year, preseason, near Wrigley Field. It doesn't get any better than that.

My bride Afton and I made an agreement about my career in sport. She liked it when I played at Mount Nadir. We were dating then and she came to the games, and I said some of my best things to her walking back from the Vo-ed field to the dorms. When we got married, I said I'd like to give it a try. She said, "How long is a try?"

I thought about it. We were living in an apartment in Coalseam, a nice little place, and we had our expenses screwed down tight, and Afton was clerking for the dentist, and I told her, "Three years. If I don't get called up in three years, I'll let her go, and we'll go back up to Fidelity River and take my dad up on his offer to farm there."

"And we'll have those kids," she said.

"Right," I said. "There's room for all the kids we want. But for now, I'll play my heart out and see what happens."

Well, what happened was what happened. I'm a good ball player and I love it, and I found out that there are about one million good ball players who have the same personal feeling for the sport. I did an inventory last year of the skills and abilities and talents and special dexterities that single me out from the infielders I was running across, and there are none. I was doing just fine, and then two vampires join the team and they glisten every game. They make the infield look like it was a birthday present and they had the pretty paper, the scissors, and the tape.

You stand at third base as the pitch goes in with only two thoughts in the world: *hit it to me right now because I am so ready and hungry to join the contest*, or *please please please do not hit it to me or near me or anywhere at all really for I am fearful and not prepared*. These two thoughts fought for space in my head like kids playing king of the hill; they were my constant companions. Every time I looked over at Dracula and Dracula, they were showing their teeth having a wonderful time.

I asked Coleman why he doesn't show up for our day games, and he looked real surprised. "I've got something to do," he told me.

"Like a job?" I said. We were in the dugout spitting sunflower seeds waiting to see if Kaiser was going to let Benito Porch steal second. We were playing the

Herons in Lake Catbite, where there is no lake and never was, and if we won, we'd be above five hundred and get a good seed at the Jubilee Tournament. Benito was dodging and hopping, and he had a good six foot lead. He could run. Then the Heron left-hander just stepped and threw to first. Benito hadn't moved, and Kaiser picked up the Tupperware of orange juice off the shelf and started out of the dugout because he knew, as we all did, what was going to happen next. Benito Porch went face down in the dirt. He'd forgotten to check his blood sugar. When he falls, it is beautiful, like a kite on a broken string. Just down. No kaboom.

Coleman packed his mouth with sunflower seeds, showing me his beautiful incisors, and he grabbed his mitt as we took the field. "I'm finishing my second year at Lavender Craft."

"In heating and air-conditioning?" I asked him.

"God, no," he said. "I'm making teeth for the cosmetic dentistry industry; it is exploding. All the teeth in Chicago come from Lavender." He ran off to play ball, and I stood at third base, wondering.

We won that game but it took eleven innings. We scored on three errors in that inning, and then Three-fingers Whisper came in and struck out the side. His pitching was way off, but he kept showing his hand and scaring the guys and it worked. So much of being at the plate is about fear.

On the bus back home, I went back and sat by Devlin and told him good game, though he didn't look too happy. He never really looked too happy. He had a long face from the get-go. "Devlin," I said. "Why don't you come to our day games?"

"I've got school," he said. This surprised me because he was like twenty-five.

"Are you at Saint Permission?"

"No, I'm at the seminary in Fort Lunch."

"There's a seminary there? I thought it was just the theme park. What are you going to be?"

He tapped his backpack on the floor and said, "I'm going to read these books and then god only knows."

"What about the weekend games?" I said. He wasn't fooling me.

"Retreats," he said. We were driving past the weigh station outside of Catbite and the panes of light flashed across his doleful face. "Different places," he said. "We were over in Mount Nadir two weeks ago." I was going to tell him I went to school there, but thought better of it. We were silent. The long dark bus rides are twenty guys sleeping with their iPods in, and Coach Kaiser up in front with his lighted clipboard going over the box score. They are comfortable as a team gets, but I wasn't comfortable.

I had one more gambit. I pulled my little silver crucifix from my pocket and showed it to Devlin in the dark bus. "You wear these?"

He turned on his light and held it in his two fingers. "No," he said. "We don't." I was astonished that he could let it touch his skin, if that was his skin. "And you shouldn't either," he said. "I saw a guy in More put one into his breastbone when he rammed the catcher sliding in at home. *I'll bet you did*, I wanted to say, but I held my tongue.

I keep a lot of things to myself. Such as, I would never really tell anyone how much I want to play ball, because first of all, I couldn't express it with dexterity. Secondly, I would get about half way through it and start to cry. I still cry. Another thing I hadn't spoken about to anyone was the fact that I promised a three-year shot at the baseball, and this was it. The third season was over and there was one more week of baseball in my whole life forever and ever amen. Afton knew it, but she hadn't said anything or done anything like X out the days on the calendar or put any countdown on the fridge. She supported me and every time I grabbed my kit to go off to play, she'd say, "Play your heart out and come home to me." She even said that at home games where I could see her in the stands, sometimes with my folks.

I also keep my worries to myself and my suspicions, but I decided to sample them to Afton the night before the team was going off to the tournament. I had packed my duffel and oiled my mitt and I got into bed and Afton kissed me and snuggled up. She'd always liked the smell of leather oil and I did too. I said, "Do all the teeth in Chicago come from Lavender?"

She put her hand on my chest and pushed herself up. "What?"

"Do all the teeth in Chicago come from Lavender?"

She laughed a little and said, "Not all. There's a lot of teeth in Chicago."

"You know what I'm saying," I said.

"I don't know what you're saying, Eddy, you dear man, but yeah, a lot of the crown work and full bridges are made out in Lavender. It's sort of famous for it."

"Okay," I said. She lay back down and was still sort of laughing.

"Is there a seminary over by the theme park in Fort Lunch?"

"Eddie," she said. Now she was just laughing at her husband. "You mean over by Calvary World?"

"Yes, a seminary."

"Are you going to take me and the kids over to Calvary World when they're old enough?"

"What?" I said.

"You know," she said, "ride the wagon train through the mountain tunnel and do that canoe ride and eat there in the barracks?" I remembered when we'd gone over to the place when we were dating.

"There's a lot of splashing with those canoes."

"I want to go," she said.

"Well, then, I do too."

"Do you want to go to the seminary there?" she said.

"There is one," I said.

"Yes," she said. "There's been one for a hundred years. The seminary was before the Fort Lunch."

"Devlin said he was at the seminary, studying."

"He would be," she said. "His dad was minister at Mercy for years." She lay back down and said, "And the log slide." She kissed my neck.

I'm a ballplayer, but I'm not dumb as a door. I knew what was going on. "We are going to have a baby," I said.

"We are," she whispered.

"What is it?" I asked.

"It is a boy or a girl," she said.

"Perfect," I said. "That's my choice," and as I said it I knew it was true. Bring on the boy. Bring on the girl. I'll go into it with my whole heart. Boys and girls play ball with talent, skill, adroitness, and dexterity.

"Perfect," she said to me there in the bed.

That win over the Herons put us in fair shape for the Jubilee Tournament in Blister, which includes all seven teams in the Bird League, as the Mid American Prairie League is called in the papers. It's shorter, but none of the players call it that. It's a four-hour bus ride and I could sense the anticipation. I could sense my anticipation. Coach Kaiser went up and down the aisle a few times talking to the guys, his hand on our shoulders. Benito asked him if Fergus Finity would be there. "He will," the coach said. "This is one stop shopping for that guy. You'll be in his notebook before Saturday," the coach said. He said that to a lot of us. It was good to hear.

The field in Blister is the toughest place we play. The infield is fine enough for mowed bunchgrass, but the outfield is all stubble alfalfa and left center is low and marshy. With the rain there can be some standing water and you've got to play the ball in the air or it hits like a hockey puck and shoots into the tall grass. There is no homerun fence. There's a three-strand barb wire way back by the surplus canal and always twenty black angus standing there like umpires chewing it over. In the night their eyes glowed.

We beat the Eagles the first night, nine to nothing. Mikel Antenna, who hadn't homered all year, hit two. It made you wonder if he'd been holding back until the scouts were seated, but a win's a win. The next night we beat the Loons three to two on a sacrifice squeeze. Coach Kaiser should have been scouted for that call. It was thrilling. Each night was a double-header, and so by Friday there were just three teams left. The Wild Turkeys drew the bye and that meant we faced off against the Robins to make the playoff.

The Robins were all corn fed and big, and they played big. I've never seen such swings. These guys stood legs apart and stepped toward the ball like they were on the SWAT team breaking down a door. When they swung and missed, you heard the noise, like an angry ghost going by your head. They hit a homer every inning, these balls lost in the far swale and one causing a minor stir in the supreme court of cattle by the back fence. But, they were big in the field too, and it took them a while to get to anything out of the infield, so we had seven doubles by the sixth inning and were only trailing by two runs.

In the top of the seventh, their catcher hit a double into right which splashed and stuck in the mud in front of Benito Porch. There was a short delay as the umps dried the ball with a towel and put it back into play. I didn't like this catcher being on second. They were calling him "Hammer" from their dugout, and I hoped it was not an earned nickname, but that he might be from a polite family of Hammers who knew the rules of sport and etiquette. I had already pissed him off by accidentally tapping his hand on the backswing when I had been up in the fourth inning. I hadn't helped my case by looking at him hunkering there and saying, *So move.*

Now the two thoughts contended in my ballplayer's noggin. *Come on, big guy, try to steal and meet your certain fate under my mortal tag* and *Please Please Please do not steal, don't come this way at all or even look in this direction.* When I would glance at him between pitches, though, he was looking in my direction. He looked, in fact without exaggeration like he was coming for me. Harry Whisper threw the next pitch hard, his famous three-finger drop, and our catcher bobbled the ball, not much but just enough to give Mr. Hammer the idea that third base would soon be his. It was only three giant steps away and he was after all a giant, and he was now coming right at me. I ran to the bag and crouched for the throw which was low; it one-hopped and found my glove just as Hammer slid headfirst into my waiting knee. His momentum rolled us both up and over the bag, and I was underneath him, trapped. I looked up and saw the umpire's thumb. Out! He was out. Literally. Suddenly I couldn't breathe under this bleeding giant. I lifted my head enough to see the doleful Devlin sprinting over, not looking so doleful now, but with a clear vampire's lust in his eyes. He too looked like he was coming for me. Hammer's mouth had struck my knee and his face was all blood, as was my jersey now, as they rolled him onto his back and Devlin knelt above him. It looked like he was feeding. Coleman came over and pushed Devlin away and put his fingers into the bloody mouth. "If we straighten these teeth right now," he said, inches from Hammer's face, "he won't lose them." And he worked on the man there for twenty minutes in the Blister night.

We beat the Robins by four runs, proving that twelve doubles will beat nine homeruns, but it was an uneasy night for me in the old village. It's never easy for a ballplayer to have great stripes of blood on his shirt when his teammates, some of them, are vampires.

The championship game was at two in the afternoon on Saturday. We had known this from the start. I knew we'd be without our vampires, and it ended up being the difference. Fergus Finity finally showed up and we saw him talk to Coach Kaiser before the game. I wondered how Devlin and Coleman felt knowing the scout wouldn't see them—the only two guys on our squad who really had a chance. Finity was a little skinny guy with his hair combed back severely as if it were a lesson. A couple of the guys went up and shook hands with him. Mikel did. Finity came down the dugout and asked my name and I told him. He said, "Third base," and I was glad he knew that.

"You should see our short and second, though," I told him. We were alone there for one minute and I could speak. "Coleman and Devlin," I said. "Not one ground ball got through this season. Not one."

"I'll make a note," Mr. Finity said. "Good luck," he said.

A few minutes later, Coach Kaiser said, "Play your hearts out, boys."

I guess we did. The Wild Turkeys beat us six to four in a pretty good game. The sun had dried portions of the outfield, and Benito Porch had an easier time of it. Two of the cows went around and got onto the field so there was a little break in the fifth. Afton and my folks came down and saw my last at bat in a uniform. The pitch was inside and I stepped out and got it all in a line drive down the baseline for a double. Standing on second I could see the whole world.

A person has his hopes and his illusions and he does what he can to foster them. I had mine. I played baseball for a while on a good team; two of our best players were vampires for a while. Now, I've turned practical. My father grows flax, but next season we're going to put in ten acres of sunflowers; this is perfect soil for them and there's a market. In three years some of them will be in the red and blue buckets in the dugouts of Fenway Park and Yankee Stadium. It helps knowing—even at this distance—that we'll be part of America's game.

Cecilia Tan has been writing about baseball since she recorded Dave Righetti's no-hitter in her high school diary in 1983. She is the author of *The 50 Greatest Yankee Games* and has edited the Yankees Annual every pre-season since 2007. In 2011, she became publications director for SABR, where she edits the *Baseball Research Journal* and directs the SABR digital books program. Her short fiction has appeared in *Ms. Magazine*, *Asimov's Science Fiction* magazine, *Best American Erotica*, and many other places. In this story, Tan balances the hope of a Red Sox spring training with the reality of the game no matter how informally it is played, as a young player works to reverse the curse in his own small way.

Pitchers and Catchers

∞

Cecilia Tan

THE INFIELD WAS BAKED red clay, that Georgia clay found on fields all over the country, brought in by the truckload. Kirby could smell it from the runway to the dugout, such a familiar smell. It was the smell of Little League, and the field behind the school near his uncle's house, and the smell of learning to block balls in the dirt.

He emerged from the damp shade of the dugout into the bright but weak February morning sun. The breeze was cold but the grass was green; a ground-skeeper trimmed the verge beyond third base with a manual push mower. Beyond him, the jigsaw puzzle of advertising signs that made up the outfield wall shone bright and riotous. Kirby shifted his bag on his shoulder. He should have gone straight to his locker to put it down, but something made him want to see the field first. His first spring training with the big club.

The crunch of a set of spikes on concrete behind him made him turn, and there was Mike Greenwell, suited up in uniform pants and a ratty gray T-shirt. His dark moustache was matched not so much by a goatee as an untamed off-season lack of shaving.

"You're here a little early, aren't you?" Kirby said, without thinking.

"Eight a.m.? Not really," Greenwell replied as he went up the dugout steps to the grass.

"No, I mean, isn't it just pitchers and catchers today?"

"Like I have something better to do . . . ?" Greenwell joked as he began a jog around the warning track.

It was only later, when Kirby found the locker with his name on it and saw Greenwell's was across from his, that he realized he hadn't introduced himself. *Wouldn't want to seem like a brown-noser*, he thought, after the fact. The locker, the one with "Wilcox" over it, written with a magic marker on a wide strip of what looked like medical tape, had a pile of brand new catching equipment in it. The elation over the new equipment almost overcame the letdown of seeing his locker tag was temporary. Of course it was—just his first invite to Red Sox camp; he told himself not to get overexcited.

Catchers tended to get the invite to the big club sooner than other position players. It was just math—there were so many pitchers who needed to work out, put in bullpen sessions, non-roster invitees auditioning for jobs. Probably more than thirty pitchers in camp right now. Maybe forty. Prospects were there, too, starters and bullpen guys—pitchers everywhere. That meant a lot of catching to be done. Kirby knew that, but he'd still felt privileged to get the word that, just a year out of rookie ball, he would be lockering with the likes of an All-Star like Mike Greenwell.

Other guys were filtering in now, some he knew from rookie ball, some not. Now introductions were okay, he decided, since they were mostly new guys, both the pitchers and the catchers. Ever since Tony Peña had gone, there had been something of a revolving door at catcher for the Sox, and every guy there knew it. Kirby's heart started to beat harder just thinking about it. Who knew? Make an impression on someone, maybe someone else tweaks a muscle, anyone could be behind the plate on Opening Day, wasn't that right? He pictured himself crouching behind the dish, Roger Clemens on the mound, the big green wall visible through the bars of his mask, Clemens' leg kick . . .

There was Clemens now, big Texas guy, his hair in need of a trim, shaking hands and exchanging back slaps with some of the other players near his locker. *Yes*, thought Kirby, *this is where I belong*. He decided to dump the worry about brown-nosing and went to join the circle around Roger's locker, but halfway there he saw a satin-jacketed coach tacking up a white piece of paper. There were always too many coaches and assistant coaches to keep track of in Spring Training, but anyone with gray hair and a field jacket was probably in the know. Kirby veered toward the bulletin board. The notice had the day's workout schedule and rotation. He and ace pitcher Clemens were in a group together and he couldn't help but take that as a little ego-boo. *Maybe they do like me, after all,* he thought.

An hour later he was in the bullpen, his gear on, while Clemens and two other starters prepared to take the mound under the watchful eye of a coach. Kirby kept forgetting the names of the other two guys. One of them he should have known, too, because they had faced each other in college. But try as he might, the name Gar Finnvold was too ridiculous to stick in his brain. The other one, same problem, Nate Minchey, for whatever reason it was like these two guys could not be for real. Finnvold took the mound first and tweaked something in his landing leg within the first five pitches. He and the coach went off in search of the trainer, and Minchey took a seat on the bench to wait for his return.

"C'mon," Clemens said to Kirby, "I'll have a go. It's not like I'm really going to air it out on the first day."

Kirby crouched behind the plate and tamped down the spike of anxiety in his throat. He had caught plenty of fireballers in his time and besides, as Clemens said, he wasn't going to be trying to light up the radar gun today.

Still, the first fastball popped loudly in Kirby's mitt, and he felt the sting in his left hand. He plucked the ball out and lobbed it back to Clemens who stood waiting at the bottom of the mound, his glove bobbing impatiently for the return throw.

The next pitch was the same, and soon he and Kirby sank into a rhythm. All Kirby did was think about catching it, throwing it back, catching it, throwing it back. That was plenty to think about. He didn't know Clemens' form, his habits, his tendencies, any of that stuff. His job right now was singular: get the ball back to Roger.

"All right if I try Mister Splittee?" Roger called as the ball sailed back to him.

"You sure?" Kirby asked, tipping his mask onto the top of his head so he could talk. Pitchers typically didn't start on the breaking stuff until later in the spring. But maybe Roger didn't count the split-finger fastball as a breaking pitch.

"No, are *you* sure?" was Roger's reply, "meat?"

"Bring it on," Kirby said with a smile as he yanked the mask back down. He pounded the glove for emphasis.

The first one, as Fate would have it, got by him. Bounced in the dirt right at the plate, and then went through his legs and hit the chain link fence, startling some reporters on the other side. Kirby felt his cheeks burn under his mask. *That's baseball,* he repeated to himself, the mantra he had picked up long ago when he learned that it could be a humiliating game. *That's baseball.*

No more balls got by and after a few more minutes, Roger was done. Minchey shrugged, not wanting to throw until the coach came back. So Roger and Kirby sat together on the bench, companionably sweaty and drinking water out of Gatorade cups.

"So how did it look to you?" Roger asked.

"Good," Kirby replied.

"Good?"

"Good." Kirby shrugged. "I've never caught you before so . . . what do I know?"

Roger crumpled the lime green cup in his hand and tossed it on the ground. "You were a Gator, weren't you."

"How did you know that?" Kirby had, in fact, gone to the University of Florida, Gainesville.

"I play golf with a sports administrator from there, nobody you'd know," he said, which didn't answer the question. "Did you always catch or were you converted?"

Was I that bad? Kirby wondered. "I caught and pitched in high school . . ."

"Red, hey Red!" Roger shouted to a coach passing by and gave him an exaggerated hieroglyphics-style shrug. "What gives?"

The coach, a wizened fellow with a shock of white hair Kirby didn't recognize, pointed back the way he had come.

"C'mon," Roger said then, giving Kirby a slap on the shoulder, and jogged off to the practice field where the next phase of the workout was beginning.

That night Kirby found himself at the local steakhouse the players favored, sitting around the square of a bar in the center with six or seven other guys, all pitchers except for him. He ordered a beer, a steak, and a tall glass of iced tea, "Hold the tea." The bartender was a cute blond who didn't get it, but the pitcher on his left, a bullpen hopeful named Hiram Green, burst out laughing.

"Just do it, honey," Green said to her. "In fact, put that cup of ice on my tab."

That got a smile out of Kirby. Green, despite his name, wasn't—he had been bouncing around the league for a good number of years already before getting the invite to Red Sox camp. Kirby didn't know much about him.

When the ice came, Kirby clamped his swollen left hand around the glass, and sighed.

"You catching Roger today?" Green asked.

"Yeah."

"Thought it was you. Can't really tell you guys apart with the fucking masks on, of course. What number you wearing?"

"Eighty six."

"Well, my sympathies to both of us, brother. They gave me sixty seven." Hiram shuddered. "If I get a chance I hope to switch it up."

"Why?"

"How old are you? Aw, you would have been only two. But sixty seven, that was a cursed year for the Red Sox, didn't you know?"

"Uh, eighty six wasn't such a great year either," Kirby said, still not quite sure what Hiram was going on about.

"Cursed," Hiram said, shaking his head sadly. "You don't want nothing to do with that number."

Kirby felt a shiver run through him as the image of that ball going through his legs earlier in the day suddenly popped into his mind. It wasn't anything like what happened to Buckner and yet . . . ? He shook himself. Snap out of it. Ridiculous.

He sipped his beer in silence and let the pitchers indulge their superstitions. Catchers had to be better grounded, squatting down instead of perching up on the mound like flamingoes surveying their domains. He was used to this kind of thing. Pitchers, when in groups, invariably talked about three things besides women, and that was breaking balls, jinxes, and hitting. Yes, hitting. Even American League pitchers seemed obsessed with it. The rumor that Major League Baseball was going to institute interleague play during the regular season within a few years persisted, and of course here in Spring Training, when they played a National League team, they would use the National League rules.

So Kirby wasn't surprised when, halfway through his steak, the pitchers started talking about wanting more cage time. "Yeah, I want to get my cuts," Hiram said. "But I'm a bullpen guy. Like I'm going to be out there more than one inning anyway."

"Don't say that, Green," a blond, red-faced lefthander named Jones said, a little breathless. "Some of those split squad games, they don't bring that many guys. If you come in to face the last batter of an inning, and then have to pitch the next inning, and the pitcher's spot comes up to bat . . ."

"Keep dreamin'," Hiram replied. "'Cause that's the only way you or I are getting any licks in this spring. Really. No way, José."

One of the Latin pitchers jumped in at that, though Kirby hadn't determined if the guy's name was José or not. He stopped listening. Everyone knew pitchers couldn't hit. The National League clung to their stupid rule out of tradition, but they were pretty much the only ones at this point. Kirby had been a fairly good pitcher in his time, but one of the reasons he had given it up was that his hitting talent would have gone to waste. Well, that was the rational reason his coaches and he gave. The less rational reason was that he somehow knew that *because* he could hit, he did not belong in the fraternity of pitchers. His eyes scanned the bar. Where were all the other catchers tonight? Did they have some other watering hole he didn't know about?

The pitchers around him, egged on by booze and the presence of the blond bartender—her baby blue shirt seeming to grow tighter as the evening wore on— were now actually bragging to one another about which one was a better hitter than the next. Kirby put a twenty dollar bill on the bar and stood up to leave.

"You ain't goin' now, are you, man?" said José, or whatever his name was.

"Catchers have early *cage time* tomorrow," he said, unable to resist making it a subtle dig.

"Okay, mister high and mighty," said Hiram. "But just wait until you see how I hit."

Kirby didn't mask his chuckle, which was maybe a tad on the condescending side. He figured it was all in good fun, but he hadn't counted on how much Hiram had drunk, or maybe why Hiram—despite deceptive stuff and a high strikeout to inning ratio—never stuck with a club.

"What are you laughing at? Are you laughing at me?" Before Kirby could answer, Hiram proclaimed, "I'm sure I hit better than you pitch, meat."

"Don't bet on it," Kirby said and walked out.

*   *   *

The next day went much like the first, bullpen sessions, fielding practice, wind sprints, the usual. It was some time around noon when Kirby realized he was the subject of a larger than usual number of stares and looks.

"What is that all about?" he asked Roger, as they walked back to the foul line to start the next wind sprint.

"Heard any trade rumors?"

"No."

"Have a hot date last night?"

"No."

"Then it's probably nothin'."

But when Kirby got back to the clubhouse, he found Hiram and a small cabal of pitchers hanging around his locker. Kirby's locker, that is. A twenty dollar bill was tacked next to Kirby's name tag.

"So, when are we getting it on, amigo?" Hiram said, his smile and his arms wide. He was wearing only a towel around his waist and his shower flip flops.

"Sorry, Hiram, you're not my type," Kirby replied, drawing guffaws out of some of the guys.

"No, no, man, our bet."

"What bet?"

"Don't you remember? At the bar last night, you bet me twenty dollars that you can pitch better than I can hit." Hiram indicated the sawbuck with one long finger.

"No, I didn't," Kirby said. "That twenty was to pay my bill."

"Don't you remember? I said I was paying for you last night."

Kirby paused for a moment. That wasn't the way he remembered it. But his argument clearly wasn't going to get him anywhere, not if they were all in on it. He just wasn't sure what kind of clubhouse prank this was leading to. It wasn't that he didn't expect a little hazing—that came with the territory—but he really wasn't sure where this was going. "That was just talk," Kirby said, pushing his way through the group to the locker. He sat down on the stool and started unlacing his spikes. They were caked with red infield dirt.

The group did not disperse, looking to Hiram to take the lead. "All I know is, we have a bet, you and me, and we ought to find a time and place to see who wins it." There were murmurs of approval from the others. "I mean, who said pitchers couldn't hit?"

Did I say that? Kirby wondered. He didn't think he'd actually said it. "Later, Hiram. I gotta go lift."

"Oh, right, build up those muscles so you can get that fastball of yours by me," the pitcher sniggered, but sauntered away.

* * *

By the time the regular position players showed up at camp, Kirby's hands, knees, and his throwing arm were more sore than they had ever been in his life. Thank goodness for the trainers, who had a ready supply of ice, liniment, analgesics, and rubdowns. He didn't mind being sore when it meant being taken care of so well. And he was catching Roger Clemens every other day, which he figured if nothing else he could tell his grandchildren about. All in all, Kirby was in baseball-player heaven except for one thing: Green and his bet.

Somehow things had escalated to the point where now half the pitchers in camp were getting ready to take swings against him, and the other half were placing bets themselves.

He knew it was at the point of no return when Clemens himself said, on one of those wind sprint walk-backs, "Heck, I'd like to get in there and take some cuts against you myself."

"Can you hit?" Kirby replied.

"I dunno," Clemens shrugged. "I've been in the American League all my life. But I never back down from a challenge."

Kirby sighed. There hadn't been any challenge, but everyone was acting like there was, and in a team situation you had to go with the group's idea of reality. "Can I ask you something?"

"Sure." The Rocket spat onto the grass.

"Can you show me how you throw the splitter?"

* * *

A couple of days later in the showers Kirby snapped Hiram on the ass with a towel and said "So when are we getting it on?"

"Whenever you're ready," Hiram replied, clapping his hands with glee, ignoring the welt on his ass, and scrubbing his head with vigor under the spray of the high showerhead.

"What about tomorrow, since it's a light day." Kirby started the flow on the next showerhead over. They were the big ones, like sunflowers, and they never ran out of hot water.

"Sorry, couldn't hear you," Hiram said, shaking water from his hair and ears like a dog. He raised his voice. "Did you say *tomorrow?*"

"Yeah." Kirby grabbed the soap and began to lather his chest, gently because there were a couple of bruises there from getting crossed up and taking bouncers in the dirt off his equipment. "I hear there's some other guys want a piece of me, too."

"Yeah, me!" shouted José—it turned out his name was José—from across the cinderblock room.

"Fine." Kirby ducked his head under to wet his hair and then turned to Hiram. "Get as many guys together as you want."

Hiram had raised an eyebrow and was unsure what to say now that Kirby had made such a dramatic about-face. "So what's the bet then? You gonna pay us each twenty bucks if we get a hit off you?"

Kirby shook his head. "Even a blind chipmunk finds a nut sometimes."

"So, what, no lucky hits?"

"Hiram, Hiram," Kirby said, not sure where the confidence in his voice was coming from, since he didn't actually feel it. "Have you really thought about how this is going to work? We gotta do it schoolyard style."

"What do you mean?"

"Any ground ball on the infield is an out, any pop-up is an out. Line drives, anything that lands on the warning track, hits the wall, or goes over, is a hit. You guys get twenty seven outs. Every three outs clears the bases." He ducked his head again then came out blinking water out of his eyes. "I'll give you twenty bucks for every run you score."

"You're on," Hiram said, and they shook on it, ghetto style, to the whooping of José in the background.

* * *

Kirby found, much to his annoyance, that he could not sleep that night. He was housed in a two-star motel a couple of miles from the park, the same place most of the other low-paid players and coaches stayed. Nice little place, the kind with a breakfast room and a coffee dispenser that ran 24 hours. Kirby was as perky as the coffee when midnight came around. It wasn't as if he really cared whether Hiram, or any of the other pitchers, got a hit or a run off him. It was Hiram's ego, not Kirby's, that had a lot at stake.

But something one of the coaches had said to him in the lobby had started him worrying. As he was grabbing a little iced tea from the dispenser there, Red had come up and wished him good luck.

"Oh, you know about it?" Kirby had said.

"Kiddo, everyone knows about it. Didja think you were just going to waltz out there and no one was gonna care?"

"Well, I . . ."

"Even the groundskeepers are going to be out there. Heh, should be fun."

Kirby lay in bed after that wondering how he could have missed the fact that he was now the center of everyone's attention. That hadn't been his intent. He just wanted to get it over with, in fact, so that he would *stop* being the recipient of so much attention. But he couldn't call it off now, he just had to get out there and do it. Just like any other day in baseball, he told himself. Sure, it was something out of the routine, but it was still baseball. The whole key to success was just being in the moment and doing your best in that moment. Right? *That's baseball.*

The next morning he arrived to find the other catchers—or someone—had festooned his locker with red, white, and blue bunting, and there was a ball stuffed into one of his cleats. He shook his head—he knew what the ball meant. In the old days, before strict pitching rotations, managers used to leave a ball in the shoe of that day's starting pitcher so he'd know it was his turn.

There was a glove there, too, a pitcher's glove. Kirby picked it up gingerly, as if it might be booby-trapped, but it appeared to be free of joy buzzers, roaches, or dog poop. He turned it over and saw the name on it was "Clemens." He had a moment of panic, wondering who stole it from Roger's locker and looking around to see if he might be able to slip it back in there without Clemens noticing. But then Clemens himself came up beside him, clapped him on the shoulder, and said "I thought you might need that."

"Holy crap, Rocket, thanks."

"No problem, man. Now let's get out there."

Kirby found it hard to concentrate on the workouts that day. He had to catch Hiram, for one thing, and everywhere he went, people were full of cracks and comments. He found himself blushing under his mask a lot. He tried to shut it out, stay within himself, but he couldn't.

He paid for it when catching Roger in the bullpen around noon. They got out of synch, Kirby got crossed up, and Roger let go a forkball when Kirby was expecting the fastball, or maybe it was the other way around. Either way, Kirby didn't see what he expected, caught the pitch awkwardly, and the next thing he knew Roger was leaning over him asking "Are you okay?"

Despite the fact he was scrunched up on the ground like a turtle he automatically replied "I'm fine, I'm fine." It's what he and every other athlete always says when asked "are you okay?" despite the fact that they are not. Then the trainer and some coaches were there with more specific questions like "Can you stand up" and "Can you take your glove off"—the answer to both being "not yet." Kirby was hunched over the hand inside his glove, his eyes squeezed shut like he could somehow wish away the pain if he just tried hard enough.

Now there was the long walk from the bullpen, along the foul line, down the dugout steps, and Kirby felt like if every eye hadn't been on him before, they were all watching him now. The trainer walked on one side and Roger on the other, holding him by the elbows like it was his leg he had hurt, not his fingers. The midday sun was hot like a spotlight, and it seemed to Kirby like the whole camp had paused to watch his slow march to the trainer's room. The normal sounds of a spring workout, the smack of games of catch, the steady chop of wood in the batting cage, all were silent.

As they went up the tunnel he thought he heard Hiram's voice from across the grass, "Aw, *man!*"

* * *

Twenty minutes later Kirby was breathing a sigh of relief. They had an X-ray machine right there, and nothing was broken. Hell, it was only his pinky, and it was only sprained. He might have dislocated it but it had popped right back in. He had it wrapped in ice and resting on a shelf as high as his shoulder when Roger came in.

"So, Doc, what's the prognosis?"

The trainer told him. "He won't be catching for a while."

"Yeah, but can he still pitch?"

The trainer looked at Roger like he had grown another head.

"Can you just tape the two fingers together?" Kirby asked. "I don't really use my pinky very much."

"You're a catcher, right?"

"Right." Kirby caught Roger gesturing at him from behind the trainer's back. "Am I cleared to do other things besides catch, though? Like can I still do my running and lifting?"

"Oh, I suppose," the trainer said with a sigh and reached for a roll of white medical tape. "Let me see it."

* * *

And so it was that Kirby "Nine Fingers" Wilcox, pumped full of ibuprofen and wearing Roger Clemens' glove, took the mound in Fort Myers to face a motley lineup of eleven pitchers who were all milling around the on deck circle, fiddling with their stiff, new batting gloves and their borrowed bats. Three different catchers sat in the shade of the visitor's dugout with their shin guards on, playing rock, paper, scissors to determine who caught first.

Kirby hadn't expected to have a catcher. Then to his surprise he saw he had fielders, too. Scott Hatteberg, another catcher, stood at first base, one of the other guys out of the minors at third. And how about Mike Greenwell and Roger standing in left center, talking? When they saw him look back at them from the mound, they jogged apart. Kirby blinked. Roger was going to play center field?

There were whistles and cat calls from the rest of the team, players, coaches, and other employees sitting behind home plate, but back about twenty rows so they were under the shade of the roof. Rich Rowland crouched behind the plate and gave Kirby the sign to start his warm-up pitches. Red stood close by, working his chaw absentmindedly, until Kirby had thrown his eighth warm-up pitch, when Rowland and Red shouted simultaneously, "Coming down." And just like before a real inning, the catcher threw the ball to second base, and then Red stepped up in the role of umpire.

Hiram tapped his bat on the plate, unperturbed by this turn of events. He must have known there would be an umpire, a team. Kirby took a deep breath and tried to put out of his mind the thought that everyone else knew more about what was going on than he did. He cleared his mind of all thoughts except the one that he was grateful to have a catcher. Having a target made it so much easier.

He kicked, and threw his fastball. Hiram stared at it, it hit the glove, and Red called out "Hype!" and raised his fist.

Hiram waggled the bat, exchanging looks with his teammates, the other pitchers who had now taken seats in the home dugout. "You've seen him now, you've seen him now," one of them shouted.

Kirby kicked and dealt. This time Hiram swung, late, and missed.

"Hype-*oo*!" Red shouted.

"What was that!" Hiram called to Kirby, jokingly, as if Kirby had thrown some trick junk pitch. But it was just a fastball, a plain fastball.

Kirby blinked; Rowland had just put down a sign. Two fingers. And Kirby heard Roger's voice from behind him, in center, where he had probably seen the sign, too, shouting "Come on, give it to him, now, come on now!"

Kirby threw the forkball. He held onto it a tad too long, and the ball bounced in the dirt, but Hiram had started his swing early, and he golfed at it and missed.

"Hy-ee! Yer out!" Red screamed and gave a theatrical flourish as he pumped his fist.

Hiram didn't joke now. He stared at Kirby all the way back to the dugout. The guys on the bench gave him a hard time, some of them imitating that last duck-assed swing, and laughing. José was next.

Rowland called for the fastball and Kirby threw it. And again, and again. And José went down swinging, though it was a better swing. Hoots were coming from the stands now—"I told you none of you could hit the side of a barn!"—and the pitchers were starting to sit up a bit on the bench. Their jocularity was undiminished, but each man began to pay a bit more attention to Kirby's delivery. They groaned wildly when the third of their number also went down on strikes.

Rowland jogged out to the mound. "So do we take a break between innings or what?"

"I just need some water," Kirby said, and Rowland motioned for one of the bat boys to bring him a bottle. He took a swig, resettled his cap, and was ready to throw again.

The first batter to hit a ball into fair territory came in the fourth inning, when Hiram came to bat again. This time he swung late at a pitch, but got wood on the ball, and hit a soft three-hopper right to Hatteberg at first. An easy out.

"Thank god!" Roger shouted. "We're starting to get bored out here!" But he did not sound bored.

Kirby, for his part, had stopped counting the outs. There had been no one on base so there had been no need to know when the third out came and cleared them. The breaks were brief. In one, a new catcher came in, had a brief chat with Rowland, but to Kirby nothing had changed. He would set, look for the glove, throw, and then wait for the ball to come arcing back to him. Sometimes he would grip the ball across the seams, sometimes along the seams—that was the only change in his world. Oh, and sometimes the batters were left-handed, but even that didn't seem to matter since none of them could hit him.

When it got to be the end of the sixth, he started to hear the shouting again. There was a lot of it, and more of it was aimed at him. "C'mon Kirby, attaboy!" Things like that, from voices he did not recognize. But it echoed against the inside of his skull—he heard it without noticing it. He was too intent on just keeping his motion the same, his leg kick, his follow-through.

Here was Hiram again. There were no jokes from him this time, no smile on his face. He dug in and waggled the bat. Kirby blinked as his brain did the math. If they had eleven men in their lineup, and this was the start of the third time through, then Hiram was the twenty third man. Almost done.

Perhaps the thought broke his rhythm or perhaps he was tiring, but the next two pitches were wide of the strike zone by an obvious margin.

"Whatsa matter, Wilky?" Hiram called, suddenly animated again. "Afraid I've figured you out?"

The catcher called for time and came jogging up to Kirby. Kirby was shocked to realize it was Hatteberg, which meant someone else was at first base, now. He filed that away in his brain as he tried to hear what Hatty was saying. "I'm flying open?"

"Yeah, your shoulder. Down and hard. Come on." He gave Kirby a pat on the butt and then jogged back behind the plate. Kirby blinked. It was word for word what he had told many pitchers, many times. Surreal.

Hatty pointed at him with the glove, pounded his fist in it, and called for the fastball.

Kirby kicked, fired, it went in for a strike, right down Broadway. Hiram shook his head as if to clear it. Kirby could almost imagine what Hatty was saying, under his breath, to Hiram then, because it was what Kirby would say. "You just don't expect it to be right there, do you?"

So now, come back with it again, or try the splitter? The splitter. Kirby nodded, kicked, and brought his arm through his motion. Hatty caught the ball just below Hiram's knees and then whipped his glove up an inch or two.

"H—" Red began, but then thought better of it. "Ball three."

"Nice frame job," Hiram said to Hatteberg.

Kirby kept his eyes trained on Hatteberg's hand and his glove. *Okay, again.* This time Hiram tried his golf swing again, but fouled the ball off. Full count.

Come back with the fastball, Kirby thought, and nodded as Hatteberg thought the same thing. Kirby was already visualizing Hiram's swing, how he would swing late on this extra-fast fastball, and have to go back to the bench, defeated. The sun was hot—the morning breeze always died by mid-afternoon—and Kirby could feel sweat making the sleeves of his undershirt stick to his armpits. *Here it comes,* he thought.

As soon as he released the ball, he knew he had made the classic mistake. Trying to put a little extra on it, he had muscled up and instead slowed the ball down, flattened it out. Hiram put a huge swing on it and the ball sailed up and up, straight over Kirby's head.

"Roger!" Kirby wasn't the only one shouting.

Clemens turned this way and that, everyone on the field, in the whole ballpark thinking, that's the toughest play a center fielder has to make, the ball hit straight to the middle, but Roger kept going back and back, and finally turned, backpedaling and then stretching back over his head, giving half a leap and snaring the ball in the edge of the webbing of his glove. He somersaulted backwards and then sat up, holding the glove in the air to the whoops and hollers of all assembled.

"Hot shit! Sign that kid up!"

"Rocket, who knew?"

"Yahoo!"

And Hiram's voice, too. "No way! No fucking way!" He had already passed second base when Roger made the catch, and as he jogged back to the dugout he did not make eye contact with Kirby.

Kirby waited for the ball to come back to him, then got a drink. He glanced into the pitchers' dugout and found most of them sitting in dejected postures, batting gloves strewn about. Hiram was shaking his head and still saying "No way, no way."

Red hollered. "Four outs to go."

José stood in, and barely waved at three pitches before going sheepishly back to the bench.

"Aw, c'mon!" Hiram chastised him. "Didn't you see that drive! We're getting to him now!" But none of the others looked like they really wanted to go through with it. "Gimme that bat."

Kirby just shrugged when Red gave him a look like "is this in the rules?" If Hiram wanted to make the last three outs, that was fine with Kirby. Hiram was jazzed now, surely he'd overswing—and indeed, they got him to pop up a high fastball which Hatty caught right between the plate and the backstop.

"Two to go," Red said.

"Dammit," Hiram said, digging in again.

They went after him again, with a similar result, this time the pop-up went to Kirby himself. He felt it land in his glove and his pinky twinged horribly. He shook it off, climbed back up on the mound, and waited for Hiram to get back in the box.

This time he tried to start him off with a splitter, but it bounced in the dirt, Hiram didn't swing, and it was ball one. Kirby tried to come back with the fastball but it sailed outside, and it was ball two.

Hatteberg visited the mound, his red eyebrows pale in the strong sunlight. "Do you want to walk him?"

"What?"

"Is this the unintentional intentional walk, or are you really just so gassed that you can't hit the strike zone anymore?"

"I don't know. How many pitches do you think I've thrown?"

"Ninety? A hundred?"

They both thought about that a moment and Hiram shouted "Come on, guys, we haven't got all day!"

"Jerk," Hatteberg said, but where only Kirby could see it. "Hang in there, let's get him."

But the next one was a fastball that Kirby overthrew and Hatteberg had to jump up out of his crouch to make sure it didn't hit Red.

Hiram began to crow. "He's got a perfect game on the line and he's going to walk me? Lil' ol' me?"

Kirby coughed. *Perfect game, my ass*, he thought. *This isn't a game. In fact, I don't know what it is.* Then he realized he was about to walk a pitcher, for god's sake, and if there are cardinal sins in baseball, that had to be one of them, no matter what the situation.

What am I doing out here, anyway? he thought. *This is all about Hiram's ego, not mine. Maybe I ought to just cookie one in there, let him hit the damn thing, that'd make a good story, wouldn't it? How I no-hit them all day until the very last out . . . ?* It was tempting, like he could be Fate for one moment.

But then he could hear Roger screaming. "Come on, damn it, Kirby, let's finish this and go home! Just put him away already! Don't make me come over there and do it!"

And the people in the stands, the other players, the office girls, everyone, they were all shouting. It didn't matter this was just a lark, that it didn't "count." Kirby suddenly didn't want to disappoint anyone, either.

Just throw the ball, he thought. *That's the only part I can control. Just throw the ball.*

Hatty dropped down two fingers. Kirby adjusted his grip, kicked his leg, and let it fly.

Hiram, who had gotten stiff standing there while Kirby mused, swung late, just got a little wood on it, and it was another pop-up. Hatteberg screamed "I got it! I got it!" Flung the mask away so hard it hit Red in the stomach and doubled him over, and then he did get it, the ball landing nicely in the round pocket of the catcher's mitt.

Hatteberg leaped in the air "Yes!" and ran to give the ball to Kirby. Kirby had pumped his fist as the ball came down, but now seemed bewildered by the rushing, jumping teammates all around him, slapping him on the back—no, *pounding* him on the back—and shouting. And the next few minutes were a blur, of Hiram shaking his hand and saying well, you know, pitchers can't hit worth a lick, and Roger signing the ball and getting the other guys to add their signatures to it, and asking what the date was so it could be written on there, and more slaps on the back and invitations for dinner, drinks, rounds of golf on the next off day, as the whole gaggle of players made their way back into the clubhouse finally to get out of the afternoon heat and humidity.

So it was, flushed with success but with his pinky and his arm hurting like never before that Kirby Wilcox came to his locker to stow the souvenir ball, only to find all his gear neatly packed, the bunting gone, his name gone—though the twenty was still there. Hatteberg stared with his mouth open, but Roger just shook Kirby's hand—the one without the sprained finger. "Thanks. That was fun. Keep the glove."

It was Red who came by and told him he was on the disabled list, officially, and so was booted to minor league camp.

Kirby ripped down the twenty, suddenly feeling like a gate-crasher. His ticket had been revoked. He couldn't leave fast enough. He handed the twenty to the bat boy on his way out the door, as he repeated to himself over and over, *That's baseball, that's baseball.*

Edo van Belkom is an award-winning author and editor. He has published eight novels and more than two hundred short stories. He has edited several anthologies, including the influential *Baseball Fantastic*, which he co-edited with W. P. Kinsella. This story was his first short-story sale and was reprinted in *Year's Best Horror Stories* in 1991. The story asks, is there a limit to how much arcane baseball knowledge one person can retain? Dr. Doubleday doesn't think so.

Baseball Memories

∞

Edo van Belkom

THERE WAS NOTHING WRONG with Sam Goldman's memory. Not really.

He forgot the odd birthday or anniversary but no one ever thought him more than slightly absent-minded.

Sam remembered what he wanted to remember. His wife Bea could tell him a hundred times to take out the garbage but he never took notice of her, especially when he was doing something important—like watching a baseball game on television.

Sam liked baseball, not just watching it, but everything about the game. He was a fan in the truest sense of the word—he was a fanatic. He was also a student of the game and as a student he studied it with a peculiar passion that made everything else in his life sometimes seem secondary. Sam was never absent-minded when it came to baseball. Where baseball was concerned, Sam's memory was an informational steel-trap, a vault containing all sorts of trivial information. Inside Sam's head were the numbers for hitting averages, home runs, stolen bases, RBIs, and ERAs for just about anybody who was or had been anything in the sport.

Sam's head for figures made him a great conversationalist at parties; as long as the talk centered around his favorite subject he was fine. Once he got his hands on somebody who was willing to quiz him or be quizzed on baseball trivia, he never let them out of his sight. The only way to get rid of Sam at a party was to ask him how much he knew about hockey—which was nothing at all.

Some of Sam's friends began calling him "Psychlo" because he was a walking, talking encyclopedia of baseball to which they could refer to at any time to clear up some finer point of the game. His friends would be sitting in a circle on the deck in Sam's back yard talking baseball over a few beers when some statistic would come under question and the discussion's decibel level would get turned up a few notches. It was up to Sam to turn the volume back down and restore order with the right answer.

"Sammy, what did George Bell hit on the road in 1986?"

".293," Sam would say without hesitation.

"And how many homers?"

"Sixteen of his thirty-one were hit on the road."

"See I told you . . ." one friend would say to another, proved correct by the circle's supreme authority.

Sam considered himself gifted. He thought that what he had was a natural talent for numbers, something that might, at the very least, get him on the cover of a magazine or onto some local talk show.

It had begun as a hobby, something he liked to do with a cup of coffee and a book late at night after the rest of the family had gone to bed. Lately, however, it had become something more, something abnormal, if you asked Bea.

But even though Bea wasn't crazy about baseball or her husband's love affair with the game, she put up with it as most wives do with their husband's vices. She thought it was better for their marriage if Sam spent his nights at home with his nose buried in a baseball fact book instead of in a bar flirting with some woman with an "x" in her first name.

"As long as he sticks to baseball it's pretty harmless," she always said.

And then one day she began to wonder.

The two were sitting at the breakfast table one Saturday morning when Sam said something that put a doubt in her mind about her husband's mental well-being.

"Why don't we take a drive up north today and visit your cousin Ralph?" he said.

Bea was shocked. She looked at Sam for several seconds as if trying to find some visible proof that he was losing his mind.

"Ralph died last winter, don't you remember? We went to the funeral, there was six inches of snow on the ground and you bumped into my mother's car in the church parking lot. She still hasn't forgiven you for it."

Sam was shocked too. He could remember how many triples Dave Winfield hit the last three seasons but the death of his wife's cousin had somehow slipped his mind.

"Oh yeah, that's right. What the hell am I thinking about?" he said and then added after a brief silence. "I better go out and wash the car."

* * *

Things were fairly normal the next few weeks. Sam was still able to wow his friends with his lightning-fast answers and astounding memory. As long as baseball was in season Sam was one of the most popular guys around.

A co-worker of Sam's even figured out a way to make money with his head for figures. Armed with *The Sports Encyclopedia of Baseball*, they'd go out to some bar where nobody knew about Sam and bet some sucker he couldn't stump Sam with a question.

"Who led the Cleveland Indians in on-base percentage in 1952?" the sucker would ask, placing a ten-dollar bill on top of the bar.

"Larry Doby, .541, good enough to lead the American League that year," Sam would answer. After a quick check in the encyclopedia, the two had some pocket change for the week.

Sam was astonished at the financial rewards his talent had brought him. He had always thought himself something of an oddball, but if he could make some money at it—tax free to boot—then why the hell not. The prospect of riches made him study the stats even harder, always looking to increasingly older baseball publications to make sure he knew even the most trivial statistic.

"Well, would you look at that," he would say as his eyes bore down on the page and his brain went through the almost computer-like process of defining, processing and filing another little-known fact. It took less than ten seconds for him to remember forever that a guy by the name of Noodles Hahn led the Cincinnati Reds pitching staff in 1901 with a 22–19 record. Hahn pitched 41 complete games that year and had two-hundred and thirty-nine strikeouts to lead the league in both categories. No mean feat considering the Reds finished last that season with a 52–87 record.

The information was stored in a little cubbyhole deep within Sam's brain and could be recalled anytime, like a book shelved in a library picked up for the first time in fifty years. The book, a little dusty perhaps, would always tell the same story.

* * *

Bea went to see Manny Doubleday, their family physician, the morning after Sam did another all-nighter with his books.

While it was true Sam had bought her some fine things since he'd been making money in bars, Bea felt the items were bought with tainted money. The fur coat had been hanging in the hall closet since the day Sam had bought it for her, not because it was the middle of summer, but because she was ashamed of it. She never showed it to guests, even those who might have thought Bea the luckiest girl in the world—and Sam the greatest husband.

Bea sat quietly in Doctor Doubleday's private office, waiting. The office was decorated like a tiny corner of Cooperstown. On the walls hung various team photos and framed press clippings about Manny Doubleday in his heyday. On the desk were baseballs signed by Mickey Mantle and Hank Aaron, even one signed by Babe Ruth, although the authenticity of it came under suspicion since the "Bambino" signed his name in crayon.

From down the hall the doctor's melodic whistling of "Take Me Out To The Ball Game" pierced through the space made by the slightly ajar door. Moments later the door burst open and in strode the portly doctor. Doctor Doubleday had been the Goldmans' family physician for what seemed like forever. He had delivered both Sam and Bea into the world and always looked upon the couple's marriage as a match made by his own hands. He was also a former minor league pitcher and big baseball fan, something that had cemented a friendship between the doctor and Sam since Sam was a teenager. The doctor knew of Sam's ability to remember statistics and thought it was simply wonderful.

"What seems to be the problem, Bea?" he asked, picking up a dormant baseball from his desk and wrapping his fingers around it as if to throw a split-fingered fastball right over the plate.

"It's Sam, I think he's—"

"How is the old dodger?" the doctor interrupted as he took a batter's stance and pretended to swing through on a tape-measure home run. "You know I've never seen anyone with a memory like his. It's uncanny the way he can tell you anything you want to know at the drop of a hat."

"Yes, that's what I mean. I think he's overdoing it a bit," Bea said, sitting up on the edge of her chair anxious to hear some words of support.

"Nonsense," replied the doctor.

Bea slumped back in her chair.

"What your husband has is a gift. He has a photographic memory that he's chosen to use for recording baseball statistics. It's harmless."

"It used to be harmless. He used to do it in his spare time but now he's obsessed with it. He lets other things slide just so he can cram his head with more numbers. He's beginning to forget things."

"Bea," the doctor said, putting down his invisible bat. "Forget for a minute that I'm your doctor and consider this a discussion between two friends.

"Most people are able to use about ten percent of the brain's full capacity. Your husband has somehow been able to tap in and exceed that ten percent. Maybe he's using twelve or thirteen percent, I don't know, but it happens. He could be making millions at the black jack tables in Atlantic City but he chose to use his gift for baseball. Just be happy it's occupying him instead of something more dangerous. I'll talk to him the next time he's in. How are the kids?"

Bea was brought sharply out of her lull and answered in knee-jerk fashion. "Fine, and yours?"

* * *

She was satisfied, but marginally. It was one thing for the doctor to talk about Sam's mind in the comfort of the office, it was another thing entirely to sit at the dinner table and watch Sam try to eat his soup with a fork.

"Honey," she'd say. "Why don't you try using your spoon? You'll finish the soup before it gets cold."

"Yeah, I guess your *right-handed batters versus lefties*," Sam would reply and then sit silently for a few moments. "Did I say that? Sorry Bea, I don't know where my head is."

Sam knew he was spending a little too much time with his baseball books. He was weary of the numbers and after a couple hours study, some nights the inside of his skull pounded incessantly and felt as if it might explode under the growing pressure. But he loved the game too much to give it up.

Anyway, the money he earned on the bar circuit was too good to give up. It was so good in fact that he could probably put the kids through college with his winnings; something he could never do just working at his regular job.

Sam worked as an airplane mechanic in the machine shop at the local airport. He was good at his job and always took the time to make sure it was done right.

One day he was drilling holes in a piece of aluminum to cover a wing section they had been working on. The work was monotonous so Sam occupied his time thinking about the previous night's study.

Pete Rose hit .273 his rookie year, .269 his second, .312 his third. . .

The drill bit broke and Sam was brought back into the machine shop. He stopped the press, replaced the bit, tightening it with the key.

Lou Gehrig hit .423 in thirteen games for New York in 1923, .500 in ten games in 1924, .312 in his first full season in 1925 . . .

Sam started the drill press and the key broke free of its chain, flew across the shop and hit another mechanic squarely on the back of the head.

He was once again brought into reality. He shut the drill off and rushed over to see if his co-worker was still alive. A crowd had gathered around the prone man and all eyes were on Sam as he neared the scene.

"What the hell were you thinking of?"

"You gotta be more careful."

"That was pretty stupid."

The other mechanics were crowing at him in unison and Sam felt like a baseball that had been used too long after its prime. His insides felt chopped up and unraveled as he looked at the man lying on the floor.

A groan escaped the downed man's lips. "What the hell was that?" he asked. The crowd around him let out a collective sigh. Sam felt better too, but just slightly. The shop foreman walked up to him, placed a comforting hand on his shoulder and told him to go home.

"Why don't you take the rest of the day off, before he gets up off the floor and these guys turn into a lynch mob."

"Sure boss. I'll go *home run leaders for the past twenty years.*"

"What?"

"Nothing, nothing. I don't know what I was thinking of."

* * *

On the way home, Sam stopped by The Last Resort, a local sports bar with big-screen TV and two-dollar draughts. He needed a drink.

After what happened at the shop, Sam thought he might be going crazy. Baseball trivia was fun but if it turned him into an accident waiting to happen, he might as well forget all about his baseball memory.

He sat on a stool in front of the bartender and eased his feet onto the brass foot-rail. Comfortable, he ordered the biggest draught they had. As he sipped the foam off the top of the frosted glass, he overheard a conversation going on down at the other end of the bar.

"Willie Mays was the best player ever to play the game, and believe me, I know . . . I know everything there is to know about the greatest game ever invented."

Sam watched the man speak for a long time. He stared at him, trying to see right through his skull and into the folds of his brain. Sam wanted to know just how much this blow-hard really knew.

"Go ahead, ask me anything about the game of baseball, anything at all. I'll tell you the answer. Heck, I'll even put ten dollars on the bar here—if you stump me it's yours."

"How many home runs did Hank Aaron hit in his first major league season?" asked Sam as he carried his beer down the bar toward the man.

"Awe, that's easy, thirteen, Milwaukee, 1954. I want some kind of challenge."

"All right, then. In what year did Nolan Ryan pitch two no hitters and who did he pitch them against?"

"Another easy one. Nolan Ryan was pitching for the California Angels and beat Kansas City 3–0, May 15 and Detroit 6–0, July 15, 1973."

Sam was startled. No hitters were something he'd studied just the night before. This guy was talking about them like they were old news.

"Okay, now it's my turn," the man said, massaging his cheeks between his thumb and forefinger. "But first, would you care to put a little money on the table?"

"Take your best shot," Sam answered, slamming a fifty-dollar bill down on the bar.

"Well, fifty bucks," the man said impressed. "That deserves a fifty-buck question!"

The man looked into Sam's eyes. A little sweat began to bead on Sam's forehead but he was still confident the bozo had nothing on him.

"Okay, then. Who was the Toronto Blue Jays winning pitcher in their opening game 1977, and what was the score?"

Sam smiled, he knew that one. But suddenly something about the way the other man looked into his eyes made his mind draw a blank. It was as if the man had reached inside and pulled the information out of Sam's head before Sam had gotten to it. The beads of sweat on Sam's forehead grew bigger.

"I'm waiting," said the man, enjoying the tension. "Awe, c'mon, you know that one. I only asked it so you'd give me a chance to win my money back."

Sam closed his eyes and concentrated. Inside his brain, pulses of electricity scrambled through the files searching for the information, but all pulses came back with the same answer.

"I don't know," said Sam finally.

"Too bad. It was Bill Singer, April 7, 1977, 9–5 over Chicago. Fifty bucks riding on it too. Better luck next time, pal."

The man picked up the money and walked out of the bar. Sam stood in silence. He'd never missed a question like that before—never! He finished his draught in one big gulp and ordered another.

* * *

Sam said nothing about the incident to Bea over dinner. He ate in silence, helped his wife with the dishes and told her to enjoy herself bowling with the girls.

When she was safely out of the driveway, Sam dove in his books. He vowed never to be made fool of again and intensified his study. He looked up Bill Singer and put the information about him back on file in his head. He studied hundreds of pitchers and after a few hours their names became a blur.

Noodles Hahn, Cy Young, Ambrose Putnam, Three Finger Brown, Brickyard Kennedy, Kaiser Wilhelm, Smokey Joe Wood, Wild Bill Donovan, Twink Twining, Mule Watson, Homer Blankenship, Chief Youngblood, Clyde Barfoot, Buckshot May, Dazzy Vance, Garland Buckeye, Bullet Joe Bush, Boom Boom Beck, Bots Nickola, Jumbo Jim Elliot, George Pipgrass, Schoolboy Rowe, Pretzels Puzzullo, General Crowder, Marshall Bridges, Van Lingle Mungo, Boots Poffenberger, Johnny Gee, Dizzy Dean, Prince Oana, Cookie Cuccurullo, Blackie Schwamb, Stubby Overmire, Webbo Clarke, Lynn Lovenguth, Hal Woodeshick, Whammy Douglas, Vinegar Bend Mizell, Riverboat Smith, Mudcat Grant, John Boozer, Tug McGraw, Blue Moon Odom, Rollie Fingers, Billy McCool, Woody Fryman, Catfish Hunter, Vida Blue, Goose Gossage, Rich Folkers, Gary Wheelock.

Sam slammed the book shut. His head was spinning.

He felt like he couldn't remember another thing, not even if the survival of baseball itself depended on it.

But then a strange thing happened.

Sam swore he heard a clicking sound inside his head. His brain felt as if it buzzed and whirred and was suddenly lighter.

He reopened the book and looked at a few more numbers. He took them in, closed the book once more and recited what he had learned.

"We're back in business," Sam said out loud and returned, strangely refreshed, to the world of statistical baseball.

Bea came home around eleven o'clock and found Sam in the den asleep with his face resting on a stack of books.

"Doesn't he ever get enough?" she muttered under her breath and poked a finger into his shoulder, trying to wake him.

"Huh, what . . . *Phil Niekro, Atlanta Braves 1979, 21–20 at the age of 40. Gaylord Perry, San Diego Padres 1979, also 40, 12–11 . . .*"

"Sam, wake up! Isn't it time you gave it a rest and went to bed?" Bea said, pulling on his sleeve, hoping to get him out of his chair.

"Who are you?" asked Sam, looking at Bea as if they were meeting in a long narrow alleyway somewhere late at night.

"Well, I'll say one thing for you, Sam, you still have your sense of humor. C'mon, time for bed."

"Which way is the bedroom?" Sam asked. He thought his surroundings familiar but wasn't too clear about their details.

"Into the dugout with you," Bea said, caught up in the spirit of the moment. "Eight innings is more than we can ask from a man your age!"

After the two were finally under the covers, Sam lay awake for a few minutes looking the bedroom over. The pictures on the wall looked familiar to him and he thought he might be in some of them. Comfortable and exhausted, he finally dozed off.

* * *

Sam's brain was hard at work while the rest of his body rested in sleep.

It had started with a faint click but now his brain hummed and buzzed with activity. After being bombarded with information over the past months, every available cubbyhole in Sam's brain had been filled. There wasn't room for one more ERA, one more home run, not even one more measly single.

But like an animal that has adapted to its environment over the course of generations, Sam's brain was evolving too, and decided it was time to clean house.

The torrent of information it had been receiving must be essential to the survival of the species, the brain reasoned. Why else would so many names and numbers be needed to be filed away? So the brain began a systematic search of every piece of information previously stored, from birth to present, and if it did not resemble the bits of information the brain was receiving on a daily basis, out the window it would go.

Sam's brain decided it wasn't essential that he remember how to use the blow-torch at work so the information was erased to open up new space for those supremely important numbers.

By the time Sam awoke, a billion cubbyholes had been swept clean.

Sam walked sleepily toward the kitchen where Bea already had breakfast on the table.

"What's that?" Sam asked, pointing at a yellow semi-sphere sitting on a perfect white disk.

"Are you still goofing around?" Bea answered. "Hurry up and eat your grapefruit or you'll be late for work."

Sam watched Bea closely, copying her movements exactly. He decided he liked the yellow semi-sphere called grapefruit and every bite provided a brand new taste sensation on his tongue. Sam's brain couldn't be bothered to remember what grapefruit tasted like, not even for a second.

Bea helped Sam get dressed for work because he said he couldn't remember which items on the bed were the ones called pants and which were the ones called shirts.

Bea decided she'd speak to Dr. Doubleday the moment she got Sam out of the house and insist he come by and give Sam a check-up. She nearly threw Sam out the door in her rush to call the doctor.

As the door of the house closed behind him, Sam tried to remember just exactly where he worked and what it was he did for a living.

He also wanted to go back to The Last Resort and show that joker at the bar that Sam Goldman was no fool.

If only he could remember how to get there.

David Sandner's poetry and fiction have appeared in *Asimov's Science Fiction* magazine, *Weird Tales*, *Pulphouse*, and elsewhere. He is the editor of *Fantastic Literature: A Critical Reader*, and co-editor of *The Treasury of the Fantastic* with Jacob Weisman. Sandner is an assistant professor of Romanticism and Children's Literature at California State University in Fullerton. Jacob Weisman is publisher of Tachyon Books, an independent publishing house specializing in genre fiction. As publisher and editor he has been nominated for the World Fantasy Award several times. As a writer he has published stories in *The Nation*, *Realms of Fantasy*, and elsewhere. This story by Sandner and Weisman follows an elderly man and his young friend as, somehow, they find themselves reminded that baseball's long history can be very real, indeed, for those who know and love the game.

Lost October

∽

David Sandner and Jacob Weisman

DEROSA WATCHED THE BOYS play baseball in the street below. They played with a tennis ball. First base was a rear tire of a car. Second base was a dark patch of asphalt in the middle of the road, the pitcher's mound another. Third base was the tire of the car across from first. Home plate was a crushed tin can.

DeRosa rested in a large deck chair on the balcony of his third floor apartment, his right knee turned inward and his ankle twisted around the front chairleg. Only his eyes moved, following the high, bounding hops of the tennis ball.

One of the boys drove a deep fly ball that sailed the length of the street and bounced several times before coming to rest beneath the wheel of a parked car. An outfielder closed on the ball, chased it down and threw a two-hopper to the plate. The catcher caught the ball to his right, pivoted violently to his left, throwing himself to the ground to make the tag. An argument ensued.

The arguments always bored DeRosa. The balcony swirled in sunlight. DeRosa lay back, content in the brightness, sitting as still as empty bleachers. He dozed, listening to shrill voices punctuated by the womp of a flattened tennis ball.

DeRosa awoke uncomfortably, the tough fabric of the chair biting into his arm, etching deep, criss-crossing patterns into the flesh. He had on only a short-sleeved shirt, faded green, unbuttoned to his white undershirt. DeRosa rubbed his arm tenderly. His head swam. Gingerly, he turned his neck from side to side. He slipped his black socked feet into a pair of white leather shoes and stood slowly, keeping his hands firmly on his knees for support. He opened the sliding glass door and crossed the living room to the kitchen to splash some water on his face.

Standing at the sink, water dripping from his chin, DeRosa looked out his open kitchen window over the backyard. The trees were deathly still, yet he heard the branches creaking. It seemed unnatural to him, put him on edge. A German Shepherd crossed into the shade of a eucalyptus and sniffed at the trunk. It had been too close to the house to be seen before. The dog was old, gray mixed in his soft colored tan and brown coat. He was big shouldered.

DeRosa leaned out the window, holding tight at the sill.

"Hey," DeRosa called. "Hey. Get out of there. Shoo."

The dog turned, eyeing DeRosa evenly before moving across the yard to a hole in the fence. He looked back again and the sun glowed in his eyes, then he ducked through the hole and was gone.

DeRosa drank a glass of water and sighed. He felt tiredness heavy in his eyes and shoulders. Maybe the heat had gotten to him, or maybe he was still sluggish from sleeping on the balcony. He shuffled to the couch, sat, lay back and slept. He dreamed of the trees, full with thin, earth-tone eucalyptus leaves and overfull with the moist, drunken smell of spring.

DeRosa awoke to footsteps and then the doorbell chimed. Eugene Kelly opened the door and walked in carrying an overstuffed bag of groceries. He dropped it on the counter.

"You looked good playing ball out there, Eu," said DeRosa, sitting up. "You're really starting to give the ball a whack. How much do I owe you?"

The bill came to twenty four dollars. DeRosa came up to the counter and counted out the money.

"Thanks, Eu."

DeRosa stuffed the crumpled bills into Eugene's hand, grasping the boy's hand in his own. Eugene's hand was smooth and small.

"That was a great play you made behind the plate today."

"Yea." Eugene shrugged. "Thanks."

DeRosa walked over to a closet by the door, reached in and grabbed his jacket, holding it by the collar until he had extracted another five. DeRosa saw his own shadowed face reflected in the mirror hanging inside the closet door. He thought he looked worried. Deep lines cut down his cheeks, bruises weighted under his eyes and wisps of white hair stuck out from atop his head at odd angles. He wondered what Eugene must think of him, looking the way he did. DeRosa hung the jacket back in the closet.

"Something for you," he said, dropping the wadded bill on the counter between them.

"It's too much." Eugene turned his head.

DeRosa backed away.

"Take it." He smiled and nodded his head too much.

Eugene rubbed his nose. His face was blank, unreadable. He took the five and wiped it flat. He folded all the bills together and tucked them in his front pocket.

"I've got to go," Eugene said, turning his shoulder away from DeRosa toward the door.

"I was hoping you'd catch a few with me." DeRosa came forward, leaned his bare forearms against the edge of the counter to support himself. He grinned at Eugene. "Still plenty of time before the game. You are coming back up for the game?"

Eugene shrugged, nodded without turning. "I'll be back around five. I've got some homework to do."

"Homework? You can forget about that right now." DeRosa moved back into the closet. He took down a ball and glove from a shelf. The mitt was old, dark from many oilings, with short, squat fingers that barely covered DeRosa's hand. "These are the Giants in the World Series. Doesn't happen very often. We almost won it, you know, back in '62."

"Yes," Eugene said with a trace of boredom. "If the Yankees' second baseman doesn't catch McCovey's line drive in the seventh game. I know."

"That was Bobby Richardson, an excellent second baseman. Think about it, will you? That was twenty-seven years ago. Haven't been back since. Besides if Whitey Lockman had just sent Matty Alou home from third on Mays' double, McCovey wouldn't even have gotten up to the plate."

"I don't know," Eugene said.

"Come on." DeRosa put his jacket on, turning the collar down. The nylon rustled as he strapped the Velcro straps around his wrists. The jacket had Giants scripted in black across the back. The orange had worn to white at the forearms. The gold lining had dirtied.

They walked down the front stairs and set up in front of the garage. DeRosa warmed his arm up slowly, his pitches barely reaching Eugene who squatted on the balls of his feet fifteen feet away. Eugene looked bored, but then the ball started to break. It would cross the plate, flutter, and shift suddenly, all at once, exploding in all sorts of directions.

"Could you show me that?"

DeRosa moved forward and took the ball.

"Hold the ball by your fingertips. Don't use your knuckles."

Eugene walked out and threw the ball a couple times, nothing.

"The ball should barely have any rotation at all," DeRosa said. "Too much rotation or no rotation at all and nothing happens. If you throw it right, you should be able to see the ball tumble." DeRosa demonstrated, turning the ball an inch on its axis. "Try it again."

The sky was clear, without a trace of clouds or wind.

"It's a great day," said Eugene, wiping the perspiration from his cheek.

"Not really," DeRosa said. "Not really."

"What do you mean?" Eugene licked his lips.

"Nothing. It's just bad luck to have weather like this in San Francisco, that's all. It's no big deal. Throw the ball."

* * *

DeRosa's dream was sharp as morning light. He was sitting on the warm grass outside the stable where the milk men parked the horses after the morning run, watching Joe DiMaggio. Not the Yankee Clipper. Not yet. Not even the pride of the Seals or Galileo High School.

DeRosa's older brother, Monty, was hitting batting practice to a bunch of his friends, while the younger DeRosa sat in foul territory watching the players and guarding the extra equipment.

DiMaggio played third, his usual position back then. He was tall and gawky, thin with a strong but erratic throwing arm. It was only when he batted that one could see the savage, slashing swing that would one day lead him to stardom.

On this day, DiMaggio played more fluidly than usual, handling even the toughest short hops effortlessly with soft hands, gunning the ball over to first with perfect crisp throws. DiMaggio's delight was obvious. Unlike his later days with the Yankees, when cameras hounded him everywhere, DiMaggio was relaxed without even a hint of self-consciousness. Baseball was his escape from the world, from his family's fishing business, from his father.

The morning light swirled warmly about DeRosa's cheeks as he laid back in the shallow grass. Dom DiMaggio sat next to DeRosa, pounding his fist into his tiny child's glove, longing for his chance to play. DeRosa picked up an extra ball, stained green from overuse, and tossed it to Dom. Dom smiled and threw the ball back, lobbing it gently, allowing his arm to loosen up slowly.

They continued throwing the ball back and forth, looping high arcing tosses and sharp ground balls, forcing one another to move left or right into the hole or back for a high fly ball. Even as they threw, DeRosa knew Dom would be great, eventually following his older brothers, Vince and Joe, into the major leagues, leaving DeRosa behind to scan the box scores over his morning cereal before making his way to work.

* * *

DeRosa awoke with a start. The kitchen door was rattling loudly. He stood up and a force bigger than himself knocked him back. Spider web cracks burst suddenly through the plaster board walls with a crack like the snap of a whip. A green glass ashtray fell from a kitchen counter, ringing off the linoleum. Stacks of magazines slid from a shelf and spread across the floor. A glass on the table beside DeRosa rocked, waves of brown ice tea sloshing over the rim, tipped and spilled, clanging on the table. Plates and glasses clinked in the kitchen cupboards and the whole house, the walls and floors, and below the floors, rumbled like heavy machinery.

Before DeRosa struggled to his feet again, it was over. He was breathing heavy.

"That was a big one," he said.

Books leaned askew on their shelves; ice tea drained noisily from the table to the hardwood floor; a photograph finally tipped off the edge of a mantel and fluttered down to where the baseball rocked, slowed, stopped.

"The game was just starting," Eugene said.

Eugene surveyed the room from where he sat in front of the blank television set. Eugene knelt in front of the television and clicked the on/off button several times. DeRosa turned a switch on a lamp beside the couch. Stepping over the puddle of ice tea, he walked over to the open counter between living room and kitchen and picked up the phone receiver.

"Dial tone," he said. "But no power."

Eugene stood and walked, steadying himself along the wall and doorframe, into the bathroom.

"Let's go outside," DeRosa called, retrieving his Giants jacket from the couch and shuffled over to the door. Eugene emerged from the bathroom.

"What about the mess?"

"Leave it, come on."

They walked downstairs and out into the street. Neighbors were emerging, or standing staring at their houses; a group had gathered down the street around a portable radio to listen to reports and exchange stories about the quake.

"You O.K.?" someone asked without bothering to stop, moving toward the throng. A man with a wrench offered to turn off DeRosa's gas line. DeRosa conferred with him, then stared up at his house. No cracks along the foundation. Eugene returned from talking with his mother.

"Look," Eugene said. "What's that?"

DeRosa turned and looked out from Telegraph Hill. Off to the left, towering over the row of houses and trees, he saw something dark and menacing. He had to walk further down the street before the image took shape. Thick smoke mushroomed over the Marina.

DeRosa headed for an old white fifty-eight Cadillac and unlocked the driver's seat.

"Get in. I'll turn on the radio."

They sat in DeRosa's car and listened to the radio until the main news stories, the fire in the Marina, the cancellation of the Series, the collapse of the Bay Bridge and the I-80 expressway, began to repeat. Out in the Pacific, the sun set— canary yellow spreading over the sea.

"Come on," DeRosa said. "Let's drive."

"They said not to," Eugene said. "There's no street lights or signal lights."

"It's all right. We won't go far."

DeRosa started the car and pulled out into the street. Tipping over the edge, they rolled downhill.

They drove in silence, slowing down only when something caught their attention: the fallen brick of a house front, long cracks in the sidewalk, or the long drifts of smoke rising over whatever remained of the Marina. The city was quiet as the sun melted away like margarine, sickly yellow burning to black.

As the sky darkened, no lights came on anywhere. The city felt strange and empty, somehow different.

"I've never seen anything like it," DeRosa said. "A night like this could promise anything. You could remake the world on a night like this. Just fold it up and start over. Look at it. No lights to anchor it down and make you believe in it."

Eugene rubbed his leg and looked out the window, away from DeRosa.

DeRosa smiled. "This is history you're seeing. Living history."

Eugene didn't respond.

"O.K., I guess it's time to head back."

"What's that?" Eugene asked.

"What?"

"That."

A bright light lit up the sky, obvious and out of place in the dark city.

DeRosa drove towards the light, sometimes losing it altogether behind houses and hills, sometimes just following the glare in the sky. DeRosa rolled down the dark streets, winding his way to the light, finally turning a corner and heading straight into the glare. For a moment, he couldn't see a thing.

"Hey," DeRosa said.

"What is it?"

DeRosa leaned forward over the dash and looked up, as if getting closer would clear his vision and make the stadium and the lights resolve and disappear.

"That's Seal stadium."

"How come the lights are on?"

"They tore it down years ago. There's supposed to be a Safeway here now."

Eugene turned and looked at DeRosa.

"I don't understand."

DeRosa stared up at the lights.

"Neither do I, but it's really here."

DeRosa turned off the engine of the car, flipped off the car lights.

"Let's take a look," DeRosa said, stepping out, leaving the door hanging open. He walked in front of the car and stared upward. A cheer sounded from inside.

Eugene sat and watched DeRosa, who was smiling, bathed in an even white sheet of electric glare.

"Let's go in," DeRosa said. "Sounds like there's a game going on."

Eugene got out slowly, pushed his door closed with both hands. DeRosa had already swept off into the deep shadows around the edges of the stadium.

"Wait up," Eugene said, then hurried after him.

They entered the ballpark along the first base line. The thick, richly colored grass, lit up by the lights, glowed like an emerald. A series of goose eggs on a narrow hand-held scoreboard in dead away centerfield showed the score tied at zero midway through the sixth inning. Seals and Oaks. Pacific Coast League.

They found a pair of empty seats farther down the left field line among a swirl of orange pennants.

The Seals wore white uniforms with navy pinstripes and the letters "ea" and "ls" written inside the upper and lower halves of a large letter "S" to form the word "Seals." The Oaks wore more conventional navy blue uniforms with Oaks inscribed across the chest.

"Pretty nice," said DeRosa, looking around. "That's Joe Marty, the Seals right fielder at the plate. He played a couple of years in the Major Leagues. A friend of mine once went to his bar in Sacramento, said he was the most foul-mouthed person he'd ever met. That's what can happen, I guess, when you get to be around my age."

"Who's pitching?" asked Eugene.

"I don't know," DeRosa admitted. The Oakland pitcher looked young, baby fat still resting heavy in his cheeks. "Might be Ed Walsh, Jr."

Marty lined a two-two pitch down the line at third. The third baseman dove to his right, picked the ball off the short hop and gunned a throw to the bag at first, beating Marty easy.

"Nice play," said Eugene. "These guys are good."

"Yes." DeRosa smiled, not the shy smile that Eugene was used to, but rather a big grin.

A Seals left-hander lined out to deep right for the third out of the inning. The Oakland outfielder caught the ball on the dead run, took off his glove and threw it behind him as he walked off the field into the dugout.

"What's all this doing here?" Eugene asked.

"What? This game? I don't know."

"Are you here. I mean, do you think you might have been to this game before?"

"You mean as a kid? Maybe. I hadn't thought of that."

DeRosa scanned the people in the seats around them.

"What did you look like then?" Eugene asked.

"A lot like I do now, only younger."

"That's a big help. What color was your hair?"

An Oaks batter lashed a line drive into the gap between right and center. DiMaggio seemed miles away as he charged the ball, closing the gap slowly with long, loping strides. DiMaggio caught up with the ball suddenly on the third hop, extended his glove effortlessly across the width of his body, changed directions in midstride, and threw a strike to second base, holding the batter to a long single. The crowd stood to cheer.

"I thought he didn't have a chance," said Eugene.

"He made plays greater than that when he played for the Yankees. The fans in New York took it for granted after a while."

DeRosa's palms began to sweat and his body felt light and a little strange. He rubbed his hands against his legs, his nerves starting to feel the heightened tension of a scoreless game.

Marty doubled off the right-centerfield wall to start the eighth, but was thrown out at third on a perfect relay throw from the Oaks second baseman who went out onto the outfield grass in rightfield to take the throw.

Still tied, 0–0 with one out in the ninth, the Seals' shortstop, Hal Rhyne, beat out a bunt down the first baseline, bringing up DiMaggio. DiMaggio knocked the heel of his bat against the ground, dislodging the circular weight around the barrel and walked intently toward the plate, head down, but with his eyes up, tracking the pitcher.

"Watch this," said DeRosa, pointing.

DiMaggio dug in, redistributing the dirt around the back of the batter's box. He fouled the first pitch straight back, missing the ball by less than an inch. His swing was pure and savage—his weight shifting forward, his face contorting in expectation.

The second pitch, just off the outside corner, was called a ball. DiMaggio stepped out of the box, looked over at the third base coach who flashed a long series of signals.

DiMaggio took a sharp curve ball, just catching the inside corner above the knees, for another strike.

DeRosa shifted nervously in his seat. Eugene rubbed his hands together.

DiMaggio ripped a line drive down the third base line that just hooked foul. He fouled off the next couple of pitches before laying off a ball in the dirt—evening the count at 2–2.

"I don't know," muttered Eugene.

DiMaggio stepped back out of the box, turned to face the fans behind home-plate. His face was young; his hair was dark. He looked more uncertain than DeRosa ever remembered seeing him before. He couldn't be much more than nineteen or twenty years old, his whole life ahead of him.

"Get him, Joe," yelled DeRosa.

DiMaggio stepped back in, took a fastball, high, 3–2. The fans rose to their feet.

The catcher threw the ball back to the pitcher, walked slowly out to join him on the mound. The manager popped his head out of the dugout, walked out toward the mound, pausing for a second as he passed over the foul line. He said a few words to his catcher, looked over to the bullpen where a pair of righthanders warmed up, before focusing his attention back to his pitcher, gesturing with sharp movements of his hands how he wanted DiMaggio pitched. At last, the home plate umpire broke up the meeting, starting in toward them, waving his arms.

The manager jogged slowly back to the dugout. The pitcher milled about behind the plate, picked up the rosin bag while the catcher settled back behind the plate. The fans stood up. DiMaggio stepped in.

The catcher stuck his bare right hand out to his side. The crowd booed loudly.

DeRosa snorted. "They're going to walk him." The pitcher delivered the ball two feet outside and the catcher stepped outside to take the throw—ball four. DiMaggio tossed his bat and jogged to first.

"Damn," DeRosa muttered. "Looks like extra innings."

The Seals' next batter, Ernie Sulik, received a smattering of applause when his name was announced, but it was clear that the fans' hearts weren't in it, thinking instead to the top of the tenth when the Oaks would send the heart of their order to the plate against the Seals' ace Walter Mails.

Sulik swung at the first pitch, in at the hands, pulling it down the line at third. The Oaks third baseman dove to his right, fielded the ball, dropped it, picked it up again, spun on his knees, throwing over to second for the force out on a sliding DiMaggio—wide! The ball kicked off the fielder's glove and out into center field. The runner at second, running all the way with two outs, scored easily and just like that the game was over and the Seals had won.

DeRosa and Eugene sat in silence while the crowd filtered past them out of the stadium, neither of them looking at the other. At last power was cut to half of the lights, and the playing field dulled, lost its luster.

"We better go now," said Eugene.

"Sure, Eu." DeRosa's voice was tired, defeated. He made no attempt to rise out of his seat.

"Here," Eugene said. "Lean on my shoulder."

"I'll be all right, Eu. Just give me a second."

"No hurry." Eugene stood, stretched, waiting for DeRosa.

"All right." DeRosa stuck out his hand and Eugene helped him to his feet. A soft wind greeted them as they exited the stadium. DeRosa led Eugene across the street to a large tree-filled park where he sat down on a short concrete embankment. The lights, still at half power, cast sharp, elongated shadows across the illuminated landscape of the park. They watched the silent empty ballpark as the lights winked out entirely. The power in the city was still out except for the soft emergency lights of a hospital in the distance.

"I can't believe they walked him," said DeRosa, his voice muffled in darkness.

"It doesn't seem fair, does it?"

"No, it doesn't."

"What would you have done?"

"You mean if I was the manager? I don't know. I might have walked him, I suppose."

"Their manager lost the game because of the walk. He put the go ahead run at second base where the runner could score on the error."

"I just don't understand, Eu. I get a chance to go back fifty years and . . ."

"And it doesn't come out the way you wanted it to, does it. That's all right. We saw a good game, a great game. When's the last time you saw anything from the thirties that didn't look ancient? Everything always looks so scratched and grainy, without color, from another era. Tonight was real. Isn't that enough?"

"Yes, I guess so." DeRosa took a deep, heaving breath. Footsteps echoed down the long, dark street. Eugene helped DeRosa back to his feet.

A tall, angular figure approached, obscured in darkness.

"Is everything O.K.?" the figure asked. "Do you need any help?"

"Joe?" asked DeRosa.

"Do I know you?" The figure's hands were tucked casually inside the pockets of a heavy, wool jacket with alternating vertical stripes of navy and orange.

"You did, once."

"You do look a little familiar. Must have been a long time ago, though."

"Ages. I knew your parents," DeRosa lied.

Together Eugene and DiMaggio led DeRosa across the street, around the corner, to the car. Someone had closed and locked the door DeRosa had left open. DeRosa searched in his pockets for the keys, found them, fumbled with the lock.

"You're a young man, Joe," said DeRosa. "You should be out celebrating."

"The rest of the players went over to the Double Play for drinks. I won't turn 21 for another year." DiMaggio shrugged, averted his eyes down to his feet.

"Don't worry, Joe. Next year you'll be able to drink anywhere you want. Just don't forget where you come from." DeRosa finally got the key in the lock. He got in and opened the passenger door from the inside.

They pulled up in front of DeRosa's blacked-out building just past midnight. A neighbor must have watched them approach and now appeared to greet them.

"Is he O.K.?" the neighbor asked.

"He's fine," Eugene answered, "just a little tired. It's been quite a night."

Eugene helped DeRosa up the stairs and into his apartment, fumbling in the darkness. DeRosa smiled at Eugene, placed a hand heavy across his shoulder. "Don't forget where you come from, either, Eugene. Don't forget."

Eugene shook his head.

DeRosa lay back on the couch, too tired to undress and get into bed. He closed his eyes and listened to Eugene move through the apartment, shut the door softly and retreat into darkness. That night DeRosa's sleep was dreamless.

Rick Wilber is an award-winning editor, novelist and writer whose short fiction often appears in *Asimov's Science Fiction*, *Fantasy & Science Fiction*, and elsewhere. He is at work on a trilogy for Tor Books, and also continuing to work on a series of counterfactual stories about famous ballplayer and spy, Moe Berg. The first of those stories, "Something Real," won the Sidewise Award for Alternate History in 2013. Wilber has published some fifty short stories, many of them touching upon baseball in one way or another. In this supernatural story, a man claims to be Stephen Crane, the nineteenth-century author who was a pretty good college baseball player before he became famous for writing *The Red Badge of Courage*, "The Open Boat," and others. Crane offers our narrator some pointed advice about writing, about base ball (as Crane spelled it), and about reality.

Stephen to Cora to Joe
∽

Rick Wilber

O N A SUNDAY AFTERNOON in September that threatened a downpour, in the top of the eighth of the last game of the season, with no one on and two outs and things pretty much looking okay, suddenly I couldn't find the strike zone.

Control tells you the truth about yourself. You go along thinking you know exactly where to place the ball and you're always getting it in there, and then suddenly you can't find the damn plate. Sliders that painted the black just the inning before start missing wide or are down in the dirt, and your fastball—such as it is—loses the corners, coming in so fat that you have to quit using it or risk someone coming back up the middle with a line drive and taking your head off.

I walked the first guy in the inning on four pitches, two of them way wide and two in the dirt. He was their number seven hitter and I'd gotten him out three other times on easy groundballs. Now I'd walked him on four straight. Steve, back behind the plate, was not happy about that.

As the batter trotted down to first, Steve came clanking out, the broken metal clasps of the cheap shinguards I'd bought him at the used sporting goods store rattling loosely. There was an ominous rumble of thunder from a squall line out over the bay. I looked that way, took a deep breath, tried to think my way through my control troubles by looking at the scenery. A rainbow was just forming, a thin arc of color emerging in front of the charcoal sheets of rain. Just a bit south of that, a huge mass of low blue-gray clouds boiled, the sky running from pewter to dangerous shades of green and black.

"Looks quite mean and low out there, David, don't it?" Steve said in that Bronx jargon he put on for laughs sometimes. "But, hully gee, I don't think she's blowing our way." He slipped his catcher's mask up on top of his head and then held the ball out to me, nestled in that wide Rawlings mitt I'd bought him. "So, ya mug," he added, "how ya feeling?"

I looked over toward the stands. Cora was there, watching us, wearing a Rays cap in our honor, and sitting up straight on the bleacher seat so I couldn't miss the tight scoop-neck T-shirt, those glossy sports shorts she likes, and her granny sunglasses set up on the top of that blond hair. She looked gorgeous. She saw me seeing her, gave me a quick wave of her hand, and smiled. Next to her on the grandstand bench was a small overnight bag. That, I thought, was a good indicator.

I turned to look at Steve. "I'm fine," I said. "Just lost it for a second there, that's all. It's been a long day."

Steve had seen where I was looking. "David, Cora's a real looker, got a real shape on her, she does." He grinned. "She's got everything an old gent like you could want, including that ample bosom; but if you don't start worrying about your pitching, I'll lam the head off ya. Got it? We're two runs in front and this is the bottom of their order. Just throw the old pellet in there and let them hit it, right? Let your fielders do their job."

I nodded. "Sure. Let them hit it." That plan, I thought, gave our defense more credit than it was due, but I didn't say that. It was always hard for me to argue with Steve.

He leaned in close, stared at me hard, eyes narrowing. "Don't be rum, David. We don't have anyone in relief. It's your game, win or lose, all right?"

"I'm fine, Steve. Really. Let's get this guy." I was tense, and he could sense it. He was good at that. He smiled. "Loosen up," he said, "and just throw strikes."

He turned to walk back, stopped, turned back. "Did I ever tell you what my friend Joseph said about America's love for baseball?"

I smiled back. "Joseph? Conrad? No, you never did." Steve loved telling those stories about his circle of friends when he lived in England: Henry James, Ford Madox Ford, H. G. Wells, Conrad—they were all his pals there at Brede Manor down in Sussex, south of London, in that last year of Steve's life as he slowly died from the consumption that destroyed his lungs. Must have been quite a group when they got together on a Saturday evening to drink, smoke, and play cards and listen to the rattle of Steve's cough.

I wanted to hear the story, but then the ump walked out and made us break it up and get back to the business at hand. I walked the next guy, too, and then gave up a double and a single before finding my nerve and settling back down with us a run down. We tied it up on Steve's single in the ninth before the squall line hit and the rain came down and everything got very confused.

I never did get to hear what Conrad had to say about baseball.

Her Upturned Face

I first met Cora on a Monday morning as I walked across campus from my office in the Arts Building to Cooper Hall, where I taught a 9 A.M. class in Fiction Writing 402, Advanced Techniques for the Short Story.

She sat on the low brick wall that marks the path between the two buildings, reading a thin, little book. She wore a tight T-shirt that showed off her breasts, a pair of plaid walking shorts, and those platform sandals that are so popular with the coeds these days. She had broad features—there's nothing delicate about Cora—with that wide mouth and her red lipstick. It was too much makeup, but she wore it well.

As I walked by, she looked up at me; that beautiful upturned face, her eyes wide, those lips pouty and full. "Professor Holman?"

I just smiled at first. I'd been teaching a long time, and you develop a kind of immunity to the sexual displays of the typical undergraduate. But then, I swear it, she said this: "The burnt sky thundered its rejection of Sean's entreaty. Nature, inimical Nature, arched her back and hissed at him. Her claws were out. He felt small, and still shrinking. Great cracks of fury pounded him, reducing him, until he was gone."

My jaw must have dropped. "Wow," I said. "You've actually read that?" It was from "Hide the Monster," the title story from my thin little collection, part of my Big Break five years before: a two-book deal, the short-story collection with the novel to follow. The collection got some nice reviews in places that matter and sold well; the novel I'm almost done with and my agent and my editor love what they've seen of it.

"I love that story," she said, and held out the book she was reading. It was the collection. "I've memorized whole passages from these stories. Will you autograph the book for me?"

I laughed. "Does rain fall from the cracked sky? Hand that over, dear."

And I found out her name so I could sign: "To Cora Taylor, A Beautiful Reader." She giggled at that when she read it, then thanked me, said she thought the book was the best thing she'd read in years and that she'd been surprised to find I was teaching right here on campus. I thanked her again, and we kept talking. She flirted. I flirted back, and then met her for drinks a few hours later and we wound up in bed.

It was all very simple, very effortless. Have you ever noticed how all the best things seem to just fall into your lap and that the things you try for the hardest are the ones hardest to get? It's always been that way for me, and Cora was a perfect example. A girl like that? Wanting to bed a tired, old writer like me? It was laughable until it happened, and then it all seemed perfectly normal, like I knew what I was doing, like I had it all under control.

Active Service

There was a time when I could really play The Game. Pitcher for the national champs in college at Southern Illinois, four years in the minors after that in places like Paintsville, Kentucky, where I met Emily, the perfect girl for a young pitcher; and then in Lakeland, Florida, and Medford, Oregon, where I could show her off along with my skills. And then came my cup of coffee in The Show when the Cardinals called me up in September with the expanded roster and I got my shot. It didn't take me long to figure out that I was good, not great, on a pitching staff that took the Cards to the World Series. My career stats: no wins, two losses, an ERA of 4.05.

I was on the big league roster for spring training the next season but couldn't stick. Then I went down to Triple A and couldn't find the plate. Same at Double A and while I kept at it for another year or two after that, the two truths I discovered were these: the downslope is a slick one and twenty-eight is an old man for a minor leaguer. So before I was thirty, I had to face doing something with the rest of my life. I thought I'd make a good college coach, and that meant getting some degrees, so I went back to school, got one degree and then another and then still another while I got interested in words and how they're put together, and I started caring about writing. Baseball—that other life—disappeared into my past until finally, on the day I sold my first short story to the *Mississippi Review*, I didn't pay attention to it anymore at all. It was fifteen years before I came back to it.

Fast Rode the Knight

Steve rowed up to practice the day I met him. We were two weeks away from our first game, and I was running in the outfield, trying to loosen up some old tendons and build up a little endurance at the same time. We play in an over-thirty league, all very amateur; doctors and lawyers and teachers and mechanics and salesmen and even one politician, a city councilman who has his eyes on the mayor's office. We all just play for the love of the game, but there's some real talent around too. My first baseman played in the minors, same for the shortstop. All four of our outfielders played college ball, and our one other pitcher, like me, even made it to the big leagues for a half-season or so. So while we're out here for fun, we take it seriously once the ump says play ball.

It was at the end of one halfhearted wind sprint that I stopped for a moment to look out past the left field foul pole toward the little harbor there and the bay beyond.

It was an absolutely perfect blue-sky day, the way it can be in Florida in the spring, the sun hot but not as deadly as it gets in July and August. Someone was out there in a rowboat, I noticed. I was happy for any excuse to stop and look for a minute or two instead of running those interminable halfhearted outfield wind sprints. You get to forty years old and getting into shape isn't the fun it used to be.

As I watched, the rise and dip of the oars and the boat's forward motion spent out a series of small whirlpools that bordered a peaceful wake, the bright sun bouncing off the tiny wavelets. It was mesmerizing, and I kept watching as the boat reached the dock and the guy inside tied it off, stepped out, started walking from the dock across the two-lane street to where I stood at the ball-field's low fence.

"You're playing base ball?" he asked. He looked a little lost.

I nodded, added "Yes. We're a semipro team, just play for fun."

He was thin, under six feet tall, had a small moustache, wild dark hair parted right down the middle and then pulled back behind each ear. He brushed back that dirty hair. "You need a player?" he asked. "I play a pretty decent catcher."

"Well," I hesitated. We had a lot of guys who tried out for the team, but the truth of the matter is that most people just can't play the game. We weren't some fantasy camp, where they coddle wannabees and give them uniforms and a chance to pretend. This wasn't slowpitch softball where everyone's a hitter and anyone can play. This was baseball. Hardball. The real thing.

But, on the other hand, we could always use a guy who could handle himself behind the plate. Truth was, nobody our age seemed to want to put on the tools of ignorance for more than a few innings, so this guy was worth a look. "Sure," I said, "c'mon on in and give it a shot."

And he did. And within the hour I knew we had the new catcher we needed. He was a natural, with a bullet arm, a great glove; a singles hitter but he always made contact.

He called himself Steve Crane, and I thought that was pretty funny, rowing up in an open boat and all that.

And then I realized he really meant it.

Her Blue Hotel

I met Emily in Paintsville, Kentucky, my first year in professional ball. She was drop-dead gorgeous and bored to tears in that tiny town, a prom queen turned part-time student at the local junior college while she worked for her daddy's insurance business. I was a star at that level of the game, and there was no competition in Paintsville. It took us something like ten minutes to go from hello at the Blue Hotel bar to oh, yes, back in my little apartment. She was the most beautiful thing I'd ever seen, and if the sex wasn't that good, the looks were compensation. I saw her as the perfect ornament. She saw me as her ticket out, her lifetime pass to the big leagues, and that was okay by me. Hell, I saw me headed that way myself, and she made for one great-looking baseball wife, all perfect blond hair and those tight jeans and that luscious accent, y'all.

But then I didn't quite become the ballplayer she'd figured on. Or the famous sportscaster either, though I gave that a try for a few years. Or even, later, the Famous Writer.

I didn't become much of anything and one day, five years into the marriage— she was patient with me, I'll give her that—I came home to packed bags and a note about what I hadn't turned out to be. Later, I found out she had a boyfriend who made more money than he knew what to do with in software sales, so Emily finally found somebody who could succeed at something, and that gave her a chance for a new beginning. That's how she told me to see it in that note: A New Beginning.

A Girl of the Streets

Cora wanted to know about my writing. It started with the how-many-words-a-day questions and went on from there, growing in complexity, some of them personal and some of them about the work. She wanted to be a writer herself and kept talking about how she was willing to pay her dues to get there. I should have thought that through a little better when she said it.

She had stories to tell, God knows. I found out this: She was a local girl, Catholic elementary school at St. John's Parish out on the beach. Then four years at St. Petersburg Catholic High School, where she played on the softball team and edited the yearbook.

She was a good Catholic girl from a solid family—father a pediatrician, mother a teacher, two little brothers who played soccer. She was on her way to wherever it is good Catholic girls go for their careers when she got hooked up in college to a boy with the wrong kind of dreams and the wrong way to reach them, and she found herself in trouble—drugs and pregnant and the boyfriend got mean. I didn't get all the details but there was no child and a nasty little scar on the back side of that gorgeous left cheek.

So she'd come back from all that. Back in school, wanting to write, looking great. And paying her way through as a dancer at the Club De Dream out on the beach. I started going there every Tuesday and Thursday night. She went on at ten, this good Catholic girl, and oh, my.

A Sense of Obligation

Halfway through the season I had a terrible Sunday pitching, getting roughed up for nine earned runs on the way to losing 15–2. We have a ten-run mercy rule in this league, and it was a good thing for us, since it ended the game early. Most of us went to the Little Regiment bar afterward, a dark-wood paneling faux-British pub not far from the field. A few pints of Guinness sounded pretty good to me at that point.

We weren't in there more than fifteen minutes when Cora left to play some pool with Humphrey Regis, our shortstop. He was fresh from a recent tough divorce and had been oh for four at the plate, so a little eight-ball with Cora must have seemed heaven sent.

That left me and Steve alone at the table for a few minutes. Steve pulled my collection out of his bag and told me he'd read it.

I stared at him.

"This is the copy you signed for Cora," he said. "She asked me to read it."

I nodded.

"It's good work," he said. "I like it. But. . ."

"But?"

He gave me a slight smile. "I know a little something about writing, David. I did well at it there for a while."

I nodded. "Sure. I know. You're Stephen Crane, *the* Stephen Crane."

He shrugged those thin shoulders. "You know what I mean, all right, David." He leaned back in his chair, sipped on his beer. "Look, David, I don't know how or why this is happening, either, chum. I think I recollect something that Herbert said, about that machine of his."

"Sure," I said again. "H. G. Wells and his time machine."

He laughed. It sounded bitter. He started to rise. "All right, then, David. I'm sorry I tried to monkey with this. Cora thought you'd appreciate my advice, that I should try and help, that your career—"

"Cora thought?" I shook my head, waved at him to sit back down. "Please, Steve, stay. Look, I appreciate what you're trying to do, really, but my career is fine. Just about got my novel done, and my agent says she's close on the next deal. I might get to quit teaching if things really take off, you know."

"Bully for you, David," he said. Then he smiled at me. "David, can I tell you a story?"

"Sure," I said. "Tell me a story. Something about the Civil War, right? About red badges, about fighting and dying and all that."

I knew that sounded mean even as I said it. This poor guy really did think he was Stephen Crane; he'd convinced me that he really believed that, at least. And here I was teasing him, acting like I was hot stuff just because I'd written a few books and won a few awards.

He was staring at me. I tried again, nicer. "I'm sorry. Sure, absolutely, I'd like to hear a story."

He shook his head slightly. "The 'Red Badge,'" he said, then paused for a moment. "You know, I'd never seen war when I wrote it."

I nodded. "I knew that."

"I thought I could tell the truth about war when I wrote it. I thought I had some talent."

"You did, on both scores."

He shook his head again. "No, not really. You know, it's hard for a man to realize these things about himself." He paused, sipped on his beer, went on. "I didn't know the truth from an electric streetcar. I came to realize that in May of 1897, the Greco-Turkish War. The *New York Journal* hired me as a correspondent, and it was there, at Velistino, that I finally saw the truth of war for the first time."

"And?"

He smiled, shrugged. "Death is very real." He took a sip of beer, smiled again. "I wonder how close to the truth I might have come if I'd lived past twenty-nine."

"Now you'll get to find out. You're writing aren't you?"

He shook his head. "No. That's the rum thing. There's no time."

"No time? We practice a couple of times a week and we play a single game on Sundays. What are you doing with the rest of your time?"

He frowned. "What am I doing?" There was a long pause. "I don't know," he said. "I'm trying to think about it right now, trying to remember, and I don't know. When I'm not at the park, playing the game, it's all gray, blank."

"Oh, c'mon." The poor guy, I thought, was Looney Tunes. "You're here now, with me and there's nothing gray."

"Yes, I am at that." His eyes widened. "Maybe it's you, David. Maybe it's you that's brought me back, you that makes me real."

I laughed. "Right. Me and my magic powers, that's it. Okay, then, here," and I grabbed the paper placemat from under his plate, flipped it over to the blank side, pulled my antique Waterman pen out of the reading-glasses case where I keep it, and handed it to him, calling his bluff. "Abracadabra, Steve. Here's your chance. Get writing. I'll just hang out here and make you real for a while, while you scribble."

He chuckled. "It might work at that, my friend," he said. He held up the pen to look at it—an 1893 Waterman #25, eyedropper filled, a classic with a tapered cap and gold-filled bands around the barrel. Emily splurged and bought it for me to celebrate my first contract. He gave me the damnedest look, part smirk, part wonderment, then reached over to put his finger on the placemat, slid it back his way, and started writing. I shut up and for the next couple of hours just sat there and watched him write. It was my job to keep the beer coming for both of us.

His handwriting looked clean and legible, but I couldn't read it from where I sat, beyond being able to see that it was prose. He wrote steadily, the motion of pen against the paper was so fluid, so constant, that I could see the story taking shape before my very eyes. There was no hesitation, no long moments where he was lost in thought, no getting up to wash the dishes or cut the front yard and vacuum the carpet or stare out the window or any of the other tricks I used myself to stall for time in the middle of a writerly panic. It was utter confidence at work—dumbfoundingly utter confidence.

As he got toward the end of the second paragraph, he coughed, the first one I'd heard from him in the couple of months he'd been around. It was just a sharp, quick bark, that first one; but a few minutes later came another and then another, each one looser than the one before, like his lungs were filling with mucus right there in front of me. Finally, maybe an hour into that writing session—on his fourth or fifth placemat by then—the cough was so rattlingly hard that he had to stop and get it over with. I got up from my chair and came around the table to help him but he waved me away, then grabbed one of the big paper napkins from their holder on the table and held it to his mouth as he brought the mucus up. He spat into it finally, and his lungs seemed to clear. He tossed the napkin back on the table and went back to writing as I sat back down. Later, when the waiter came by to clear away the empty beers and the used napkin, I saw the red stains on the paper napkin.

The coughing eased after that; there were still some fits but nothing so dramatic as that one, and then, finally, he seemed to hit a stopping point. He set the pen down, leaned back in his chair, reached over to pick up his beer, and took a good, long pull. He smiled. "You, of all people, must understand just how good that felt, David."

"That's a hell of a cough," I said.

He waved my concern away. "No, not that. The writing. It was . . .," he searched for the right word, "it was real; do you know what I mean?"

"Sure," I said. But I didn't. Not then.

"David, everything's square with us, right?"

"Sure."

"Then I wonder," he started to say, but then he fell into that cough again, a quick bark that built to a loose rattle that he covered with another big paper napkin, his whole body convulsing with it.

"You ought to get that looked after," I said.

He laughed, and that brought him to a cough again for a minute. Then he smiled, nodded. "Yes. Get it looked after. Damnable thing."

Then he reached over to take my hand. Holding on to my hand, gripping it tighter as he spoke, he said this: "David. Why are you playing base ball? A fellow your age—you're the oldest chap on the team by a good ten years—you could be hurt, pull a muscle, break an ankle. It doesn't make any sense really, does it?"

"No, I suppose it doesn't."

"But you're playing."

I smiled. "Yes. I'm playing."

"Why?"

I thought about it, started tossing out reasons, possibilities, excuses. "Hanging on to my youth? Getting some exercise? Still learning to hit a curve? Hell, I don't know. Because I enjoy myself. Because I can quit worrying about other things when I'm out there pitching."

"What do you think about when you're on the mound?"

"The game. The situation. The next pitch. Whether or not my catcher can throw that runner out at second."

He smiled, the cough gone. "To the last question, the answer would be yes, old chap."

It was my turn to laugh. "I don't know. I play because I love it. There's no excuses, nothing gray out there. I pitch and they hit or they don't, that's it. At the end, it's all very definite, very real."

"Real?"

"Yes, real. I can feel the ball, the glove, the rubber, and the hole I've dug with my right foot in front of it; the downslope of the mound, the feel of the ball's stitches against my fingertips, the way it comes off the side of the knuckle of this finger," I held up the second finger of my right hand, "when I throw a curve, or off this spot," I touched a spot a little higher up on that same finger, "when I throw a slider. It's all about physical sensations and concentration, lovely, lovely concentration. It's reality. Unarguable reality. I love it for that."

He nodded. "Unarguable reality. I like that." He leaned back in his chair, put his hands behind his head, and said this: "Art—your art, my art—is involved in that terrible war between lies and the truth, David, and the truth must win out. Describe it truthfully. Make it real. That's all I wanted to say."

He leaned forward. "If you're truthful about the surface, if you get the details right, then the interior is revealed and you can get close to the bone, get inside the bone, to the marrow, and tell the truth. That's all. This is something that took me years to figure out. Only at the end, lying there at Brede one day in the sun, dying, knowing I was truly dying, did I finally begin to figure it out. And then it was too late."

He let go of my hand, took the paper he'd been writing on, filled now with tiny scribblings that filled the page, folded it once, twice, and then put it into the pockets of his pants. He looked at me. "You have these skills, David. They're very impressive, just like that little speech about base ball.

"But they're all a bit too, too . . ." he hesitated, came up with the word, "too pyrotechnic. I can't find the truth of things in there anywhere. I don't see anything that really matters. That's all I thought I might say. All right?"

What was I supposed to say to that, to this man who thought he was an invention of mine, someone I'd brought to life, created from the ether? "Sure," I said. "It's fine, Steve. Thanks for the input. I appreciate it, really."

"All right, then," he said. And he got up and left, waving once as he walked out the door.

Okay, I thought, finishing off my beer, that would be irony, right? A guy like him, a guy who thinks he's a dead writer, preaching to me about the truth.

I set my empty beer glass down on the table, tossed a twenty on top of it, and went over to the pool table to shoot some eight ball with Cora. Later, we headed back to my place at the beach, the one with the second-story deck that looks out over the dunes to the Gulf of Mexico so I can watch for the green flash that comes with some sunsets here. It's a bright emerald moment that shoots straight up from the final instant of the sun's disappearance into the Gulf. They're wonderful and rare and require concentration, focus, to see. Some people watch for years and can't get the hang of seeing one. I'd seen a lot of them—dozens— over the years.

I wondered, as I got into my Lexus with Cora, if I'd ever get to see what Steve had written on those placemats. By this time I'd read everything Crane had ever written. I'd know in a heartbeat if this guy was the real thing. I wondered about that all the way home. Later, the green flash was terrific. So was Cora.

Yellow Sky

"He was just trying to help you, David," Cora said to me on a Sunday morning a week later, the early light coming in the bedroom window to backlight her, so I couldn't see much of her face, just the penumbra of that long, blond hair around her, a vision, a miracle.

She rolled over on her side to face me, propped herself up on one elbow, shook her head to clear her hair out of her eyes. We'd argued about her telling Steve that I was a writer, too. Now she wanted to explain herself. "He likes you," she said, "and when I told him you were a writer, he said he'd like to see your work; that's all."

I stared at her. "You really believe it's him? You do know that Stephen Crane died in a sanitarium in Badenweiler, Germany, in 1900, right?"

She stared back, slowly smiled. "So he's back from the dead, or some kind of ghost? I don't know, David. You tell me. You're the fiction writer. You're the one who makes all this stuff up."

I played along. "I wonder how he got here, then," I said. "He keeps talking about H. G. Wells and his time machine. I looked it up to make sure. *The Time Machine* was Wells's first novel, that's all—an allegory about the British caste system in the Victorian Age."

"So what?" she said, leaning over to kiss me on my stomach. It tickled. Laughing, I pushed her back, then reached up to touch that perfect chin, run my fingers across those lips, as beautiful in the morning on their own as they were during the day when she'd put on her lip gloss and lined it in. She was young and perfect and I wasn't either one. And she'd actually bought a copy of my short-story collection, which made her one of about a thousand people in the whole damn country. Part of me felt pretty awful about having an affair with a girl of twenty-two. But part of me felt I was not to be blamed. At least, with Cora, I was alive again. I was even writing again. Not particularly well, I thought, but bad words on the screen are better than no words at all.

I didn't know how long the bubble would last, floating along there in the metaphoric breeze with me inside it, playing these kids' games—sex with a twenty-something, baseball with a guy who claimed to be Stephen Crane.

Cora laughed. I watched those breasts move as she sat up on her knees and looked down on me. "You should get him to come guest lecture in your short-story-writing class. Now that would impress the students."

"They'd believe it was really him," I said. "All that stuff about Conrad and Ford Madox Ford and Henry James and all the rest—they'd lap that up. And the part about Wells and his time machine, they'd go crazy for that. All most of them want to write anyway is sci-fi and fantasy."

"He is pretty damn convincing," she said.

"And good looking too," I added, "in that dangerous kind of way."

She reached down to feel me. I was ready and she moved over on top, concentrating, her eyes closed as she eased on down. Then she opened her eyes—those perfect eyes—and smiled. "Yes," she said in a whisper, "he is kind of good looking, and dangerous."

And then she started moving, up and down, and I started to lose control again.

That afternoon she came to the game to watch. It was the first time she'd done that. She didn't miss a single one after it. She even started keeping score.

One Dash—Horses

The next game, Steve turned a single up the middle into a sliding double when the center fielder took his time fielding the ball and coming up to throw. Steve saw this as he rounded first and just kept going, sprinting hard for second. His slide was showy and maybe a little risky, spikes up pretty high, but he got in there safe and then I brought him in with a single of my own two pitches later. That moment, when he raced like a thoroughbred across the plate well ahead of the throw from left to score the tying run for us, was the second happiest I saw him in the six months he was here. His narrow face with that dour, scraggly, wild look on it finally lit up in a huge smile and he clapped his hands and shouted happily as he scored. His cough was gone. Never once in a practice or a game did I hear the faintest hint of that deadly rattle.

Later, in the dugout, he said this to me:

"I love running, lungs full of air and legs flying. It's an honest measure of a man, isn't it, David?"

I smiled at him, nodded. "Sure. An honest measure."

"You know, David," he said, crossing his legs there in the dugout and pulling out his pipe to suck on it dry, since the league rules didn't allow you to smoke. "You know, near the end, when the consumption had about claimed me fully there at Brede, Herbert would come visit."

"Herbert? Oh, H. G., right?" I said. "You know, he once said that 'The Open Boat' was an imperishable gem."

He smiled. "Really? Nice of him. That was a true story, you know."

I nodded. "The *Commodore* went down off the Florida coast. You were on your way to Cuba to cover the insurrection and you and the captain and a few others wound up in a lifeboat. You drifted just off the coast for a couple of days and then finally tried to ride it in through the surf. One guy died."

He smiled, nodded. "Close enough, David."

"And the month before that, waiting for the *Commodore* to be ready, you stayed in Jacksonville, Florida. That's where you met one Cora Stewart. She ran the Hotel de Dream."

He smiled. "She was stunning, David. A big ample bosom, that blond hair that she would loosen and let fall around her shoulders." He sighed. "I forgot everyone else."

"The drama critic for the *Chicago Daily News?*"

He nodded. "Amy Leslie. Lovely woman."

"But Cora?"

"Better. By yards old chap, by yards and miles."

Then he went on. "Herbert would come visit Cora and I there at Brede, and he'd bring along a whole group of nieces and nephews so we could play rounders. I taught them how to play base ball instead. With a cricket bat and no gloves. That was the closest I came to baseball over there. Rounders, with a cricket bat." He shook his head, smiled again, and waved toward the field. "This, this splendid game. It's wonderful, David. You know that, right, how utterly splendid it is just to be out here playing baseball on a Sunday afternoon?"

I did know it, and told him so. You start to get a little older and suddenly things like a good hard slider down low and away, a hard-hit double off the wall, or even a scratch single up the middle—sure, they matter. Like making love to a beautiful woman in her twenties, like getting good reviews on your short-story collection, like writing well and knowing you're in that zone: like all those things, it matters.

"Are you still writing?" I asked him.

He shook his head, then stood up, took in a deep breath through his nose. "What do you smell, David? Right now, take in the air and tell me what you smell."

I smiled, took a long, deep sniff. "Fresh air," I said, "and green grass."

"Leather," he said, holding up the glove I'd bought him, a good Rawlings catcher's mitt, an XPG 2000. "And sweat. And the dirt of the infield. I missed all this."

"Is it still the same?"

He laughed, picked up one of our metal bats, Louisville Slugger Terminator, thirty-four inch, thirty-ounce. He held the bat up and laughed again.

"Yeah," I said, "me too. I miss the smell of the wood. We still had those wooden bats when I was a kid, you know."

He sat back down, slouched back against the bench. "It's close, old chap. It's nearly the truth. It smells like my childhood, like my father, the preacher, before he died. It smells like learning the game, throwing and catching and hitting out in the vacant lot next door. It smells like college, like playing for Syracuse and throwing out that Colgate man who was trying to steal. My God, I could play, David. I could really play."

"Why did you quit? Your health?"

He shrugged. "I suppose. Life. Death. My writing. Finding the truth. They all mattered, too. And baseball is, after all, only a game."

"True enough."

"I'm on deck," he said, and stood, picked up the metal bat, walked out to the on-deck circle, and slipped the weighted doughnut over the barrel. I watched him as he took a few swings to loosen up. He was thin, but healthy; God, he glowed with it. Then Tommy ground out and it was Steve's at bat again. He turned once to look at me, smiled, and then stepped into the batter's box. Two pitches later he slapped a single up the middle. The look on his face as he stood there at first, happy with his base hit—there was some truth, some reality, in that too, I thought.

The Monster

I've lied about a lot of this. I drive a gray Honda Accord, not a Lexus. I've never seen the green flash at sunset. Cora wasn't really that good looking, or that young, or even a student. She didn't dance at the Club De Dream; she worked in customer relations for the phone company, and she was well into her thirties if she was a day; and her breasts sagged and she hadn't read my short-story collection and she didn't flirt with me and we never made love. My earned run average in the big leagues was really 7.50. I was only up for one game, not one month, and I got ripped by the Mets for three very long innings. In fact, I was never in the big leagues at all, but was lucky to spend three years in the lower minors, trying to get by with breaking balls. I never did have very good control.

My short-story collection sold six-hundred and fifty copies and the reviews were awful. My novel? In four years I've written about ten thousand words. Are they good words, at least? I don't know. I don't think so.

I make it all up. That's what fiction is, I thought—all lies. It's not real; it's safer than that; there's more distance.

Here's the truth about Emily, my ex-wife. She wasn't nearly as good looking as I said, and she was a great deal nicer. In my second year of minor league ball, in Medford, Oregon, we had a baby, a perfect little girl, Annie, her hair as red as her mommy's.

A year later I was in Lakeland, Florida, playing A ball for the Lakeland Tigers in the Florida State League. It was ten in the morning and Emily was at work; her job as assistant manager at the Pancake House paid our bills while I struggled to find the strike zone. There was a fire in our apartment complex. I crawled in through a bedroom window and rescued Annie, but my face was ruined in the effort and by the time my wounds had healed, my baseball career was over, my wife and child had left. I wound up homeless. I died penniless at twenty-nine.

Or maybe it was this way: Emily was a hooker, working the streets of New York. I rescued her from that and we had a child, a beautiful little blond Annie and for a while everything seemed fine. But then I was let go by the Cardinal organization and I couldn't find work, and Emily went back to what she did best and little Annie died and Emily was murdered by her pimp and I was a crackhead and I died, penniless, in the gutter, at age twenty-nine.

Or, no; our child was abducted and I found her, dead, in the woods, her body placed against the rotten trunk of a downed tree that lay in a bower, her body framed by the overhanging branches so that the autumn sun came through like cathedral lighting. There were ants on her face, crawling in and out her nostrils, the empty sockets of her eyes. I was shattered by that sight. No, I was the murderer, and I turned myself in and I was executed in Florida's Old Sparky, smoke rising, sparks flying, the smell of burnt flesh. I was twenty-nine.

No. We were all in a small boat together. Me, my wife, our daughter, adrift after our cruise ship sank off the coast of Florida. We could see the shoreline, huge breakers rolling in just a few hundred yards away, so big we didn't dare try to get through them to safety. Finally, exhausted, we had to try. I made it and dragged Annie to safety; but Emily, poor Emily drowned and I've never forgotten the look on her face, the rage of it, as she slipped away. She wanted so badly to live. It broke my heart. She was twenty-nine.

No. Those are all lies too, of course. Here's the real truth:

My father was an agent for Farmer's Insurance in Edwardsville, Illinois. He was good at his job. Mom taught English at Ward Junior High. We had a good life there, my brother and sister and I. I played Little League and we won more than we lost. I went to Mary, Queen of Peace for grade school and survived the nuns, then Edwardsville High School where I played football, basketball, and baseball for the Tigers and did fine. Then off to major in English at Southern Illinois University, where I discovered Crane, and myself, and a good changeup that got us to the Division II national championship game, where we lost to Cal Poly when I gave up a scratch single to their worst hitter at the wrong moment.

My two best friends went to Vietnam while I played baseball in college. One of them came home alive; the other in a box. I was lucky in the first draft lottery and didn't go. Instead, I started that minor league career, which stayed minor league in writing, in life. I married a nice girl. We have a nice family. I have nice degrees from nice colleges and did a nice master's thesis on the truth in Stephen Crane's fiction. I teach at Pinellas County Community College, where I'm head of the creative writing program. I've sold exactly three short stories—one to the online version of the *Mississippi Review*, one to *Elysian Fields*, and the third to *Alabaster*. That makes me well published by community-college standards. I make a nice living. When I write, I really use that antique Waterman that Emily bought me. It connects me, somehow, to the man I studied so much.

I play baseball on weekends with some other nice people. We lose more than we win, but I'll be damned if it isn't fun. Just like Steve said, it's an honest measure of a man, this splendid game. When you face a good hitter, when you're at bat facing a hard slider, when that sharp grounder comes your way or that sinking liner loops toward you in right—you can't hide; you can't lie; you can't fake it. You make the play or you don't. Reality sounds pretty boring, doesn't it? But that's it; that's me; that's the truth of it.

A Notebook

And there's this too: Stephen really did come rowing in that Sunday in May. He tied up his rowboat and walked over to watch us and we gave him a glove and a ball and a bat and, my, he could play The Game. We finished with two wins and twelve losses the season before he came. We won ten this past season, with Steve catching and hitting third. He made me a better pitcher. I learned things from him, some of them about baseball.

I looked up his stats, which is what we do in baseball. He played in the Knickerbocker League for the New Jersey Athletics. They played at the Elysian Fields. He gave the professional game five good years before he turned to writing for a living, where he finally made a lot of money and married a rich, young socialite named Cora Stewart. They moved to England, where he became a real man of letters and lived a long, productive life.

No. I lied about that. He played baseball for Lafayette College his freshman year and at Syracuse University the next year, where he said, "The truth of the matter is that I went there more to play base ball than to study." That's the way they spelled the game in those days, like two words. I want this to be accurate.

He flunked out of Syracuse, drifted into purposeful poverty in the Bowery, and emerged from there with a self-published short novel, *Maggie: A Girl of the Streets*. That got him the chance to do more, and so he wrote his *The Red Badge of Courage* and became famous, if not rich.

The Red Badge was in 1894. In 1897, a famous writer at age twenty-six, he met Cora Stewart, already thirty years old and a failed socialite who ran a discreet bordello, the Hotel de Dream. They fell in love. He truly did survive the sinking of the *Commodore* and wrote a news story that became a short story that is generally said to be the best thing he ever did—and every word of it a kind of truth: "The Open Boat."

Three years later he was dead, his frail lungs doing him in. Those last few years he traveled as much as he could, but called England his home. Henry James, Ford Madox Ford, Joseph Conrad, H. G. Wells—they all loved him and his work. They thought him important. In 1899 he declined rapidly. They sought a cure in Germany. Cora was with him at the end. You can look all this up if you don't trust me, and I wouldn't blame you.

And this is the truth too: There really was a rainbow that last day in September, and those dark clouds to the east over the gray chop of the bay, and that small rain that down could rain to soak me, sneaking up on me until I realized, at game's end, that the rain, my sweat, the lies, my curveball, my lack of control—that all of it was a lie, that nothing was real except, maybe, Stephen and his stories and Cora, his and mine, there in the stands.

Wounds in the Rain

In the bottom of the ninth of that final game, Steve got me through it and I slowly found my control again. I let in enough damage that they tied the score, but we answered with a run in the top of the tenth and then all I needed was three outs in the bottom.

I was so tired, so hot and wet that I couldn't think straight. Steve, behind the plate, was calling the pitches. I trusted him completely. We were up by that one run and I had no relief. Slider, slider, slider to the first guy and he went down swinging on all three, thank God. One out.

The next guy up had hit a double in the seventh and here he was again. Okay, then, slider wide, slider inside, fastball down the middle and he ripped it—another double, this one into the corner in left.

Steve came clanking back out again. "Got that one up," he said.

I nodded.

"I'd like to win this one, old chap, wouldn't you?" he asked.

I was too tired to care, but you can't say that to your catcher. "Sure," I said. "Let's get two more outs and we'll all go home happy."

"Yes, that's it," he said. "Everyone goes home happy." And he grinned at me, tossed me the ball.

This is probably what happened after that. I came in with a slider again, low and inside, but the guy went down and got it, drilled it right down the line. Foul.

Another slider, over the plate some more, and a hard groundball, but right at Randy Miller, our first baseman. He fielded it cleanly and stepped on the bag while the runner moved over from second to third.

Two outs and a man on third. Okay, more tired sliders, then; Steve with his two fingers stabbing at the red dirt behind the plate. Ball one. Strike one.

And then, like I meant it, like I could pick my spots like that, like I had that kind of control over my pitches, over myself, my life, I came in with a good pitch, low and outside. Strike two. Steve, back there, shook his fist at me, good pitch.

Same call, same pitch and the guy hit a two-hopper right back at me. I gloved it, pulled it free, tossed it to first and that was that. We win. Season over. First damn place for the first damn time in the five years I'd been playing again.

No. Same call, same pitch and the guy hit a two-hopper right back at me. I gloved it, pulled it free, and threw it fifteen feet over my first baseman's head. Runner scored from third. Game over. Season over. We lost. We came close, but we lost. I lost.

It was raining, I realized. It had been raining lightly for two innings and I hadn't noticed until the game ended and the rain started coming down harder, with a distant flash of lightning and a rumble of thunder.

I walked over to shake hands with the other team, like we always do in this league. Nice game, I told them, which was true. Good job, they told me, and there was some truth in that too.

I got back to the dugout and Steve wasn't there. I looked in the stands. Cora was gone. I dropped my glove into my athletic bag and saw some paper folded in there. Those placemats. His scribbling. The antique Waterman I'd loaned him was clipped to the folded sheets, holding them together. I pulled the pen free, opened the pages. The first page had this on it in that careful handwriting of his:

None of them knew the color of the sky. Their eyes glanced level, and were fastened upon the waves that swept toward them. These waves were of the hue of slate, save for the tops, which were of foaming white, and all of the men knew the colors of the sea. The horizon narrowed and widened, and dipped and rose, and at all times its edge was jagged with waves that seemed thrust up in points like rock.

That's the opening passage from "The Open Boat." I looked at the second sheet. It began like this:

The great Pullman was whirling onward with such dignity of motion that a glance from the window seemed simply to prove that the plains of Texas were pouring eastward. Vast flats of green grass, dull-hued spaces of mesquite and cactus, little groups of frame houses, woods of light and tender trees, all were sweeping into the east, sweeping over the horizon, a precipice.

That's the opening passage from "The Bride Comes to Yellow Sky."

I looked at the next sheet and it was the opening from "The Blue Hotel." All that writing that day, I thought, all of that just copy work, scribbling down what he'd already done. I shook my head, tossed those first three sheets back into the athletic bag. Held the fourth and fifth in my hands, looked at them.

And didn't recognize them.

I'd read every story that he'd ever written and this one wasn't among them. He'd been editing on it; you could see the scratched-out words and their replacements, see whole lines scratched out and rewritten. My hand started shaking as I read it. I got dizzy, then steadied myself, put those precious pages and the pen he'd used back into the athletic bag, then walked out of the dugout and stood there for a few minutes, looking up to feel the rain on my face.

Last Words

Okay, then, this is the truth as I know it: We lost, but losing is part of winning and they both are part of what's real. Maybe I threw that ball away on purpose so Steve wouldn't be able to let it go at that, so he'd be back in February when we start the next season. Maybe he'll have Cora with him, and maybe Conrad, so I can finally find out what he thinks of The Game. They'll show up that first practice, rowing into the harbor in that little boat, emerging from the haze and fog of February's heat over cold winter water. I'll walk over there, and say hi, and help them out of the boat, help them tie it up to the dock.

And then we'll play catch, take a little infield, some batting practice, catch a few flyballs, and just play the game, loosening up for the season to come, ready to find whatever realities, whatever truths, there are out there on the diamond. I think maybe it will happen that way.

At that moment, I stood there, face wet in that cool spray. Then walked over to the low fence, hopped it, and jogged to the harbor. The open boat was just thirty yards away, heading toward the gray sheets of rain sweeping in from the bay. Steve was in it, rowing. I could see the happy smile on his face. It was the happiest I ever saw him. Cora, there with him, turned around to look at me. I raised my hand. They both raised theirs, and then they waved, and then the rain came down harder and the gray closed in and they were gone.

Although he has often written about Native peoples in Canada's Hobema Reserve and has a deserved reputation for that work, W. P. Kinsella is best known for his baseball fiction. His *Shoeless Joe* novel in 1982, and the movie adaptation of it, *Field of Dreams*, in 1989, dramatically altered the landscape of baseball fiction, opening the door to speculative baseball fiction from the strange and wonderful to the supernatural and fantastic. As the writer most responsible for the mainstream popularizing of fantasy and baseball, Kinsella was extremely productive through the 1980s and 1990s before an accident nearly ended his career. He has more recently returned to writing with the award-winning *Butterfly Winter*. In this story from early in his career, Kinsella displays a wonderful sense of the absurd in a witty, gently mocking, study of a high-school student who finds success with Leo Durocher and the New York Giants.

How I Got My Nickname

W. P. Kinsella

IN THE SUMMER OF 1951, the summer before I was to start Grade 12, my polled Hereford calf, Simon Bolivar, won Reserve Grand Champion at the Des Moines, All-Iowa Cattle Show and Summer Exposition. My family lived on a hobby-farm near Iowa City. My father who taught classics at Coe College in Cedar Rapids, and in spite of that was still the world's number one baseball fan, said I deserved a reward—I also had a straight A average in Grade 11 and had published my first short story that spring. My father phoned his friend Robert Fitzgerald (Fitzgerald, an eminent translator, sometimes phoned my father late at night and they talked about various ways of interpreting the tougher parts of *The Iliad*) and two weeks later I found myself in Fitzgerald's spacious country home outside of New York City, sharing the lovely old house with the Fitzgeralds, their endless supply of children, and a young writer from Georgia named Flannery O'Connor. Miss O'Connor was charming, and humorous in an understated way, and I wish I had talked with her more. About the third day I was there I admitted to being a published writer and Miss O'Connor said "You must show me some of your stories." I never did. I was seventeen, overweight, diabetic, and bad-complexioned. I alternated between being terminally shy and obnoxiously brazen. I was nearly always shy around the Fitzgeralds and Miss O'Connor. I was also terribly homesick, which made me appear more silent and outlandish than I knew I was. I suspect I am the model for Enoch Emery, the odd, lonely country boy in Miss O'Connor's novel *Wise Blood*. But that is another story.

On a muggy August morning, the first day of a Giant home stand at the Polo Grounds, I prepared to travel into New York. I politely invited Miss O'Connor to accompany me, but she, even at that early date, had to avoid sunlight and often wore her wide-brimmed straw hat, even indoors. I set off much too early and though terrified of the grimy city and shadows that seemed to lurk in every doorway, arrived at the Polo Grounds over two hours before game time. It was raining gently and I was one of about two dozen fans in the ballpark. A few players were lethargically playing catch, a coach was hitting fungos to three players in right field. I kept edging my way down the rows of seats until I was right behind the Giants dugout.

The Giants were thirteen games behind the Dodgers and the pennant race appeared all but over. A weasel-faced bat boy, probably some executive's nephew, I thought, noticed me staring wide-eyed at the players and the playing field. He curled his lip at me, then stuck out his tongue. He mouthed the words "Take a picture, it'll last longer," adding something at the end that I could only assume to be uncomplimentary.

Fired by the insult I suddenly mustered all my bravado and called out "Hey, Mr. Durocher?" Leo Durocher, the Giants manager, had been standing in the third base coach's box not looking at anything in particular. I was really impressed. That's the grand thing about baseball, I thought. Even a manager in a pennant race can take time to daydream. He didn't hear me. But the bat boy did, and stuck out his tongue again.

I was overpowered by my surroundings. Though I'd seen a lot of major league baseball I'd never been in the Polo Grounds before. The history of the place . . . "Hey, Mr. Durocher," I shouted.

Leo looked up at me with a baleful eye. He needed a shave, and the lines around the corners of his mouth looked like ruts.

"What is it, Kid?"

"Could I hit a few?" I asked hopefully, as if I was begging to stay up an extra half hour. "You know, take a little batting practice?"

"Sure, Kid. Why not?" and Leo smiled with one corner of his mouth. "We want all our fans to feel like part of the team."

From the box seat where I'd been standing, I climbed up on the roof of the dugout and Leo helped me down onto the field.

Leo looked down into the dugout. The rain was stopping. On the other side of the park a few of the Phillies were wandering onto the field. "Hey, George," said Leo, staring into the dugout, "throw the kid here a few pitches. Where are you from, son?"

It took me a few minutes to answer because I experienced this strange, light-headed feeling, as if I had too much sun. "Near to Iowa City, Iowa," I managed to say in a small voice. Then "You're going to win the pennant, Mr. Durocher, I just know you are."

"Well, thanks, Kid," said Leo modestly, "we'll give it our best shot."

George was George Bamberger, a stocky rookie who had seen limited action. "Bring the kid a bat, Andy," Leo said to the bat boy. The bat boy curled his lip at me but slumped into the dugout, as Bamberger and Sal Yvars tossed the ball back and forth.

The bat boy brought me a black bat. I was totally unprepared for how heavy it was. I lugged it to the plate and stepped into the right hand batter's box. Bamberger delivered an easy, looping, batting-practice pitch. I drilled it back up the middle.

"Pretty good, Kid," I heard Durocher say.

Bamberger threw another easy one and I fouled it off. The third pitch was a little harder. I hammered it to left.

"Curve him," said Durocher.

He curved me. Even through my thick glasses the ball looked as big as a grapefruit, illuminated like a small moon. I whacked it and it hit the right field wall on one bounce.

"You weren't supposed to hit that one," said Sal Yvars.

"You're pretty good, Kid," shouted Durocher from the third base box. "Give him your best stuff, George."

Over the next fifteen minutes I batted about .400 against George Bamberger, and Roger Bowman, including a home run into the left centrefield stands. The players on the Giants bench were watching me with mild interest often looking up from the books most of them were reading.

"I'm gonna put the infield out now," said Durocher. "I want you to run out some of your hits."

Boy, here I was batting against the real New York Giants. I wished I'd worn a new shirt instead of the horizontally striped red and white one I had on, which made me look heftier than I really was. Bowman threw a sidearm curve and I almost broke my back swinging at it. But he made the mistake of coming right back with the same pitch. I looped it behind third where it landed soft as a sponge, and trickled off toward the stands—I'd seen the play hundreds of times—a stand-up double. But when I was still twenty feet from second base Eddie Stanky was waiting with the ball. "Slide!" somebody yelled, but I just skidded to a stop, stepping out of the baseline to avoid the tag. Stanky whapped me anyway, a glove to the ribs that would have made Rocky Marciano or Ezzard Charles proud.

When I got my wind back Durocher was standing, hands on hips, staring down at me.

"Why the hell didn't you slide, Kid?"

"I can't," I said, a little indignantly, "I'm diabetic, I have to avoid stuff like that. If I cut myself, or even bruise badly, it takes forever to heal."

"Oh," said Durocher, "Well, I guess that's okay then."

"Yon shouldn't tag people so hard," I said to Stanky, "Somebody could get hurt."

"Sorry, Kid," said Stanky. I don't think he apologized very often. I noticed that his spikes were filed. But I found later that he knew a lot about F. Scott Fitzgerald. His favourite story was "Babylon Revisited" so that gave us a lot in common; I was a real Fitzgerald fan; Stanky and I became friends even though both he and Durocher argued against reading *The Great Gatsby* as an allegory.

"Where'd you learn your baseball?" an overweight coach who smelled strongly of snuff, and bourbon, said to me.

"I live near Iowa City, Iowa," I said in reply.

Everyone wore question marks on their faces. I saw I'd have to elaborate. "Iowa City is within driving distance of Chicago, St. Louis, Milwaukee, and there's minor league ball in Cedar Rapids, Omaha, Kansas City. Why, there's barely a weekend my dad and I don't go somewhere to watch professional baseball."

"*Watch?*" said Durocher.

"Well, we talk about it some too. My father is a real student of the game. Of course we only talk in Latin when we're on the road, it's a family custom."

"Latin?" said Durocher.

"Say something in Latin," said Whitey Lockman, who had wandered over from first base.

"The Etruscans have invaded all of Gaul," I said in Latin.

"Their fortress is on the banks of the river," said Bill Rigney, who had been filling in at third base.

"Velle est posse," I said.

"Where there's a will there's a way," translated Durocher.

"Drink Agri Cola. . ." I began.

"The farmer's drink," said Sal Yvars, slapping me on the back, but gently enough not to bruise me. I guess I looked a little surprised.

"Most of us are more than ballplayers," said Alvin Dark, who had joined us. "In fact the average player on this squad is fluent in three languages."

"Watch?" said Durocher, getting us back to baseball. "You watch a lot of baseball, but where do you play?"

"I've never played in my life," I replied, "But I have a photographic memory. I just watch how different players hold their bat, how they stand. I try to emulate Enos Slaughter and Joe DiMaggio."

"Can you field?" said Durocher.

"No."

"No?"

"I've always just watched the hitters. I've never paid much attention to the fielders."

He stared at me as if I had spoken to him in an unfamiliar foreign language.

"Everybody fields," he said. "What position do you play?"

"I've never played," I reiterated. "My health is not very good."

"Cripes," he said, addressing the sky. "You drop a second Ted Williams on me and he tells me he can't field." Then to Alvin Dark: "Hey, Darky, throw a few with the kid here. Get him warmed up."

In the dugout Durocher pulled a thin, black glove from an equipment bag and tossed it to me. I dropped it. The glove had no discernible padding in it. The balls Dark threw hit directly on my hand, when I caught them, which was about one out of three.

"Ouch!" I cried. "Don't throw so hard."

"Sorry, Kid," said Alvin Dark and threw the next one a little easier. If I really heaved I could just get the ball back to him. I have always thrown like a non-athletic girl. I could feel my hand bloating inside the thin glove. After about ten pitches, I pulled my hand out. It looked as though it had been scalded.

"Don't go away, Kid," said Leo. "In fact why don't you sit in the dugout with me. What's your name anyway?"

"W. P. Kinsella," I said.

"Your friends call you W?"

"My father calls me William, and my mother..." but I let my voice trail off. I didn't think Leo Durocher would want to know my mother still called me Bunny.

"Jeez," said Durocher. "You need a nickname, Kid. Bad."

"I'll work on it," I said.

I sat right beside Leo Durocher all that stifling afternoon in the Polo Grounds as the Giants swept a doubleheader from the Phils, the start of a sixteen-game streak that was to lead to the October 3, 1951 Miracle of Coogan's Bluff. I noticed right away that the Giants were all avid readers. In fact, the *New York Times* Best Seller Lists, and the *Time* and *Newsweek* lists of readable books and an occasional review were taped to the walls of the dugout. When the Giants were in the field I peeked at the covers of the books the players sometimes read between innings. Willie Mays was reading *The Cruel Sea* by Nicholas Monsarrat. Between innings Sal Maglie was deeply involved in Carson McCullers's new novel *The Ballad of the Sad Cafe*. "I sure wish we could get that Cousin Lyman to be our mascot," he said to me when he saw me eyeing the bookjacket, referring to the hunchbacked dwarf who was the main character in the novel. "We need something to inspire us," he added. Alvin Dark slammed down his copy of *Requiem for a Nun* and headed for the on-deck circle.

When the second game ended, a sweaty and sagging Leo Durocher took me by the arm. "There's somebody I want you to meet, Kid," he said. Horace Stoneham's office was furnished in wine-coloured leather sofas and overstuffed horsehair chairs. Stoneham sat behind an oak desk as big as the dugout, enveloped in cigar smoke.

"I've got a young fellow here I think we should sign for the stretch drive," Durocher said. "He can't field or run, but he's as pure a hitter as I've ever seen. He'll make a hell of a pinch hitter."

"I suppose you'll want a bonus?" growled Stoneham.

"I do have something in mind," I said. Even Durocher was not nearly so jovial as he had been. Both men stared coldly at me. Durocher leaned over and whispered something to Stoneham.

"How about $6,000," Stoneham said.

"What I'd really like . . ." I began.

"Alright, $10,000; but not a penny more."

"Actually; I'd like to meet Bernard Malamud. I thought you could maybe invite him down to the park. Maybe get him to sign a book for me?" They both looked tremendously relieved.

"Bernie and me and this kid Salinger are having supper this evening," said Durocher. "Why don't you join us?"

"You mean J. D. Salinger?" I said.

"Jerry's a big Giant fan," he said. "The team Literary Society read *Catcher in the Rye* last month. We had a panel discussion on it for eight hours on the train to St. Louis."

Before I signed the contract I phoned my father.

"No reason you can't postpone your studies until the end of the season," he said, "It'll be good experience for you. You'll gather a lot of material you can write about later. Besides, baseball players are the real readers of America."

I got my first hit off Warren Spahn, a solid single up the middle. Durocher immediately replaced me with a pinch runner. I touched Ralph Branca for a double, the ball went over Duke Snider's head, hit the wall and bounced halfway back to the infield. Anyone else would have had an inside the park homer. I wheezed into second and was replaced. I got into 38 of the final 42 games. I hit 11 for 33, and was walked four times. And hit once. That was the second time I faced Warren Spahn. He threw a swishing curve that would have gone behind me if I hadn't backed into it. I slouched off toward first holding my ribs.

"You shouldn't throw at batters like that," I shouted, "someone could get seriously hurt. I'm diabetic, you know." I'd heard that Spahn was into medical texts and interested in both human and veterinary medicine.

"Sorry," he shouted back. "If I'd known I wouldn't have thrown at you. I've got some good liniment in the clubhouse. Come see me after the game. By the way I hear you're trying to say that *The Great Gatsby* is an allegory."

"The way I see it, it is," I said. "You see the eyes of the optometrist on the billboard are really the eyes of God looking down on a fallen world . . ."

"Alright, alright," said the umpire, Beans Reardon, "let's get on with the game. By the way, Kid, I don't think it's an allegory either. A statement on the human condition, perhaps. But not an allegory."

The players wanted to give me some nickname other than "Kid." Someone suggested "Ducky" in honour of my running style. "Fats" said somebody else. I made a note to remove his bookmark between innings. Several other suggestions were downright obscene. Baseball players, in spite of their obsession with literature and the arts, often have a bawdy sense of humour.

"How about 'Moonlight,'" I suggested. I'd read about an old time player who stopped for a cup of coffee with the Giants half a century before, who had that nickname.

"What the hell for?" said Monty Irvin, who in spite of the nickname preferred to be called Monford or even by his second name Merrill. "You got to have a reason for a nickname. You got to earn it. Still, anything's better than W. P."

"It was only a suggestion," I said. I made a mental note not to tell Monford what I knew about his favourite author, Erskine Caldwell.

As it turned out I didn't earn a nickname until the day we won the pennant.

As every baseball fan knows the Giants went into the bottom of the ninth in the deciding game of the pennant playoff trailing the Dodgers 4–1.

"Don't worry," I said to Durocher, "everything's going to work out." If he heard me he didn't let on.

But was everything going to work out? And what part was I going to play in it? Even though I'd contributed to the Giants' amazing stretch drive, I didn't belong. Why am I here? I kept asking myself. I had some vague premonition that I was about to change history. I mean I wasn't a ballplayer. I was a writer. Here I was about to go into Grade 12 and I was already planning to do my master's thesis on F. Scott Fitzgerald.

I didn't have time to worry further as Alvin Dark singled. Don Mueller, in his excitement, had carried his copy of *The Mill on the Floss* out to the on-deck circle. He set the rosin bag on top of it, stalked to the plate and singled, moving Dark to second.

I was flabbergasted when Durocher called Monford Irvin back and said to me "Get in there, Kid."

It was at that moment that I knew why I was there. I would indeed change history. One stroke of the bat and the score would be tied. I eyed the left field stands as I nervously swung two bats to warm up. I was nervous but not scared. I never doubted my prowess for one moment. Years later Johnny Bench summed it up for both athletes and writers when he talked about a successful person having to have an inner conceit. It never occurred to me until days later that I might have hit into a double or triple play, thus ending it and really changing history.

When I did take my place in the batter's box, I pounded the plate and glared out at Don Newcombe. I wished that I shaved so I could give him a stubble-faced stare of contempt. He curved me and I let it go by for a ball. I fouled the next pitch high into the first base stands. A fastball was low. I fouled the next one outside third. I knew he didn't want to go to a full count: I crowded the plate a little looking for the fastball. He curved me. Nervy. But the curveball hung, sat out over the plate like a cantaloupe. I waited an extra millisecond before lambasting it. In that instant the ball broke in on my hands; it hit the bat right next to my right hand. It has been over thirty years but I still wake deep in the night, my hands vibrating, burning from Newcombe's pitch. The bat shattered into kindling. The ball flew in a polite loop as if it had been tossed by a five-year-old; it landed soft as a creampuff in Peewee Reese's glove. One out.

I slumped back to the bench.

"Tough luck, Kid," said Durocher, patting my shoulder. "There'll be other chances to be a hero."

"Thanks, Leo," I said.

Whitey Lockman doubled. Dark scored. Mueller hurt himself sliding into third. Rafael Noble went in to run for Mueller. Charlie Dressen replaced Newcombe with Ralph Branca. Bobby Thomson swung bats in the on-deck circle.

As soon as umpire Jorda called time-in, Durocher leapt to his feet, and before Bobby Thomson could take one step toward the plate, Durocher called him back.

"Don't do that!" I yelled, suddenly knowing why I was really there. But Durocher ignored me. He was beckoning with a big-knuckled finger to another reserve player, a big outfielder who was tearing up the American Association when they brought him up late in the year. He was 5 for 8 as a pinch hitter.

Durocher was already up the dugout steps heading toward the umpire to announce the change. The outfielder from the American Association was making his way down the dugout, hopping along over feet and ankles. He'd be at the top of the step by the time Durocher reached the umpire.

As he skipped by me, the last person between Bobby Thomson and immortality, I stuck out my foot. The outfielder from the American Association went down like he'd been poleaxed. He hit his face on the top step of the dugout, crying out loud enough to attract Durocher's attention.

The trainer hustled the damaged player to the clubhouse. Durocher waved Bobby Thomson to the batter's box. And the rest is history. After the victory celebration, I announced my retirement blaming it on a damaged wrist. I went back to Iowa and listened to the World Series on the radio.

All I have to show that I ever played in the major leagues is my one-line entry in *The Baseball Encyclopedia*:

W. P. KINSELLA   Kinsella, William Patrick "Tripper"

BR TR 5'9" 185 lbs. B. Apr. 14, 1934 Onamata, IA.

| | | | | | | HR | | | | | | | Pinch Hit | |
	G	AB	H	2B	3B	HR	%	R	RBI	HB	SO	EA	BA	AB	H
1951	NY N	38	33	11	2	0	2	6.0	0	8	4	4	0	.333	33	11

I got my outright release in the mail the week after the World Series ended. Durocher had scrawled across the bottom:

"Good luck, Kid. By the way, *The Great Gatsby* is *not* an allegory."

Acknowledgments

An anthology of this nature, one that collects and reprints classic material from writers past and present, is very much a team effort. A necessary collaboration takes place between the anthology editor, the various writers and their agents, and even, on occasion, the original publisher of the story at hand. It is the sort of time-consuming work where patience is a virtue, though a sense of urgency is also required.

I'm very grateful for the perfect balance between those two extremes shown by Skyhorse Publishing editor Jason Katzman, who kept me on track throughout, and Jarred Weisfeld of Start Publishing, for seeing the potential of this project from the very start. I'm also very grateful for the generosity and support of talented writer and publisher Jacob Weisman, who brought me into the project and offered sound advice along the way, and to Night Shade editor Jeremy Lassen, who initiated the entire project.

My agent, Bob Diforio, was extremely helpful with advice, counseling, and some critical communication with other agents, and I'm most appreciative of that help. Special thanks, too, to Roxana Aguilar, who worked some critical magic with the scanner at just the right moment; and to Bradbury scholar Donn Albright, whose advice is greatly appreciated.

Also, my wife, Robin, and my daughter, Samantha, have always been supportive of my writing and editing work, and I greatly appreciate their support on this project. My son, Richard Jr., is a big baseball fan and unmatched supporter of the Tampa Bay Rays. His hugs, encouragement, and consistently positive outlook on life were important to me in completing this project.

And, finally, I owe a huge debt to the writers of these fine stories, who have, one and all, entertained and deeply informed all of us who love great literature and the game of baseball. I'm deeply appreciative of the opportunity to reprint their work.

The conversion of reprinted material from its original source to the version you see here in *Field of Fantasies* is a demanding task. A number of people have worked to make that conversion a clean one and I thank them all. Any errors or omissions, of course, are mine.

Rick Wilber
May 2014

Permissions